Violeta Treciokaite "The Secret of One Grave"

I0563611

VIOLETA TRECIOKAITE

THE SECRET OF ONE GRAVE

Violeta Treciokaite "The Secret of One Grave"

You can also order this book at the address:

Jurate Somerville
224304 E 421 PR SE
Kennewick, WA 99337
(509) 582-6403
eagleview1@live.com

Printed in the United States of America

ISBN: 978-0-692-50117-7

Library of Congress Control Number: 2015948304

This book is dedicated to one of the most extraordinary people in Lithuania - Kazimieras Treciokas - who lived and created during the Soviet times.

If I may say so, this book is a mixture of "The Hunchback of Notre-Dame" by Victor Hugo and the "An American Tragedy" by Theodore Dreiser, only in the Lithuanian version of it!! It is especially so because much of the action in the book is taking place in one of the most famous churches of Europe that is located in Vilnius, Lithuania.

Believed to have been built on the site of worship to Milda, the pagan goddess of love, this breathtaking Late Baroque masterpiece was commissioned to celebrate victory over the Russians in 1668 by Michael Casimir Pac, the Grand Hetman of the Lithuanian armies, who never lived to see its completion. Financed by two of Pac's cousins and completed under several master craftsmen including the Polish Jan Zaor and Italian Gianbattista Frediani, the rather plain façade betrays an interior by Giovanni Pietro Perti and Giovanni Maria Galli that is quite simply out of this world! Containing over 2,000 astonishing stucco mouldings representing miscellaneous religious and mythological scenes, of equal magnificence is the 20th-century altar containing a wooden figure of Christ, *Antakalnio Jėzus* (Jesus of Antakalnis) which features a real human hair brought from Rome in 1700 and the Latvian chandelier made of brass and glass beads and dating from 1905.

The book is truly worth reading if you are into the genre of the historical romance. Enjoy..

Upon coming home after her classes at gymnasium, Julija threw her backpack with the textbooks on a sofa. This time, she didn't sit down to do her homework at her little desk as she had usually been doing on any given day. Moreover, she didn't even wait for dinner that her aunt regularly served her after her coming from gymnasium.

Julija had been living with her aunt after a catastrophe that had taken place on railroad tracks where her mother and father died.

After that unfortunate event, her mother's sister sheltered Julija, the ten-year old orphan, after what she had been living with her for six years now.

Julija's aunt had been extremely nice to her, probably because she never had children of her own. Over the years following her sister's tragic death, Julija's aunt got used to bringing her niece up. Julija wasn't a burden to her at all. On the contrary – she was always a pleasure to be around.

After her niece's mother and father had passed away, Julija inherited a big farm located not far away from Vilnius city, in Verkiai area. In addition to that, her parents had owned a big and very profitable women tailoring shop on Didzioji Street. This business had provided the family with twice as big revenue as the revenue they had been receiving from the farm. Now, after Julija's parents' death, her aunt and uncle had been making use of all these assets while raising their niece.

Besides, Julija's uncle himself had a decent job at a government office.

No wonder Julija seemed to have nothing to complain about since her aunt never hurt her; she took care of her just as a real mother would. Thus, Julija was growing up while surrounded by her aunt and uncle's sincere guardianship that felt like her real parents' caring. The other words, she lived the trouble free life because her aunt and uncle took care of every little thing for her.

Julija's only responsibilities were to do her homework after coming home from gymnasium and, also, attend her evening music lessons that took place on Antakalnis Street. She had begun taking those classes since she had moved to live with her guardians in their home in Sapezinka.

Julija's aunt had not wanted to live in her deceased sister's luxurious apartment located on Didzioji Street. For some unknown reason, her aunt had decided rather staying in her husband's little, modest house in Verkiai that he had inherited from his parents together with a rather big and well taken care of orchard.

Most likely, Julija's aunt was afraid of memories haunting her about her sister. Therefore, she let her husband influence Julija in staying together with them in their home, especially because he himself didn't wish to part with his parents' house and their assets. This house with all its surroundings reminded him not only of his childhood but also of his entire life he had spent in this beautiful, peaceful place.

There was more than enough room for the three-people family in the six-room house with the pretty big entrance-hall. Every summer they would spend a lot of time in Verkiai, too, and Julija got used to living the entire summer there. She would only come to Vilnius occasionally in order to meet with her girlfriends during her summer vacation.

This afternoon, after returning from gymnasium, Julija didn't wait for dinner to be served. Instead, she lifted a cover of a piano, sat down on a little, round stool, and began spinning on it, time from time pushing herself with her foot up the wooden floor and making her body turn a few rounds on the piano stool, which helped her to distract herself.

She liked to spin on this little stool when she was extremely joyful - at those times when her heart would be singing with happiness.

At this moment, also, she effortlessly and promptly pushed herself off to spin while sitting on her stool. After quickly making a couple of rounds turning, she energetically hit the piano keys pretty hard with the fingers of her both hands. The sounds of the piano surged across the rooms filling the silence there with the strange, vibrating ringing.

Even Julija's aunt toiling behind a few doors in the kitchen heard these unusually loud accords of the piano. Instantly, she ceased doing her chores there and rushed to the room thinking that maybe the piano fell down or something else tumbled over the top of it.

However, as soon as she opened the door of the room, she saw Julija sitting at the piano with her dexterous fingers adroitly flying over the keyboard.

Julija could not see her aunt because she was sitting with her back facing the door. Therefore, she didn't cease playing when the aunt appeared in the doorway.

Her aunt also calmed down seeing that nothing bad had happened. She didn't want to hinder Julija from having her passionate moment. Therefore, she just silently closed the door and returned to the kitchen in order to finish up preparing a meal. She had to hurry since her husband was going to be home for lunch at any moment now.

Julija was in such high spirits as she had never been in during the past few months. It felt as if something unusual, significant, and big was just about to happen to her that she had never experienced before! It even made her play the piano passionately; it appeared as if the song was coming right from the bottom of her heart, which was longing to be as free as the music floating in the air. Finally, that nagging her feeling gently gushed out, and the silent humming was heard merging with the soft sounds of the piano that were filling up the empty rooms. It was very intoxicating - like aroma of a big bouquet of flowers.

Without anyone or anything interrupting her, Julija for a while was absorbed in this 'narcotic' of the music and living in the moment of its pleasant giddiness. Her uncle, however, managed for a brief moment to dispel that wonderful dizziness when he entered the house upon returning home from his work.

After eating lunch with her aunt and uncle, Julija went back to the piano room where she again sank into the vertigo of the music.

This time, however, no one interrupted her, and she could enjoy the 'intoxication' of the music to her heart's content. And she really took advantage of it. Once in a while, though, she would run quickly to another room in order to glance at the wall clock, which was an indication she was pushing the time under the compulsion.

She had nobody to share her secrets with because she had no such close girlfriends whom she could reveal her deepest thoughts to. And she didn't dare to brag about her happiness to her aunt, either. Therefore, she kept her amusing secret to herself waiting for afternoons to come every single day now!

At three o'clock she always had her music lesson with a music teacher she had been taking the private lessons from.

It had been a week now she had become acquainted with a boy who had broken stillness of her monotonous life by infusing totally new feelings into her soul. Because of this, Julija was feeling so amazingly good that she could not even put that feeling into words even if she wanted to describe it; she had not only been enjoying her life to the fullest now, but she began to idolize it greatly as well.

The one to blame for her feeling this way was that recently met youth, who had very unexpectedly intruded into Julija's world together bringing into her life fresh forms of pleasure the existence of which she had no awareness about before.

It had happened when she was walking home from gymnasium, when some youth had started a conversation with her. He persisted to see her home for two days in a row until he managed to talk Julija into going to the movie together with him.

After this victory of his, he not only began seeing her home from gymnasium every day, but he also started coming to see her again after her lunch in order to accompany her on her way to the music lessons. There, he would also wait for a couple of hours until Julija was done with her lesson so just he could walk beside her.

While walking together with her in the street, he would brag about being very rich and about his father having a lumber processing factory. He would make up various stories in order to seduce Julija. He also told her that he was the only son of his parents and that he was going to inherit all their assets after his father's death. In addition to that, he said he already was helping him with management of his business at the factory because his father was getting too old and could not longer do all the work by himself. Therefore, he was entrusted with taking care of his father's business and, at times, he even thought he was doing a better job than his father!

However, the truth was that his father had been working in that lumber processing factory only as an ordinary worker. As about the youth himself, he only had heard from his father about the big revenue that the real owner of the factory had been deriving from his business. Thus, the youth was making up those fantastic stories himself and, in a meanwhile, he kept inquiring Julija about her personal life in attempt to learn about the environment she was living in as much as he could.

She, on the contrary, created just the opposite story about her being a poor girl, who was living under her aunt's guardianship after her parents' tragic death. And she did not even mention anything about her inheritance. Julija wished to move her supposedly rich admirer to tears to the point where he would start feeling overwhelmed with compassion for her and would fall in love with her without measure!

The only true thing the youth could find out was that Julija's aunt had a little house with some land that had been turned into an orchard. And it seemed good enough to him, having in mind that her aunt and uncle did not have any more children. This way, Julija was supposed to inherit their property after her guardians' death.

After learning this, the youth was feeling happy to have acquainted with such a rich girl! That was precisely the reason he continued following her all the time.

Today, too, he was waiting for Julija in an alley located in a neighborhood not far away from the place where she lived.

In a meanwhile, Julija continued playing piano while trying to kill the time until three o'clock in the afternoon came. She was daydreaming at the same time and making up in her head various scenes of meeting with him while swaying to the sounds of the music.

When the handle of the clock hit three o'clock, she like a bullet rushed to the street where cool but pleasant autumn air greeted her.

Nevertheless, she didn't notice the beautiful surroundings because her mind was preoccupied with totally different things.

Soon, she broke into a run along a narrow, sandy alley that was enclosed with a tall fence on its both sides, resembling a tunnel. Julija slowed down only when she saw the one, who had constantly been on her mind the entire last week.

Turning red on her face, she slowly approached him. Not having enough courage to start a conversation, Julija came to a stop a few meters away from him.

However, he was the first to rescue her from the puzzled situation. He smiled and said, "I already thought you are not going to show up."

"Robertas, how couldn't I show up when you know well that every day at this time, I attend the music lessons? Today, I'm not being late, either. Anyway - how long have you been waiting for me here?"

"It's been about ten minutes, but the time was dragging so slowly; it felt as if I've been standing in this alley for eternity! I think it seemed to me this way because I knew that you were so close but, at the same time, you were still away from me. Well, let's go, or you are going to be late for your music lesson. You tutor wouldn't be very happy if you didn't show up on time. I know how it feels because I had myself a student before."

"There is no need to rush. We still have a half an hour, and it's going to take us just twenty minutes at the most to get there. We can walk slowly, and still we will have to wait for another ten minutes there. I am very punctual and don't wish to show up at my teacher's before the time is up. But why are you here so early? Don't you value your time? You are the one who constantly complains about devoting too many hours of your time in order to take care of your father's business, which robs you of time for the leisure. You knew well I was not coming here before three o'clock."

This way, upbraiding each other, both of them slowly came to Antakalnis Street. After talking with him for another five minutes, Julija went to her music class.

Left alone in the street, Robertas began lounging about while stopping once in awhile to think what to do next. Soon he began walking away his dull gaze fixed ahead of him.

People were hurriedly passing him by, and the cars were moving both ways in the street. He remembered telling Julija, upon separating with her, that he would return to his factory in order to take care of some important matters there, which should give him sufficient amount of time to help his father while she was in her music class.

However, since neither he nor his father had a factory, and moreover, he had nothing to do at that moment, either, he didn't have the need to hurry at all. Therefore, he spent the entire two hours pointlessly walking in the streets of Vilnius.

The time approaching when Julija was supposed to come out of her music teacher's house, he came to the Church of St. Peter and St. Paul where he began observing the front door of the house across the street while hiding in one of the bay's of the stucco fence surrounding the church.

Soon Julija appeared outside. He waited for a few minutes longer and stopped a coachman who was passing by. Upon climbing the horse-carriage, Robertas yelled at the driver asking him to hurry. He promised to pay him generously for the ride. The driver as fast as a wind, drove his carriage after Julija. As they approached her, Robertas ordered the driver to stop.

Then he took out the only zloty he had in his pocket and shoved it into the driver's palm to pay for this incredibly short drive.

Robertas promptly jumped out of the carriage and said in a very loud voice, making sure not only the driver of the carriage but Julija as well could hear him saying, "Keep the change for yourself! Thank you for the ride!"

"Oh, my God. I was so busy – I almost missed meeting you, Julija," he complained walking fast towards her.

"You didn't need to hurry. I could have waited for you. I have the whole evening free today. To tell the truth, my homework is not done yet, but I can spend a couple of hours before sleep doing it. That should give me enough time to take care of everything."

"How long have you waited for me?" he asked.

"It wasn't long at all. In fact, I've just left the class."

"I'm glad I didn't make you wait for a long time. The rest is just the minor things. Let's better discuss more important topic, for example, let's talk about you! What are you going to do after you finish your music classes? Obviously, you have some plans and dreams for your future."

"Yes, I do have many various dreams. But what good does it do if they are just illusions - the dreams that never come true?"

"Share with me at least one of your wishes. You've got me wondering now about what you are up to."

"I have the rich imagination, but it's all that it is – just the empty dreams. Still – no one is forbidden to dream," she said.

"If you were less strict, then who knows... it might be possible for me to turn those dreams of yours into reality," he said with confidence as if he was in power to control her destiny.

"I don't think so," she continued, "I think it is impossible because my wishes are too big. In fact, they are so magnificent that they could come true only in my fantasies."

"Well, why don't you tell me about them? You never know – I might be able to help you accomplish them."

"No one can help me because what I dream about is to be like those ancient women, for example, Cornelia, the mother of the Gracchi, or I would like to be just like Aspasia, the wife of Pericles, who had become famous for her great education and strong will. In spite of having difficult life with an old husband (he was the Greek statesman and had to drag the burden of the responsibilities for his country alone), she was adored by the citizens. Nevertheless, I could also settle for some hetaera – rich, beautiful, and admired by young patricians. Now, you see how wild my dreams are, and that's not all. Do you still desire to listen to my fantasies?"

"Yes, I do! You are the first girl I've met, who has such big dreams. What about Jadwiga, the queen of Poland? Would you want to be like her?"

"Oh, no! I definitely wouldn't want to be like her! I think she was too downtrodden by the politicians; she could not decide anything on her own. Even her destiny was being managed the way it had been more suited for the government affairs. I would rather be like Judith from the Bible, who showed her unheard equanimity by cutting off the Holofernes' head."

"I think the horrible character of Judith doesn't match your angelic appearance. The Roman hetaera sounds much better! She is always happy and worshiped by others."

"Really – it would be such a great life! I could go to the Coliseum, play chess, or just lie half way on my side on a plank-bed incrusted with gems while listening to hexameters that had been created in the honor of me! And what about you, Roberas – what is your idol?"

"What can I say? I this case, I would also like to be in the Roman times since there is nothing I wish more than to be with you! I would love being Gaius Julius Caesar. I would like to have the opportunity to conquer my opponents one after another and then notify the Roman Senate about my victories by making the laconic writing – "Veni, vidi, vici", which means, "I saw, I conquered, and I came". Another character that I'd like to be is Marcus Tullius Cicero, the first Roman orator. All consuls then would be listening to me with their mouths open during the meetings of the senate, and no one of them would dare objecting my words. So what do you think about my dreams!?"

"You have also chosen the strong figures to imitate!"

"Julija, if we had the right to choose, then it would be better for us to pick the biggest and the most famous ones! However, there are limits to everything. For example, I wouldn't want to be like the King Vladislovas Jogaila, who had betrayed his nation and this way he became the monarch. In this case, I would rather be a slave or a gladiator and kill my partners in an arena of the Coliseum! Or better yet it would be for me to end up in a manege among the beasts of prey and vanquish them one by one. In that case, I would also get bouquets of flowers that some hetaeras would throw down at me from their seats above as the sign of the reward after winning the battle with death. I could also be the gladiator Spartacus, who had led a slave revolt against the Romans. It's definitely better to be the gladiator than the dishonorable king! But the best of all it would be to become an emperor, the unlimited monarch. Then, I also could change my surname into some divine one. Just like Octavianus after conquering all his opponents received another name – Augustus. After becoming such an authoritative figure, I would definitely build for you, Julija, a monument on the top of the Esquiline Hill that no other empress in the world has ever had!"

"Robertas!" exclaimed Julija, "after becoming such a famous figure, you wouldn't even remember me, the poor orphan girl!"

"How could the emperor forget his hetaeras?! On the contrary – you and me would go to the coliseum together and watch the slaughter of the gladiators down below from our boxes there, encrusted with precious stones. Nobody would dare to condemn us for anything!"

"Robertas, our imagination is so incredibly vivid! If only a little part of our dreams came true, we could be the very happy people."

Thus chatting, both of them slowly came to Julija's house where they talked for fifteen more minutes at the gate, and they separated after making arrangements to meet the next day.

Robertas lazily walked away turning back a couple of times. However, Julija was already gone behind the closed front door.

As soon as she walked into the room, she threw her music sheets onto the same sofa where she had her backpack still sitting exactly in the same place where she had put it when she had returned from gymnasium in the early afternoon.

Then she sat down at the piano and began playing joyful music. But soon she woke up from her dreaming state of mind when she remembered that she still had to do her homework.

Without any delay, she concentrated on it and spent an hour studying which enabled her to go through all the exercises. In addition to this, she did her all music lessons as well.

Next day, she was supposed to meet with Robertas at three o'clock sharp. Julija decided to leave home a little bit earlier because she always used to find him already waiting for her. This time, she wanted to be there before him. Therefore, she left home fifteen minutes before three, but how surprised she was when she saw Robertas waiting for her there again!

Julija walked up to him and asked in a surprised tone of voice, "Have you been waiting for a long time?"

"Not really."

"Why do you always come here so early? As far as I'm aware, the time is very precious to you because of your business!"

"Julija, no matter how little time I have left to do my business, I have to admit that the time I spend being with you is the most precious time to me! And I don't regret because of using it this way since you are and always will be dear to my heart."

"I'm afraid I can bore you very soon," Julija said blushing and not having enough courage to look him straight in the eye.

"I see my words make you feel uncomfortable," noticed Robertas. "Let's better talk about something that interests you, just like we did yesterday. You seemed to be in such high spirits then! But I hope, Julija, you not always dream only about the rich hetaeras. Once in a while, probably, thoughts about poor people cross your mind as well. Thinking about those misfortunate should make you suffer together with them. Would you like to elaborate something on that?"

"I won't deny I have the moments when my heart overflows with compassion for the poor. Then, I truly want to be together with them! Not long ago, I've read a book "The Hunchback of Notre-Dame" written by Victor Hugo. The gipsy Esmeralda made a huge impact on me! She saved the poor poet from being hung during the Middle Ages. No one sympathized with the bell-ringer, who had been given a thrashing all the time. People had had an aversion for his ugly appearance, and they didn't even wish to come anywhere near him.

Nevertheless, the little, frail Esmeralda didn't get frightened and even brought some water to the beast. She gave the drink to the thirsty Hunchback. I would love to be like Esmeralda – the lively street dancer of Paris."

"In this case, I would agree to be the Quasimodo!"

As soon as Julija heard that, she interrupted him surprised, "Why would you want to choose to be such a bugbear? If you wish to stick to this story, then in my opinion, it is better to be Gringoire. Don't you think it would be much nicer to experience the life of the Esmeralda's husband instead?"

"I wouldn't want to be her husband," Robertas quickly disputed her. Having puckered his brows, he cast a fast glance at perplexed Julija. Then he went on explaining, "I don't think that Esmeralda loved the poet. She had married him only out of pity, so that he wouldn't be hung in the city square. Don't you remember she even had a lover who was an officer? Now you know why I wouldn't agree to be Gringoire! Besides, he also didn't really love her. At least, it was nothing like the love of that of the Quasimodo, who later saved her from clutches of the crowd of raging citizens that were just about to kill the innocent gipsy! He sacrificed himself because of his burning love for her, and after her death, he himself ended up in a basement of the Gibbet of Montfaucon where he buried himself together with his beloved Esmeralda. Do you see why I've chosen this ugly creature, the bell-ringer Quasimodo of the Notre Dame Cathedral in Paris, over the Esmeralda's husband?"

"I think our yesterday's conversation was much more pleasant than it is today," Julija replied. "Everyone sometimes dreams of being big, distinct, and famous, so that others would look at them with envy. But what person in his right mind could dream about being the true ugliness like that of Quasimodo!?"

"Yes, he was ugly. So what?! But his soul was as pure as the crystal spring water. It you took a close look at the souls of most of other people, especially those of the dignitaries, it wouldn't take you long to notice they were full of hypocrisy. Even though Quasimodo had been wronged by the nature on his outer form, the good was hiding inside of him, deep down in his soul. But the noble men, as a rule, were always just the opposite. Therefore, I feel for Quasimodo. I don't find him to be ugly at all! Think how much good he used to bring to the people of Paris when he, three times per day, was announcing the beginning, the middle, and the end of the day with those mighty sounds of the bell ringing in the church tower high above the city. But especially the common Parisians used to be delighted when he would ring that mighty bell during the holidays and celebrations! And what usefulness people could derive from those wealthy few? The only thing the indigent people had experienced from them was the ongoing exploitation."

"Okay, you won!" Julija agreed. "I've even begun feeling as if I myself am falling in love with Quasimodo."

"No, you don't have to love Quasimodo. What I am trying to stress is that we should notice and respect decency and see the difference between good and evil. We should propagate the first and unmask the later. This would help tremendously to those suffering all over the world. Such is my outlook on life."

"You, Robertas, sound like a real philosopher, but as far as I can remember my classes of philosophy at gymnasium, the famous Greek philosopher Homer used to walk through ancient villages and beg for food himself!"

"It was so long ago. A lot of things you read about in your school textbooks are, of course, true. However, you are in title to your own opinion, too. As far as his epic poetry the Iliad and the Odyssey goes, I agree with his phrase: 'Et omnia in philosophia, omnes in philosopho continentur', which stands for 'all things are contained in philosophy, all men in the philosopher'. I always wondered myself why he had gone begging. As far as I remember from my own classes of the philosophy, he used to write a lot during those trips out in the country. Most likely, namely while he had been doing his traveling on foot, he had written most of his immortal epopees! If he had been a professional mendicant, he would have definitely preferred to sit at the entrance of the Acropolis in Athens because that's where all the aristocracy used to pass through on their way to the temple. Most likely, he would be collecting more money this way than he had while knocking about the world. While he had walked on foot across the entire Greece, he had not only begged, but he also had collected the needed material for his works. By just sitting at the gates of the Acropolis, he wouldn't have been able to gather so much useful material. Even if some big money had come to him while sitting there, no one of those noble men would have talked to him. Therefore, Homer would not have a chance to enrich himself by expanding his view. The circumstances had allowed him to derive much more when he had found himself among the simple, poor countrymen where he had had an opportunity to fill himself with the knowledge. Those common, local people had considered themselves to be equal to him, thus, allowing Homer to get all the knowledge out of the inexhaustible source of the divine information that had opened up right before his eyes. This way, he could gift to humanity his first and greatest epic poems of the world! Even today, after reading his poetry, any cultured person remains captivated by his ancient chef-d'oeuvres."

"Again, we have wandered away from the subject," finally interrupted him Julija.

"Julija, every person is sublime in his or her own way. For example, Julius Caesar ruled Rome. The Greek philosopher contributed to the world by writing the immortal epic poetry the Iliad and the Odyssey. Viktor Hugo created the well known characters Quasimodo, Esmeralda, and others. Alexandre Dumas wrote the Graf Monte Cristo and created the characters of The Three Musketeers. Moniuszko wrote the opera Halka. Jonas Mateika painted the famous painting the Battle of Zalgiris. I could go on and on since there are huge numbers of the talented people, and it's virtually impossible to mention them all. So, all these majestic figures, every one of them according to their possibilities brought something valuable to the world's granary. Now, the entire mankind can find use of it. The same pertains to both of us – it is our responsibility to give to other people all we can, having in mind each of our abilities and talents we possess in order to contribute to the happiness of all. Of course, not every one of us is a genius, but at least, we can be righteous, decent, and diligent people. This is just by itself is already the honorable goal to follow."

Thus talking, they came to Julija's place where she lived. When Robertas returned home, it was already almost completely dark. No one at home asked him where he had been all day long since his father was still at work, and his mother was not there, either. She was at her own job where she had been working as a janitor.

After having finished gymnasium a couple of years ago, Robertas couldn't continue his studies because he had no means to go to the university. Therefore, he with no occupation and no particular things to do, day by day, kept strolling about the streets. His meager education was the main obstacle for him to find a decent job. Moreover, it was very difficult to find any kind of work in Vilnius even for those with the higher education or those who had mastered some skills in the field of various trades.

What could have Robertas expected after graduating only the gymnasium? Thus, he became a victim of the lack of the education. And he had no chance to obtain any higher schooling, either, which could enable him to derive knowledge regarding some profession for his future. Now, without having that knowledge or any experience working, all his efforts searching for a good job were in vain.

The only option he had was to try to find some simple, physical work, but he kept driving the thought about that away.

Therefore, he proceeded roaming around the city without anything in particular to do. True, he wasn't a spoilt youth even though he didn't work and, for the most part, he kept sponging. Continuing to live this way, could complicate his future even more making it difficult for him to achieve any kind of progress ahead.

Being so young, he didn't realize the implication of his behavior on his destiny; he assumed this kind of life was harmless. He was confident he could do better than carrying logs like his father had together with the other simple, uneducated laborers in a sawmill.

In addition to this, even his own father and mother didn't force him to undertake this kind of work because they, too, saw their son's humiliation in that. Therefore, both of them preferred waiting for a better opportunity to come to him in the nearest future.

Luckily, he happened to meet Julija, and now, he was preoccupied with their exciting relationship. It's been several days he had been coming at three o'clock to Sapezinka in order to accompany her to the music teacher in Antakalnis Street after what he also would see her back home.

Thus, they kept spending more and more time together every day, and that time was flying imperceptibly fast for both of them.

Julija fell helplessly in love with Robertas, and hours spent without him were making her feel sick and tired.

But as soon as she found herself walking beside him, she would gladly listen to his wise reasoning again. He was very eloquent and enlightened enough as well. Therefore, the time spent with him never bored Julija.

He had read a lot of books, and he knew not only the history of the world well but he, also, was versed in geography. Even when still at gymnasium, he had been one of the best students there. The teachers had big expectations for his future. They had no doubts about him going to the university and graduating it successfully.

However, Robertas' destiny turned just the opposite direction. Even though he was the talented student, but it had not been easy for him to graduate even the gymnasium. The reason for this was his parents' multiple debts that they had incurred while he had still been studying there. Therefore, his dreams about entering the university were deemed to fail - this kind of education required even more money!

Being able to win and even to completely enthrall the heart of Julija in such a short amount of time, he became very attached to her himself.

In the beginning of their relationship, he was seeking only entertainment so that he could have a good time and not feel lonely.

However, when he learned she had been living with her aunt and uncle, who never had children of their own, thus, enabling Julija to inherit their six-room home surrounded with the pretty big orchard, he got even more interested in her.

Nevertheless, he still wasn't aware of the huge assets that Julia's parents had had before their fatal accident. Her guardians' assets were only a shadow in comparison to the estate her parents had managed, and Julija was the first in line to inherit all this as well two years down the road!

In spite of this, Julija was hiding from him the matters of her inheritance, portraying herself as the poor orphan girl being brought up by her relatives. She wanted to move Robertas to tears since she believed that his father was the well-off business person.

In her wildest imagination, she could never think Robertas was only pretending to be rich! Therefore, she didn't even give him the benefit of the doubt when he'd caught up with her in the street the other day and threw to the carriage driver a zloty; she had not realized then it had been the last zloty Robertas had that he needed so badly for himself!

However, Robertas didn't want to appear worthy of compassion in the eyes of Julija. On the contrary, he pretended to be full of confidence, just as the Polish saying went "coto ja, coto moja kamizelka!', which meant 'I'm so good looking, and so is my vest!'.

They both kept seeing each other, and Robertas didn't even notice when he himself started missing her more and more every day. The time would drag so slowly without Julija!

Often, he remembered the first time he had seen her when he had started a conversation with her in an attempt to tease her. Back then, he had no intention to get into a close relationship with her.

Nevertheless, both of them got equally tangled up in the cobweb of love. Within the period of two weeks they became so attached to each other that they attended a few movies and performances at the theatre together.

This time when Sunday came, however, they didn't know what to do. All day long, both of them walked in the streets of Vilnius without having any purpose in mind. As lunch time came, they parted for a few hours after deciding to meet again at four o'clock at the Sts. Peter and Paul's Church where they had already met a couple of times before.

Not feeling anything ominous coming up, Julija just as usually, waited anxiously for their meeting at four while cherishing her high hopes. Running out of patience, she finally left the house a half an hour earlier, thinking to wait for Robertas by the church.

To her big surprise, he was already there walking back and forth when she saw him from the distance. She broke into run towards him, "Oh, I'm so glad I've left home early! How long have you been waiting for me?"

"Only five minutes or so."

"So where are we going to go now?" she asked all beaming.

"We could go to the concert. But it's exactly the same one we saw last week. I don't think you would want to listen to the same stuff again." Saying this, Robertas was feeling worried she could agree to listen to the same concert since he had not even one zloty in his pocket this time.

"You are right, I wouldn't want to see the same thing the second time in a row. Where are we going to go? We can't stand here by this church any longer."

"I'm not totally sure about the best way to spend our time today," he said while scratching his head.

"Robertas, wouldn't you like to go somewhere out of the city?! We could catch a coachman, and he would take us there as fast as a wind! What do you think about that?"

"Well, I don't know," turning red on his face and feeling confused, Robertas stressed his every word. He wished he could please her, but that was possible only if he had some money! Of course, he couldn't tell her he didn't have it without ruining the image he had been so diligently creating about himself and his family. What kind of son of the rich factory owner he was if he had no money in his pocket and could not satisfy Julija's simple whim!? Now, he was intensely, almost feverishly thinking how to get away from her unexpected offer.

"It would be nice to go somewhere out-of-town. But I'm not sure if it's appropriate for us to be walking somewhere in some unfamiliar location. Exactly the same way, we could also go for a walk in our local environs, for example, behind your house in Sapezinka. It's right beside your home, and there should be some more people walking there. This way, no one could think anything dirty about our behavior."

"Sure, we could do that," she agreed.

Robertas took a deep breath feeling relieved because he so easily succeeded talking her into submitting to his wish.

Julija noticed his loud sigh of relief. However, at that moment she could not think of any other reason why he was reluctant to go with her out of town. His argument regarding the decency in the eyes of the public opinion seemed convincing enough, and she quickly backed him up in her mind.

Thus, both of them walked all the way from the Sts. Peter and Paul's Church to the Sapezinka area.

Julija was trying to start a lively conversation, but for some reason, it wasn't working very well. Before leaving her house, she had prepared herself to say some important things to Robertas. Despite this, all her efforts now seemed to be in vain, and their conversation wasn't taking shape.

Robertas appeared somewhat sour and lost in thought. Maybe he had a reason for that. Soon enough, Julija also became silent, and for some time, they were walking without saying a word to each other, just trying to guess one another's thoughts.

In silence, they passed a military cemetery, after what they began climbing a steep hill behind it that was overgrown with pine trees.

At last, Robertas realized he must find the way to break this awkward silence reigning between them, and he took heavily heaving Julija by her arm, trying to help her climb the hill.

She gave a start for some unknown to him reason when he touched her. No one ever before had done it to her. Moreover, Robertas himself had never walked so close to her too. He didn't realize she had been dreaming about that kind of gentle and at the same time manly touch. And now just of a suddenly it was happening to her in reality! The pleasant, hot shivers rippled up and down her entire body, and her cheeks turned red.

She didn't get scared of Robertas' sudden move and didn't shy away from him either. She only seemed to become a little more confused, when she her head lowered and looking to the ground was taking weak, unsteady steps.

Robertas, too, noticed how uncomfortably she was feeling since he felt her startle-response to his touch. He decided to break the silence that was beginning to cause a little tension between them.

"Julija, you are going to gymnasium and taking your music lessons in addition to that. What are your plans for the future; do you intend to study further?"

"I haven't given much thought about studying further yet since I still have two more years to go until I will have finished the gymnasium. I have plenty of time to decide what I'm going to do after that. As about the music, I like it a lot. My music teacher predicted me the future of the pianist. However, it takes a lot of time and efforts to become one! Much water will have flown under the bridges until I need to choose one or the other goal in my life to proceed with. Which career would you, Robertas, advise me to pursue?" Julija lifted her face that still had some sign of redness in her cheeks. Having fixed her inquiring gaze on him, she was waiting for the answer.

"This is a pretty big responsibility for me to give you an advice regarding your life's goals. I need to do some serious thinking before I answer your questin."

"You don't have to give me an answer right now. There is no rush; I can wait. But I will be more than happy to hear it whenever you are ready to give me your opinion about that. It seems you posses a lot of knowledge that you've acquired by extensive reading, and I highly value your opinion."

"I'm very pleased to know you trust my opinion, Julija, and I will be glad to help you making the right decision even though I don't think I have the right to consult you in such an important sphere of your life." Then, he cast down his eyes not being able to look straight at her face and resumed talking while faltering at the same time, "After finishing gymnasium, I could not further my education. My father's business at the lumber mill didn't allow me to continue with my schooling even though my dream had been to study philosophy. Unfortunately, the circumstances in my family's business didn't let me to pursue my dream."

Now, Robertas could no longer feel at ease. There was no sense in elaborating his story any further because he didn't wish to reveal all the truth to Julija. He tried to save the situation, but it seemed as if he was just further digging himself deeper into the hole. Utterly lost, not knowing what to do or say next, he began stuttering and gesticulating with his hands.

Luckily, to his big surprise, Julija unexpectedly saved him from the puzzled situation, "I understand you, Robertas. Your father has a lumber processing factory, and that by itself requires a lot of attention! Of course, he is lucky to have you helping him. Therefore, it's not surprising you have no time to go to school. Otherwise, your business could be shaken or even fail all together. Your choice is self explanatory! You are the manufacturer, the rich person. Therefore, you can get away without the higher education. In fact, in your particular situation, by striving for more education, you could lose much more than you could gain if you went to school! Another advantage of yours is that you are not a woman because life is much easier for a man. In comparison to yours, my situation is just the opposite. Therefore, I must choose the right path for my future."

After taking a breath of relieve, Robertas began talking with ease, "You have guessed my thoughts correctly, Julija, even though I tried to conceal them from you. I have to admit that, at one point in the past, I felt very sad because of not being able to continue with my studies. Then I decided I must view things in a sober light because destiny could at times be very cruel to those who make mistakes by disregarding its call. At this time, however, things could not be any better at my father's mill! I think it has to do a lot with me personally contributing to the business. How could I go against my family's will anyway and risk losing everything?! Furthermore, my parents are not going to get any younger either. In addition to that, now I've met you, Julija. You can't even begin to imagine how wonderful I feel being surrounded by your aura. I don't know how to even put this into words in order to describe the warmth and light that is coming from you!"

Being very excited, Robertas with Julija didn't notice when they climbed the tall hill to its top which was not as densely covered with the trees as its sides were.

"Well, this must be the highest point of the hill," he said. "Should we sit down and rest a little bit? You are breathing so heavily. Are you tired? Look how pretty it is over there!" Robertas stretched out his arm the direction of the old part of the capital where graceful towers of various churches could be seen through the branches of the thinly growing trees.

"It's so romantic. I'm glad you've brought me here!" Julija exclaimed.

She was the first to sit down next to a trunk of a thick pine tree. Robertas settled next to her placing his arm around her waist.

Now, Julija's heart fluttered again. At the same time, she felt some uneasy feeling creeping into her heart as if there was a presentiment of a danger looming in the air. Nevertheless, she was powerless to free herself from his embrace.

"What a beautiful view! Look, Robertas, the entire city is sinking in the mist."

"Julija, it's not the mist. This is the smoke. You can't compare mist to this turbid smoke of the city. Once I was lucky to see the real fog. It was such an incredibly beautiful view that I have no words to describe it! It happened three years ago. After passing my examinations and graduating from gymnasium, my classmates and me decided to leave the city for a few days. We wanted to celebrate our upcoming summer vacation. I have to admit this trip made an impact on me. I felt this way probably because for the first time in my life, I was out in the country. All the environs there seemed new to my eyes, and all the sounds were also new to my ears. There were about twenty of us, the young graduates. We found a nice, flat, grassy area by a lake where we danced, sang, and swam almost until midnight. I can't even remember everything we were doing then, but we sure had a lot of fun! I can vividly recall that moment there when as soon as a red disk of the sun touched tips of trees on the other side of the lake, the fog began rising above the surface of the water. It was becoming denser and denser until the water totally disappeared under the fog's whitish sheet. Only the very peaks of the rush growing on the edge of the lake could be seen for a while, peaking out of this soft fog resembling down blanket which was beginning to turn somewhat grayish after the sunset. Even when the sun completely hid itself, the fog kept climbing up, and it spilled out onto the grass growing nearby the lake. Finally, even the meadow together with the all of us in it was covered with that thick blanket of the fog. However, we didn't leave our beautiful place. Instead, we kindled a few bonfires. A couple of us went to the village and brought some milk that was so fresh, right form under the cow. It was still warm. In addition to that, one of our classmates got a huge loaf of bread. So our feast began. The sliced up bread had probably been baked the same day as well since it was spreading such a pleasant smell! It appeared the entire area up at that lake became permeated with that heavenly smell of the fresh bread and milk. Later in the evening, our clothing turned somewhat damp, but it wasn't a problem because, soon, we all moved close to the camp-fires that were already merrily crackling. Our singing resumed and lasted almost without an intermission until the sunrise. And only when the sun's warm rays began caressing the ground after it had climbed the dome of the sky, we fell asleep lying scattered on the grass all over the place. However, not even two hours passed, and our camp came back to life. I forgot to mention that before the sun had come up, the fog began rising again. I remember it appeared so white and soft then. And as soon as the first sunrays illuminated the sky, it turned even whiter – now, it looked like foam of that milk we had been drinking the night before. When I look at this view of the city at this very moment, I can tell that this is the smoke mixed together with dust. Through the distance, this substance gives the false impression of romantic, panoramic view. Just by looking at it, I want to exclaim in Latin a phrase I've read not long ago in one book. It goes like this 'Per umbras magna voce. Omae male sua terrorem inoutit spectantibus!' which when translated into English, means something like this 'It speaks loud to us in twilight and terrifies with its grandeur!' Well, I don't care too much about that kind of 'mist'. It seems to me that over the years, this smog of the city has penetrated me down to my very bones."

"I still find such smoky smog in the city to be very romantic. This view makes me even want to express my excitement with it in some way," Julija protested.

"What do you mean?" Robertas fixed his inquiring look at his beautiful interlocutress.

"Robertas, I can't show my feeling as good as you do. Deep down in my soul, however, I also sense the beauty of the nature. I would love to be able to put what I am feeling right now into Latin phrases like you do, but I don't know this language."

"Julija, you don't have to feel ashamed. I'm not a member of some kind of an exam commission!"

"No, I'm not ashamed of you. I am just worried I could say something wrong or stress the wrong sealable of some word. If you were to point out my mistakes to me, it would probably be more painful than if a real teacher did it during the real examination."

"It's not worth worrying over 'nothing'. To tell the truth, I myself sometimes pronounce words in Latin wrong. However, I don't intend to give up this difficult and at the same time wonderful language because of some triviality. On the contrary – I would even feel graceful to someone who corrected my Latin. I don't want you feeling bad or uncomfortable about it, though. Therefore, we could change the subject. Which lessons at school do you like the most?"

"It's difficult to say. My favorite classes are music and literature. Also, I love poetry!"

"Can you sing something for me from an opera or some operetta?"

"I can't brag I have the perfect voice, but I really like an aria of a duke from "Rigoletto". If you want, I could try to sing it for you."

"Please, sing it."

Julija began singing in a timid, quivering voice:

"Woman is flighty.
Like a feather in the wind,
She changes in voice
And in thought.

Always the lovely,
Pretty face.
In tears or in laughter,

It's untrue."

Without finishing the song, she fell silent.
"Why have you stopped singing?" he asked.
"I don't know the words behind this point."
"May I continue?" Robertas asked.
"Do you know the words?"
"I think I still remember them," he answered.
"Well, go ahead. It's a nice song," she noticed.
"Nice song being sung by the trite duke," he added.
"Don't worry about that; it's just a piece of poetry mixed with music," Julija said.
"Okay, I'll try," he said and began singing,

"Always miserable
Is he who trusts her,
He who confides in her
His unwary heart!

Yet one never feels
Fully happy
Who from that bosom
Does not drink love!"

When Robertas finished singing, he asked, "Julija, what is your favorite poet?"
"My favorite poet is Adomas Mickevicius," she answered, and without being asked, she began reciting:

"During a happy hour filled with joy and sweetness,
You chatter as a birdie, you twitter, and you coo.
Your singing sounds so heavenly –
I don't dare to miss a word.
Captivated by your voice,
I would like to listen to that singing forever..."

As Julija ceased reciting, Robertas took over,

"When you talk, your eyes sparkle,
Ravishing reddishness floods your cheeks.
White teeth like pearls between your beautiful lips,
Those charming eyes – they charge me up...
I'm moving closer to the lips... no strength is left...
Now, kissing, only kissing is left!"

Uttering the last words in a quivering voice, Robertas put his arms around Julijas' waist. Exciting, pleasant shudders flooded her entire body, and she was unable to resist his wishes. She only pleaded quietly," Robertas, please don't... someone could see us..."
However, Robertas either didn't hear or didn't wish to hear her pleading; his arm wrapped around her slim waist kept pulling her closer and closer to his body.
As Julija saw in front of her a stagnant look in his eyes, she became frightened. She felt an impulse to jump to her feet and run, but his strong arms pulled her back, and his soft and exceptionally sweet words calmed her down. He was using all his eloquence in order to capture her attention.
"Julija, dear, don't push me away. I can't imagine how I would be able to survive without you. You are everything to me in this gray world – you are the sun, the light, the air, and the life itself. Before I met you, I had been at peace. All my days had been similar to each other like drops of water, passing by monotonously. However, as soon as your presence penetrated into my routine, I lost my sleep. Your appearance in my life has taken me by the storm, and I no longer can find peace. Julija, if you only knew how much I'm in love with you. I don't know how to put my feelings for you into words. The only way I could prove this is by devoting my body and soul entirely to you."
Julija was trembling with her whole body not knowing what to do. She wanted to run away, but his strong arms continued pulling her closer to him. Not being able to withstand his fiery gaze, she wanted to close her eyes. For a split second, she saw an image of a

fiery, big, red disk of the sun hanging above the bell-towers of the churches that were still dozing in the bluish smog. It seemed the sun was angry watching Julija's indecent behavior.

The next thing, her eyes were covered with a dark shroud.

Even when Robertas very gently kissed her hot lips, Julija didn't open her eyes as if being afraid to see something horrible in front of her. Then he for the second time glued himself to the still opened her mouth, thus, preventing her from uttering a word for a quite a while.

When Julija came to her senses and finally opened her eyelashes, the red circle was already gone as if hiding itself from her. Only the sky remained lit up, drowning the towers of the city in its bloody glow.

Pretty soon, it also faded away, and now it became dark. The night's mantel enveloped the two lovers still leaning against the trunk of the pine tree.

Maybe the dark fall night was to blame for everything that was taking place on the top of this hill since it was hiding the two of them from the eyes of the world. After the first successful Robertas' steps, his other attempts to seduce her followed. Finally, Julija became submissive. She gave up herself to him completely, and he took advantage of the situation, not being able to control his own feelings and desires.

After this incident Julija took her downfall deep into her heart; she didn't know where to put herself so that she could find peace of mind. The thought how she could have done something of this nature was tormenting her every minute of the day.

As a few more days went by, however, she began feeling more at ease. Now, different than before ideas began haunting her. One of them was especially troublesome. Namely, she was paranoid that after reaching his goal, Robertas could leave her all together.

Every day, she lingered at gymnasium in order to avoid coming home and looking in the eye of her aunt and her uncle. She didn't know that Robertas was coming to see her and waiting outside of the gymnasium after her classes were over. He would patiently wait for her until most of the student left.

Not being able to catch Julija for three days, he began thinking she had caught a bad cold or flu. Many times other troubled thoughts, too, like some black shadows crossed his mind. He even imagined the totally outrageous thing that Julija had commit suicide! At that moment, he cowered out of fear thinking the police could show up on his doorsteps and accuse him of ruining the innocent girl's life. Every time this thought crossed his mind, he broke out into a cold sweat.

In addition to that, anxious dreams tormented him also at night. Lately, he had the dream that a policeman tied him up, and he was begging him to be released. Then, in his dream, he tried to free himself by force. The tension built so high that Robertas woke up with his fists clenched and his forehead covered with big drops of sweat. In the morning he was feeling tired and was depressed all day long.

Finally on the fourth day, he was lucky to see Julija leaving the main entrance of her gymnasium. As soon as he saw her, he felt as if a heavy stone rolled of his heart. The sense of sudden relief replaced it, and he smiled ear to ear.

However, he didn't dare to approach the girl, who was the dearest one of all the other girls streaming outside. At that moment, she seemed to be also the closest and the most precious person to him in the entire world!

For a while Robertas followed her from behind. Then he caught up with Julija and spoke to her, "Boy, you seem to be in a big rush. Are you running away from somebody?"

Without lifting her head to look at him, Julija growled out in an angry tone of voice, "That's right! I'm running away from you!"

"Julija, why are you saying this?" asked Robertas feeling stupefied. "I'm not stalking you. You've never said things like this to me before."

"You've never treated me in such an impertinent way before, either. Therefore, I had no reason to reproach you back then. Before, I used to wait for you impatiently. But now, you appear like some vampire, who is stalking me!"

"I hope you don't really mean this. Do I look like a vampire? I've never expected to hear anything like this coming from those lips of yours. You know what – I feel more like a pilgrim at this time in my life!"

"I'm not quite sure who you really are. But don't pretend you are a meek lamb either! After performing your feat of valour, you remind me more of Don Juan than a poor pilgrim. Now you can be proud of accomplishing your goal, and please, leave me alone!"

"Julija, dear, why are you acting on the offensive? I don't feel as if I have committed some crime. Whatever happened between you and me, I think, was the cause of our both inability to suppress our feelings of love for each other. All people are creations of God that have been meant for love. Therefore, the feelings are given to us so that we could enjoy them. If there is somebody to blame for the recent incident, then we both are responsible for it, but not just me alone! I admit I'm week, and I gave way to temptation which, at that moment, was the most powerful thing I've ever encountered in my entire life! I've never realized that some feeling could be stronger than one's mind. But where were you then – why didn't you stop me from doing that!? All you had to do was just to say one word. There was no way I would have been making love to you against your will! Nevertheless, despite of everything that has happened, I beg you to forgive me for losing my mind which tuned me then into helpless weakling."

Julija didn't answer. She was weighing Robertas' words to herself. At first, she considered it to be the biggest insolence for him to say things like that. However, little by little, her rage went down. And finally, she even began justifying him. Now in her mind she was reasoning that if she herself had showed more resistance then, nothing would have happened between the two of them. Therefore, she wouldn't be worried now and she wouldn't have to blame Robertas for something that most likely was her own fault anyhow, either. Moreover, Julija also became frightened he could get mad at her and leave her in these shameful circumstances. Thus, she lost the desire to reprove him.

Walking beside him while suffering immense heartache, she only moaned quietly and uttered in a barely audible voice, "I hope neither one of us is going to suffer the consequence of our thoughtless behavior."

"Julija, stop eating your heart out! What makes you think there should be any consequences?"

"But what if something bad happens? What will I do then?! Just the mere thought of it makes me go crazy. I would not be able to handle that — I would probably kill myself!" Julija resumed pouring out her frustration.

"Julija, don't say things like this! It makes me terrified. If anything bad ever happened, I'm sure, we could think of something in order to remedy the situation."

"I hope everything is going to turn out okay, and I won't have to blame you for anything."

"You'll see — everything will be just fine. I'm sure your worries are in vain."

Thus, Robertas was able to calm himself and Julija down a little bit. He saw her home where they as usually stood for a while talking in the alley.

For a while, it seemed to Robertas all the problems were left behind. Anxious dreams ceased tormenting him, and intrusive thoughts causing bad mood no longer disturbed him, too. Most importantly, however, his relationship with Julija had not changed even though he had been concerned about that happening. On the contrary — they became even more intimate now.

Without feeling shy, he was making love to her to his heart content almost every day and enjoying every minute in this paradise that, he reasoned to himself, was being sent to both of them from the heaven even if it was lacking the blessing of the Heavenly Father.

Three weeks passed by, and both of them were in time to forget about their worries that they had been so preoccupied with before. True, some far away inside echo reached Julija's mind again when she fell a little ill, but she didn't pay much attention to it. She thought she was just getting sick with flu.

Since her sickness continued causing occasional episodes of throwing up, Robertas remembered his anatomy classes he had attended at gymnasium a few years ago. Cold sweat stood out on his forehead as he understood the reason of Julija's ailment. He suddenly realized what processes were happening in her body. However, he could not bring himself to ask her about it.

The long awaited opportunity to talk with her on this subject presented itself by chance when Julija again complained about feeling nauseous. Then Robertas asked her, "Julija, do you have anatomy classes at school?"

"We do. Why?"

"I think it's good that this discipline is included into the gymnasium program together with the other subjects to be taught to the students. This way, they can get some kind of understanding about their bodies and diseases in relation to them."

"Yes, currently we are studying about the circulation of blood in a human organism and the work of the human heart when carrying the blood through the veins," Julija elaborated.

"I always loved my anatomy classes," Robertas continued talking about the subject matter, "even though they often caused me to find some abnormalities in my own body. However, it always later turned out to be false since it appeared I had only imagined all those symptoms happening to me."

Robertas had to use all his keen wits in order to approach the subject in a round-about way. He wanted her to discover for herself about the gynaecology so that she could find out some answers regarding her sudden indisposition.

He wasn't sure how to put into words such a delicate matter. Finally, after some searching for the right phrases in his mind, he started, "I find the anatomy classes to be of the most importance and usefulness to any student."

"For some reason, I don't feel any inclination for the human anatomy," she objected.

"As about me, I've always been interest in gynaecology."

"Eek! You are such an inveterate person! Why are you interested namely in this aspect of the anatomy?" she inquired.

"There is nothing surprising in this; I think every cultured person should know as much as possible about his or her body. It can only benefit every one of us."

"But the gynaecology pertains to womanly diseases and not to those of men."

"That is exactly why namely women should be interested in it more than the men!" he stated in a loud voice.

"For some reason, I've never been interest in this subject."

Robertas further insisted, "But you should, and then, you would know more about your body."

Robertas came home feeling very distressed. As soon as he crossed the threshold of his room, he began rummaging in a pile of textbooks and manuals that he had not touched for a period of at least a couple of years. Only now, being forced by his circumstances, he pulled out an old school book of anatomy and got absorbed in it. However, he didn't find any solace in doing that. The other way - all that had been happening to Julija recently didn't appear promising to him after the reading some pages.

He didn't sleep all night long; he wished he could share his findings with Julija. However, he already knew her outlook on her situation, and he also understood he could not touch this subject anymore.

Little did he know it was not necessary for him informing her about her current status because as soon as Julija returned home, the first thing she did was she, too, found her textbook of anatomy.

Not even an hour later, she already knew one particular lesson so well that she, without any doubt, would have received the highest evaluation in the class if there was a test about it.

At that moment, however, her entire body was shaking, and tears began rolling down her cheeks obscuring her mind. Unbearable heartbreak shackled her heart, and a bitter cry escaped Julija's mouth.

Only now she realized why Robertas insisted about her learning the anatomy. It meant he also had sensed the cause and the reason of her current condition.

Not having had a wink of sleep and feeling worn out, she left the house with pale face and hurting head the next morning.

Julija with difficulty waited for her classes to end, after what she was the first one to run outside. As she saw Robertas standing on the other side of the street, she decidedly crossed it, walked up to him, and politely greeted him trying to suppress her excitement.

Julija didn't show any sign of worry even when the school building remained far behind them.

Nevertheless, as soon as she realized both of them were alone, she couldn't help but to start reproving him again, "Robertas, I was so stupid yesterday because I didn't catch right away why you were talking about the gynaecology. Looks like you had caught my 'disease' earlier than I had. I don't know what to do now. Just the mere thought of the possibility of such a thing terrifies me. What if our apprehension is real?!"

Julija didn't get an answer to her question. For a while, both of them were walking in silence, and neither one dared to break it. It was obvious the situation was getting tenser, and it was taking on a darker shade than ever. Julija and Robertas both knew at any given moment now, the tension could burst; then, neither one of them would probably do without tears and hysteria.

However, their negative feelings kept still growing and filling up the air around them that resembled a big, dark cloud similar to that which usually forms high in the sky before a storm.

Robertas and Julija were feeling the same way. They realized the silence had to come to an end. At the same time, one and the other were worried because they didn't know how their conversation was going to turn.

Julija uttered the first, "Robertas, say something. Please, talk to me. I need to hear some comforting words!"

Just a few minutes ago, she wanted to attack him. However, things turned out the opposite way – now, she was begging for help.

"Robertas," she continued pleading, "why aren't you talking to me? I feel as if I'm going out of my mind! It seems the entire world is against me, including you!"

"Julija, it's all just in your mind. Pregnancy is such a thing that sometimes women can be mistaken about it."

She abruptly interrupted him, "There is no doubt I'm pregnant! We need to discuss this situation seriously. All this guess-work of yours is in vain. One way or the other, we've gone too far. Therefore, we must decide the future course for us. We can't afford making any more mistakes!"

"I still think you shouldn't draw the conclusions beforehand. We have plenty of time to decide what to do next," Robertas sounded irritated.

"I agree with you - this is not an emergency situation. It's not like we are having a fire. But still, we ought to take our relationship seriously and, at least, make up some kind of plan for the nearest future. I don't want you to sit with your hands folded, looking cool and indifferent."

Robertas snapped out, "Oh, stop it! What if everything is fine?! Why would I have to burden myself by making some senseless plans and taking some dumb measures that, most likely, are going to turn out to be completely unnecessary? We will probably laugh later when we remember all this."

"I wish your words would come out to be true, so we don't have to make any arrangements in regards to this. It would be such a relief!"

Robertas and Julija parted without having any mutual consent. All their other meetings were not any better, either; they also turned out to be fruitless. Robertas remained adamant since he maintained she was tormenting herself without any reason.

Two more months passed by, and right after the New Year's, brutally freezing weather set in. In addition to that, a lot of snow blocked the roads making it almost impossible for them to meet. Many enterprises in Vilnius, including Julijas' gymnasium, were closed.

The timing was cruel to Julija driving her insane. Her situation every week was getting worse - more threatening and horrible.

Finally, she decided to do something appreciable in order to remedy it.

When Robertas and she met outside the St. Peter and St. Paul's Church where they often used to meet before, she right away began her conversation, "Robertas, I no longer wish to remain in this kind of uncertainty. We must decide today how we are going to go about the situation. We already know that I am expecting a baby; there is no reason to delay!"

"Of course, we have to do something about this. But first, we have to weigh all the pros and cons. Tell me, please, how are your aunt and uncle going to react upon learning you are pregnant?"

"I have no clue. I'm afraid to even think about that! In the worst case scenario, they could just kick me out on the street where I would definitely perish with no one there to help me."

Julija was deliberately exaggerating her fears since she knew well her aunt and uncle loved her beyond love. Moreover, they valued the possibility of managing her huge inheritance. Both of them understood that if they forbade Julija staying with them, some other relatives would certainly provide her and her newborn child with the shelter. Julija herself realized that well. Nevertheless, she continued pretending she was an indigent orphan in order to evoke Robertas' compassion.

"Wow! I've never realized your aunt and uncle could be so cruel to you. What do you think you could do in order to avoid this from happening?"

"I know, Robertas, what needs to be done."

"What kind of plan have you conceived now?!" Robertas cried out.

"I think the only way out of this situation is for me to get married," she said gazing pleadingly into his eyes.

Robertas had never thought about the possibility of marrying Julija even though he was truly in love with her. However, he also knew well he could not marry her at this time in his life. The circumstances in his own family were working against him. Therefore, the possibility of marriage was out of the question.

No wonder, as soon as he heard her words, his entire body began shaking hard as if thunder hit him on his head. Suddenly he became utterly confused and could not utter a word for a long time.

Only after Julija repeated her request, he answered in a dispirited voice, "Is this the only solution you can think of? There must be some other way to remedy this situation."

"What ideas can you offer in this case?" she asked sounding very disappointed.

"I don't know yet. It just seems to me that the marriage is not the answer at this moment."

Julija was becoming desperate, "Don't you love me? You are rich, and we have nothing to worry about!"

"What good do those riches do for me if I'm still not in title to be the master of my parents' property?! I can't manage their assets independently. If my father found out everything about our situation, I don't know what he would do. It could bring huge conflict between him and me, and the outcome of it would probably be very undesirable! I don't wish to lose my entire inheritance. Therefore, I can't afford to make my father upset. Don't despair, though, Julija. We are going to get married later, but we must wait for a better time to come in order to do this. In a meanwhile, we have to come up with something other than that. I think, the most rational solution for now should be to get rid of the pregnancy by making arrangements with a doctor."

"Is it possible to do this?" she asked in a frightened voice.

"Anything is possible. You just need to want it. I think this is the best way out of the situation. If you agree, I will find a doctor who is going to take care of everything."

"Okay, find a doctor for me. I no longer care. My situation is really bad; in fact it's so bad that it can't get any worse! I just want to get rid of this disaster."

Having found the means to solve the situation, both of them parted. Julija had a couple of nights of peaceful sleep since she expected to get rid of her pregnancy with the help of Robertas very soon.

And he wasn't just feeding her with the empty promises because he was really searching for that kind of doctor who could do this for her. First of all, Robertas came to the maternity hospital. However, his visit there turned out to be a total failure. The doctor he talked with at the hospital explained to him it was against the law to perform abortions there. Moreover, he insisted in finding out the

name of the woman who was thinking of doing the abortion.
Therefore, Robertas as fast as a bullet left the hospital.

In spite of his unsuccessful first attempt, he didn't cease looking for other opportunities to find the right doctor for Julija.

After having difficult time, he finally found one, but the problem was that the doctor asked him to pay a fee of one hundred roubles before providing his service.

Of course, Robertas could only dream about such a big amount of money. Despite that, he didn't refuse to accept the offer. He came home and got out the only suit he had in his wardrobe that had already been worn well enough and took it to the city market in order to sell it.

However, only one person showed interest in his suit, and he offered only ten roubles for it, which was just one tenth of the amount of the money the doctor had asked Robertas to pay for the abortion. Robertas understood that even if he sold his costume, he would still have to worry about where to get the remaining ninety roubles.

Thus, without having sold the suit, he returned home.

In spite of experiencing another failure, he continued puzzling over how to get the money for the doctor. Suddenly, he recalled seeing his mother's golden bracelet a few years ago. He also remembered seeing some of her rings.

After rummaging all the corners at home and not having found anything, Robertas decided to ask her about them himself. He walked into the kitchen where she was preparing lunch. However, the food wasn't spreading a pleasant smell which was sending him the message that the meal was going to be meager, just as the hostess was herself.

His mother was standing by the kitchen table and slicing bread. She was a little over forty years old, but her hair had already been grown somewhat gray. And her clothing looked so worn out that even the patches on both elbows of her blouse were holey.

When Robertas walked in, she lifted her smiley, tired face and uttered, "You are probably hungry, sunny. The food is almost ready."

"No, I'm not hungry. Besides, this smell doesn't give me an appetite," he said.

Then he looked at her tired face and apologetically added, "Most of the time, though, I like everything you cook for us."

"Son, it's difficult to prepare a decent meal without any meat. No wonder it doesn't smell good to you. I wished we had enough money to buy more food. Lately your father has been earning very little money. Therefore, right now we must content with what we have."

"It's too bad because we had better times before. Back then, you used to dress up. I remember you even wearing a bracelet, rings, and earrings. Where is all your jewelry now?"

"Oh, sonny! They have been long gone. I sold them when you were graduating from gymnasium. Remember - I bought you your suit then? That's where my money for the jewelry had gone. The only thing that has been left of my jewelry is my wedding ring since I couldn't bring myself to sell it, too."

Robertas no longer wished to stay there and listen to his mother talking. He was feeling heaviness on his heart. Without saying a word, he walked out of the kitchen.

When he came back into the room, he opened the door of the wardrobe that was half way empty with only a few worthless rags hanging inside of it. Now he realized how hopeless his situation really was. He understood that even if he sold everything in this house, most likely, he still wouldn't be able to collect the right amount of money.

Not knowing what to do next, Robertas was spending the remaining part of the day at home depressed, but he didn't want to go anywhere either.

When his father came home from work and they sat down to eat supper, Robertas still didn't utter a word even though his parents accosted him a few times. He just didn't feel like talking to them, since he was still trying in his mind to find a solution to his problem. Moreover, without even finishing his meal, he got up from under the table and went back to his room.

His mother and father came to a conclusion that their son was unable to find work again, and therefore, he was upset because of this reason.

Robertas didn't meet with Julija for two days, which turned out for her to be an eternity. Now she regretted she didn't know where he lived. Otherwise, she would have definitely gone looking for him. However, she was not aware of his address or even his surname, and there were literally thousands of men by the name Robertas in Vilnius which wouldn't have done any good in her search!

Julija still was not able to properly evaluate her situation. She believed in Robertas. Therefore, she could not imagine he was capable of leaving her in this kind of condition.

For the second time now, they had been separated for a long period of time. She was beginning to get angry at Robertas.

Nevertheless, as soon as Julija saw him, she instantly forgot all her negative feelings. She was so happy that she even forgot to ask him what was his surname or address. Having rejoiced at him, she soon again returned to the same old subject of how to get rid of her pregnancy.

As she fixed her inquiring gaze on Robertas, he cast his eyes down. Before she even began talking, he knew what to expect; he had already prepared himself for this conversation way beforehand. Thus, he started explaining to her his findings in a most gentle manner possible, "Julija, I've found the doctor. To tell the truth, it was not easy for me to accomplish this task because abortions are against the law. Nevertheless, I think everything is going to work out, but we need to wait for a couple more weeks."

"I can wait for two more weeks even though, in my situation, it's going to cost me a lot of stress. But I'm determined to do anything that is needed so that everything would work out okay."

"We can't lose hope. You'll see - this nightmare is going to be over in two weeks, and we no longer will have to worry about it!" he reassured her.

Robertas didn't spend much time with Julija that evening. Right before leaving, he promised to meet with her in a week since the weather was very cold, and it was virtually impossible to stay outside even for a half an hour. However, in his heart and mind, he already knew this was their last meeting.

Before their separation, he kissed and caressed her for quite a while, and Julija totally settled down.

As Robertas with an aching heart found himself near the Sts. Peter and Paul's Church, he decided to walk inside. Even though he wasn't a pious person by nature and, once in a while, he even doubted in existence of God, now he came to Him looking for comfort. Being weighed down by this huge disaster, he was forced to turn to the Almighty at least for some inner guidance since there was no one around to give him humanly advice.

Being alone in the middle of this magnificent, empty home of God, he was pleading in his heart for the answer to his prayer. His steps echoing in the tall arches, vaults, and central dome lavishly decorated with ancient paintings of saints and countless white sculptures of angels and architectural ornaments, Robertas walked up to the barrier of the main altar. He got down on his knees, chained the fingers of his both hands together so firmly he started feeling pain, and whispered, "Credo in Deum, dominum nostrum omnipotentem!" ("I believe in God, the Father!").

Tears flooded his eyes as he was pronouncing these words, expressing all his trust in God. Robertas expected that if He really existed, then He really could answer his prayer.

However, it was very quiet around, and suddenly he got overwhelmed with horror. For a split second, he got frightened that God Himself was turning His back on him.

Then, Robertas lifted his eyes at the altar, lowered his elbows onto the top of the barrier covered with a fancy, white sheet, and loudly hailed the St. Virgin Mary, "O salve, Regina, Mater misericordiae!" ("Pray for us, O holy Mother of God!").

His voice resounded throughout the vaults of the entire church, and only the echo of many little voices from all the corners answered him. Then again, dead silence shrouded him.

Only now Robertas understood his cry for help was a voice in the wilderness; his words were seemingly dissipating like smoke in the wind.

Robertas got up off his knees, looked around, and he felt ashamed because of asking for help those who couldn't help even themselves. How could then they help him?! It seemed to Robertas his own destiny now was against him.

Feeling distressed, he came home where he could not find peace also.

Julija, in a meanwhile, remained home thinking her heartbreak would end soon enabling her to take a breath of relief. In general, she was feeling at peace; the only thing that made her unhappy, though, was that she could not see Robertas.

A week went by, and he didn't show up. Julija began worrying. When a few more days were gone with him not coming to visit her, she became afraid he didn't love her anymore. At the same time, she was angry at him and thought of heaping reproaches for not coming to see her.

As one more week passed by, Julija totally broke down. Thousands of various horrible thoughts kept crossing her mind. However, the only thought she refused to let into her heart was that he could abandon her.

Therefore, she started justifying him against her own assault on him by all manner of means. She even invented a theory he had most likely been sick and, thus, could not come and see her.

However, the time passing by, the circumstances themselves dispelled her erroneous thoughts.

Finally, Julija realized Robertas had left her. For a long time, she didn't want to accept that thought, and she kept cherishing some unknown hope. But Robertas still wasn't showing up, and she finally exhausted all her efforts.

During the freezing winter weeks she had thought he had been avoiding to catch a bad cold. Nevertheless, it was already the end of March; the sun was shining brightly high in the sky, warming up the air more and more every day.

In the beginning, the melting snow turned into creeks that were carrying the troubled waters along the streets of Vilnius.

After another week passed by, only the scarce patches of dirty, icy snow could be seen lying here and there on the ground that the sun was mercilessly finishing to melt away as well.

The sunshine was beckoning citizens to go outside, and it was almost impossible for anyone to remain at home.

No matter how much distressed Julija was, but as soon as she found herself in the vortex of the waking up nature, her weeping heart cheered up also. At times when she became depressed, though, she would go out to their orchard where she walked and imagined Robertas walking next to her, just like they often did a few months ago. During those moments, she always saw herself in her mind talking with him in a friendly way where she no longer upbraided him with anything.

However, this was only daydreaming that was lulling her mind to sleep; those were the illusions that she was able to experience only in her head.

Oddly enough, she still had a slight glimmer of hope deep down in her soul that their holy love had not been completely lost. There was no room for any anger left in her heart. Most likely, if she saw Robertas, she would have not dared to say a word for rebuke and she would have definitely forgotten all the troubles.

Lately, Julija had been reproving herself for hiding her inheritance from Robertas. She reasoned he probably had left because he had been afraid to make his father angry. Most likely, he would have been dismissed from his leading position at the lumber mill if he had gone against his father's wishes. There was also a possibility he had had a conversation with his father about Julija after what he really was discharged from work. Therefore, not having any money to pay for the abortion, he had left her all together.

Now, she truly regretted she didn't tell him the truth about being rich, richer than his father! She realized there was no reason for them asking his father for reprieve. If not for her shams, Robertas wouldn't have to suffer the humiliation from his own family.

Julija decided once and for all to find him and tell him the truth about her real status. She was going to explain to Robertas that she was rich, and that there was no reason to worry about his father's cruel behavior. Thus, they could get married, and Robertas would become the master of her significant assets, including the big tailor's shop. Therefore, even when they had their baby born, it wouldn't be such a big deal. Now it seemed to Julija there was nothing serious to be worried about. On the contrary - giving a birth to their child - could bring them closer together. Julija was convinced that if everything worked out this way, she would be gladly performing her motherly duties which would definitely crown her with halo of happiness!

She was determined not to delay even one more day and find Robertas. Julija was palnning to explain everything to him and finally tell him the truth. At the same time, she had a slight fear he could disagree with her decision to keep the baby and continue pressing her to go to the doctor in order to get rid of him. Julija also knew that if he insisted on this, she wouldn't dare resisting his wishes. One way or the other, she needed to find him as soon as possible!

After her classes at gymnasium ended, she hurried out to a sawmill the address of which she had learned a few days ago. Since this was the closest sawmill in the entire vicinity, she was almost sure Robertas had been managing namely this place.

As soon as she found herself in the territory of the mill that had not been fenced in, she saw piles of logs. The workmen there were hauling the logs out of the river, rolling them onto the bank, and piling up in the place about one hundred meters away from the water.

Sounds of piercingly screeching saws, while cutting the wood, were coming from the shed. It was impossible to talk in this kind of noise since no one could hear a word being said.

Julija was standing in the middle of the yard, littered with sawdust, and she was searching with her eyes for some office there. She thought there ought to be some kind of premises or at least a room where she expected to find Robertas. However, she could not see anything even remotely resembling an office.

Then, she walked up to two laborers who were rolling wet tree-trunks and uttered, "Excuse me, please, where could I find Robertas?"

The men ceased working. One of them pointed the direction of the shed and said in a hollow voice, "You can go inside of this building where you'll see his father. He knows where you can find Robertas."

After hearing this, Julija cowered since she didn't want this visit with his father, whom she had always been so afraid of, to happen. However, now she didn't have a choice. She had to talk to Robertas' father even though there was no time to prepare for what she could say to him. Julija wanted to leave, but she noticed the two sets of eyes of the workers observing her with curiosity. Under the pressure of the circumstances, she with trembling legs walked inside the shed.

It was rather dark there, especially after leaving the sunny lumber yard outside.

She stood by the door for a minute until her eyes got used to the twilight reigning inside of the shed. To her big surprise, she saw only one person laboring near a pile of logs. He was cutting some planks. It was a middle aged man all covered with sawdust to the point where it was impossible to even distinct his facial features.

Julija didn't know what to do; she was reluctant to start a conversation with this scary looking man. She already wanted to turn around and leave but it was too late because the laborer lifted his head and spotted her.

He walked up very close to Julija, leaned with his entire body towards her, and asked loudly trying to out-voice the squeal of saws now coming from outside, "What are you looking for here, miss?"

"I've come here to talk to the owner of this sawmill or to his son."

"The owner was here not long ago. Maybe he is still somewhere outside. But it's not likely you could ever find his son here; he almost never shows up at this sawmill. To be exact, I've never seen him here myself."

After getting such unexpected answer, without feeling her legs, she walked out of the mill. She wasn't paying attention to the mud in the yard when she walked straight across the puddles of water not looking for a dry spot to step on.

Having lost all hope, she left the lumber territory with her head hanging down, not feeling ground under her feet. At that moment she was feeling totally lost in life.

As she found herself back in the street, she could not comprehend where she was going. Her instinct was steering her ahead. Tears kept flooding her eyes, which made her walk almost fumblingly. Some big lump was lodged in her throat that she could not swallow no matter how hard she tried.

Julija didn't feel when she crossed the Neris River through the Green Bridge and found herself by the Gediminas' Castle Hill. But she continued walking until she felt as if being woken up from some sleep when she saw the Sts. Peter and Paul's Church that was lit up by the bright spring sunrays, and now it was glowing in the blue of the sky. It appeared as if this chef-d'oeuvre of Baroque style was mocking her because of her grief.

She stopped by the tall stucco fence surrounding the entire territory of the church and remembered how many times she had met here with Robertas. She didn't want to leave this spot where she had spent so many happy minutes chatting and laughing with him.

Through the black iron gate of the churchyard that was also beautifully decorated with the fanciful ornaments she slipped inside the church. The interior of it was even more magnificent looking like a very expensive, exquisite pearl with all its statues and architectural ornaments painted white!

Soon, with trembling legs due to the excitement and respect to all this beauty surrounding her Julija was walking through the black and white checkered stone floor.

As she was fearfully looking around, it seemed to her that all those countless stone figures of the saints, protruding out of the walls, were following her with their intent, censuring stares.

Julija persisted walking toward the main altar located in the centre of the front wall of the church, and she ended up exactly in the same spot where Robertas had been kneeling a couple months ago upon separating with her. Then, he also had come to this worship place asking for help. However, he left from there feeling the same heartache as he had been feeling upon entering this God's home. It appeared as if destiny had already prearranged all the events for both of them.

Julija was kneeling in the exact same place hoping to find solace here. She just like Robertas before, with tears in her eyes and holding her hands in the position of prayer, was gazing at the altar where Jesus Christ had been nailed to the huge cross. His head was hanging low on His chest.

While on her knees, she was asking for mercy the Highest, Who Himself was in much worse condition than Julija right in front of her eyes. A thought suddenly crossed her mind – how could he help her if He could not defend Himself from the tortures of the villains!?

Now Julija began feeling as if she came here not to ask the Lord to help her but she had come here to have pity on the Martyr, Who had been too weak to control His destiny even though He had been the Son of God.

However, Julijas' difficult status was still holding her soul undermined. Her outlook on religion differed from that of Robertas. She blindly believed in God and all the saints, and she had prayed not only when in church but, also, when at home. She would never forget to say a short prayer to the Almighty upon getting up every morning and, then, upon going to sleep at night, too.

Therefore, when she was kneeling on the bench in this church, her lips automatically began whispering in Polish while calling upon all the saints to help her, "O sventa, Marija, pomue mne. O borze ojeze ratuj mne!" ("Oh, Saint Mary, help me. Oh, God Almighty, help me!")

However, it seemed to her that the words she uttered in Polish language commonly used by everyone in order to pray at the church were not affective enough to reach those Heavenly Beings. Therefore, she changed the language to Latin which appeared to be the more divine talk in order to get their attention, "Pater noster ir Ave Maria ir Credo in Deum patrem omnipotentem!" ("Heavenly Father and Virgin Mary and I believe in God Jesus Christ Almighty!").

But her words again crashed against the high walls of the church sending only icy echoing back to her with no answer from the Holy Spirit Itself. It seemed not even the saints, staring at her with curiosity from the ancient paintings hanging on the walls in the fancy, golden frames, heard her words; they weren't reacting to her prayers.

Having noticed this, Julija ceased crying quarter since the saints continued only looking at her indifferently from all the directions. She could even perceive irony in some of their gentle smiles.

However, Julija had no strength to get up and walk away from there. Thus, she remained kneeling in this splendid sanctuary. She no longer had any power left entreating the Almighty, also, in order to hear His judgment on which her entire future was supposed to depend.

Obviously, the saints were not in any rush with their reward for her prayers. On the contrary – it appeared as if they were waiting for something, or maybe they just could not come to an agreement among themselves.

Suddenly, she heard someone's whispering into her ear, "Get up and go because these stone hearted statues are not going to help you with anything."

Julija obeyed this unknown voice. She got back to her feet and walked through the empty church with her arms hanging down on both sides of her body. It was obvious just looking at her face she was feeling disappointed not having got anything for her pains.

Now she was absolutely sure there was no one in the entire world to help her. The only person she still could rely on was only herself. She had to make the final decision.

Having lost all her hope, she left the cold church where she was able to sense also some faint smell of mould, which oppressed her even more.

Therefore, when she found herself in a more joyful environment where everything had been waking up after the deep winter's sleep, she gladly looked up at the sun still shining high in the blue sky.

But this bubbling with spring environment also couldn't completely dispel her horrible apathy that was about to reach a culmination point. Very little was needed for the most horrific transgression to happen. The other words, Julija was within a hair's breadth from committing the suicide.

Only because no one besides her and Robertas knew about her current situation, she was reluctant to go against herself. Her beloved could not do any more harm to her since he had not only disappeared himself but he also had taken her secret together with him.

Nevertheless, Julija realized that no matter how hard she tried to conceal her pregnancy, sooner or later, it would come out to the surface since it would be impossible to hide something as obvious as this.

She kept walking along the street lit up by the warm sun rays, but she wasn't paying much attention to the waking up nature.

After crossing the road, she headed straight towards the Neris River where she descended to its bank and walked down to the widely overflowing river-bed.

For a long time, Julija was gazing at the flowing turbid water that in some places was whirling in vortexes and, then, flowing speedily away from her, after what the new vortexes were forming right in front of her eyes and flowing away, too. It appeared as if those vortexes were inviting Julija to come into their embrace.

However, she still didn't dare to jump into this cold, muddy water. She was waiting patiently for something as if expecting to get a better opportunity to die.

Julija stood there for about a half an hour and, finally, she sobered up. She even shook her head thinking to herself how dumb she was to harbor such a stupid idea of killing herself! Nothing would have come out of it anyway.

First of all, it was not deep enough right by the bank of the river. Second, there were a lot of people walking on the sidewalk that was located right on the top of the precipice that was running along the busy street. In fact at this very hour, people kept ceaselessly streaming both its directions. Therefore, somebody would have definitely dragged her out onto the bank after having snatched her right out of the clutches of death. And third, the problem was that she knew how to swim which would make it difficult for her to drown.

In spite of all this, Juliga didn't completely renounce her intention to commit the suicide. She just was contemplating over the other more assuring ways of dying when no one could save her!

Soon, she herself stepped into that stream of people in the street and quickly headed toward the center of the city.

She walked over the bridge across the narrow Vilnele River and continued walking along its bank overgrown with bushes and, in some places, with tall grasses. Being led by instinct, Julija began climbing the Hill of the Gediminas' Tower.

As she reached its halfway, it was difficult for her to breathe since she had still been carrying a heavy bag with her school books. She stopped to take a breath and remembered how, once before, she had walked together with Robertas the same path winding to the very top of the Gediminas' Hill. The difference was that back then both of them had been full of happiness. She had also got tired that time while climbing this hill, and Robertas had helped her to walk by holding her hand.

This time, though, she was climbing the hill not to enjoy the view of Vilnius, but feeling forgotten by everyone, she was walking to the top with the intention of committing the big sin. No person in the world could interfere with her from making this horrible act; it was the only thing she was contemplating about. Only once in a while Robertas' shadow would glide past her and leave her far behind.

However, as soon as Julija found herself on the very top of the Gediminas' Hill, she didn't rush to the place that she had chosen to jump off. Instead, she turned to the ruins of the Gediminas' Castle where she had once stood with Robertas. Being in his embrace, she'd enjoyed the view of Antakalnis' Hills with red domes and white towers of the Sts. Peter and Paul's Church parading itself right in front of them, nestled below among the transparent verdure.

This time, just like at that time with Robertas, the fine scenery had been opened right in front of her eyes. Shrinking back, she leaned against the big, cold stones of the castles' retaining wall and submerged in the pleasant memories of the still recent past. They were so vivid now! She could almost feel his hands on her waist and hear him saying in Latin, "De praedestinatione Dei et libero arbitrio." ("The destiny and the free will.")

Now, Julija was thinking that if she could start her relationship with Robertas all over again, her answer to that phrase of his would be, "Id est cibi, potus, somni, venus, omnia moderata sint." ("Self-control is needed everywhere: when eating, drinking, sleeping, and making love.")

However, Julija knew well those times were gone forever. Being oppressed by her thoughts and ready for anything, she left the place at the ruins of the Gediminas' Castle defense wall.

Now, she was climbing a narrow, spiral stone stairway inside of the Gediminas' Tower.

When she reached the top of it, she walked outside to the very edge of its flat surface and looked down leaning far over a barrier going all the way along the perimeter of the ground circle area of the tower.

Far down below, a horrible precipice opened up before her very eyes luring to swallow her. She instantly jumped away from this fathomless pit as if some imperceptible power would have thrown her back from the opened jaws of Death Itself.

Suddenly, she woke up from the apathetic downfall of her soul. She heard monotonous sounds of the city pulsing with life all around far below. Her eyes began nervously running around enabling her to see only life in its full swing.

Smoke was coming out from chimneys of many houses located in the old part of Vilnius, and people were hurriedly crossing the big Cathedral Square right at the Gediminas' Castle foothill.

Julija lifted her eyes and saw the intensely blue sky filled with sunlight, and it was enticing her to live.

A dark grave flashed through her mind making her to shake with horror. In a split second, life seemed so precious to Julija she could not believe she was thinking of raising her hand against herself just a few minutes ago.

Looking down at the smoke coming out of the chimneys into the blue sky, she mumbled under her nose, "How many girls just like me live under those red tile roofs? I must live. I shall survive!"

At run she descended the Gediminas' Tower, and without looking back, she hurried down the Gediminas' Hill, the place of her potential guillotine, where so little had been needed the black veil would have covered pupils of her eyes preventing her from enjoying life on this Earth forever.

On the way home, she began feeling lightness that she had not experienced for a long time; it was slowly but surely creeping into her heart, thus, completely waking her up for life.

Julija didn't know yet that the man who had been cutting boards in the lumber mill was really Robertas's father. Judging by his son's boasting, she always imagined his father being the owner of a much bigger factory than the one she had just seen, where there were only two sheds with the saws droning non-stop. Moreover, there was no office at all in any of those sheds.

However, Julija didn't go into the heart of this matter. She just for a little while wondered with curiosity if there could be so much work in this tiny mill as Robertas had portrayed it to be. She thought that it wasn't necessary for two people to be managing such a small business in scope. Rather, it appeared that even one person would not have much to do there! Nevertheless, Robertas always pretended to be so busy and so swamped with work! She had noticed there was not even one third of activity at that lumber mill her family had currently been dealing with in her tailor's shop even though only one administrator and one supervisor were able to manage all the business there. In addition to that, there were probably ten times more workers for just the two of them to manage in her sewing-shop.

Thus, Julija came home too late for supper and without being able to figure Robertas' business out.

Robertas' father forgot about Julia as soon as she had left through the mill door. Then lunch time came, and the saws had to be stopped. They just like humans also needed to get some rest. In addition to that, just like the laborers of the saw mill, who needed to eat lunch, those saws, too, needed replenishment of the oils for their rotating assemblies.

As usually, all the work crew gathered in one place to eat lunch they had brought with them to work from home. During winter time, the men used to eat their food in a watchman's box being used as a shelter for someone in order to guard the logs, boards, and planks during the night. Most of the time, it would be warm inside of it due to the heat coming from a wood burning stove. But during the summertime, they liked to eat their food outside.

This time, too, they sat down onto the logs just under a roof of a porch of the shed in the heat of the sun. Everyone unfolded their bundles with the food and began avidly eating. Those were the only times the men could talk a little since, during the day, they would be very busy and rarely could exchanged a word or two between themselves. In addition to that, the saws always hummed tiresomely making it difficult to hear anything.

Most of the time, they would just tease each other while eating their lunches. The workers who worked outside of the shed in the yard had more opportunities to talk, but mainly the real conversation would begin only during the lunchtime upon everyone gathering together.

Therefore, today after Julija's visit right before the lunchtime, they were anxious to discuss this rare event in their workplace.

One of the workers, whom she had asked to help her find Robertas, said, "Antanas, how come that beautiful, young lady was looking for your son?"

"She wasn't looking for my son; she was looking for the son of the owner."

"But she said Robertas. That's why we sent her to you!"

"I don't know what she asked you but to me she said she was looking for the owner of the mill or his son."

This time, the lumbermen apparently were not inclined to tease because they were too preoccupied appeasing their hunger. Therefore, the food was more important to them then the empty twaddle.

For a while, silence reigned being disturbed only by the smacking of the lips and intermittent coughing. Only after good five minutes, the conversation restarted, just on a different subject.

However, the fact that the young lady was looking for his son would not escape Robertas' father. Even after the lunch, the thoughts about the unfamiliar girl didn't leave him alone. Thus, even while running the saw, he was all the time thinking about her visit. He kept puzzling over why she had asked the workers in the yard about Robertas and later him about the son of the owner of the lumber mill. Soon enough, he was nervous wreck!

Not being able to come up with any kind of explanation, he came home a little distressed, bringing together with him the event of the day at work.

Already on his way home, he was planning first to notify about the incident his wife. However, when at home, Robertas' father couldn't find the convenient moment to mention about the young lady's visit since his wife began serving supper. And as soon as all three of them sat down at the table to eat, the conversation turned the same old way about how poorly life had been treating their family. At last, there was a moment of silence making it possible for Robertas' father to tell about the visit of the unknown girl at his work which had still been bothering him.

Therefore, taking advantage of the previous subject of the conversation coming to an end, he without waiting filled the gap, "Today, some young lady came to the sawmill asking me about a son of the owner. Then, one of my co-workers asked me about you, Robertas. I don't understand what this visit could have to do with you."

After his father mentioning about the unknown, young lady, Robertas right away understood who that was. He got so frightened he could barely control himself and almost gave himself away that this incident made an impact on him. He shrugged his shoulders a few times. Then, he tried to utter some words, but he choked over his food and began coughing.

Finally, he cleared his throat and brought himself to ask, "I don't know what you are talking about. How did she look like?"

"She looked like a student probably seventeen or eighteen years old. Pretty. That's all I can tell you."

"I wonder who that was," Robertas said even though he knew well that was Julija, and he had an idea why she came, too. However, he continued pretending he had no clue about any of this. Then he added, "Maybe that was one of my students whom I taught before. Who else could that be?"

A few times, Robertas had helped some students before their foreign languages' examinations. He had been teaching them German and Latin which he had known very well. Thus, it was convenient for him to turn the conversation this way without raising any suspicions.

"You see, Daddy, the exams are nearing," he continued. "Most likely, this girl's foreign language skills are weak. Therefore, she was looking for someone to help her. It could be someone had recommended me to her, most likely one of my old students. To tell the truth, I had told some of them that you'd owned a saw mill since I'd wanted to gain indisputable authority over them."

Robertas' father was completely reassured by his son's explanation since his words sounded sincerely.

They were still sitting at the table when the bell rang at the front door. The sound of it made Robertas' heart stop beating in his chest. Big drops of cold sweat appeared on his forehead, and a piece of bread that he hadn't been in time to swallow got stuck in the middle of his throat. The thought 'Julija!' hit him like a lightning on his head. Then, he began wondering how she was able to find him without knowing his address or his surname.

Some unfamiliar woman showed up in the room all dressed up in fancy clothes. Robertas' heart slacked off a little bit. However, a black mantle quickly shrouded it again. The thought crossed his mind this woman could be Julija's aunt, who came here after learning about their inappropriate, unmarital relationship.

As soon as Robertas' mother uttered, "Robertas, this Madame has come to see you," he jumped off his seat as if being bitten by a venomous snake. He was terrified that right here in front of everyone she would reveal his horrible secret.

While politely nodding his head, he invited her to another room where nobody could listen to their conversation.

Robertas offered the unfamiliar woman to sit down. However, she remained standing and approached the matter at once, "Mr. Robertas, I have been referred to you by Madam Psibilevska. Last year before the graduation exams, you had taught German her son. She spoke very highly about you. Therefore, I decided to ask you to teach my son, too. Madam Psibilevska also had told me you are fluent in Latin as well. Therefore, I would like you to start teaching Latin my daughter also. Would you be available to do this and when

can you start? My husband and I are generous people, and we are
going to pay you well for your efforts."

"Indeed, I helped Madam Psibilevska's son to get ready for his
examination. He was a little mischievous student but at the same time
he was very gifted, too. I hope your son is not lacking talent, either.
As far as the pay goes, I charge everyone the same amount of
money per hour. I hope it won't be too much money to ask from you.
You have to understand that it takes me a lot of work and time to
prepare myself for every lesson."

"I'm not going to be petty regarding the pay. Therefore, I'll pay
as much as I have to."

"Okay."

"When are you available to come to our house?" she asked. "I
would like to introduce you to my children."

"I could start in a couple of days. There is no reason to delay
and waste the precious time."

When the elegant woman left, Robertas' father completely
calmed down in regard to Julijas' visit at his work. However, Robertas
was now both excited and sad due to that day's events that had been
so unexpected to him. They made him to give it a serious thought
about his present life and the future.

He regretted he could not solve his problems right away.
Nevertheless, he still was happy about the little winning the life
presented him with the same day! The opportunity to teach German
and Latin the children of rich parents made him rethink the possibility
of helping Julija to get rid of her pregnancy. Even though he still didn't
have the amount of money needed to accomplish this, he went to talk
to the same doctor.

This time, though, the doctor once and for all refused to perform
the abortion because of how far Julija's pregnancy had already gone.

As Robertas with his head down was walking back home from
the hospital, an unexpected thought crossed his mind to leave
Vilnius.

He knew he would always have the responsibility to Julija as
well as his fatherly obligation to his child. He could not marry her; he
had neither a steady job nor a place where he could harbor his family.

Robertas was also worried about his parents' outlook on his current situation. Even though his father had a job, he could barely support his own family. Thus, Robertas decided the only way out of the situation was to save some money while teaching German lessons and move away from the city.

He impatiently waited until Thursday afternoon and went to the place where he had an appointment to teach his German and Latin lessons. Standing in front of a tall, wide door in Adomas Mickevicius Street, he with trembling hand pushed the button of the doorbell. Soon he heard steps behind it. As the door opened up, he saw the same madam, who had come to his parents' house a couple of days ago.

"Please, come in, Robertas. You are so punctual; I highly value people who respect the others' time."

"You hired me to teach your children. Therefore, this is my responsibility to come on time," said Robertas feeling in a good mood.

She led Robertas in to a big salon, excused herself, and went to look for her children in order to introduce them to Robertas.

He left standing in the middle of the huge room with a grand piano in one of its corner. There was a small statue of half way naked young lady holding lyre in her hand on the top of it. Behind the piano, there was a widely branched out ficus plant sitting on a stool with three ornamented legs. On both sides of the walls, fancy chairs covered with beautiful tapestry were lined up. But the focal point of the room was definitely a colorful chandelier with golden plated frames that were shining more than glasses in an ancient hutch standing in the center of one of the walls. Robertas' eyes also scanned a small, round table standing on one, thick leg by the door. Its surface was covered with glass, most likely in order to protect the wood from wear and tear when using the table. Also, there were three little, round stools without backs placed around it. A marble statue of a teenage girl standing in the opposite corner of the room on a half meter tall pedestal also didn't escape his attention. Whoever the author of the stature was, he had done a great job capturing the movement of the girl in the marble. She appeared to be running while holding a bow in one hand and an arrow in her other hand.

There was the door in one corner and a huge oil painting that was taking up a half of the remaining side of the wall. Robertas had already seen another reproduction of the same painting which was depicting lions' hunt by Rubens. The opposite wall of the hall had three tall windows that allowed a lot of light to come inside since thin curtains weren't interfering with it.

After scanning such a luxurious hall he had never seen before, Robertas realized he came to a noble family.

He had no more time to look around since the door opened up widely, and the hostess brought her children in. Her son appeared to be about eighteen years old, and the daughter - maybe a year younger than he.

Then she announced, "Please meet my children – my son Teodoras and my daughter Gertruda. Kids, this is Mister Robertas. He is going to teach you languages. He will help Teodoras with his German and Gertruda – with the Latin." Then she turned to Robertas and said, "I'm going to pay three roubles for two lessons if that is okay with you, Mister Robertas."

"Madam, I usually ask for a half of a rouble per lesson. I don't feel comfortable taking so much money from you. You've offered me three times more!"

The woman objected, "Mister Robertas, I'm not going to worry about the pay. I've decided to pay you that much so that you would do the best for my children you can. I must also warn you, Mister Robertas, that my daughter Gertruda is rather a spoilt girl. Therefore, you should be strict with her. As about my son, I'm not worried about him at all – he is a responsible boy. Well, I'm leaving you with my son." After saying this, she turned around and walked out of the salon taking her daughter away together with her.

Robertas was graceful to the destiny this good luck had fallen right into his lap seemingly out of nowhere. The only thing that was hindering his total enjoyment of his happiness was Julija's pregnancy.

Three roubles for the two lessons three times a week amounted to nine roubles a week! In Robertas' financial situation, it meant a huge amount of money especially because his pocket had been empty for a very long time. And he had not been expecting to earn any money any time soon, either.

Luckily, this sudden happiness smiled upon him at the very right time! Now, he could begin to think about putting into reality his new idea of saving some money so that he could eventually move to live to some other city.

Nevertheless, a black shadow of poverty soon started following him again since he decided to refuse from one of his classes, namely, from teaching Gertruda Latin which made him in turn to fear that he could lose his German class, too.

When in two weeks the children's mother handed the first pay to him enclosed in a beautiful blue envelope, Robertas used this opportunity to voice his concern, "Honorable Madam, I need to tell you that I must cease teaching your daughter Latin. I highly regret I must resort to such a strict measure since I need money badly, but I don't know how else I could remedy this situation."

"Mister Robertas, may I ask you to explain me what has made you come up with this decision. Is my daughter lacking the talent?"

"Oh, no! I didn't notice anything like this. On the contrary, I find her to be a highly gifted and talented young lady. In fact, I think she supersedes Teodoras in languages."

"So what is the problem then? Please, tell me; don't feel shy."

"Madam, it's not easy for me to discuss this subject, but I feel I must tell you about it. She is doing pretty well in Latin. During the past two weeks, she has made a significant progress. What bothers me, though, is that during our lessons, she often tries to deviate from the Latin into the other subject that has nothing to do with the learning Latin. For example, she says that she likes music lessons more than those of Latin. Last time, she even sat down at the grand piano and began playing for me sonatas and etudes. She told me she has been learning to play music for ten years now. Of course, she plays piano beautifully, and I love listening to her playing. Moreover, I have to admit I'm proud of her achievements in this field. But still, she hardly listens to me explaining her grammar rules of Latin. It seems that lately she has been talking only about music! It almost appears as if she is teaching me music and not I'm teaching her Latin. Being afraid to get behind our curriculum program, a couple of times, I spent with her almost two hours instead of one hour when I devote only one hour of my time to Teodoras when teaching him. However, I would like to spend more time with your son teaching him German since he is not as good as your daughter at absorbing the information. However, Gertruda uses all the available time up. Besides, I wouldn't want to arouse anyone's suspicion because I spend twice as much time with your daughter than I have to according to my employment agreement with you. I don't want you thinking I have some other intentions. Therefore, I dare to refuse from teaching your daughter Latin."

"Mister Robertas," said the hostess, "I'm glad to hear my daughter is gifted and clever. I find it to be the most important thing. Please, don't worry about all the other things. I've already warned you she is a naughty girl. However, if you find it to be a problem any further, I promise I'll take care of it. In fact, during your next lesson with her, I could sit together with you in the room. Maybe that would prevent her from playing pranks."

"I don't want to cause you any inconvenience," said Robertas feeling ashamed.

"Mister Robertas, I am a mother, and this is my responsibility to make sure she listens to you. I still would like you to continue teaching her Latin."

Robertas returned home feeling completely calm because he knew his conversation with the mother of his students was going to take care of this problem in his favor.

Next time he came to his Latin class being in a very good mood and on time as usually. Gertruda's mother as she had promised was in the same room during her daughter's Latin class. To Gertruda's biggest surprise, her mother was sitting quietly at the round table and knitting something without interfering with the lesson.

Robertas did his best teaching his class to Gertruda after what he didn't delay even a minute and was getting ready to leave the house. As he said to both of them goodbye, Gertruda offered to see him to the very door of the lobby. She said, "Mamma, I will see Mister

Robertas to the door because he might not know how to open it. We had a new lock installed this morning."

"Sure, go ahead, Honey," her mother answered.

Robertas courteously gave way for Gertruda to walk through the door of the room and followed her to the hallway that was lit up by a bright light spreading all directions from a fancy, ancient chandelier hanging in the middle of the ceiling.

However, Gertruda wasn't in a big hurry to open the front door. Instead, she obstructed his way out with her entire body and stated in a rather impertinent tone of voice, "Good job on complaining about me to my mother! Not a very honorable thing to do. My soul is crying for you. Why are you going against me? Even though I am only seventeen, I know already a lot of things about life. For example, I understand that my family's position in the society allows me more than you can think of! Therefore, I don't want to see you triumphing because of your little victory over me. I want you to know it's going to be the way I want it to be every time. I have to admit, though, that I liked you from the very first time I saw you. You are handsome, well educated, and poor which not necessarily is a deficiency in this case because it makes me feel stronger as a representative of the weaker sex. I would like to get to know you better; it would be nice if I could not only listen to your lectures of Latin, but also go to dances and the theatre together with you. I want to make my girlfriends jealous because you are much smarter and better looking than their cavaliers. And as far as your social status goes, it's not marked on your forehead. But it doesn't mean that, now, knowing my feelings toward you, you have right to take advantage of me. I always anxiously look forward to our Latin classes, and as soon as I hear your voice in the hallway, my heart begins throbbing. I'm going to get even with you now for complaining about me to my mother!"

Without waiting until Robertas comes to his senses, Gertruda twined herself with her hot, bare arms around his neck, and her moist lips glued themselves to Robertas' lips.

He was in time to grab her by her waist in order to push her away, however, not only her lips had been sucked into his, but now her entire body was also flattened against his.

At that exact moment, the door of the salon opened up, and Gertruda's mother sprang up in the doorway. Even Gertruda herself was utterly at a loss. Her arms now hanging down on both sides of her body, she didn't know what to do or say.

"Gertruda, behave yourself!" her mother gave a scolding in a rather austere voice.

In spite of the situation turning totally unexpected way, Gertruda managed to quickly regain her equilibrium. Trying to stand her ground, she cunningly kissed Robertas again right on his lips and said to him, "This is revenge. No more complaining about me to my mother."

Then she promptly opened the door and pushed through it totally lost Robertas outside.

"Gertruda, I can't believe you are acting like this. You don't even know him well enough!"

"I think you, mother, should be ashamed of yourself! Besides, I'm already a grown up; I'm over seventeen years old. The other girls of my age are already married. Moreover, you yourself got married exactly at that age. Why are you persecuting me now?"

Thus, Gertruda walked into the salon holding her mother by her arm and trying to say these harsh words in the most gentle way possible.

"Gertruda, you should find yourself someone who is higher or at least equal to you by your status in society."

"Mama, don't you remember what happened between you and dad? Back then, you were also only seventeen, and my father was thirty five. Almost twice as your age! Why did you marry him? But you don't have to tell me this because I already know the answer. My father likes repeating 'Rich people can do anything they wish'. Dad married you not because of your assets since you had very little of them. He had fallen in love with you because you had been young and beautiful, and you married him because he had been very rich."

"That's not why I married him! I had been in love with him then, and I still love him today!"

"I believe you, mamma. He hadn't been a bad looking man. In addition to that, he had been in his very prime. Living luxuriously for so many years, you got attached to him. Therefore now, you just feel sorry for him. I don't want to make the same mistake you had done. I could do just the opposite and marry a handsome, young, smart but poor man because I love him!"

"Gertruda, it's too early for you to think about the marriage!"

"According to you, mom, I have to wait until I will be thirty five and, then, marry a man like Robertas, or I could marry now but only some prominent owner of a factory or a landowner. Is it so? In spite of what you or dad want, I have my own head to use, and I don't want at this moment in time to marry anyone – neither Robertas nor some other dandy. I will marry the man I will fall in love with. It would be enough for me the money I will have. Mamma, I don't want you watching me during my Latin lessons. I feel being underestimated which, in turn, makes me want to rebel. I want you to know that I like Robertas, and I want to date him. He would be an excellent companion to go to the theaters and parties with. He is good looking, clever, well educated, and young which is good enough in order to represent me in the society. Yes, he is poor, but no one will know this. I could create some stories about him, and nobody would ever suspect anything. You can't imagine how much the other girls would be biting their lips with jealousy upon seeing me shining with him beside me in those parties they keep throwing every month!"

"But he can fall in love with you."

"Fine! He can love me all he wants. It's not like love is some kind of an incurable disease that I could not get rid of!"

"You also could fall in love with him," her mother objected.

"Mom, I'm not that stupid to fall in love."

They talked for a long time, and Gertruda's mother still didn't want to agree with her completely. However, after the persistent her daughter's arguing back she finally gave way to her. Gertruda, in turn, promised to behave appropriately in Roberas' presence.

Even though Gertruda's mother submitted to her daughter, she decided to make a secret agreement with Robertas so that the relationship between her daughter and him could be broken if it was necessary.

In a meanwhile, Robertas standing outside their front door, didn't know what to do – go back and talk to the hostess and apologize to her explaining that all this had been Gertruda's fault since she herself had kissed him by force or just spit upon this entire deal and never show up in this house again. At the moment he was feeling totally out of control of the situation; it appeared as if neither one of them really took in consideration his feelings or his opinion.

However, the money issue didn't let him do the later since he badly needed it. Therefore, as soon as the next his class was scheduled, he again was standing outside the same door he had been pushed out through lately.

A few times he reached up with his hand in order to push the doorbell. However, every time he drew his hand back as if being afraid that the electric current could strike him dead.

He had no choice, though, but to come inside. Robertas already had some explanations prepared for Gertruda's mother. At this moment, however, he didn't know which one of them would sound the most convincing, and in general, he was in doubt if they would even want him to continue with his lessons.

His hand trembling and sweating profusely, getting ready for anything, Robertas at last pressed the doorbell. Then, he quickly pulled his hand away. It drooped down heavy as if the electric current really entered through his palm and into his arm.

He didn't have to wait for long, and a maidservant showed up in the doorway. She was as usually in a good mood, but for some reason, her glare appeared unfriendly.

Robertas asked getting flustered, "May I come in?"

"Please, come in," she quickly moved to the side giving him the way.

As soon as Robertas found himself in the salon, Teodoras walked in. Their lesson started which Robertas performed with utmost care.

When his German lesson was over and Teodoras left, Gertruda came in. She just as before tried to talk about the outside matters right from the beginning of their Latin lesson.

In spite of this, Robertas remained persistent and demanded her to stay on track with the Latin. However, she also tried to insist on doing her own thing.

"Miss Gertruda, please pay attention to what I'm saying to you, or I will leave. I am going to dictate to you what to write", and without waiting any longer, Robertas began, "Cessat doctorum doctrina, discipulorum disciplina." ("The erudition of the scholars and the obedience of students come to an end.")

"Robertas, I know the other phrase: "Sclus cum solo non dogitabuntur orare Pater noster." ("A man and a woman left alone in the room together are not going to pray together 'Our Father which art in heaven'.")

"I'm sorry, Gertruda, but it's not going to work. Let's not torture each other."

"Okay, Robertas, I give up. I'm already writing 'cessat doctorum doctrina, discipulorum disciplina'.

Robertas continued dictating, and she continued writing. After checking her work, he was pleasantly surprised to find only two mistakes. It was pretty good having in mind such a short time of learning the completely new language!

He said, "Wow! You've made a significant progress! I feel bad to lose such a great student!"

"What do you mean to lose?!" exclaimed Gertruda. "Are you going to stop teaching me Latin? You just said I've made progress. This pertains not only to me but to you as well. It means the time has been spent well. I don't want you ceasing to teach me. I promise not to talk about other topics during your lessons."

"Okay – the last try. I doubt it's going to work, though, but I'll give it a try."

"Maybe I look flighty, but I'm capable of keeping my word," Gertruda reassured him.

"The time will show if I can believe your words. Now, I would like to see your mother so I could apologize to her for the last time."

"Robertas, you didn't insult my mother. All this was my own fault. Therefore, I'm going to straighten this matter myself."

"This matter calls me to obey simple rules of decency, and I feel I need to talk to her myself."

"Okay. I will take you to her. You can follow me."

Gertruda took him to her mother's room and knocked on the door, "Mamma, Mister Robertas is here to talk to you."

"Sure, come in please."

Before he started the conversation, he asked Gertruda to leave the room. Her mother encouraged him to sit down next to her on a sofa.

Without waiting a second, he began talking in a trembling voice, "Madam, I regret the last incident. I don't dare to blame your daughter. However, I feel I must explain what happened so that you wouldn't make wrong assumptions. What I mean by saying this is I'm afraid you could think I was taking advantage of my position of the teacher. I had never expected she could throw herself into my arms. If I had known she was going to do something like that, I would have never let it happen. She did this not because of her feelings for me; she was just playing pranks."

"Don't worry, I have nothing against you. If you remember, I had warned you about my daughter's behavior. She is like this because of our family's social status. What I'm worried about, though, is that she is still very young and inexperienced in life. I would like to discuss this with you, and I want you to be honest with me."

"I appreciate you for believing in me; I will do whatever it takes to earn your trust."

"Robertas, I want you to listen to me very carefully because I'm not going to repeat it twice."

"I'm listening to you very attentively," Robertas said obediently.

Gertruda's mother straightened herself up in her seat and began talking, "Robertas, my daughter and you could get very close and fall in love with each other. However, you don't have to let yourself to fall in love because nothing good could come out of that relationship anyway. I can assure you right from the start you are never going to be her husband. Her social status serves as an obstacle for that to happen. And if you ever tried to strive for it, then you would have to deal with the rich people who are more powerful than you! I can give you just a few examples on how easy it would be to get rid of you. Number one – a catastrophe could be organized during which you would die. Number two – riots can also be arranged, and after you get killed, you could be accused even after your death. There is also always an option to send Gertruda to live abroad even if it takes to do this against her own will. Besides, some people can do thousands of other things for the money as well."

"Madam, you don't have to threaten me. I've never had intentions to seduce your daughter. On the contrary – I was going to refuse from teaching Gertruda all together. This way, I could put an end to all those worries. At this time, she has just being naughty. But you are right – not giving any more lessons of Latin to her, could be the best medicine of all."

"Robertas, I want you to understand that I'm a mother. Therefore, it's natural I want to know as much as I can about my daughter. I would like to make a deal with you. I would pay you good in return for your information. But you can't take advantage of my trust in you, too, or you are going to be in trouble. I'm not against Gertruda's and your relationship. In fact, I would like you to attend the parties that her girlfriends organize and go with her to various shows and operas. My goal is to keep track of what she is doing and make sure she is safe. I understand it's not an honorable thing to do to spy on your own daughter, but she is still so young. I no longer can keep her at home by force. By knowing she is with you, I would have peace of mind because I would know you won't let anyone to hurt her. So what do you think about my offer?"

"To tell the truth, I am not very fond of working as a spy agent, but I do need money badly. Therefore, I agree."

"I'm glad we've gained the mutual agreement."

Now, Robertas didn't have to worry anymore. Luckily, Gertruda had also changed a lot. She wasn't naughty during her Latin lessons anymore. Quite the opposite – she was acting like a very modest girl now. Robertas could hardly recognize her. However, he still didn't have an opportunity to go out with her, and he began getting worried because he didn't have anything to report to Madam about her daughter's behavior. And he already had his payment received practically for nothing.

Finally, the long awaited day had come when Gertruda graduated from gymnasium. She successfully passed exams, and Teodoras also entered his second year at the University even though it didn't come easy to him.

Seizing this opportunity, their parents were making arrangements in order to celebrate this double success of their both children.

A lot of guests were invited. There were also friends of Teodoras and Gerturda among them who belonged to the parents of the higher society.

Thus, that Sunday late afternoon, guests began pouring in. By the evening, there were so many of them gathered that Gertruda's parents' big home was reveling and swarming like a beehive.

Their faces shining, Madam and her husband were chatting with their relatives and the noble guests. Teodoras was tossing about the entire apartment joyfully accosting his own friends from the university.

Only Gertruda stood out of the entire crowd; she appeared a little anxious often casting her glance at the door. Nevertheless, she managed to cover up her feelings so well that no one could suspect she had been waiting for someone. Most of the guests were preoccupied with talking anyway, and no one paid too much attention to the young hostess' moods.

Of course, the party was organized in honor of Teodoras as well. But everyone unanimously noticed Gertruda's beautiful attire that evening. There was no other girl in the room who could compete with Gertruda. Her beautiful, bare arms were decorated with golden bracelets studded with diamonds, and a ring with a big diamond was shining in electric light. She was wearing a white, silk dress, and only the very tips of her shoes were showing from underneath of it as she was adroitly walking across the salon.

When she was dancing, her white shoes with shiny brooches once in a while would show from under her dress for everyone to admire. Her beautiful shoulders were slightly covered with a stylish imitation resembling short sleeves. Also, a modest décolleté of her dress, up to the top of her neck, was covered with a compact, soft, transparent net over which two rows of beads made of pearls paraded while changing the colors in the artificial light of the chandelier.

No matter which room Gertruda appeared in, she like some young goddess captured everyone's attention with her white, shimmering dress and expensive jewelry. All the girls were envious seeing her so beautiful that night.

Gertruda as if looking for someone was walking from one room to another feeling uneasy.

As soon as the music began playing again, she was asked to dance. Soon, she was flying with the other like couples across the parquet floor that had been specially polished for this particular event.

Gertruda didn't even notice when Robertas showed up in the doorway dressed in a black suit that he had rented the day before. As she inadvertently looked at him, she was stunned since she had never seen him looking so good. He appeared almost like a young prince! Even though his attire was modest, but at the same time, it was elegant and very tasteful.

She felt a little disappointed because she couldn't walk up to Robertas in order to meet him since she was still in the vortex of the dance.

The other two people among the great number of those in the salon who knew Robertas were only Gertruda's mother and Teodoras. However, it didn't do him any good because, besides Gertruda, no one else had noticed him. She wanted to leave the dance floor badly, but the music as ill luck would have it, kept playing nonstop.

Gertruda noticed he was feeling a little lost while standing alone in the corner. Nobody met him or even said hello to him. She felt sorry for him since he looked as if being caught doing something shameful.

She badly wanted for the music to stop so that she could be standing right next to the one her heart had been longing for.

However, it seemed the circumstances themselves were either playing pranks or going against her.

As soon as the music ceased playing, she took a deep breath, exchanged some official words of politeness with her dancing partner, and without delay walked to Robertas.

"Salvus, salvus, Robertas!" ("Hello, hello, Robertas!") she greeted him in exciting voice.

"Salve, salve, Maria Stella!" ("Hello, hello Star of the Sea!")

Robertas' face was beaming as he greeted the one who was the first to appear next to him at this critical moment when he was standing lost among the strangers as if caught in the act of committing some crime.

"Robertas, you look gorgeous tonight! The real Apollo! You are going to conquer hearts of all the girls here."

"Thank you for the compliment, Gertruda. If you are going to be among those to be conquered by me, I will be very glad; you are the brightest star of this evening. I don't want to win the other hearts. I would be satisfied with just one heart..."

"You can consider it's yours..." she said looking deep into his eyes.

"Oh, I didn't know it could be so easy."

"Yes," she agreed, "a good Don Juan is capable of piercing a few hearts through at once with just one arrow."

Robertas quickly disagreed, "I can't brag too much about my accomplishments in this area. I haven't had enough experience doing this."

Their conversation was cut short by Teodoras' appearance, who walked up to them and politely greeted Robertas. Then he jokingly said, "Gertruda, keep Robertas busy for a while so that he wouldn't feel lonely among all those boring people around. I have no time to entertain him. Besides, he would be bored with me. You could also introduce some of your girlfriends to him."

After uttering those few phrases, Teodoras disappeared. Gertruda, walking arm-in-arm with Robertas, whispered into his ear, "I will rejoice in my happiness alone. I will just monopolize it so that the other girls could not steel you from me. I would rather have them be jealous of you than vice versa."

As soon as the music began playing lively, Robertas with Gertruda were the first to dance in the middle of the fancy salon that looked especially festive this evening. It was all buried in the garlands and flowers.

When most of the young people filled the entire dance floor, this way hiding Gertruda with Robertas, he pressed her entire body to his while tenderly looking into her eyes. It seemed to her she could dance like this all night long swaying to the waltz music.

Soon, all the guests were invited to the spacious dining room where a few long tables were covered with snow white tablecloths and loaded with all kinds of dishes. Strong and soft drinks were lined up among them in the middle.

The guests being encouraged by the hosts were filling in the seats at the tables in the middle of the room. The huge chandelier hanging above brightly illuminated everything around with its great number of electrical lights, making it appear as if it was still an early afternoon of the sunny day.

Robertas sat down in the corner a little away from the other people. He didn't notice when Gertruda appeared in front of him on the other side of the table. She was smiling right at him her pearly teeth gleaming between her pink lips.

Soon all the glasses were filled with champagne, and Gertruda's father urged everyone to have a drink to his daughter's graduation. The other toasts followed to some prominent guests and the hosts' health. For awhile, only clanking of the forks and knives and ringing of the plates could be heard.

One hour later, some little tipsy guests with red faces were already unceasingly trying to convince each other about the truth of some cock-and-bull stories.

After emptying a few little glasses, Robertas also found a couple of friends to talk with. Surprisingly, even though they had been holding themselves dignified in the beginning of the party, now, both of these young men were acting like his best friends. At times, they were even too friendly. Their affection for Robertas interfered with his attention towards Gertruda.

As he finally glanced at her, he understood just by looking in her eyes across the table that she wasn't too fond of the prevailing situation. However, both of them had to wait patiently for a better opportunity to present itself in order to get back together.

Robertas was still feeling hungry, but he was at the same time shy to rush to the food as if he hadn't been eating for the entire week.

There were so many different dishes being served that it was difficult to enumerate all of them. Many of their names Robertas didn't even know.

After he had some more drinks of hard liquor, his head grew dizzy, and his eyes became overcast with some strange mist that not only obscured his imagination, but it also stirred up his consciousness. Never in his entire life, he had felt anything like this before.

A reddened face of Gertruda kept flashing in front of him once in a while changing its expression - her smile to melancholy and vice versa.

However, Robertas could not react to her feelings the way he should since he was feeling intoxicated. His imagination was altered to the point where he could not comprehend how to respond properly in the first place. Of course, he was trying to be polite to those who talked to him, but his eyes also turned the direction of Gertruda less often, who now kept staring at him almost without an intermission.

Finally, she became so enraged that she decided to get even with him for being so insensitive towards her. Therefore, as soon as the music started playing loud, she cast askew glance at Robertas and demonstratively got up from under the table hoping he would notice this. However, Robertas didn't react to her move at all but continued talking to his neighbor.

Pretty soon, she was spinning on the dance floor among many other couples. Now it was the hot tango. In spite of this, she couldn't completely give herself away to the romantic mood of the dance because some anxiety kept nagging her; she unceasingly kept glancing through the opened door to the dining room.

Robertas, however, wasn't paying attention from his seat at the table to those dancing on the floor where a few middle-aged couples were spinning among the young.

At last, the musicians ceased playing. The entire hall suddenly became quiet, and the dancers began breaking up and slowly scattering to the borders of the room. Some of them went to the dining room again where a few elderly men were sitting and sipping their hard drinks while chatting rather noisily. It was obvious their faces were pretty heated already.

Gertruda also found herself in this stream of the people. On her way, she got rid of a couple of admirers and walked up to Robertas, who didn't seem to notice her again. She placed her trembling hand on his shoulder and nervously shook him suddenly interrupting his conversation with his neighbor.

His dull eyes showing no feelings got fixed on her face that was all red from long dancing. The expression on his face reflected surprise that she was already back.

"Robertas, I'm sorry; I need to talk to you. Mister Bzezinskis, please excuse me for taking away your collocutor."

"That's fine, Miss Gertruda. We've already spent too much time chatting and didn't even think Mister Robertas could be doing something better tonight," he said smiling and winked at her.

Gertruda took Robertas' arm and walked with him to the middle of the dancing floor. Musicians soon started playing a lively waltz melody that was just beckoning into the vortex of the dance. The other couples one after the other kept flowing on the middle of the floor being lulled by the intoxicating melody of the waltz.

"Let's dance, Robertas."

"We can dance, but I thought you wanted to tell me something first."

"I wanted to ask you why you came to the party at my house," she said.

"What do you mean?" he asked stunned and fixed his eyes on her. "Teodoras had invited me, and so had you."

"Robertas, I had not invited you to get drunk and stare at those old men."

"I'm not that drunk."

"Maybe it seems this way to you, but I personally feel ashamed of you."

"Well, I beg your pardon. Maybe I really had too much to drink today. I guess, I should just leave now."

He nodded his head, turned around, and walked towards the door. However, he wasn't able to get very far since Gertruda caught up with him and blocked his way.

"Where are you going?"

"I'm going home. There is no room here for the drunks."

"Robertas, wait. I won't let you leave. Besides, you are not that drunk. Most likely, your head is spinning just a little bit. Let's go to the balcony. In the fresh air, all this will go away."

"What's the point staying here any longer? Best thing for me to do is just to go home," he insisted.

"Robertas, can't you see what you are doing to me?! Or maybe you are just pretending you don't care? If that's the case, then you are free to leave. But I want you to know I care about you. I want to spend as much time with you as I can, especially on a special day like today. I anxiously waited for this day to come, counting not only days but even the hours. Therefore, if you walked out now leaving me alone, you would cause such a terrible pain to me!"

Being stunned by Gertrudas' words and not knowing what to say, he was standing his arms hanging down on his both sides.

"Robertas, please, stay. Let's go outside and talk. You'll feel much better after getting some fresh air. It feels really stuffy here."

Gertruda took him by his arm and walked him across the floor into another room. While Robertas was listening to her soft voice filled with compassion, his brain almost instantly sobered up.

Then, she took him to a far room in the back which was rather dark and pretty big in size, where he had never been before. She released his hand and walked to a tall, glass door, opened it widely, and let him into the balcony, after what she closed the curtains and the door itself behind both of them.

The balcony was rather big in size as well with thick colons crown molding it on all three its sides. It was facing the street, and dark branches of a tall maple tree were hanging over one corner there.

Robertas could almost reach those branches with his head. In the very far corner of the balcony, there was standing a middle size statue made of white marble, and a wide, branched out palm tree its leaves in some places intertwined with those of the branches of the maple tree. On the other side of the balcony, right next to the wall, there was a bronze statue standing on a small pedestal depicting the half naked women holding a lamp above her head.

It was dark outside. The lamp on the statue was not turned on, which was making Robertas feel a little dizzy again while trying to get familiar with the environment.

"Sit down," Gertruda with her hand pointed a wide, wattle-bench with a comfortable back to lean on, standing along the wall. There was also a little, round table made of the same material in front of it.

She didn't have to ask him for the second time since he obediently sat down passing his cold hand over his hot face. Gertruda landed next to him on this gently waddling bench.

For a while, both of them were silent, plunged in some thoughts.

At last, Robertas took his hand off his face and lifted his eyes to look at Gertruda. No matter that it was dark around, as soon as their eyes met, some flash of inner light illuminated brightly the distance between the two of them making everything look and feel like during the daytime again.

Gertruda and Robertas were so close to each other they could feel the air being warmed up by their breathing.

"How do you feel?" she asked. "Isn't it better here than in the stuffy salon?"

"No doubt, I feel much better here, in the cool, fresh air. But you are probably cold."

"Robertas, I would not be cold with you even if we were in Siberia now. You are like the Volcano Vesuvius to me that is capable of heating me up, especially when the distance is so small between us. Besides, I don't believe you would let me freeze here."

"Of course, I won't let you freeze. Thanks to God, this is not Siberia. I will give my jacket to you," he said his eyes sparkling with happiness.

He already unbuttoned the jacket of his suit but wasn't in time to take it off because Gertruda leaned with her back on his chest. Then she grabbed both his arms and covered herself by crossing them over her torso.

"There!" she said. "I don't want you freezing because of me. This way, we both should stay warm."

The conversation came abruptly to an end.

Leaning against Robertas' chest, Gertruda was listening to his heart beating hard like a little bird locked in the cage. While warming her body in his embrace, she was enjoying the pleasant feeling accompanying that warmth. She wanted to turn around and kiss Robertas hard almost to the point of suffocating him.

Nevertheless, Robertas wasn't feeling any passion towards Gertruda while holding her in his embrace. For some reason, she appeared to him more like a stranger. Therefore, he answered her ardent touches passively and without any desire. In general, he wasn't feeling the same gravity to her like that he had felt toward Julija. Of course, Julija was much more beautiful and attractive, but Gertruda wasn't bad looking, too. Gertruda also dressed more stylish. Especially this night - she just radiated with her smartness.

However, it was not enough to evoke his feelings towards her.

Not being able to get any kind of response from him, she began feeling more and more disappointed. His hand didn't start to caress her body even though she had expected she would have to defend herself.

Overwhelmed with vexation, she pulled herself away from him and reproached him, "Robertas, why are you so cold towards me? The other person wouldn't miss such an opportunity. Any man would show more initiative after a girl having expressed such intimity."

"I don't know what the others would do in this case, but my duty is to remain an honorable person. I have no right to take advantage of the situation; this could lead to a disaster."

"You seem so cold toward me which scares me."

"Gertruda, I perform my duties with integrity and don't try to do anything beyond that point. That is what I've been getting paid to do by your parents."

"Robertas, I don't want you mentioning about your duties any more. My love for you is so strong that it seems to me I could not live without you. Whatever I told you during our Latin lessons has nothing to do with what I am saying to you now. Those were just the pranks of the spoiled girl. Before, I was planning to show off with you against my girlfriends. But now, I no longer want them to see you so that they could not steel you from me. I'm afraid I'm jealous. My situation has changed because I've seriously fallen in love with you. Robertas, please tell me – maybe you are in love with someone else? I promise I'm not going to get mad at you. I will just do my best to make sure you will forget about her. I hope you realize no girl can even compare herself to me. I would conquer them all; I would not spare any of them. You know what, Robertas?! I could talk my father into letting us go on vacation to Switzerland. I heard about so many fantastic places there - one couldn't find such even in heaven! Being there with me, you Robertas, would forget about everything you left behind. You can't even begin to imagine how rich my father is! He is a prominent manufacturer, and he owns a huge textile factory in Lodz city in Poland. He is engaged in trade; he also belongs to big corporations about which I don't understand much. I only know he has a lot of money in different banks in Vilnius and Lodz. Also, he has a large amount of money in the bank in Switzerland. Have you noticed how my mother looked tonight? She was literally shining with gold and gemstones. All the women were envious of her riches. She could consider herself to be the happiest woman!"

"Gertruda, you are not lagging behind your mother as far as the jewelry goes. I can't even compare myself to you and your family. Can you believe – I don't even have a suit. Before coming to your party, I had to rent this one."

"Robertas, what would you want to have?"

"I don't have anything, and I don't even want anything because I couldn't obtain it anyway."

"Well, but still," she continued probing, "every person strives for something. Everybody has some dreams."

"Yes, I had dreamed a lot before, but my dreams never came true."

"What did you dream about? Or is it some kind of a big secret?"

"No, it's not a secret at all. When I had finished the gymnasium, my dream was to study further. However, dreaming didn't do me any good since I could not accomplish my dreams."

"But what about now – would you like to go to school now?"

"Of course, I would, but that doesn't change anything."

"Robertas, I will help you to bring about your dreams, but please, don't be so indifferent towards me. I'm ready to do anything for you!"

"Thank you, Gertruda, for your generous offer. I don't want to burden you with my problems. Most likely, God created me in order to have someone carrying the failures. All these problems are not solvable - at least, not at this time. Let's better go dancing. We must have one more dance together. Our separation from other guests can call everyone's attention which could make people say same nasty things about us. People at times can be incredibly mean; they can think of something so drastic that neither one of us could ever imagine!"

"I don't care about the gossips – I follow my dreams. Besides, I don't believe there could be those in my home who would dare to talk bad about me in public," Gertruda said.

"You are right – they probably would be afraid to talk dirty about you, but what about me? Or you don't care?"

"Robertas, don't say this. You know well I care about you! If someone said something bad about you, it would definitely affect me, too."

"We don't need to let it get that far. Therefore, let's go to the dancing room where no gossips can chase us. It's not appropriate to stay here away from everyone. I feel totally normal now, and you are probably cold, too."

Finally Gertruda gave way to Robertas under the condition he would have to dance with her all the time and not sit in the dining room talking with other people.

They went to the dancing room and right away mixed in between the other couples. Soon being overwhelmed with youthful passion, this gorgeous couple was already flying through the entire salon with the other couples gazing at them.

Gertruda was right – no one dared to express their opinion in public. Many guests just enviously followed them with their eyes.

Only at dawn, guests began breaking up. Seizing an opportunity, Robertas also politely said goodbye and got ready to leave this hospitable home where everything had been submerged in luxury.

Gertruda saw him to the front door, but then, she agreed to let him go only after he kissed her a few times on her cheek.

The distance from Gertruda's to his home was about two and a half kilometers. He felt somewhat relieved having found himself being free from that pressure of love imposed on him by Gertruda; she had haunted him the entire evening.

He was walking slowly remembering one after the other the events of this night. Robertas wasn't too fond of them, but at the same time, they appeared very promising. He had a thought that if he had met Gertruda before Julija, he would not only have excepted Gertruda's offer, but he would have strived to win her love himself.

However, the truth was he was in love with Julija, and Gertruda's endearments had not given him any pleasure. On the contrary, he had felt somewhat irritated every time she had touched him. Even the warmth of her body had caused him some unpleasant feeling.

No matter of that, he couldn't express his thoughts loudly, just like the rest of her guests, and had met her wishes by embracing her. A few times, he'd even agreed to kiss her on her lips seemingly very passionately to her.

Even though Robertas had not felt any pleasure in doing this, but he also had not experienced any aversion or hatred for her either. In a way, he was feeling sorry for Gertruda because she wasn't suspecting he had been doing all those little things for her just because of necessity. He knew he had no other choice but to lie to her.

With those gloomy thoughts, his head down, Robertas was walking home this early morning when the entire city was still absorbed in deep sleep.

Different ideas kept flooding his mind. He was thinking that if he obtained a significant amount of money from Gertruda and gave it to Julija, then she would still be able to get rid of the pregnancy. But most likely, it was already way too late since the doctor had refused to help her after discovering the fetus had long been developed beyond the allowable limit for the abortion.

Then, another thought crossed his mind about the opportunity of going with Gertruda abroad which would enable him to hide away from Julija. Also, he was not ready to cancel a possibility of marrying Gertruda no matter how difficult it was for him to picture himself living with her because of that simple reason that he just wasn't in love with her.

However, there was no use of his relationship with Julija, either. Despite of having her on his mind all the time, he could not marry her. He was reasoning that Gertruda more than Julija was in the position to make him happy if not through her feelings for him, then through her riches. In this case, the new horizons could open up for him including the opportunity to go to the university and have a great job after graduating it, at the very least.

Gertruda gave him beautiful hopes while asking for so little in return - the only thing she wanted from him was to love her.

In spite of this, Robertas in the very core of his soul remained faithful to Julija. Their love for each other lent him warmth and comfort. Deep in his heart, he felt he didn't want Gertrida's riches or her feelings that were strange to him.

He didn't even feel when he began talking to himself aloud, "If I can't have happiness with Julija, I don't need love from Gertruda, either. I can try to make it on my own. Until it's not too late, I better leave Vilnius, and I won't have to worry about either one of these girls!"

With those unhappy thoughts, which he couldn't share with anyone in the world, Robertas reached the street he lived on. It was already the daylight when he was at his house, but he still didn't want to go inside. Instead, he sat down on the cement stairs that had become cold during the night. They were also a little wet and covered with dew.

Not paying attention to the surroundings, he was sitting and thinking about his situation and trying to decide what course to take for his life in the nearest future.

Robertas brushed his face with his cold as a dead person's hand. He discovered that after such a long night, during which a lot of alcoholic beverages had been consumed, his arm was hurting a little bit. He closed his eyes trying to remember some scenes of the last night that were still so vivid in his memory. In his sleepy consciousness, he saw Gertruda's jewelry sparkling in the bright light of the chandelier. Even her face was radiant with triumph.

Then her image began growing cloudy, and soon, it completely died out disappearing into the far distance. His mind became blank seemingly with no end to the vacuum that replaced that vivid picture. However, he didn't long for the Gertruda's image; he even felt some lightness on his heart. For some reason, presentiment was whispering into his ear she should come back soon which gave him an uneasy feeling.

He lifted his head and looked at the sun that had just begun climbing the dome of the sky, and he saw contours of someone moving forward. For a split second, the thought crossed his mind that Gertruda was coming after him.

His instinct prompted him to hide in a little corner on the very top of the cement steps.

The aura around the person moving towards him kept decreasing but the silhouette itself was growing in size. At first, that someone's diamond sparkles dazzling him.

Robertas started blinking fast standing in the cold shade of the corner, and he saw a familiar modest bearing of Julija so close to him. Her half way smiling face was gazing seemingly right through him into unknown distance.

She was walking straight at him. Soon, she came up so close that it appeared to Robertas she almost brushed him with her clothing on his side. Thus, all shimmering she passed right by him taking together with her the light of the rising morning sun and glowing of her jewelry somewhere into the mist ahead.

Suddenly he wanted to jump out of his lurking-place, catch up with her, fall on his knees, and beg her for forgiveness. However, he didn't have strength to free himself out of his hiding corner.

Pretty soon, Julija was barely noticeable, and he realized she would be gone out of his life forever!

The thought of losing her hit him like lightning, and he instantly got overwhelmed with despair. Having collected all the strength he had, Robertas tried to call her, but no sound came out of his mouth as if some imperceptible power was holding him by his throat. He fluttered with his entire body overwhelmed with desire to free himself out of those unappreciable chains. He wanted to catch up with Julija and grab her by her hand while she was still visible.

Having lost his last hope and being broken down by the immense grief, he began to weep. His own loud cry made him jump to his feet.

The first thing he saw was a tip of the sun coming up above the Antakalnis Hills which totally woke him up from his dream. He realized it had just been an incredibly beautiful vision that shook him to the core of his soul!

Robertas slowly walked up to his front door and pulled out a key from his pocket, but he could hardly get it into the keyhole.

At last, he succeeded unlocking the door and walked on his tip toes inside of the room where his father with his mother were sleeping. He had to cross this room in order to get into his own room.

"Robertas," his mother lifted her head off the pillow, "you are probably hungry. Go to the kitchen; I left something for you to snack on there."

"Thank you, mama. Don't worry – I'm not hungry. But I would like to have something to drink. I'm really thirsty."

"If you want, go down to the basement. There is a bottle of beer on the shelve there."

He headed straight to the kitchen, got a hold of a chain on the floor in the corner, and lifted up the lid that had been covering the opening which was leading down to the basement.

It was pitch black around him when he was walking down the small, narrow cement steps. Robertas had to hold onto the walls going along on his both sides. Soon he already could feel the coolness and stuffy smell of mold there.

He gropingly struck a match and began searching for the bottle of beer that his mother had told him about.

Not being able to locate it and thinking his father must have drunk the beer earlier, he was getting ready to leave. But then he decided to give it another try.

A little head of a match covered with sulphur gave a loud sputter, and the light suddenly lit up the small area of the basement. Now, in the corner of it on the middle shelve, he noticed the bottle. Robertas grabbed it and threw the burned up match onto the cement floor.

When back in the kitchen, Robertas filled the glass up to its rim. The beer was very cold, and soon after drinking it, he felt it was becoming brighter in his eyes. He finished drinking the remaining beer and went to his room where he quickly undressed and fell into his bed that had been prepared for him by his mother the evening before.

Without waking up, he slept good four hours. When Robertas opened his eyes, he heard some unusual noises in his head and felt a little dizzy.

For a while, he couldn't get up, and he was ashamed to call his mother in order to ask her to hand him a cup of water so that he could moisten his palate which had been so dry he probably would not have been able to utter a word if he tried.

He closed his eyes in attempt to go back to sleep, but nothing good came out of his efforts. Every little sound could be heard in the room since it was already a midday. In the yard, children were yelling in different voices while playing ball, thus, making a lot of noise. Obviously, there was no sense to continue lying in bed with all the chaos going outside.

Not being able to get enough sleep, he was feeling irritated. Various recent dreams were all the time interlacing in his head. He was trying to decode their meaning. However, he could not remember all their tiny details, and in general, now they appeared somewhat insipid. He even began doubting if they were the same dreams he had seen tonight or they were the dreams he had seen some time ago especially because, lately, the anxious dreams had been tormenting him almost every night.

Nevertheless, he overcame his worries, got out of bed, and put on his pants. Then he got into his slippers and stumbled into the kitchen while yawning and scratching his head.

He wasn't surprised to see his mother there, who was getting ready to make lunch.

"Are you already up?" she asked.

"Actually I'm still sleeping, but my thirst is the one that is up and making me to look for something to quench it."

"We, sonny, have nothing to quench your thirst with. If you wanna wait, I will run to the store and buy you some beer."

"That's okay, mom. There is no better medicine for me than the cold, plain water."

He turned a tap on and poured himself a full cup of water that he drank without stopping to take a breath. Then he washed his face and moistened his chest. After rubbing himself with a towel which made his skin red, he returned to his room.

However, this time, he didn't get under his blanket; he just lay down with his arms under his head and his eyes fixed onto the ceiling, plunging into reverie.

Now, Julija was on his mind. The most aggravating thing for Robertas seemed to be that he was unable to help her in any way in this most difficult time in her life. He realized well that every month passing by was going to bring them closer to that catastrophic day he had been dreading to even think about. Nevertheless, he knew it was coming fast!

The only thing that provided him with some comfort was that he wouldn't be able to see this tragedy with his own eyes and hear with his own ears the complaints of the girl, whom he had placed himself in this pitiful situation in life.

Lying in his bed, Robertas was reasoning that if he could only somehow avoid this shame, than his parents would not be able to find out about that. He knew their reproaches were going to completely destroy him. In order to escape dealing with all this misery, however, he had to leave Vilnius as soon as possible and find another place to live somewhere far away where nobody could find him when this critical day came and Julija had to give a birth to their child. He realized he should do it now, until it was not too late and others didn't get suspicious about his situation or about his plans. He didn't want anyone to begin searching for him already.

An unexpected, scary thought crossed his mind what would happen if Julija killed her newborn child?! Now, he wished even more to escape abroad. Instantly, the other thought replaced it that maybe a better option for him was to come back to her, fall on his knees, and beg her for forgiveness. As he continued on thinking, he still couldn't see the way out of the situation; he couldn't come up with any kind of plan what to do next, where to find a shelter for them, or where to get the money in order to feed her and the baby.

Poverty that Robertas was living in was to blame for his actions. His inability to take care of Julija because of the lack of the money was forcing him to deny the love of his life. Not being able to find the way out of his situation, he decided it would be the best if he left her all together. Thus, there were no longer any doubts in his mind he had to move away from Vilnius and burry his memories about the girl, who was the most precious to him out of all the people in the entire world!

For some reason, no thoughts came into his mind about what was going to happen to Julija when everything that both of them had been hiding from everybody around came out.

If he just gave the serious thought about her precarious situation, he would probably have the strength to change his mind about running away to some distant place in order to hide from all the troubles.

After the party in Gertruda's home, Robertas ceased coming there to teach Latin and German. Now, he was bound and determined to move away from the city. The only thing that remained for him to do was to find the place to go to – Moscow, St. Petersburg, or maybe Warsaw in Poland. However, he was still contemplating and delaying his drastic move. He already had some money put aside that he had earned while teaching languages, and he had been painstakingly saving it and didn't spend a kopeck. He was planning to notify only his parents before his leave.

However, events took an unexpected turn because Gertruda mixed up all his plans.

One day, she came to his house. Trying to get rid of her, Robertas told her he didn't love her. He also said he was in love with someone else whom he could not live without.

Gertruda's reaction to his hopeless dodging was strange. The fact he had been in love with another girl didn't seem to bother her much, but she really wanted to know who that lucky girl capable of winning his heart was.

"Robertas, you can't imagine how much I love you. If I only liked you, I would have never come here. Even though you've told me you don't love me and you love someone else, I'm still not going to disavow you. I know you don't want to tell me who she is. Nevertheless, I intend to find out this anyway. I will do everything so that you would belong only to me!"

"Gertruda, what's the point? I've already told you that I don't love you. Can't you understand – I love another girl?! If you hurt her, I will despise you forever!"

"Robertas, I'm not planning to hurt her or you. I will simply make you fall in love with me and will make her to forget about you! I just need some time to accomplish this."

Robertas began entreating, "Gertruda, no one needs these kinds of comedies. It would be best for you to go home. Please, don't come here anymore. It's not appropriate for you to do this. People can start thinking something bad not only about me but about you, too."

"Okay, Robertas, I can leave now. As far as my visits go, I don't have to come here if I make you feel uncomfortable. However, I would like to set a condition for you in exchange for your request. You must tell me where we are going to meet the next time."

"Nowhere!"

"We could meet Thursday wherever you want to. I won't move from here until you tell me where we are going to meet! Do you understand?"

"Okay, we could meet in the Bernardinai Gardens, only not on Thursday but on Sunday at two o'clock. Would that work for you?"

"I agree. Are you going to devote your time before our meeting to that other girl?"

"It seems that no matter what I say, I can please you. That one day of the week, the Sunday, is always worth more than all the rest of the days of any given week, and I am devoting it to you! Moreover, please, remember that you are steeling this precious day from my beloved one."

"I understand. I'm not going to bother you any longer today. Give me a kiss, and I'll leave," Gertruda said.

Robertas walked up to her and gently kissed her on her cheek.

"Is that how you kiss your 'beloved one'?" she asked.

"I've never told you that you are my beloved one," he answered.

"If I have to steal your feelings, then I'm gonna go for the love and nothing less than that! Kiss me passionately on the lips as if I was your true love, or I won't move from here!" she said in a definite tone of voice and turned her head slightly on one side putting out her beautiful, pink lips.

Turning red, Robertas merely touched her lips with his lips.

"What kind of kiss is this?! I haven't felt any passion coming from you at all. I've seen people kissing better in the movies at the movie theatre."

"This is not the movie."

"Then, kiss me the way a man should kiss a woman, or I won't leave!"

Robertas' face flushed even more when he touched her hot lips with his own again. This time, though, she grabbed his head with her hands and kissed him back a few times. However, her kisses were not any better, resembling those of an inexperienced, young student girl.

He let out a sigh of relief only when he returned to his room after seeing her through the door.

However, he couldn't enjoy the peace for very long since he was anxious about the upcoming hapless date with Gertruda on Sunday. Robertas debated for some time to go or not to go, and for a while he was thinking not to show up there at all.

Nevertheless, as the Sunday came, he went to their assigned place in the afternoon.

Gertruda was already waiting for him there. Even though he was pretty late, she didn't seem to mind it because she didn't complain.

Instead, she seemed to be in a high spirit when all beaming she chattered merrily, "Here you are! I'm so glad to see you! Let's go for a walk in the park."

"We can, but first, let me get tickets for us," he offered in an unhappy voice.

"I already bought the tickets. Here they are!" exclaimed she lifting her hand up with the two yellow tickets in it.

"Why did you buy the tickets beforehand? You had known I might not come. You know well that I've done this under compulsion and not by free will."

"I knew you are a gentleman, and thus, you were going to keep your word to me. That was precisely why I bought the tickets. If you didn't show up, I would have just thrown them away. I wouldn't go to the park alone."

"Okay, since you already have the tickets, let's go inside. We can listen to the music."

"I would like to walk not only to the outside stage, but I would also love to check out the pond in the park. I heard people talking there are two black swans swimming there together with the white. It's supposed to be this year season's surprise for the public. I've never seen live, black swans yet! Have you?"

"I haven't either. I know there are black storks in the world, too. However, I haven't had much luck of seeing even the white ones," Robertas answered.

"You are kidding! There are no black storks! The storks have black tails, but the rest of their body is white," explained Gertruda enthusiastically.

"In addition to that, their legs and beaks are red," he added. "Why don't you believe me there are black storks in the world? Well, I haven't seen them myself, but I don't think people would just say this if the black storks didn't exist. I don't want to be like some ostrich that buries his head in the sand, meaning that if I didn't see something, then it doesn't exist at all."

"I'm not going to argue with you," interrupted him Gertruda. "That's not why we've come here. If the black storks really live somewhere in the nature, then I imagine they look rather funny. But also, they could make the same impression on people like those black swans in this park do, which in this case, make everything appear more romantic."

Thus, halfway talking halfway arguing, they came to the outside stage where they found two empty seats to sit down. For a while, they were listening to live, joyful music, but soon, both of them became bored. Robertas was feeling irritated because he had to stay in the park against his will, and Gertruda was just anxious to leave in order to look at the swans. Therefore, she kept stirring in her seat as if she was feeling uncomfortable while sitting there.

Finally, her patience ran out, and she said, "Can we go to the pond? It's rather boring here."

"I would like to listen to the music. I like it. It evokes some pleasant memories of my past," he lied. Deep in his heart, he was laughing at her thinking that he would be glad to leave her alone in this park.

At that moment, he remembered Julija and thought she would be glad to listen to this light, joyful jazz since it had been one of her favorite genres of music.

He was staring at the lady pianist whose fingers were quickly running back and forth along the keyboard, and his heart was trembling when dreaming about Julija. For a little while, he closed his eyes and imagined that she was the one sitting at the piano and playing this musical composition especially for him; he even caught himself enjoying this piece of jazz music.

While Robertas was sitting submerged in the music, Gertruda was also patiently waiting. She let him glut his appetite with it.

Finally, Robertas said, "I loved this composition! I guess we could go. There is a Russian proverb that sounds something like this: "Everything is good in moderation."

"And I've heard another Russian saying: "A nightingale can't satisfy his hunger with singing."

Robertas didn't answer. He was first to get up off the bench and, without even waiting for her to stand up, still feeling a little sad, he headed the direction of the pond.

Soon, both of them were already walking on a small decorative bridge that had been dividing the pond into two equal parts.

Gertruda right away saw the two black swans at the end of the pond and joyfully exclaimed, "Robertas look – here they are! Aren't they gorgeous?!"

The two magnificent, big birds with their wings puffed up were swimming straight at Robertas with Gertruda standing on the little bridge.

"Oh, my God! They are so beautiful! They look like a happy couple, just like you and me," said Gertruda taking his arm and pressing her side against it. She cast a tender, quick glance at him.

"If they love each other as much as we do, then I'm not sure if they are really a happy couple," he answered rudely while looking at the swimming towards them swans without hiding his irony.

Then, he himself became overwhelmed with shame because of such his behavior.

In spite of his rudeness, Gertruda didn't show her vexation to him; she continued looking into his eyes in the same gentle, pleasant manner that forced him to be more polite with her.

She regretfully uttered, "It's too bad I don't have anything to give to them. Probably, they've come to us for some treats."

"I wished I had some bread," he said politely as if trying to put himself right. Those words poured a little warmth into Gertruda's soul, and she presented him with a beautiful smile in return for this.

The swans were right under the bridge stretching their long necks towards both of them. As if asking for something, they were circling in one place, once in a while glancing at Robertas and Gertruda with their little, round, black eyes. However, soon they realized their efforts were in vain, and they gracefully swam away.

"Well, Gertruda, maybe we should go home? We've had enough time together today."

"Robertas, we've just come here! Please, keep me company a little longer. I spent an entire hour with you at the stage when you were listening to the music."

Robertas was trying to suppress his anger when thinking to himself how senseless had been their today's date. He didn't like being fooled by her to come here against his free will.

However, he didn't say a word about that. Moreover, he remained with her for two more hours in the Bernardinai Garden.

"Gertruda, let's go home. It's pretty late. The sun is going to set very soon."

"Don't exaggerate. It's not that late. It's not like you are going to go somewhere else tonight," she resisted.

"How do you know that I'm not going to go anywhere?"

"I know. You have spent the entire week cooped up at home, and just of a suddenly, you are going to go somewhere?!"

"Who told you I had not left the house for a week?! Maybe I went out every single evening. Who could forbid me going wherever I want to go, anyway?"

"I know you didn't see her last week," she insisted.

"No, you don't know!"

Gertruda continued, "I'm not going to argue with you. Can you at least accompany me home? Hopefully, you are not going to get mad at me and leave me here alone."

"If I should get mad at someone then it would be me."

"Robertas, you didn't do anything wrong. It's all in your head. I don't see anything wrong with someone like you taking a walk with a girl like me in the park."

"Well, you have your truth, I have mine," he said.

"Okay, if you want to get home so badly, we can go. Just tell me now when we are going to meet again."

"I can't tell you that at this exact moment."

"Why?"

"Because I don't know."

"Are you available next Wednesday? If you can't come, then I will come to see you at your house again."

"Please, don't do this. You don't need to resort to this kind of behavior. I will come here again the next Sunday at the same time as I did today."

"Only on Sunday? We are not going to see each other before that?!" she sounded disappointed. "You are so cruel to me; the entire next week is going to be like a torture to my poor, longing heart."

"I think I treat you in a more gentle way than you treat me no matter that I'm putting up with my difficult fate," he said sounding indifferent.

"Easy…" she said quietly as if complaining to herself and fell silent.

Robertas saw Gertruda to her house but didn't linger talking with her there for long.

It wasn't still completely dark, and he was already sitting in his room holding his head with both of his hands trying to prevent it from exploding with helpless thoughts. His situation was getting totally out of control and even becoming more and more threatening. Robertas was completely sure he had to do something about it very soon! He had to make the final decision. He just got to the point to where he no longer even cared if it would be the right decision or not because he couldn't remain in this kind of situation any longer.

His head spinning, Robertas was sweating over what he should tell his parents and also about how to soften the harshness of his answers to them when they were going to inquire about his plan to move away from home.

He couldn't sleep all night long tossing from side to side in his bed. Nevertheless, he was determined to end this nightmare once and for all now!

Next day during breakfast, he mentioned about his plans to leave trying to portray his fabricated reasons in most bright colors possible.

However, neither his mother nor his father wanted to hear anything about his strange plans. Thus, without making any conclusions, they parted.

Nevertheless, this was only the very first Robertas' try which meant the foundation for the further discussion on this subject had already been made.

After that, he continued habituating his parents to the thought it was the time for him to start living his own life independently. A few times, he even had to resort to gentle threatening until finally he succeeded convincing them it was absolutely necessary for him to move out. He talked a lot about his dreams for the future and better job opportunities in the other cities that were bigger than Vilnius.

Finally, he succeeded proving to his folks this was his best opportunity to get a job while he was still young and unmarried and had his entire life ahead of him. He insisted he no longer wanted to be a burden to them by being their dependent.

At last, all his past - Vilnius, his parents, Gertruda, and Julija – were left behind him. He was sitting in a third class carriage of the train cram-full of people where, through the cigarette smoke, he could hardly see silhouettes of the men and women at the end of it.

However, Robertas wasn't paying much attention to them. Only now, he was feeling free from all the problems that had been like some huge, black clouds hanging over his head and unceasingly threatening him with the inevitable storm coming in his nearest future.

He was sitting crouched in the corner and looking through the window at the always changing views of the fields, forests, and villages.

The train was taking him to Warsaw. However, if someone asked him where exactly he was going, Robertas wouldn't be able to answer. Even though he had the train ticket in his pocket indicating the exact station where he had to alight from the train, he had no one to report this to.

In general, he was a loner. Even when still living at home, he had no friends and very few acquaintances to talk to. True, since his birth, he had lived in the same one place, but he didn't get into close relationships with the others. When still a child, he used to play with the same few boys in the same yard, in the same neighborhood. However, as all of them were growing up, their friendships kept dying out, too. Finally, when all of them turned into the adults, they went their own ways in life.

Thus, Robertas felling alone was also going somewhere far away from his birth country, not knowing what was awaiting him in the future.

Some passengers in the train carriage were already having a snack for a second time in a row. However, he didn't have any food with him even though he had spent over ten hours on the road.

It was pretty dark, but he could not tear himself away from the window. The other passengers, in a meanwhile, kept leaving their seats, ant the others were taking them. Sometimes, the carriage would get almost empty with only a few people remaining in it.

Currently, there was enough room for him to lie down and take a nap, but Robertas didn't take advantage of it. Even though he could hear sounds of snoring, it didn't arouse his desire to sleep; he continued staring through the window at the dark of the night.

Thus, not having a wink of sleep all night long, he finally drifted into the kingdom of anxious dreams while leaning against the wall of the carriage right before the sunrise when the east side of the sky filled up with the light. In the beginning, he tried not to get asleep even though his eyes kept relentlessly shutting against his own will. However, the sleep turned out to be far stronger than his wishes.

Finally, Robertas leaned into the corner and totally surrendered to the sleep. Only some loud noises woke him up later.

When he opened his eyes, it was already daylight. The sun had been up high over the far horizon, and its bright rays were streaming through the window inside the carriage of the train.

There were so many people crammed inside of his coach that not only all of its seats had been occupied but some of the passengers were sitting straight on their luggage that they had placed right on the aisle in between the seats.

There was a presentiment in the air the train was approaching the big city. And indeed, not even an hour later, they arrived at the main Warsaw train station. The locomotive, hissing and letting out the steam, was reducing its speed until the train stopped completely under the glass roof in the train station.

The passengers poured out of the train turning the platform outside into the real squash that was difficult to get through.

People were hurrying all the directions, hauling their suitcases together with them. Sometimes they would brush against each other with their luggage, thus, creating even bigger crush.

Here and there, those meeting the arriving passengers could be seen when giving away their hugs and kisses. Their faces beaming with joy, the relatives and friends of the arrivals were sawing the air with their arms widely while talking loudly.

Having found himself in the unfamiliar city where nobody was meeting him and where he had nowhere to stay, Robertas was feeling lost. However, he had no time to contemplate since the stream of people grabbed and carried him towards the entrance leading to the city where, in a big square located right outside the train station, the rows upon rows of coachmen had been lined up. Many people were putting their suitcases into those light horse-carriages and climbing inside of them themselves.

After that, the drivers were breaking up all the directions while seemingly competing with each other. Thus, the rows of the horse-carriages kept melting away.

He could see some tramways making circles around the square while letting out funny noises that resembled those of the metal bells. They were rushing towards the streets that were leading Robertas into the unknown.

However, not even a half an hour later, the entire crowd disappeared after being taken away by the horse-carriages and trams.

Robertas was still standing by the wall of some building that belonged to the train station even though only a few people were hardly passing by him anymore. He was trying to collect his thoughts and decide what to do next. For some reason, he was still reluctant to dive into the vortex of the megacity as if being afraid to let this wall of the building go.

Only now, he felt the biggest hunger that was even making his legs tremble since he had nothing to eat for over twenty four hours straight now. However, he didn't dare to start eating in this place even when he remembered his mother had put some food in his little suitcase.

He realized there was no sense staying there any longer. Therefore, he took his meager belongings with him and left, thus, giving a start to his new life in foreign country. There were just the very few most necessary things in his suitcase: some shirts, underclothing, a few pair of socks, a razor, a towel, a bar of soap, and some other miscellaneous items.

He was walking and looking around while passing the street after the street. Every time he saw a grocery store or a dining-room, a pleasant smell of being cooked food that was lingering outside would irritate his palate.

He loitered from one place to another for about an hour until he got tired. Then, he went to one dining-room that he had seen on his way before where he bought two lunches and with the biggest appetite consumed both of them at once.

After having some rest, Robertas felt stronger. Even his mood improved a little.

Having found himself back in the street, he began looking at the shop windows and reading various signs that had been fixed on the walls of the buildings there.

This way, when passing by one of the shops, he noticed a small piece of paper sticking to the glass of its window. At first, he didn't pay much attention to it and passed it indifferently. But then suddenly, a thought crossed his mind that a job offer could have been indicated on that bit of paper. And Robertas needed a job badly.

He was ready to take any kind of job - the first job he came across. He really needed to find the source that could generate him some money, and that source was supposed to be work. He no longer had his mother or his father to provide for him. There was no one to feel for him, either. Therefore, now he had to take care of everything himself.

Roberas stopped at the advertisement stand on the street and began attentively reading the ads. In one of them, there was an offer of the comfortable flat. Without thinking much, he wrote down the address.

It took a long time for him straying along the streets and asking passersby for the directions in order to find the needed address. Finally, he stumbled upon the right door the number of which had been indicated on the advertisement, and he pushed the doorbell on the right side of it.

After checking the flat, he realized that it was way too expensive for him to be able to afford it. Moreover, it would have probably been too big for an entire family since there were two big rooms in it that could easily be used as the salons. The rest four of the rooms in the flat were a little smaller; he didn't need that much room just for himself alone in either case.

After walking through the entire flat, he didn't even ask about the price. He just said that this kind of dwelling was not suitable for him no matter that the landlady tried to talk him into making a deal with her that appeared to be favorable to him.

Robertas refused vigorously shaking his head to both sides. He had no doubts in his mind that such a luxurious flat in the very center of the city was way too expensive for him.

However, the first failure did not take his desire away from him to find a place to live. Next thing, he was again loafing in the streets and reading the ads glued on the windows of the shops. There were all kinds of services being advertised in them as well.

Robertas wrote down a few more addresses of the flats for rent. The day was coming to an end, and he had to make his decision as soon as possible.

Therefore, he went to one of the places that sounded to be the most affordable and suitable for him. Having three rooms, this flat wasn't nearly as big as the first one in the center of Warsaw. However, he couldn't rent it, too, because it was suitable for a family but not for a single person. In addition to that, he had no job or friends in this big, unfamiliar city, and he didn't know if the circumstances were going to take a favorable turn in financial respect on which his entire future depended.

This time as he found himself back in the street, he was in a bad mood. Now he began looking at the glass-cases of the shops with certain fear and lack of confidence.

Therefore, often he passed the windows of the shops without even looking at them. He was thinking only about the shelter for the night. He could not make it back to the train station since it was too far away, and he was feeling exhausted. Moreover, he also wanted to sleep badly; his eyes were literally shutting. If it was possible, he would have gladly fallen to sleep in one of the corridors of the houses he was passing by. However, he knew it was not an option. Therefore, he decided to find some cheap hotel so that he could have at least one night's decent sleep. He also understood that those kinds of inexpensive hotels could be found not in the center of the city but somewhere in its suburbs.

Without feeling his legs, he was still walking along the poor neighborhoods of the outskirts of Warsaw where the houses appeared half way disintegrated and abandoned. The little streets there looked not any better too – dirty and not taken care of.

As he turned into a dirt road stretching along the Vistula River bank, he didn't have to get very far before he spotted a piece of an ad glued to a telegraph pole, with the name of the street and the number of the house. There were also some letters written on it, but that didn't tell him much regarding to what they were referring to.

Nevertheless, Robertas decided to take advantage of this seemingly the last opportunity of the day especially because he didn't even have to look for that street, since the road he was walking on happened to be the one that was indicated on the piece of paper.

The entire street that looked more like a narrow alley appeared to be half way heaped up with garbage. Robertas quickly found the house number indicated on the advertisement; he wasn't surprised that house was also halfway disintegrated, just like the rest of the buildings on the same street.

He knocked on the door, and a woman with tousled hair and crumpled up dressing-gown appeared in the doorway.

"I've come here because I saw an advertisement, but I'm not sure if it's the right address."

"Yes, I am selling a wardrobe that is still in a decent condition. It's so cheap, almost free. Please, Monsieur, come in and take a look at it. You'll see that I'm telling the truth."

"I'm sorry, Madam, I'm not looking for a wardrobe. I was expecting you were renting a room," Robertas showed her the piece of the ad that he had still been holding in his hand. "There is only a half of the advertisement left here; the other half is gone."

"I see," she uttered. "You've been looking for a room, but it's not easy to find it here. However, I think I could help you since I know someone who could rent you a room."

"Madam, if you could give me that person's address, I would be immensely grateful to you."

"In now days, one can't buy anything for the 'thank you' but, for one rouble, I would give you that address."

"I would give you one rouble, Madam, if I was sure the room was still available. How do I know it is?"

"Oh no, it definitely is available. If you want, I could take you there myself."

"I'll tell you what, Madam - if I will be able to rent the room tonight, then I will bring that rouble to you tomorrow. What do you think about that?"

"Okay, I agree. I hope you are an honorable person and won't swindle me."

"Have no doubt I will keep my promise," Robertas reassured her.

Not even fifteen minutes later, they reached an old, sooty two-story little house that looked more like a pile of scrap than a dwelling suitable for people to live in.

Without even knocking, his companion woman burst inside noisily through the unlocked front door. As soon as the door opened up widely, some unpleasant smell greeted Robertas, instantly squeezing his throat.

It wasn't surprising because the hostess herself looked and smelled not any better than her house.

"Pani Domosevskaja, ja vam psziprovadzil liokatora." ('Madam Domosevskaja, I brought the tenant to you.' Translation from Polish).

The woman, who came with Robertas, began praising him as if she had known him since his very birth.

In spite of this, the landlady still had her doubts in him since she asked him to pay for two months ahead of time.

When Robertas stretched his hand with ten roubles banknote in it, his future landlady suddenly became very pleasant. She even complained to him trying to justify herself she had to resort to this in order to protect herself from problems she had encountered before when her tenant had lived for a month and left without paying any rent at all.

The room was not the nicest one – about ten square meters in size with one window facing the Vistula River floating her waters along the dirty banks of this neighborhood.

There was also a small kitchen there that was about three or four square meters big with the rotted out floor in some places. Robertas could easily reach the ceiling with the fingers of his hand. Staying in the environment like this, could not make anyone feel good.

However, he realized he would have to learn to live with it for a while and even to appreciate it. Even though the room wasn't luxurious, but he still had the roof over his head sheltering him from rain and enabling him to have some rest during the nights to come.

The furniture was also very meager; it seemed every piece of it was hardly standing on its feet. In one corner of the room, there was a bed with a ragged mattress. A small table and a couple of chairs were sitting in another corner of it.

It appeared as if the room itself had not seen fresh paint since the day it was built decades ago. Therefore, it was no surprise to him that the stucco had fallen off the walls that were also spotted in some places. The ceiling looked not any better too.

When both women left, Robertas walked to the window and fixed his gaze on the slow current of the Vistula River. On the other side of the street, a row of the same type beggarly homes was pressing itself along the bank of the river that could be seen in the gaps of space between them.

Only far away the view was getting more exciting because on the south side of the Vistula he could see the roofs of the highest buildings of Warsaw. The bell towers of the churches were crowning the city by jumping above the rest of the buildings which had orderly been lined up on the other side of the river.

Dusk was beginning to set in since the sun was already hidden under the line of the horizon. Only on the west side the sky was still glowing red. Robertas was observing it slowly diminishing in color. No matter how tired he was, he didn't rush to get to bed that had been pulling him now like a magnet.

He could not feel his legs under his body since he had been so exhausted that they were literally bending out of fatigue, and his eyes were shutting from the lack of sleep. In spite of that, he continued standing and looking through the window at the growing dark panorama of the Vistula River where, on the other side of it, the silhouettes of the houses were still pretty easy to single out.

The air in the room was stuffy. Before moving away from the window, Robertas opened widely both sides of it, and a wave of cool, fresh air came inside bringing together with it a smell of the water of the river.

He picked his little suitcase off the bed and placed it onto the table. Then he took his food out and moved the suitcase down under the table.

Sitting and looking through the window, he began eating with relish his supper that he washed down with an entire bottle of lemonade.

After that, he no longer wanted to admire the scenery of the night, so he undressed and lay down on the mattress leaving the window opened.

The summer night was pretty warm, but he got a little cold toward the morning what caused him to wake up from his sweet sleep.

Robertas got up, closed the window. Then he returned to his bed, covered himself with his jacket, and got asleep again.

He woke up only when the sun was already high in the sky. Having opened the window, he stretched his torso a few times right in front of it. Then he took a bar of soap and a towel and walked down to the river.

For a few minutes, he was standing and observing the powerful stream moving by. Then he undressed down to his belt, rolled up his pants on his legs, walked into the stream, and washed his torso with the cold water which dispelled all his sleep making him alert right away.

His landlady greeted him with a polite smile and asked him if he had a good night's sleep when he returned home.

Having exchanged a few words, he left because he didn't want to go with her into unnecessary details about his personal life.

After having a modest breakfast, he went to the city in order to become acquainted with the surroundings there. Robertas didn't expect to find a job soon, but to his biggest amazement, one hour later he was already working!

It was just a temporary seasonal job, but after working there only for a week, he made pretty good money.

That put him into a much better mood even though it was just a simple physical labor that he had to perform there.

As he ran out of the stuff to do at his temporary employment place, however, not even two days later, he found another job at one textile factory. This time, it was the permanent work. Robertas was so happy he felt like in heaven! He knew the Lady Luck was smiling on him since it was not easy to find any kind of work in Warsaw.

Now, Robertas didn't have to count every copeck. He even bought himself new bedding and the most necessary dishes along with the other little things he needed for living. He also allowed himself to obtain a several books that he read very quickly due to boredom during the evenings after his work. Since he had no acquaintances to go out with, he read a couple of his books twice.

The days were passing by looking almost identical. At the end of every week, he received his pay that always enabled him to come home in good spirits.

This way the entire month passed. Robertas felt his life was getting pretty good. One day he had a thought to inquire about a teacher's position. Even though he didn't expect to get this kind of job, he still decided to go to school to ask about it.

On Monday, he complained at work about feeling sick and asked to be released from work after lunch. However, he didn't go home but went straight to the institution that he kept passing by almost every day last week.

Robertas was treated with respect there, but as soon as the staff learned he had no teacher's degree, they became cold toward him right away and said they didn't need any teachers at the moment.

Robertas didn't give up; he told them about his private German and Latin lessons that he had taught in Vilnius which instantly improved the situation. He was asked to come in one week to check if there were any available positions at the primary school.

He wasn't planning on getting his hopes up, but he came right at the appointed time for the meeting with the staff of the school. To his biggest surprise, they offered him the position of a teacher at the elementary school.

In the beginning, he could not believe it. It seemed to him that he was probably misunderstanding something when he heard the good news; he thought maybe they were just making fun of him. He had been dreaming about this kind of job since the day one, after he had finished the gymnasium. However, the years were passing by, and his hope was slowly dying off. And now just of a suddenly, his dream job was handed to him!

For a little while he was wondering if he was just imagining this happening, and if everything was real. At last, he realized this wasn't just a mirage when he was asked to sing a job application.

Without waiting any longer, Robertas filled out the application. And two weeks later, he received a report he was being assigned to work as a teacher. It was the biggest celebration in his life! He could not come to his senses for a few days.

Thus, he began his career at one of the elementary schools located in the suburb of Warsaw.

Julija's life in a meanwhile was going just the opposite way than his. Even the summer was not making her happy. Days, weeks, and months passing by, her situation was getting more and more complicated threatening her entire life and future.

She finally reconciled herself to her fate after learning Robertas had left her. In spite of his despise toward her, she wasn't mad at him, and she still loved him, maybe even more than before. The only thing that caused her most heartache, though, was that he walked out of her life leaving her to deal with her cruel destiny alone.

Nevertheless, she was determined not to give in and fight her destiny. She had already made up all kinds of plans, but then she decided to stick to the only one of them.

The school was already over for the current year. Therefore, she made up her mind to wait until the end of June and leave her aunt and uncle's home since her figure was changing its shape rapidly. She had been trying hard to conceal her waist that kept growing bigger seemingly every day. Julija realized the time was near when all her efforts to hide her pregnancy would be fruitless. Therefore, she had to come up with the rescue plan quickly!

Having chosen a moment during lunch time, Julija uttered in a trembling with excitement voice, "Aunt, students at our gymnasium are taking a trip to the Carpathian Mountains this year. They also are planning to visit the seaside. Can I go with them too?"

Her aunt looked at her surprised not knowing how to respond to such a sudden and unexpected request. Hiding her feelings, she asked, "When is this trip being scheduled?"

"On Thursday."

"What do you mean 'on Thursday'? This Thursday?! This is the day after tomorrow. No, this is nonsense! If it was coming in a month or so, we could think about it, but now – it's just too sudden. You don't even have time to get ready for it."

There was a silence reigning in the air for a while, and then her uncle joined the conversation, "Throw that idea out of your head! It's not the right time for us. But you could go on vacation next year. At this time, though, we don't have money for your trip. You know well yourself that in winter we bought a big hotel that required a lot of money for remodeling. To this very day, the restaurant and stables still need to be restored. We've spent all our money on various repairs. Therefore, nothing is left for this year's entertainment. Next year, we'll talk about that again. You could even go to Switzerland then. In fact, the nature there is even more beautiful, and the Alps always attracted tourists more than the Carpathian Mountains did."

"Uncle, I don't want to go to Switzerland. I would be bored there alone. It's nothing like this time when almost half of our class is going! Can you believe how much fun they are going to have?!"

"Julija, listen to your uncle. Didn't you just hear that we have spent all our money for the purchasing of the hotel and its remodeling, too?"

"You keep buying expensive real estate, but you grudge a few roubles for my trip!" exclaimed Julija desperately.

"Julija, how can you say things like this?" Uncle got up and continued talking in a trembling with vexation voice, "You know that we bought this hotel with your approval. We even put it on your name; we didn't appropriate even one copeck!"

"That's right, uncle, you indeed bought this hotel for me and with my consent. But what good does the hotel, or the tailor's shop, or the farm in Verkiai do for me if I can't go anywhere further than my yard? According to you, why would I need the Carpathian Mountains if I could feast my eyes upon Antakalnis Hills and the Vilija River that should be good enough to take the place of the sea! If I had known our class is going to the mountains back then, when we were buying the hotel, I would had not agreed to buy it! What good does this four story mansion do if it restricts me in everything?!"

Here her aunt jumped in, "Julija, stop it! Calm down. Your uncle is right."

"You are the ones with the money, so that makes you always right!" exclaimed Julija bursting into tears while resorting to her last measures.

"Okay, Julija, don't cry. You can go; I will get you some money for your trip," her uncle said. Then he pushed his chair back and left the dining room without having finished eating his lunch.

He went to his office where he sat down at his writing desk. Leaning his head on his hands, he got absorbed in his mortification. It seemed so painful to him that he had taken care of Julija for so many years, and that was how she was now paying back to his wife and him for all their efforts.

However, soon Julija sneaked up to her uncle. She walked quietly on her tiptoes into his room, approached him, and threw her arm around his neck. Then she bent down, kissed him on his forehead, and uttered, "Uncle, please forgive me for saying those harsh words to you. I don't want you thinking that I hate you. No, I still love you the same way I did before. I beg you – let me go together with my classmates to the Carpathian Mountains. I swear – I will never ask you for anything else! I would not ask for this trip, too, if not for one thing – I've already promised to my girlfriends at school way beforehand to go together with them. I can't break my word now!"

"Okay, Julija, you can go with them. I will give you some money for the trip tomorrow. You are right – you should see the world while you are still young. When you get old, you might not even want to travel at all."

Julija didn't waste any more of her precious time; she rushed onto carrying her well thought out mission further. She was glad the disturbed stillness of the peaceful atmosphere during their lunchtime was getting back to normal.

Now, she was walking hurriedly along Antakalnis Street. The Sts. Peter and Paul's Church was already behind her. Then she passed the Gediminas' Castle Hill; only when Julija found herself in Didzioji Street, she stopped at a big entrance door of the tailor's shop as if hesitating if it was worth coming in.

However, she had no other choice but to make up her mind to take this step that appeared pretty dangerous to her.

Julija without delay walked into the spacious reception-room with a few big mirrors facing her on the walls where some clients were already waiting for their appointments.

As soon as a manager of the shop saw Julija standing in the doorway, she immediately excused herself and called her assistant to continue taking the order from some lady.

She herself quickly walked to Julija, greeted her politely, and even gave a compliment to her, "Oh, hello hello, Miss Julija! You just keep getting prettier every day - blooming like a rose. I can't take my eyes off of you."

"Thank you, Madam, for the compliments. However, I've come here to take care of some business."

"Sure, Miss Julija. I consider it an honor to help you taking care of your business."

"I would like to talk to you personally. I promise it won't take long. But before I tell you the reason I've come here, I must ask you for a favor. Namely, I have to make sure no one could overhear our conversation. Do you understand?"

"Of course, I understand, Miss Julija. We could go to our store-room. No one would be able to interfere with our conversation there."

The manager took Julija to the door at the end of the waiting room, opened it, and let her walk through it first. Now they were in the big premises where about thirty treadle sewing-machines were droning on both sides.

However, before even the two of them reached the middle of the big room, the buzzing noises began to subside. Julija heard someone whispering behind her back, "This is our young owner. She is so beautiful, isn't she?"

Julija didn't pay much attention to those whispers; she didn't even turn her head to look back at the two young ladies referring their compliments to her. All her thoughts were occupied with the upcoming conversation with the manager of her tailor shop.

When both of them walked up to the store-room, the manager unlocked its massive door, let Julija walk in first again, and showed her a stool standing by the window inviting her to sit down.

However, Julija remained standing and right away got to the essence of the matter. She said, "Madam, do you know that I celebrated my seventeenth birthday this year? One more year – and I'm an adult. That is when I'm getting all the legal rights to my parents' inheritance."

"I understand, Miss Julija. It means you are going to become the full-fledged owner of your assets. Congratulations! I will be happy to serve you," the managers said.

"Madam, first of all I would like to explain you something. I didn't come here to brag to you about my assets. There is a good reason why I'm here. Can you listen to me without interrupting me?"

"Sure, I'm listening."

"I would like to know how much money you are making here."

"I make twelve roubles a week."

"And how much money do the dress-makers earn?" continued asking her Julija.

"It depends on the output they produce. I would say on average they make about six roubles a week."

"Well, it means you are making pretty good money, aren't you?"

"I can't complain about that," the manager answered.

"As far as I know, your husband also works, and you have only one child. It means you should have plenty of money for living. The reason, I'm having this conversation with you is that I need two hundred roubles that I would like to borrow from you," Julija said.

The manager of the shop didn't answer. Then Julija continued, "You see, a day after tomorrow, I am leaving for the Carpathian Mountains. One month later, I would like to visit the seaside as well. Of course, my uncle is going to give me some money for the trip. However, I would like to have some money of my own also. I'm going there with my girlfriends, and I don't want to appear pitiful in their eyes. I've been raised the way that doesn't approve suffering or humiliation in any shape or form."

"Miss Julija, this is a huge amount of money. Of course, I would give it to you without a moment's respite, but I simply don't have that kind of money."

"Madam, I want you to understand me correctly and remember my words. I'm not asking you to give me the money – I'm asking you to borrow it to me. I'm going to return it to you in one year. If it would make you feel more at ease, I could sign a promissory note for this amount of money. However, as you know I'm still under-age, and my signature would be invalid. I will come back tomorrow in the afternoon. I hope you will bring the money to me. I have to warn you, though, if you try to trick me over by telling about my visit to my aunt, I will not take that money from you. One way or the other, I will get all the money I need from my uncle. But then, remember – a year from now, when I receive my rights to the inheritance, you will not work in my tailor shop! I mean it... I'll see you tomorrow."

Julija turned around and walked out of the storehouse leaving the stunned manager, who was still struggling to come back to her senses after the unexpected blow.

As soon as Julija entered the tailor's room, some dress-maker fell on her knees right in front of Julija when she was passing by. Grasping her head with her hands, she begged, "Dear young owner, I'm asking you for intercession."

"Please, get up. I can't talk with you when you are down in this position," Julija said taking her arm and pulling her up, "tell me what is that what you want."

"Dearest Miss, one month from now, I will have to give a birth to my fifth child. I have to feed four children already, and soon, there will be five mouths total for me to feed. My husband drinks away all the money he makes, and then he beats me and the children up. Miss, I wanted to ask you not to hire anyone else in order to replace me when I'm gone to give a birth to my baby. If I lose this job, I will lose the source of our living. Dear Miss, please have mercy on me."

Julija turned around and looked at the manager, who was seemingly back to her senses now, and after having caught up with her, she was standing behind her.

"Madam, please don't hire anyone to replace this lady during her maternity leave," Julija said.

"Miss Julija, we have a lot of urgent orders. Every dress-maker is an asset to us. Nevertheless, we can't wait for her to come back since we don't know how long it's going to take for her to return to our shop."

Julija was adamant, "It doesn't matter how long it's going to take for her to recover after giving the birth. Please keep her position for her. I know you are a decent person, Madam, and you'll find the way to help her."

Julija took a few steps toward the door when an idea suddenly came to her head. She stopped abruptly, turned back to the young dress-maker, and asked, "How old is your oldest child?"

"My oldest daughter is fourteen."

"Well, she is pretty big already. She could help here while you are gone. Of course, we are going to train her, thus, she could do some simple tasks around here. I hope our management at the shop is going to do exactly that. They will know better how to properly handle this situation."

Without waiting for the words of gratitude to start showering her, Julija quickly walked out of the tailor's shop leaving completely lost manager behind, who with difficulty was trying to collect herself for the second time now. She would have gladly had a good cry now. However, she had to remain calm and return to her duties at work.

At the end of her workday, the manager came home with a heavy heart; she found her husband back from his work, too.

She was afraid to mention to him anything about the incident that had happened at the tailor shop earlier in the day. The thoughts how he was going to react to the news and if he was going to realize how serious and even threatening the situation was had been haunting her all the afternoon.

She knew she had to notify him about this event, sharing all the details of it and ask him what to do next. But she still could not bring herself to start the conversation about this sore subject.

During supper, she appeared unusually quiet and distressed.

"Mother, what's wrong with you today? You look somewhat different – not talkative, as if you are grieving over something."

"No, you are just imagining this," she answered shortly while smiling artificially at him.

As soon as the supper ended, she went to another room. Not being able to handle her pain, she fell down on the sofa there, buried her face in her palms, and began to cry.

Her husband came after her into the room. Seeing his wife in this kind of distress, he realized that his suspicions were correct. Now he had no doubts something bad had happened.

At that moment, their daughter walked in and rushed to her mother to comfort her, too. Before she began asking questions, her mother asked, "Dear, please let me and your father talk alone for a while."

As soon as their daughter walked out of the room, the husband sat down next to his wife and said in a timid voice, "Sweetheart, please tell me what happened."

"Zigmundas, we are in trouble!"

She whipped tears off her eyes with a handkerchief and told him everything in detail what had happened earlier in the tailor's shop.

For a long time, both of them were silent. Zigmundas was obviously nervous; he jumped to his feet and began walking back and forth in the room trying to find the right words to express his feelings.

Only about ten minutes later, he spread his arms widely and stated in a firm tone of voice, "You don't need to borrow her that money. Tomorrow I will go to her uncle's work and tell him everything. She is just a snot girl! Any other girl of her age would not even be able to count so much money. She just doesn't realize the price of that kind of money. That's the very brave request – to ask for two hundred roubles! Soon, she will get the two hundred she asked for, but they are coming not in the form of the bills but in the form of a spanking with a rod! That will make her forget about that money!"

"Honey, I'm scared. I saw that determined look in her eyes. In one year, she is going to become the sole owner of the entire inheritance of her parents. If you go to her uncle tomorrow, most likely soon after that, I will have to leave the tailor shop. Having in mind that I make pretty good money there, it's out of the question. There are so many things that could be done with my work place in the future. Next year when she becomes the owner of it, we could expand the business by establishing there also a salon of elegant hats. Thus, I would make even more money! Zigmundas, I beg you – don't go to her uncle. She is very rich. Therefore, it's dangerous to argue with her. This year, her uncle bought her the biggest hotel in the city. They are already working on the thorough repairs of a restaurant and abandoned stables. In addition to that, they have a nice, big property in Verkiai, too!"

"Well, if she is going to continue treating money the way she is starting now, then her inheritance is not going to last for very long."

She gave a deep sigh and uttered again, "Two hundred roubles is not the end of the world. What I'm really afraid of, though, is that after receiving this money, she could start blackmailing me while asking for more money over and over again."

"That is why I am saying to you that we need to notify her uncle about her behavior. It's going to be good for us, and it's going to teach her a lesson, too."

"Zigmundas, make no mistake! She warned me today. You have to think about your own daughter. She is growing up; she will need a job soon, too. I think I could ask Julija to help us with that. She must pay me for the today's favor somehow, so I will ask her to give some job to our daughter in the near future. For example, she could work as a waitress at that new restaurant in the hotel. You never know - it could turn out to be a very well paid job."

At last, Zigmundas ceased walking in the room. Instead, he sat down next to his wife and plunged in thought.

"I can't stand this snotty girl," he said finally, "she wants us to give her two hundred roubles and that's it! I guess, we'll have to do this. But if she later asks for some more money, we can explain to her we don't have it. I will go to the bank tomorrow and bring that money to you in the afternoon. Or maybe I should give it straight to her myself? Maybe that would prevent her from asking you for more of it in the future?"

Suddenly both of them began feeling much better after talking this out and making their decision.

Next day, Zigmundas took two hundred roubles out of his account and went to his wife's work. He had to wait there until Julija came.

This was the first time he saw her. Just yesterday, he had imagined her to be some flighty girl. However, as soon as they began talking, he had to change his mind about her. He no longer wanted to say anything insulting to Julija. On the contrary, upon handing her the money, he was very careful not to say anything that would make her want to snap out.

"Julija, you are very young and, of course, you don't have as much experience dealing with people as my wife and I have. Be smart – don't tell anyone you have all this money. There are all kinds of people. Someone could follow you or just take it away from you."

"Thank you, Monsieur, for your valuable advice. I will be careful."

Zigmundas felt being pleasantly surprised hearing her talking this way to him because he had expected to meet someone arrogant and rude.

Having such a significant amount of money, Julija was able to look her fate in the eyes with much more confidence now. She also added to it the one hundred twenty roubles that her uncle had given to her for the trip.

She rented a small room on Bernardinai Street in the old town of Vilnius. Julija would leave her room only in the evenings in order to go to the store to buy some food. She was very afraid to meet some acquaintances in the streets of Vilnius. In spite of all her fears, she was feeling better now since she didn't have to tighten her stomach with a corset any longer, and it was getting bigger seemingly every hour!

The last month of her pregnancy, Julija hired a nurse who was supposed to take care of her baby.

Finally, the long awaited pivotal time came, which happened to be on the twenty first of August. On that day, Julija felt severe pains in her stomach area. It was the afternoon when she sent her nurse to bring her a midwife that she had already made arrangements with before.

Thus at six o'clock in the evening, the midwife was already sitting next to Julija's side. As it started getting dark, horrible pains began tormenting her again.

One hour later, after the difficult delivery, two new citizens came into this world mewing loudly like some kittens, announcing about their right to live.

Had not even completely recovered, Julija got up with a slight temperature on the fourth day after giving birth to her twins. She took a little suitcase with some presents that she had bought for her aunt with her uncle a few weeks before and went home.

Julija's aunt noticed she had lost some weight. However, she thought that her niece became skinnier because of not eating properly while on her vacation. Therefore, she kept urging Julija to eat almost every time she passed by.

As the evening came, Julija wanted to leave in order to feed her newborn twins, who had seen the world for the first time in their life only a few days ago. However, her aunt didn't let her leave the house.

Julija had to comply with her request since the World War One had broken out twenty four days ago which stirred up a lot of fear at their home. She learned that her uncle a few times had gone to the gymnasium in order to ask her teachers about the trip, but they had not known anything about it.

The situation in the city was getting progressively worse since more and more army forces could be seen everywhere in the streets. The newspapers were telling stories about Germans being hit on all the fronts.

Nevertheless, locals were telling different things on the same subject; they talked between themselves about the Germans taking the initiative instead. No wonder, Julija's aunt and uncle didn't let her retreat a step from home. She had always been their only solace.

Thus, the most difficult days of Julija's life began. Every week the news from the front kept getting worse. Life in the city was becoming more difficult, too. Therefore, those who could leave were trying to escape from Vilnius out to the country where it was easier to make living during the wartime.

It was almost impossible to get food in the city. The news was spreading that the coming year was going to bringing new government as well – the government of Germans.

As the winter set in, life became twice as hard. Now, to obtain fuel was just as difficult as to get food. The majority of the city residents were not only starving, they also were freezing in their flats.

Julija with her children, too, were living not in the best conditions. True, she had succeeded to buy a couple of cart-loads of wood just as the war had started. However, it was not sufficient to heat her room for the entire winter. Situation with the food was a little better since she took her housekeeper in hand, who in turn kept supplying her with enough food. The only problem was with the delivery of that food to her room on Bernardinai Street because she had to bring it to the city herself from her aunt and uncle's home that was located outside of Vilnius, in Verkiai.

Having to carry such a heavy life's burden on her frail shoulders, Julija began missing her classes at the gymnasium, sometimes even a few days in a row. When back at school, she would make excuses she had been ill.

Of course, during the normal times, her teachers would not tolerate her doing this and would not allow her continue studying this way. They would definitely do something about it. However, with all the chaos going on in the world, they turned a blind eye on the studies of their pupils as well.

With the spring a big wave of refugees came, and many families in Vilnius were getting ready for evacuation. Some of them were still delaying a little in expectation of some miracle to happen. They hoped that the Germans would be defeated, and they would not have to leave Lithuania where they had acquired their significant assets during many decades if living.

Even though the spring came, but the waking up nature didn't fill up peoples' hearts with gladness. Many families continued to suffer from hunger. The food was so scarce it was impossible to even buy it. The money lost its value; only the golden coins' course was still stable.

Julija's uncle happened to be a very practical person, and he had had a presentiment the world had been beginning to bubble even before the World War I broke out. In addition to this, after the archduke of Austria-Este Austro-Hungarian and Royal Prince of Hungary and of Bohemia Franz Ferdinand, the successor to the Austro-Hungarian throne, and his wife had been murdered, rumors spread about the possibility of the war.

And indeed, the events began developing so fast that more far-seeing people were beginning to understand that all these arguments and civil conflicts were not going to be solved in a peaceful way.

Seeing all this, Julija's uncle withdrew his and Julija's savings from the bank turning them into the golden currency. There were two thousand his and a thousand of Julija's roubles that remained after purchasing the hotel. Her uncle knew that gold would never lose its value no matter who won the military intrigues.

Julija wasn't aware of those financial operations that her uncle had performed recently. She only heard him talking at the dinner table about the power of the golden currency. Now, she was glad she had got almost the entire amount of the two hundred roubles from the manager of the tailor shop in the form of the golden coins. Her uncle also had given her more than half of his money for the trip in gold.

When the war started, Julija began quickly finding her bearings regarding the money. Remembering her uncle's words, she preserved her golden coins, and she was spending her paper money first. True, she had to use up some of the golden coins, too. She had given some gold to the midwife for her services and also paid the same way some other of her bills.

Julija counted her golden coins fund. There were one hundred seventy five golden roubles left total that she was guarding as the apple of her eye. She not only was afraid to spend it, but she didn't even dare to touch it!

In May, the atmosphere became so hot that Julija's nurse demanded her to pay her salary in golden coins.

Julija tried to excuse herself telling the nurse she didn't have any golden coins. Then the nurse threatened to leave. She only calmed down when Julija added five roubles to the already agreed amount.

However, after getting her way, the nurse became more impudent, and she demanded Julija paying her in golden coins for the upcoming month of June. Otherwise, she threatened to leave.

Being pressed into a corner, Julija had to agree with the nanny's conditions. She had no other choice, and she also was still very inexperienced in personal relations with other people. It never occurred to Julija that during this difficult time many maids and nannies were working just for food. Julija's nanny was well aware of it, but she also knew she would be able to take advantage of Julija. And she did.

In the middle of June, Julija graduated from the gymnasium. Even though her grades were rather low, but at least she knew she no longer had this burden of going to school and doing her homework in the evenings. She was free from those responsibilities for good.

Nevertheless, she was caught by another problem. Totally unexpectedly, her nanny refused to watch her twin boys after June was over, and there was virtually no time to find another nanny.

Even though there were those babysitters who would gladly serve Julija for food, but it still required time to find them. And it was not easy for her to get away from her children to do this. She couldn't even place an advertisement in the local newspaper or anywhere else because she had to keep her situation secret. She was terrified everything could come out to the daylight.

Julija had to take measures to remedy the situation. However, she couldn't come up with any salutary idea, and she had no one to share her secret with, either. She knew that the only person she could rely on was only herself. There was no time to reason for long, too, since she had no one to leave her children with.

It had been the second day now Julija hired a woman from the same yard on Bernardinai Street paying her a golden rouble coin every twenty four hours.

Julija understood she could not last long like this. Therefore, she had to make some kind of decision immediately.

In the beginning, she was thinking to take her twins to the city's main train station and leave them there. However, she quickly refused from this plan; she was afraid that the passing by people would take her children somewhere far away. Thus, she could lose them forever, and they were very precious to her now that she had endured so much hardship during the last few months. Therefore, she didn't want to separate with them completely.

Finally, she came up with the idea to take her little boys to the church and leave them there. She reasoned those who attended the church were mostly decent people, and with God's help, her children would end up in a good home.

The decision was made; Julija waited until Sunday. Then she got up early, together with the sunrise. She told her aunt she had to go some place with her girlfriend who lived in Naujoji Vilnia because she didn't want her aunt being suspicious about her early leaving.

Julija brought in a young tattoo master with her and made the last five golden roubles' payment to the woman who had been watching her children lately.

As soon as she remained alone with the tattoo boy, she also paid him five roubles in gold asking him to tattoo two crosses about two centimeters in size on both of her little boys' right arms just above their elbows.

However, the boy got mixed up – he tattooed one cross on the right arm of one baby and the other cross on the left arm of the other little boy. Julija didn't even notice this.

The crosses turned out to be made in a masterly fashion, but the babies being pricked with the needle were crying so loudly as if the tattoo boy was slicing them into small pieces. Julija suffered deeply this operation together with her twins.

When the tattoo master left, Julija was for a long time leaning and crying on the little bed of her children where the two infants were lying content and playing already. However, she didn't have enough time to feast her eyes upon her little boys; she had to nurse them.

At last, she took her both children in her arms and hurried out the door. Soon she was walking along the still empty Vilnius streets. On Sundays, people used to get up later than on ordinary workdays.

When Julija approached Sts. Peter and Paul's Church, she looked around a few times. It seemed to her all the passersby were aware of what she was just about to do with her poor twin little boys, whom she was holding on both of her arms.

She had no time to delay. Julija approached carefully the stone wall of the churchyard, but she didn't have any more strength to walk any further. She was so nervous that she had to lean against the cold wall trying to collect herself. The twins in a meanwhile didn't have a presentiment of the disaster coming; they were just sitting in her arms and quietly waiting for their destiny to take place.

Julija looked around a few times again. After having convinced herself there was no soul alive anywhere near, she began slowly moving towards the main entrance that had still been locked.

Then she walked straight to the little gate that was next to the main entrance, but it also was locked. She shook a few times the big, black metal handle of it. However, the gate was not moving.

Sweat stood out on her back; her legs and hands began shaking. She didn't know what to do now. Julija began feeling sorry she didn't leave her twins by the door of some other church that had no fence. And there were quite a few of that kind of churches in Vilnius. She could have even left them right in the heart of the capital by the Cathedral Church, and all would have been accomplished by now.

She didn't dare to leave the infants around the corner by the gate leading to the churchyard. There was a busy street running along the fence there, and Julija was afraid they could crawl into that street and perish under the wheels of some passing by cart.

She remembered there was another little gate on the very left side of the stone fence leading to the sacristy. She often used to enter through it when going to the church.

This time, too, she decided to walk through that gate inside the churchyard. Without waiting any longer, she slinked off that direction along the stucco fence.

Luckily, she found the gate unlocked. As she opened it, she heard a loud, squeaking noise that made her heart stop. She was terribly afraid someone could see her with the children which would certainly destroy all her plans causing her terrible efforts render fruitless.

However, all her fears proved to be with no reason. There were no people in the churchyard, too. Now, she broke into run until she reached the stone cobbled grounds by the massive oak door that was framed with black iron ornaments.

Julija knew she had neither time for delay nor room for an error. Therefore, she quickly spread a little blanket on the ground right next to the door. Then she covered both little boys with the folded corners of the same blanket which she joined in the middle by pinning it in two places with two big pins so that the children could not crawl out of it. She also gave to each of them a little toy, kissed both her little sons on their foreheads, and walked backwards tears running down her cheeks.

Soon she found herself in the street where she wiped her tears away trying to hide her pain in case if she met some acquaintances.

Fortunately, it was still early, and there were very little people in the streets. She saw only a few human figures passing by, and they were unfamiliar people to her, until she reached Sapezinka where she lived with her aunt and uncle.

However, Julija didn't want to go home right away. She didn't feel like explaining herself why she returned home so early. Instead, she turned the direction of Sapezinka hills where she found the same place Robertas and her had sinned in. Because of that time spent there with him, she had to go now through so much moral pain and repent every day!

Just like that time, he sat down on the ground leaning her back against the same pine tree and plunged into a profound reverie. She remembered those beautiful days when she had just met Robertas. Now she relived his confession in love to her, passionate endearment, kisses, and all that had followed it which required her pay such a high price now.

She didn't blame Robertas for what had happened. On the contrary – she reproached herself with the consequences of her careless behavior. She thought it was her own fault she had lost him and, thus, ruined her life.

Julija was absolutely sure that if she had not yielded to the temptation back then, she would have still been together with Robertas now, and he would continue to love her. She knew he had left her only because she'd got pregnant, and the time just had not been right for them to get married.

Moreover, she felt sorry for Robertas and forgave him for everything. The image of his face overwhelmed with concern would not leave her mind. She remembered how worried he had been about her, how he had tried to help her to find a doctor to do the abortion. It served as the proof to her he had not wanted to cut short their relationship. If he had really wanted to leave her, he could have done this right away. The only thing that really bothered Julija, though, was that he had left her without saying goodbye to her.

Julija had a lot of beautiful and pleasant memories about those few months she had spent together with Robertas. However, those sweet times that had brought such a huge disappointed to her later, at the same time, made her think and learn from her mistakes.

All the suffering life presented her with could not go in vain. Her fate made her learn a lesson the hard way so that in the future she wouldn't give herself up to the pleasant passions that had already caused her so many problems. Even though Julija's first bitter lesson didn't let her forget about itself, it also didn't make her forget Robertas. At least, she could not think about him with aversion.

Deep in her heart, Julija knew that if Robertas came back to her, she would not find strength to give up her love for him. After hearing just a few meek words coming from his mouth, she would forgive him all the wrongs he had done to her, but she also knew she would not be as submissive to the temptations.

This time, while sitting on the hill, she too was admiring the far away view of the city that was again submerged into the bluish smoke. The difference between now and the time she had been here with Roberts was that back then it had been the beginning of November. Therefore, the scenery of Vilnius had appeared rather sad. Brown and reddish dry leaves had been falling onto the ground covering up the still green last summer's clothing.

This time, it was warm though. A pleasant breeze from the south once in a while would whiff just above the grass and then it would ripple over the tops of the pine trees. It appeared as if it was playing with the branches and the leaves of the plants growing on the hill.

Around Julija, joyful butterflies were diving mischievously into the air looking just as playful and careless as the breeze itself. Only when feeling tired, they would land onto some blossom of the flower and bask in the sun, their beautiful wings apart. Probably they were enjoying the warmth until another breeze blew them away of the petals of the flowers.

Only diligent bees were flying from blossom to blossom without a moment's respite and kept gathering their sweet nectar. They worked tirelessly without any days off or any holidays. Those amazing, little creatures would get up together with the sunrise and go back to sleep with the sunset. How much benefits they were providing people with by their relentless labor!

It was the first time she was truly enjoying the outdoors during the entire year since it never occurred to her to go for a walk; she didn't even have time to dream about the simple things like that. Julija had always been overwhelmed with fear and doing numerous chores that at times made her head spin.

However, she continued dragging her difficult, dreadful burden without having anyone to complain to or to turn to in order to get a speck of compassion.

Today was the first day she was sitting with no problems hovering over her head. She could think brighter thoughts and enjoy some time for herself. Now, she didn't have to rush to her children that had been taking all her precious time away from her.

At last, the motherly instinct woke Julija up. She like a roe-deer, scared by a hunter, jumped to her feet. Then she glanced at the sun that was high in the sky and again sat down feeling even more relaxed. After spending another hour, she went back to the church where she had left her twins.

Julija knew the Mass was almost over. As she walked into the church, an organist was performing the last gospel canto dedicated to the Virgin Mary.

She was anxiously waiting to hear the news about today's unexpected finding by the sacristy door.

A priest got into a pulpit and began reading a passage from the Gospel before starting his sermon. Julija wasn't paying much attention to what he was saying. On her mind, was only the fate of her twin boys, whom she had left at the church just a few hours ago. Therefore, she practically didn't hear the monotonous words dissipating into the arches and vaults of the church.

In the beginning she was searching with her eyes for something. However, after being convinced her children were not there, she cowered and got absorbed in her sorrow.

Julija was leaning against a pillar located by one of the side altars of the church and didn't listen at all to what the priest was saying.

He kept getting more and more agitated while preaching about dissolute women who were not afraid of God's wrath. He continued on saying that those women wound not succeed avoiding it. Then he made a statement that after indulging in lust, women would give birth to children without blessing of the church.

Julija was watching the priest shaking his hand in the air with his indicating finger pointing upwards while he in a threatening tone of voice announced that even though this kind of shameless women often forgot their motherly duties, they could not hide from God's punishment. He went on saying that even if they were lucky to avoid paying the price for committing their sins in this world, they would not be able to escape the responsibilities when standing in the presence of God Himself. They would have to answerer in the Heavenly Court for all the wrong doings of their past life on Earth.

Since the priest was talking about the dissolute women, Julija against her own will lent her ear to his sermon. She knew she was definitely one of those women! He was talking about her behavior. Now, Julija all tensed up was waiting for him to say something about her foundlings, too. Otherwise, he would not have chosen this kind of subject for his lecture!

Trembling with her entire body, Julija was waiting for her children to be mentioned as well with the avalanche of hatred words directed towards her.

And she was not mistaken. The priest was now menacing with his fist to the parishioners his voice growing louder and louder.

At last, the words Julija was so afraid to hear came out. He announced that two infant boys had been found on the doorsteps of the sacristy this morning before opening the church. Now, the priest appealed directly to the parishioners asking for their help in finding out any information about the twin boys. He also added that their vile mother should be found, too, and punished for her unspeakable act. According to him, she didn't have any right to call herself a mother after doing this.

Julija never expected this could take such a sharp turn. The situation was becoming more threatening by every minute. Even though there were not many people out there who knew about her twins, but there still were a few of them in the city. First of all, almost all the residents of the yard on the Bernardinai Street knew about her and the twins. But the most important witnesses were her nanny, then the woman who had watched them the last few days, and the young tattoo master, who had tattooed the crosses on the little arms of her twin boys. Thus, those people were the ones who had known the most of her and her children.

Julija was reasoning that she had paid generously to all of them for their services. Therefore, she was wondering if they could betray her after that.

All her plans regarding getting her little boys back were falling apart like some house of cards. She had dreamed about presenting her uncle and aunt with her situation in some round-about way and then, after moving them to tears, carefully talking them into taking the children to be raised in their home.

However, the harsh priest's words mixed up all the plans she had been fostering in her heart and her mind. Now, she just wanted to hide her secret from others even more. She saw the people standing around her in the church getting very indignant. It seemed that if someone pointed his or her finger at Julija and shouted, 'This is the shameful transgressor!', all the people at the church would attack her with their fists. Most likely, they would have driven her out of the church, or they would have thrown stones at her, or even would have killed her all together!

The people at the church seemed to be very angry because of the act of this unknown woman who had been so cruel to her own children. In a meanwhile, the priest just kept pouring more and more fuel into the flame making all kinds of remarks and expressing various comparisons. He even used some widely known quotations and proverbs in order to stress his words. He noticed publicly that the mother of the infants must have been crueler to her children than wild animals could ever be to theirs. Even though the later ones didn't possess any humanly feelings, there had been no known case yet where the animals would leave their newborn children to the destiny to take care of them. Therefore, this woman, who had left her children on the cold cobble-stone entranceway of the sacristy, righteously deserved to be cursed by the people and the God Himself.

Now she understood she had to take to her heels and get out of this infuriated crowd if she didn't want to be torn to shreds alive! Julija saw no one was sympathizing with her during this most difficult hour of her life. On the contrary – it seemed everybody was overwhelmed with hatred towards her. No soul alive cared about all the injustice and hardships she had to go through during the past year. Oh, if only they knew about her problems and how much she had endured so far, and how difficult it had been for her to part with her lovely, little boys! The people at the church didn't even realize that namely because Julija had given her children to the church she could not be compared to the wild animals since her intentions had been noble enough.

If all these strangers learned about her life and personal circumstances, they would not have been so harsh to her with their judgment. Then most likely many of those hearts beating in the church at that moment would have melted and have forgiven her that horrible sin which she had already paid for in full measure by drinking her life's cupful of the suffering that had been designated to her by her destiny.

Julija was still reluctant to walk out of the church since she was afraid to draw people's attention to her. It seemed that everyone noticed her agitation that was only further revealing to them who she really was.

However, she was trying to control herself while she waited impatiently for the moment when the priest was going to end his ill-fated sermon.

But as if on purpose, he continued preaching; only his tone of voice was now a little softer. Finally he got to the heart of the matter. Obviously, the thing that had been troubling this servant of the church the most was the fate of the twins. Therefore now, he began blaming the war. People at the church could even hear the faint notes of understanding being addressed towards the sinful mother. He expressed his concern that maybe because of the unfavorable circumstances due to the war, those children became the victims of the abandonment. Maybe there was hope their parents were not completely rotten after all.

He asked people to volunteer to take those poor infant boys home to raise, this way not only helping their church, but pleasing God as well. The priest insisted that such little children were totally sinless. Therefore, if they were lucky to end up in some God-fearing Christian family, they would certainly grow into decent people who would later also believe in God. In turn, the church would baptize them and not forget about them in the future as well. The priest talked a little longer about the twins, whose parents' past or religion was unclear; he promised to not abandon the children until some guardians stepped in to take care of them.

Then he finished his sermon by asking good people to come and pick up the infants at the sacristan's.

Julija didn't even feel when the current of people took her outside to the churchyard. There, she heard some people talking between themselves with indignation. They were wondering how anyone could take upon such a responsibility of raising the two little children during the wartime when the adults themselves were living half- starved. However, Julija no longer wanted to listen to those rebukes that were being expressed with hatred by some citizens and with aversion by the others.

Little by little Julija got used to her new situation. Even though she was unable to see her children, she still could find some comfort by at least knowing where they were.

Nevertheless, she avoided going to the church since she was afraid to meet someone who had known her and her children. Thus, this event with lightning speed could spread through the city turning into the real sensation! For a while, Julija didn't even want to show up in the streets of Vilnius.

A few times she accidentally heard people talking about her twins, and those talks were so horrible, even threatening in nature they were making Julija to think twice if she really had needed to leave home in order to go to the city that badly.

The current events made Julija change her lifestyle. She longed for her little sons tremendously, but she constantly tamed her feelings suffering immensely because of that.

Finally, all the gossips subsided. During this time of war when almost every day new events were taking place, one stranger than the other, it was not surprising that the news of the new outrageous things happening were in the center of the people's attention.

The big portion of the news was coming together with refugees that the city was literally swarming with. They kept enlightening the residents of Vilnius about what had been happening in the west.

When Germans occupied Kaunas, local citizens began massively evacuating to the heart of Russia. Those who lived in Vilnius were waiting with fear for Germans to show up any day now.

Nevertheless, Julija wasn't paying any attention to the scary news even though everyone around was talking only about that. An idea wasn't leaving her mind someone had already reported to the authorities she had deserted her children. She thought the day of repayment for her sin had come. Now, she was reliving the waiting period of something big to happen in her personal life that was related to her twins which did not allow her to keep up with anything else taking place around her.

Julija often saw crowds of people chasing her in her dreams at night. Not knowing how to save herself from their rage, she would jump into the water or some precipice on her way. After that, she would soon find herself sitting in her bed all sweaty and shaking with horror, and then she could not get back to sleep for a long time. And at those times when she was lucky to drift into sleep again, anxious dreams tortured her anew. In addition to this, she would hear in her sleep the cry of her twins even though they were no longer with her.

Being completely preoccupied with her grief, Julija forgot even about the war. Her aunt with uncle noticed her strange moods. When they asked her questions about that, Julija complained of not feeling good. They thought Julija was taking to her heart the World War I events that had been rapidly developing right in front of everyone's eyes. They were almost sure she was suffering all these involuntary changes in their live making her shrink into herself.

The time had come when far away shots of cannons were heard announcing to the city of Vilnius about the approaching battles, which caused such a huge turmoil it was difficult to perceive what was happening.

It was almost impossible to pass through the central streets of the capital where the tired army had been retreating every day. In addition, the refugees of war were also walking along the same streets. The institutions had been closed, the factories were standing idle, and unspeakable disorder was reigning everywhere. Many flats had also been deserted making it possible for anyone to just walk inside ant take anything they wanted.

At that time, Julija with her aunt and uncle were already living in her deceased parents' flat in Vilnius. Upon this commotion taking place in the city, though, Julija's uncle had harnessed a horse to a cart and heaped up into it everything that was of more significant value and took it to their property in Verkiai.

Julija violently opposed her uncle leaving Vilnius. She badly wanted to be close to her children. However, her uncle had his own idea of her being stubborn. He thought she didn't wish to part with the tailor's shop and their newly remodeled hotel.

Thus, Julija against her own will was taken to their Verkiai farm that was located pretty far away from the city. Her uncle figured that while the war was raging, it was supposed to be less dangerous there. Besides, having an orchard and some land, made it easier to survive just by growing their own food out in the country.

Julija's uncle was a very clever business person; he could anticipate far into the future. Therefore, he sold almost all his horses and took only a few of them to their Verkiai farm. He also disassembled and brought in all the sewing-machines from their tailor's shop in Vilnius, dishes from their restaurant, and a lot of stuff from their hotel as well. All the lofts, barns, and outside buildings in Verkiai were stuffed with all those things and furniture now.

The very next day after they moved from Vilnius, the city was bombed out of long-range artillery, making it really hot for the remaining residents there.

Now, there were pillars of smoke constantly rising into the sky during the daytime, and glow of fires were unceasingly lighting it up on one and the other side above the city at the nighttime.

Julija with fear was observing the sky glowing with firing every evening until midnight. It seemed to her that her children were burning left in the city. Sometimes it appeared as if she was hearing them crying, too.

A few times she got asleep right by the window, her head on her arms placed onto the dining table. Then she suddenly sprang up to her feet and, her hands clenched into fists next to her chest, she moved away from there with a heavy heart.

One week later, new masters came to the city of Vilnius. Life became even more difficult because the retreating Russian Army took with them more than half of all the food supply, and the rest of it was plundered by its own starving people during all this confusion going on.

Thus, the starvation was raging in the city. Everyone who had opportunity to live out in the country left the capital. Only those who had nowhere to go remained in Vilnius.

Julija's guardians didn't think of moving back to the city any time soon since they had food to eat in Verkiai to their heart's content. True, as Germans came to their farm, they took away from them two of their horses, four cows, and a couple of pigs. However, it still left their family with four cows, one horse, and four hogs. Their sheep that they had eleven left, remained completely untouched. Also, their hen-house was full of hens. Germans also took a ton of grain out of their granary – almost all of it. The only grain remaining on the farm was that which had been hidden by Julija's uncle. And that, whatever was left, enabled their family to have more than enough for them to eat.

In spite of all this comfortable life, Julija was dying to go to the city in order to be closer to her children, thoughts about whom didn't leave her alone. However, her aunt and uncle thought she was worried about their assets left in the city.

A month later, when everything calmed down a little bit, Julija and her uncle came to Vilnius to check on their property left there.

Their tailor's shop was almost in the same condition as before when they had left it. However, no one was working there or managing it; part of the furniture there was stolen. The status of their hotel was different, though, because it had been turned into the commandant's headquarters, and no one was allowed to come inside or even near it.

Julija and her uncle also checked their little house in Sapezinka where everything remained the same. That place wasn't left to its fate since their neighbor living right next door was taking care of it in exchange for some food and promises of help in the future. At that difficult time, anything could be achieved just for the food.

The war continued destroying, burning, and devastating everything on its way without any mercy in spite of all the efforts of those who had been preserving and cherishing those assets for centuries now.

The time passing by, the New Year had come. Not every family had a good holiday this year. However, Julija with her uncle and aunt celebrated it at a table loaded with a lot of various dishes. They were not lacking even alcoholic beverages on it.

They didn't invite many guests, only the closest people to them. Julija had not asked any of her friends to come. First of all, their farm in Verkiai was too far away from the city. Second, when she had begun dating Robertas, the circle of her friends began melting away simultaneously. She didn't want anyone interfering with her relationship with him.

And after Robertas left her, she started avoiding her girlfriends even more. Therefore now, also, she told her uncle and aunt that it was too far away for her previous classmates from the gymnasium to come to visit her in Verkiai.

Thus, they had just a few honorable guests visiting with them this year. It was the uncle's cousin who came from Pavilnys and also a couple of neighbors with whom they had become acquainted when they had first moved to live in Verkiai.

In this kind of setting, Julija met the New Year. It seemed the coming year was predicting difficult times. Even the toasts being made this year differed from those of the last year. The guests were wishing each other not a happy and joyful New Year as it had been customary to do every year before, but they wished to stay out of poverty and hunger this coming year.

In general, the entire New Year's Eve felt more like a funeral than the festive holiday. Neither singing nor laughter was being heard at the table.

Usually when people had too much to drink, they would forget about the worldly problems. Nevertheless, this time after having a few drinks, everyone at the table seemed to think and talk more about misery than about anything else. It appeared as if the poverty had visited every home and now kept every family hostage.

During the entire winter, Julija went to Vilnius only a few times but she didn't dare to go to the church in order to find out something about her children.

She only went to the tailor's shop which she found in the same condition as before – abandoned and forgotten. And she walked by their hotel only once. Some officer approached her there. Most likely, he just wanted to chat a little with this beautiful, young lady. After this, Julija didn't even try to check on the hotel anymore.

When the spring came, she again couldn't leave the farm in Verkiai since she had to help her aunt and uncle with various outdoor chores there.

Only during the summertime, Julija began visiting Vilnius more often. It seemed life in the city was getting back to normal. The only difficulty that remained there was for people to get the food. But other than that, some factories already opened up, thus, making it liven up a little.

However, Julia didn't see much of this coming back to life city. She still was in the clutches of the melancholy that had a strong grip of her with no intention to release her.

Nevertheless, some feelings were waking up in her heart, making her soul want to strive for happiness. Often, she could not understand herself what was happening to her. While walking aimlessly in the streets of Vilnius, she kept asking herself, 'What I'm looking here for? Did I lose here something?' Then, her inner voice would answer her painfully, 'You lost everything – your love, your children, and your future consolation.'

During those kinds of moments in her life, Julija's heart longed for something. She not only wished to see her twin boys, but she also dreamed of beautiful, big things happening to her; only she wasn't quite sure what they were. She was dreaming of meeting Robertas, too, and she knew that if she really met him, she would not be able to say a word of rebuke to him.

When the fall came, Julija again ceased going to the city. Most of the time, she would stick in her room for days. The only distraction for her at this time was the music. Now she was spending almost all her evenings at the grand piano absorbed in playing different musical compositions. Pretty soon, she was playing like a professional.

One day, some German officer came to their home and praised Julija on her piano playing. Moreover, he admitted he had never heard anyone playing so great, except during those times when he had gone to a concert hall in Germany.

This young German woke up Julija from her stagnation, especially when he began visiting her regularly once a week. He was very polite, and it was obvious from his behavior that this man had been dealing mostly with cultured and very well-bred people.

In the beginning, Julija wasn't paying much attention to his visits. She only was pleased with him listening to her playing some musical romances.

Upon leaving, he often praised her, "Fraulein Julija, you can't imagine how much I love to listen to you playing the piano!"

Julija would always answer with a smile. Stretching her hand goodbye the last time after his visit she, too, said in the most pleasant way possible, "If it wasn't boring for you to visit with us in our somber corner here, in Verkiai, please come again next Sunday to have lunch with our family. We will treat not only your soul with the music, but your stomach with some good food as well. Please, say 'yes'!"

"Fraulein Julija, I can't refuse you anything! Thank you for the invitation –I will certainly be there. I don't think it is the somber corner here, though. To the contrary, I think this is a very peaceful and safe place to live during such dangerous times for your country. Of course, you probably view me like some foreigner who had come to conquer Lithuania. Fraulein Julija, I don't want you considering me to be some bad person. I am only a mobilized officer, who had to obey the order of his government to come here and fight the war."

"Honorable Captain, I understand your mission, and I have my own opinion about the current situation in our country. Yes, the fact is you are our conquerors at this moment. But another fact tells us all that before you came here, we had had the other conquerors, too. Therefore, by pushing our previous oppressors out of our country, you had not inflicted such a big wound on us! It's still too early to say which government does a better job at ruling Lithuania."

"Fraulein Julija, I'm highly pleased to discover how bright and broad minded you are! Don't think I don't understand what hidden agenda had been on the German government's mind when they had decided to send their armed forces here. I deeply regret I have to be the part of this plan. The only thing I can tell you now is that I hope after we leave, your native county is going to regain its independence. No county in the world wants any foreign government stretching their bloody arms towards its freedom."

"Thank you, Captain, for your warm wishes to my country. Now that I know your point of view, I will be even more pleased to meet with you next Sunday. I will be waiting for your visit anxiously. Please don't forget to come for lunch."

Strangely, this German officer was the one who woke Julija up from her apathy. After hearing those beautiful wishes for the future of Lithuania, she began seeing her own future in different light. She was a little surprised that he had not sparked any feelings in her heart when he had visited her all the times before.

However, now something happened deep in her soul. Julija plunged into a reverie. While reliving a few times in a row every said word by the German officer during his last visit, Julija was feeling some unexplainable longing.

She was anxiously waiting for the Sunday to come. When it arrived, from the early morning already, she started helping her aunt preparing their fancy feast. Julija had to admit this was the first time after Robertas had left her when she was really enjoying the company of another man.

Lately, days for Julija had been going by slowly looking all identical to each other like drops of water. Therefore, she impatiently waited for this special day, however, being so busy, she didn't even notice when the noon came. There was only an hour left before Captain was supposed to show up, and she was not even dressed properly for his visit!

Julija was glad, though, lunch had already been prepared. The hot dishes had been waiting in the kindled stove, and the deserts with the appetizers were carefully displayed on a sideboard in the dining room.

Now Julija rushed dressing up herself. Her hair-do took the longest which, owing to her aunt, turned out to be very elegant and beautiful. Julija was literally blooming. Even her uncle noticed that. He smiled at her and said, "Julija, today you look more beautiful than a blossoming rose itself!"

"Don't exaggerate, uncle. I'm still the same nettle growing along the fence as I was just yesterday and the day before yesterday."

"Well," he objected, "if you don't believe me, go and look in the mirror."

"You yourself look like a strong, luxuriant oak tree," she answered.

"Oh, Julija. I resemble more a disintegrating birch-mushroom. It seems this war totally sapped me out. Most likely, I won't be able to rise up from those ruins."

"Uncle!" Julija exclaimed. "You could still compete with the young men. In fact, you could serve them as an example of a true health and manhood!"

At that moment, they heard a door bell ringing that cut their conversation short.

"Go open the door, dear. Captain has probably come."

Julija didn't need to be urged twice. However, when she opened the door, she was surprised to see Captain with some other older looking officer standing next to him.

Having noticed how confused Julija was, Captain hurried to remedy the situation.

"Fraulein Julija, I decided to take advantage of your kindness and bring my current chief officer with me. This Herr Major had been my teacher before. He'd taught me philosophy. I hope you will forgive me my brave move. We, the military men, get so lonely when at war. Herr Major couldn't remember when he had visited the civilians lately."

"Please come in," Jilija opened the front door widely. "I hope you will like visiting with my family."

Captain let Major walk through the door first. When inside of the hallway, he immediately introduced Julija to him, and as soon as they walked into the salon, they also shook hands with the hosts.

After this official part, Captain excused himself and asked Julija to play a little music for them.

She played a few romances after what both officers ardently applauded her. Encouraged by her success, Julija played some symphonies of Beethoven. When she finished playing, Major swiftly jumped off the chair acting like some young man, ran up to Julija, seized her both hands with his, and began kissing them.

"Julija, ver yut, ver vinderbar mein ziebe!.." ("Julija, my Dear, it's so fine and beautiful!") he exclaimed, at last.

For long time, he couldn't appease his excitement.

Happy Julija continued playing the excerpts from the symphonies of Beethoven, Bach, and Mozart. Then, she finished her musical part of the evening's program with the sonatas of Gluck and Haydn.

Finally, she rose up from her little, round chair and asked the guests to the table.

The first part of lunch was rather official. Everyone was trying to act very properly. However, after having a few little glasses of German rum that the guests had brought with them, they became more relaxed and began talking sincerely.

In spite of that, their guests never crossed the line of decency. Maybe because they were drinking in moderation or just because they were cultured people in general, both German officers concentrated more on the conversation taking place at the table and not on the food or drinking. Moreover, they didn't touch subjects that would make Julija or her guardians feel uncomfortable, thus, escalating some problems related to the war or anything else.

After lunch that lasted good two hours, Major asked Julija to play piano again. She with pleasure agreed to perform many romances and sonatas created by various famous composers.

Only in the evening, the content guests bid sincere farewell to Julija and the hosts. After expressing hundreds of words of gratitude, Major again kissed both Julija's hands declaring she was worth so many kisses.

Meeting with both officers, once and for all dispelled all her melancholy that she had been suffering from for such a long time. Julija felt as if she had been woken up from a deep sleep. In order to survive, she was now holding onto the ruins of her life. Stumbling, she was trying to walk on her legs that were still weak.

Through those new people in their home, she found the way out of her pitiful situation. Every day she was raising her head higher and looking up at some invisible ray of light directed at her from above.

Soon, another event poured more joy into her heart. Namely, she received two bouquets of flowers exactly one week later after the visit of the German officers. One bouquet was from Captain and another – from Major.

This noble gesture made Julija think there was a good reason to live in this world! Obviously, those two German officers were not considering her and her family to be the members of some kind of lower race on this Planet. They themselves had been very cultured and well brought up gentlemen. With their friendliness and sweetness they had managed to conquer Julija's heart. And she graciously accepted their goodness.

Moreover, after having received so much undivided attention, Julija's entire outlook on the world began quickly transforming. Before, she had had rather low expectations from people, and her perception about society and life in general were pretty negative. Now, a strong desire to live suddenly took over her entire being.

The friendship with those two high rank officers paid off to Julija's family ten times since they helped her uncle save his assets from being seizured. Many other large farmers had lost all their assets. Their owners themselves ended up on the street, and henchmen of the invaders replaced them, now playing the masters there instead. They didn't care of developing the land further by making any capital investments; they had just been after what was already available to take from the local farmers and landowners.

The same fate befell the owners of the factories in the cities. They no longer were allowed to own their assets. Instead they were doing some administrative work getting for it a salary and some incentive benefits in return for their work. All the profits went into the pockets of the conquerors.

Only in the smaller enterprises where from a few up to a few dozen people were working, the original owners had still been managing their businesses themselves. But they, too, could hardly make ends meet because they were burdened with such big taxes that many of them were not able to handle paying them. Therefore, numerous of those businesses went broke.

It wasn't surprising that under such conditions, the daily growing more and more poor industry of Vilnius, which had not succeeded in achieving very high level in this area before, too, could not meet the needs of even one third of its residents now.

The city was lacking not only food, but the condition with the manufactured goods there was not any better, either. Everything around continued to be looted and, also, many necessities were being taken to satisfy the needs of those fighting in the front. In addition to this, many assets were being hauled away to Germany as well.

Only owing to the efforts and incontestable authority of those two German officers, Julija didn't lose her assets. Moreover, when Captain learned that she was an owner of the big hotel and the modernized tailor's shop, he began talking her into reviving her business. He was sure she could derive good money from it. He even promised to help her with any legal aspects related to the renewal of it. Captain regretted only because he could not do anything about Julija's hotel since it had been occupied by his fellow-countrymen, the German military officers.

Finally, Julija agreed; her uncle helped her to get out of the barn a few sewing machines and take them to Vilnius. In the very beginning as she was trying to situate her business in the old premises of her tailor shop, she didn't know where to start since majority of the windows in the building had been broken. The floors had also been disassembled in many places by some thieves.

For a while, the tailor's shop looked as if it had suffered an earthquake. At one point, Julija already wanted to give it up as lost because the damages were so overwhelming, she didn't have any hope to revitalize her business.

Nevertheless, as soon as she met Captain again, he succeeded in talking her into starting the necessary work there. Moreover, he personally took part in it; he brought two men from barracks, and they helped Julija to put in order the waiting-room first by glassing the windows and restoring the door with the floors there. Then, the walls and the windows were also painted white, and the wooden floors were varnished. In addition to that, they ordered a new sign in two languages – German and Polish – to be hung on the outside of the front door.

One week later, the tailor's shop opened its door for the public even though the waiting-room was the only one that had been refitted properly.

Soon, the first three dress-makers who had answered an advertisement in the local newspaper for the job opportunity at the tailor's shop were already sitting at the sewing-machines. There was not much for them to do there since hardly anyone knew the tailor's shop was open again.

Even though they didn't receive any orders, Julija paid wages to her three dress-makers. Then, she told them the next week's wages were going to depend on the amount of work actually done. Her workers understood they were not going to get paid since, up to that moment, there had been no job orders at all. All three of them right away refused to come to work.

However, not having anything in particular to do, two of those women returned to work the next day.

Thus, the new life at the tailor's shop began.

Of course, Captain was again the one who helped a lot to really jump start Julija's business. He presented her with the first big order – to make one hundred military shirts.

After that, a few old clients came in and brought their coats and dresses to alter.

A month later, the two dress-makers and Julija could hardly manage all the work. Often, they had to sit at the tailor's shop during the night hours in order to meet their deadlines.

The mountain of clothes to be repaired was rapidly growing. New walk-in clients kept pouring in each day. In addition to that, Captain kept bringing in more big orders as well.

Now, he started asking Julija to hire more women to work for her so that her two seamstresses and she wouldn't have to sit over their needlework at night.

He succeeded in convincing her that working so many hours overtime was bad for Julija and her workers' health. Having in mind that their pay depended on the output, it appeared only logical to hire more people in order to handle the business expansion.

However, Julija had different idea about her business scope. She was afraid that in a month or two, the influx of the orders could dry up. Therefore, she used various excuses in order to delay hiring more dress-makers. She even resorted to lying she wasn't getting tired because of working so many hours. According to her, on the contrary – she was pleased to be occupied with some kind of activity besides sitting at home and playing the piano.

Captain remained adamant, though. Almost by force he made her hire three more women.

Even after that, all six of them were swamped with work but, at least, they didn't have to work at nights anymore.

Julija was becoming very satisfied with her business situation. She felt her life was little by little coming back on track. Also, she was glad she had been earning her daily bread herself, without anyone's help.

It was getting way too cramped in their workshop because, since the old times, it had been accommodated to receive clients. However, the five dress-makers occupied half of the entire waiting-room. The other half that was separated with movable partition-wall served as their waiting area now with one to few clients constantly present there. Julija herself took the orders, answered the clients' questions, and provided them with all other necessary services.

One day at the time when there were no clients, Julija was helping her dress-makers sewing and she didn't even notice when the front door quietly opened up, and some woman slipped into the waiting-room. Julija saw her only when she walked up close to the counter. She lifted her eyes from her needlework and glanced at the woman who appeared very sad.

Julija put the piece of clothing aside. She wasn't in time to get off her chair when she heard a timid, quivering voice coming towards her, "Good afternoon, Miss Julija."

"Good afternoon, Madam," she answered feeling a little lost. Julija was curious; she didn't even feel a question slipping out of her mouth, "How do you happen to know my name?"

"How could I not know the name of the owner at my previous job?"

"Did you, Madam, work here before?"

"Yes, Miss Julija, I did."

"Were you a dress-maker?"

"You don't remember me?" the woman asked.

"I'm sorry, Madam, I don't. Before the war, I used to come to the tailor's shop very seldom."

The woman thought Julija was only pretending she could not recognize her in order to avoid paying the money back that she had borrowed from her long time ago. And she was afraid to bring up that subject herself. Moreover, she herself had long forgotten this debt. All this time, she had considered it had been donated to Julija.

The woman's heart was aching; as soon as she saw the tailor's shop opened back to business, she was expecting to find a permanent job here that she had been needing so badly.

However, now, this hapless past with its debt was preventing her from getting this job!

Thus, she totally lost any kind of hope to find work in this poor tailor's shop that had prospered when she had been managing it. Things changed so drastically that now it seemed she couldn't get the position of a simple dress-maker here!

In spite of that, she overcame her preconceived disappointment and decided to ask Julija for a job anyway.

"Miss Julija, I had managed this tailor's shop. You probably forgot about me. No wonder – it has been so many years now. I was walking by and saw the sign above the entrance. So I thought I will go inside and ask about an opportunity of getting a job here. I need it badly. Now I remember you saying to me many years ago that you would be the owner of this place. Your dream has finally come true!"

Suddenly, something clicked in Julija's head, and she remembered her. She couldn't believe how much this manager had changed. Years ago, she had just been blossoming like a fragrant flower. She had even appeared a little too stout back then and full of life and vitality. She used to always dress tastefully, too.

But now, the woman in front of Julija more resembled a ghost with a tired, shallow, and furrowed with wrinkles face. And her clothes looked like some rags. Just by looking at her, anyone would feel a desire to express sympathy towards her.

The woman noticed the look on Julija's face, and she realized how much she had changed. She uttered, "Yes, Miss Julija, those last few years totally exhausted me. By now, you've had opportunity yourself to learn how difficult life is in the city. My personal life has been marked with a bad luck and calamities lately, too. It's been two years now my daughter has been sick, and it's nearly impossible to get medications at this time of war. A couple of times I managed to get it, but I had to pay for the pills probably as much as for some gold. The only person working in our family is my husband, and it's very difficult for us to make living and pay for the health care at the same time. I tried to get a job in order to help my husband. However, it didn't work out. All our savings are gone; we sold everything we could, and now, our family situation has reached the critical level. To tell the truth, you are my only hope, Julija."

"Okay, I've just remembered now! You are Madam Emilija. You've changed so much; no wonder I couldn't recognize you. Now you see what the war has done to our tailor's shop that had flourished before. Instead of having thirty dress-makers, we had to start with only three of them this time, and I had to help them sowing myself. Now, we are total six people working here, and we can barely cope with all the orders that keep multiplying every day. Of course, such a small collective of workers doesn't require a manager. Besides, I'm constantly worried that the scope of job orders could decrease any time, and then, there wouldn't be much to do for those few workers I have here now."

"I totally understand, Miss Julija. Therefore, I don't claim a manager's position. Such a small place doesn't need a lot of management. However, for the sake of my family, I am asking you to give me some kind of job here. If there is enough work for the five people, there should be enough for six, too. I can sew, and I have a good taste, too. I've worked in this tailor's shop for about twenty years. I remember I used to have so much clientele I could not serve all of them. Miss Julija, you have nothing to lose - if there won't be enough job orders for all of us to take care of, then, at any time in the nearest future, you could just dismiss me from work. Please, don't repudiate me, Miss Julija."

"Well, if you don't mind working as a dress-maker, Madam Emilija, I will give you the job. You've done a lot good for this place in the past. I hope you are right, and many of your old clients will come back as soon as they learn you work here. Of course, if your return serves our business expansion, I'm not going to forget about your merits. There is no doubt in my mind I would make you a manager of my business again!"

"Does it mean I've been hired?!" Emilija couldn't suppress her joy.

"Yes, Madam; if you wish, you could start tomorrow. In fact, I'm very happy you are back since I can learn a lot from you, too."

"Okay, I'm definitely coming tomorrow. Finally, God has answered my prayers!"

As Emilija left the tailor's shop, she remembered how dispirited she had been when she had left her flat the same day in the morning. Never ending sadness had been pressing on her tired soul, making her want to cry out of desperation.

Nevertheless, she came back home with her face beaming and heart filled with joy even though she didn't have a clue how much money she was going to make at work. Now, the only thing she could think about was the tailor's shop.

When her husband returned from work, Emilija rushed to brag about her unexpected success. She told him in detail about her conversation with Julija earlier in the day. Zigmundas, just like his wife, had long forgotten about Julija, whom he considered to be simply an irresponsible, young lady. However, now, after discussing with his wife this upcoming job opportunity, he changed his mind about her.

The next day, Emilija came home from work not alone but together with Julija.

After having seen her only once so many years ago, Zigmundas didn't recognize her. A gorgeous lady was standing in front of him wearing elegant clothes, which indicated the luxurious lifestyle because it had been difficult during the time of the war to even get a nice fabric in order to sew such fine clothing out of it.

"Zigmundas, receive the guest," Emilija announced letting Julija into the room where everything, including furniture and even the host himself, looked so beggarly.

He handed Julija a chair inviting her to sit down.

"Miss Julija decided to visit us even though I was reluctant for her to see how we live now," she said and looked at Julija. "Julija, you see how poor we are. Sometimes I am even ashamed to invite people here. The war and our daughter's illness had been the cause of all this."

"I haven't come here to look at how you live but to pay my debt to you. Don't think that I forgot about it. There is a saying 'a debt is not like a wound because it never heals.' I wish I could have paid you back this debt long time ago, but I had not known where you lived then. But as soon as the opportunity presented itself, I decided I didn't want to delay even for one more day, so I could throw down this burden off my shoulders. This debt had given me no rest for years now!"

Julija opened her purse and pulled out a handkerchief with golden coins wrapped in it. She undid the knot on the top of the little bundle and showed them eight new, shiny coins. Then she placed the little treasure onto the table saying, "Here are two hundred roubles. Of course, I could have given this money to your wife today at work, but then I thought I had received this money from your hands, even though I had asked your wife to borrow it to me. If you still remember, I had told you that the money had been needed to go on a trip to the Carpathian Mountains. I could only imagine what you had thought about me then. To tell the truth, it had not been the real reason I had to borrow the money from you then. But it's in the past now. I just want you to know I had badly needed the money then, and you had helped me tremendously during that most difficult time in my life."

"Miss Julija, believe me – I had not thought anything bad of you then," Zigmundas tried to reassure her. He knew he was lying. He tried to add something else in order to justify himself, but he only faltered, after what he turned red and fell silent.

However, Julija rushed in to rescue him from this puzzled situation; having noticed his embarrassment, she changed the subject of the conversation.

Nevertheless, he got right back to the same topic. "Miss Julija," Zigmundas offered, "you probably need this money for your business purposes. I thought this two hundred roubles would have perished at the bank in any case. The savings of all the other people had perished this way. We could just divide it – one half for you and the other half for me and my family. I think it would be fair."

"Of course, we all need money," agreed Julija, "and especially now, when life is so difficult. However, I feel I have no right to take advantage of your family's difficult situation. I would consider it to be cheating. You had helped me, and I will always feel grateful to you for your generous gesture. Even if it was my last money, I would be paying my duty to you. But thank God my business is doing well. Not all of my assets had been seizure. I still have my farm that won't let me go hungry. Besides, I'm aware your family needs money badly at this time. Thus, any kind of division of this money is out of the question. All of it belongs to you."

Julija got up and handed the coins to Zigmundas, "Hide this money in the safe place. You advised me to take good care of the money when you had brought two hundred roubles to my work then, and I always followed your advice when dealing with the money."

"Miss Julija, would you like to have a cup of coffee with us? Please, don't refuse us this little pleasure. You are our biggest benefactress at this time. You can't imagine how much good you've done to us by giving this money that my wife and I have long forgotten about. It almost feels as if it fell down out of the sky right on our heads! You are correct – we need the money badly. We are in a critical situation at this time."

"I'm happy to hear I could return this debt to you namely at this time when it was needed the most. It's too bad I can't stay any longer with you since I have some business to take care off. Bet before I leave, I would like to see your daughter."

"Sure, she is in another room," Emilija showed the door with her eyes.

Julija opened the door and walked inside where the environment was even grimmer. There by the window, the young, gaunt lady with a pale face was lying on a sofa. Her frightened, deep eyes, surrounded by dark circles, were fixed on Julija.

"I'm sorry, Miss Nijole, to disturb you. You mother told me you've been sick for a long time. Since I'm visiting your parents, I could not miss this opportunity to say hello to you, too. Of course, I'm not a doctor and I cannot help you, but at least, I would like to wish you to get well soon. You are so young, and you have the whole life ahead of you. I don't think your illness should last for long."

"Thank you for your encouraging words," Nijole smiled at her. "Mom, give this lady the chair to sit down." Then she looked at Julija and added, "Please don't be afraid of me – I'm not contagious."

As soon as Julija sat down next to the sofa, Nijole continued in a sad, oppressed voice, "It's well said that disease can't last forever. It must end sooner or later. I know my health is in a big trouble. I feel as if I slowly but surely keep walking towards my grave. But the most painful thing to me is that I am dragging together with me my dearest parents. During the last years, my illness almost turned them into beggars. No matter how hard they have tried, my condition didn't improve. I know that my illness will end soon... In fact, I prefer to see it end than continue vegetating like this. This way, I would be free of all this misery, and my parents would also be liberated form the unnecessary burdens. They can't help me. First of all, we can't get the medication I need. Second, we don't even have any money to buy it."

"Miss Nijole, I would like to say that you shouldn't bury yourself beforehand. Miracles do happen. You just have to believe in them. Please, don't submit to negativity. Fight for your life! Life, happiness, and good health are your birthrights. See the light at the end of the tunnel instead of setting the negative outcome beforehand. You have to understand that human life is a constant struggle for the existence. Continual course of nature, like running river, sometimes requires continual rowing and sailing against the stream. You must do everything to better yourself as long as you are alive. Don't you dare to capitulate to the first serious obstacle in your life. How old are you?"

"Twenty."

"It's only one forth of your entire life. You still have three thirds of it left to go. It's definitely worth fighting for it."

"Miss Julija, it's easy for you to say this when you are full of life's energy yourself."

Julija continued, "I feel bad we are not acquainted, and your wants and needs are unknown to me. I think that health is the most important thing for each of us. However, it doesn't mean that if one had great health, he or she would be completely happy. I know cases when physically healthy people had some emotional disorders, thus, becoming the victims of psychological illnesses. But let's return to you. Do you think you have any way out of this situation that you consider helpless? I agree that at this particular moment you are ill. But I also believe it is just temporary condition, and you are going to free yourself out of the clutches of this disease. You just need to change your thinking. I can help you. I know well one influential German officer, who could get you the needed medication. Would you like to give me your prescriptions? I would be glad to help you, my coeval."

"Miss Julija, I can't believe you have offered this to me," with tears in her eyes mumbled Nijole. "Your words sound like music to my ears."

"I promise I won't disappoint your hopes. I know myself what it means to give way to despair. I will try to get you the medications."

Julija took the old prescriptions from Emilija, heartened up Nijole for the last time, and left, in spite of them asking her to stay for the supper.

Then she indeed kept her word; she got most of the medications just in four days, which Captain brought to Julija himself. The rest of it he ordered through his mother in Germany. He wrote her a letter, and she sent it to her son in two weeks.

When Nijole received the medication, she cried out of joy and gratefulness.

Days were passing by, but the treatment wasn't working as fast as their family had expected. The good thing, though, was that Nijole's health wasn't getting any worse, either, as if her body had already reached its culmination point.

A couple of more weeks later, the long awaited moment had come, at last, when she got out of bed. In the beginning, she could make only a few steps at a time while walking on her skinny, shaking legs. However, every day she was becoming stronger, and the progress could be felt now without any doubt.

Julija visited Nijole again, who didn't know how to thank her maintaining she would always feel indebted to her for the good she had done for her.

Nijole invited Julija to come and visit her again. However, there had been so much work piling up at the tailor's shop that she couldn't get away from it even for a few hours.

Half of the work room had already been remodeled, but Julija was short of some building supplies and materials, and the entire process of the repairs had to come to a stop. The work atmosphere at the tailor's shop was heating up since she had twenty dress-makers working under its roof now.

They always had a bunch of visitors sitting in the waiting room, too, which was becoming too crowded as well, especially when some talkative women were waiting in this becoming rather cramped area. Julija often would clench her teeth and continue on working as fast as she could, pretending she was not being disturbed by the empty chattering of the clients.

Now, she had no time to help her dress-makers sewing at all. Therefore, she was glad Emilija was back helping her to oversee some of the business operations since she had been more experienced in this aspect of their enterprise management than Julija was.

The financial part of her trade required a lot of her time and efforts, and just that alone constantly kept Julija running around the city.

Upcoming repairs demanded even more time and work from Julija. She still had to finish the remaining floors and install all the remaining windows together with the frames, and she was struggling when trying to find the materials. As Julija finally stumbled on a place that was selling wood for flooring, the seller asked for incredible amount of money for seemingly just a few boards!

Finally, Julija had to resort to asking Captain to help her with her remodeling. He had been regularly visiting her every Saturday at her home. Sometimes Julija also invited him to come on Sundays in addition to that to have lunch with her as well, and he never refused her invitations. Once in a while, he would again bring Major with him. Of course, as usually, she had to play some piano for both of them. Major always listened to this soft music very attentively while sitting on the sofa submerged in reverie. He was a huge lover of the classical music.

This time, too, Julija complained to Captain at the dining table about not being able to find the affordable materials for the repairs of her tailor shop. It appeared to her they were being sold for the price of gold!

This time, again, Captain expressed his nobleness; he promised her to get some needed material. Not even one week later, he brought in a cart of boards. Then two weeks later, two more carts of wooden boards and a couple of boxes of glass were delivered to Julia's tailor shop.

Now, they only needed to get down to work. Once again, Captain had proved to be indispensable since he found some officers skilled in carpentry and sent them to Julija.

Thus, in a couple more weeks of strenuous work, many repairs were accomplished. All that had been left to do was to paint the walls and fix three furnaces which had been badly disintegrated. In many places, stucco was coming off. However, the later things were of minor importance in comparison to the floors that her workers had to walk over every day.

Now, there was plenty of space for all the twenty dress-makers in the renovated room since, before the war, there had been total thirty of them working there. Julija for quite a while had been fostering hope to place ten more sewing-machines in that room. This was namely why she kept working so hard while remodeling the premises of her tailor's shop; the business expansion was on her mind. She was dreaming of restoring her tailor shop to its previous capacity by hiring ten more dress-makers.

In spite of planning to hire five dress-makers, Julija hired only two of them.

The orders kept piling up making it impossible to deliver their services on time.

Emilija supported Julija's idea to expand their business so it could reach its pre war level. However, Julija suddenly began to linger hesitating to make her final decision.

The reason for such her behavior was unexpected mass disturbance that had been recently happening in the society. The dispersed Russian Army left the front and started quickly withdrawing into the depth of Russia. The situation was totally incomprehensible.

Julija's uncle was the first to take heed of what was happening, and he warned her to be very careful in all her business affairs.

Captain was also looking with suspicion at this quick victory. Various mass disturbances and riots spread everywhere around. In some places, the armed conflicts with Bolshevik forces were becoming severe; the news about that reflected in the German newspapers every day. Also, numerous war orders and decrees were revealing the threats of Bolshevism.

Even Captain could not say anything concrete about the situation in the country. He only advised Julija to be watchful for the rapidly developing events.

Julija waited for the usual Captain's visit on Saturday. She was getting impatient for him to come since she was never feeling sad or bored with him.

The evening approaching, it was beginning to get dark, but the Captain wasn't showing up. It appeared more than strange because he always used to be at her house early on Saturdays. Also, it was especially painful to her because, this time, she had told him she would be waiting for him coming before lunch, which had happened only a couple of times before due to some special circumstances. This time, though, she had no particular reason for asking him to come earlier.

Finally, it became totally dark but the Captain had still not showed up.

Julija realized he was not going to come this time since it was too late and, being such a gentleman, he wouldn't break the etiquette.

Sadness overwhelmed her, and she just wanted to cry. In order to avoid dealing with this heartache, she hurried to make her bed. Julija loosened the feathers of her pillow, undressed, and began combing her hair. Standing halfway naked in front of the mirror in her bedroom, she was admiring her beautiful waist.

Suddenly, she heard the doorbell ringing. Its sharp sound was rather week two closed doors away. However, it pierced her heart right through, and soft reddishness colored her cheeks making her look even more beautiful.

She didn't have much time to hesitate or think. Therefore, she mechanically thrust a thin, silk Chinese style robe on her body and, without even being able to button all the buttons, she the first hurried out to open the front door before her uncle or aunt outran her. Her heart was feeling this was Captain, and most likely, a very important, pressing cause brought him at such a late hour.

She made sure she was the one to open the door even if she had to do this in her slippers and with her hair down. In order to check if it was rally him, before opening the door, she asked in a quiet voice, "Who is this?"

"This is me, Miss Julija. Please, open," she heard Captain's voice.

"Herr Captain, is this you? It's so late. I was already going to go to bed. I don't know if it's appropriate for me to show myself to you looking like this," she said still standing behind the closed door.

"Dear Julija, I beg you to let me in. I understand my behavior seems untactful and probably even impudent to you. Please, forgive me – I didn't have another option today. I must see you and talk to you urgently!"

Frightened Julija pushed the bolt to the side, unhooked the chain with her trembling hands, and opened the door. Then she moved back a couple of steps letting him know he was allowed to step inside.

Captain right away started justifying himself, "I beg your pardon for such a late visit. Believe me – I didn't plan to come here at night. The circumstances have changed drastically seemingly overnight. I have to talk with you today or I might have no other opportunity to do this! Miss Julija, as you are aware, I am the military man which means that I don't belong to myself alone. However, I have some business in relation to your family, and yes, I do have some personal rights as well. Therefore, I would like to exercise those rights and talk to you and your guardians."

As soon as Julija brought Captain into the salon and seated him on the sofa, her uncle walked in with a beaming face. He appeared to be in a good mood. Half way joking and half way serious he greeted him, "Hello, Herr Captain. It looks like we are having the late guest tonight."

"I'm sorry for such a late visit. I know that it's not appropriate, to say the least, showing up here at night, but I have a good reason for this. Moreover, I have a very little time and so much to tell you. I would like your wife to participate in this conversation as well. Would you be so kind and invite her?"

"Sure, I think she is still up."

As soon as Julija's aunt came in, after a few official phrases, Captain got right to the heart of the matter, "I'm not sure if you are aware of what is happening in the political arena. An armed revolt rose up in Germany. It's not as bad as it is in Russia at this moment, where the Bolsheviks are trying to seize the power. However, it is still the revolution, and just like during any revolution, a lot of disorder and confusion are taking place. In the east front, too, the biggest problems are prevailing in the German Army. It's unbelievable, but fraternization is happening between the Russian and the German soldiers! Neither side wants to fight. This war has lasted too long, thus, having a bad effect on all the soldiers. It brought nothing else but suffering and hardships. Now, instead of treating each other with animosity, they suddenly became friends! Evidently, the same soldiers' destiny has drawn them together; it's not a piece of cake to keep killing each other. In a way, I'm also a soldier who has to carry the military orders. Lately, I've been waiting for the new orders to arrive every hour. The last order has been not to leave our subunit and barracks even for a short time in order not to miss any military commands from above. I think, they are preparing us to be ready to withdraw at any given moment. I don't know where we are going to be sent, but my heart feels - to Germany because, as I've already told you, there is such huge disorder there that I could not tell you for sure what is really happening. Now that you know the situation, I would like, without beating around the bush, to express my sincere feelings. I love you, Julija. I understand that our religious beliefs are quite different, but they shouldn't play the main role in our relationship. I'm ready to deal with that if the need arises. Of course, I should have done this sooner and in a different manner, but the unexpected circumstances took me by surprise, totally depriving me of time for that. It's too bad we didn't have more time to date, too. To tell the truth, I didn't dare to tell you more about me before because I was afraid you could think I was bragging. I didn't want to give the basis for you to form a bad opinion about me. However, this is my only chance now to tell you more not only about my character but also about my family. Before the war, namely, as soon as I had finished University of Berlin, I'd received conscription for the army. Back then, I had not belonged to any political organization. My father had been German and my mother – French. When my mother had got married, she had received a farm as a dowry that had been even bigger than yours. Our villa is sitting right on the shore of a lake in a very beautiful place. Along all its shore, splendid vineyards are stretching. The lake is pretty big, about ten kilometers in length. I like to spend my time on it with my yacht. As about my father's side, he had inherited from my grandfather a large textile fabric that had been giving huge profits before the war. You are probably wondering why I am telling all this to you. It's because I don't want you to think that Julija would have to live in poverty among people she doesn't know. I would cherish her and love her with all my heart and all my soul. I wanted to have this conversation with you before and under the different circumstances, but now, this new situation is making me get straight to the point. Dear Julija, please tell me if you would agree to go with me to

Germany. If you do, we have to leave without delay, most likely tonight."

"Herr Captain," began Julija in excited voice. "I respect your feelings. You did so much good for my family and me personally. Only because of you our farm has been saved. During this time of the war, it has been our main source of living. You shielded us from suffering cold and hunger; you have taken part in restoring to life my tailor shop. It has been giving nice profits lately. How could I forget it and how could I not feel grateful to you?! Moreover, I have to admit it was a pleasure for me spending time with you. Those pleasant moments will always remain in my memory. However, I have to be frank with you, too. Unfortunately, I can't accept your invitation and leave my country and my family. There are a lot of things that bind me with Vilnius as well. I feel I don't have right to leave my city; I must fight for my rights in order to get all the rest of the assets that righteously belong to me. Besides, I wouldn't feel comfortable living off of your assets."

"Dear Julija, after being united as a man and a woman, dividing property into 'yours' and 'mine', would be out of the question. Everything that belongs to me would become ours."

"Herr Captain, I know what you mean. I still am maintaining the same – I can't abandon everything I have here and go with you. I just can't cold-bloodedly leave all that my parents had been working for during their entire lives and then my guardians continued to preserve. I don't have any right to go to the foreign county selfishly just for my own benefit. I could not leave my loved ones, who had done so much good for me. I know that this war is going to leave my country in ruins, but I also realize that this kind of situation is not going to last forever. The economy eventually will rise out of the ashes and the chaos. I have no doubts life in our country is going to gradually begin prospering."

"Dear Julija," Captain objected, "take a sober look at what is happening around us. Every mistake can cost you a lot of grief. What you are saying is that you are choosing to stay here because you want to get your assets back. The city is already full of Bolsheviks, and as soon as the German Army leaves Vilnius, they will start playing 'the master'. I think I already know their program- once they are in power, you won't get anything back. Most likely, you will lose everything you have now and maybe even perish yourself. I know their attitude towards those who have significant assets."

"I agree with you, but still – I'm trying to stay positive. I haven't done anything bad to anyone. Therefore, I don't feel I should be punished for anything by taking my assets away from me. I guess I will just have to suffer the same fate as my all countrymen. And even if I die, then at least, I will know I perished in my own country."

No matter how hard Captain tried to talk Julija into leaving with him to Germany, he didn't succeed.

Julija liked Captain a lot, but she couldn't imagine herself living in another country. She had changed, matured a lot, and she knew she would not yield to the intoxicating rays of the charm of any man anymore. She believed that she could live with Captain in Germany in abundance. However, she knew her life would change in some other way drastically, too. Her body and soul was literally grown together with Vilnius. She was born here; she had met her first love here that in return enabled her to experience everlasting, irreplaceable motherly love as well. How could she part with all those memories forever!? There was no way she could forget her motherly love and live somewhere among the strangers in the foreign country!"

Captain didn't leave that night. He came the next day again right before lunch and talked to Julija for a long time, putting all his eloquence to work.

When he finally realized that all his efforts were in vain, he said goodbye to Julija and her family and walked away with a heavy heart.

The next morning he left with his subunit to Germany.

Captain's predictions came true; as soon as the German Army left the city, the Red Army occupied it. The Bolsheviks began implementing their own order. All the factories got under their government's control. No exception was made to Julija's tailor shop, also, which meant it had to be nationalized as well. Luckily, Emilija was left to oversee the work of the dress-makers.

Julija became a director now. In addition to that, a few more people were hired, among them a secretary, an accountant, two inspectors, a rate-setter, and a steward.

In spite of that, the productivity came down, and something was always lacking since the administration was unable to supply the shop even with their main materials – the fabrics. Thus, the process of the production often ceased to function because of some kind of shortage.

In a meanwhile, meetings were taking place every day, during which the management was identifying the problems and discussing how to solve them. Various examining boards were being created, but they, too, could not change anything for the better. The chaos and disorder still remained. Not being taken care of properly, the old sewing- machines began going out of order. A few of work enthusiasts perceived someone's acts of sabotage which prompted searching for those doing harm. That in return caused vengeance and faked denunciation.

A couple of dress-makers were taken into custody. However, that didn't remedy the situation, either. On the contrary - it affected morale at work in a negative way because the dress-makers had to toil in this stressful environment while receiving meager pay. All this affected the workers' family life, too, since they were bringing their bad mood from work home.

Not being able to withstand this kind of management of her tailor shop, Julija quit working there. Now, she even regretted she had put so much efforts and money into her business. Even though she was no longer at the tailor's shop, she was still keeping track of what was happening there and what moods dominated among the dress-makers.

Before the end of the war, no longer having a job, she was debating what to do next. Motherly instinct woke her up again. Mainly because of her children she had refused from the idea of going with Captain to live in Germany.

Now, she frequented going to the Sts. Peter and Paul's Church where she could see her sons almost every time she went there.

They liked to play in the churchyard, and Julija was lucky to give them some candy and even to caress them a few times.

She would look at them and discover new and, at the same time, familiar features of her and Robertas.

The children got used to Julija quickly considering her to be a good and generous lady.

The new Russian government's placemen ravaged Julija's home in Verkiai significantly.

At least, she was happy her children were living with a sacristan in the premises adjacent to the church, and they had a pretty good living there which could not be said about the sacristan since he and the dean of the church had to take pains over raising her twins.

If that had happened before the war, they would not have any trouble fitting them into some orphanage or giving them over to an abbey. However, during the wartime, nobody wanted to take care of the small children.

Being constantly urged by the dean of his church, the sacristan contacted a few orphanages, but his efforts were in vain. Then the dean himself tried his luck by going to various charity associations. However, there too, he kept finding only already empty premises or the entire association itself ready to move somewhere to the depth of Russia.

Not being able to get any help, he finally lost his hope to get rid of this trouble seemingly sent to him by God Himself.

One day, Dean talked the sacristan in to take the twins to an orphan-asylum and leave them there. However, no matter how hard he tried, he could not find any benefactors who would agree to raise the children.

Dean continued mentioning about the children to the parishioners during his every sermon. Sometimes he would talk about this subject for considerable amount of time trying to convince the people during the Mass that God would not forget their kind act, and the church would pray for them as well. Later he added, their church would also help the guardians of the children materially.

However, even this didn't lure the parishioners into taking the little boys home. There were no people who would want to merit the grace of God and at the same time take advantage of the spiritual and financial support of the church. The servant of God himself, the dean, wasn't frightened of the wrath of the Lord. He also didn't want to strive in order to ingratiate himself with God's favor which he had been so pressingly advocating to the people of his parish.

As soon as the sacristan took the children to live with him, Dean felt huge relief since the load of cares for the twins freed his shoulders. Sacristan now was the one who had not only to feed those street-urchins but to wash their clothes and to give them a bath as well.

Since Sacristan was sixty seven years old, it was no surprise he was drawn to lie down upon returning home after his service at the church. However, the little boys would not let him rest in peace; screaming loud, they played pranks and often even hurt each other.

Only the grandpa Sacristan could reconcile them by intervening in their childish conflict.

It was not an easy task for the old man taking care of these lively, little boys. Therefore, he rejoiced immensely when Dean asked him to take the twins to the orphanage and leave them there.

Overwhelmed with joy, Sacristan borrowed a perambulator from his neighbor. He seated the children in it, gave to each of them a little cube of sugar in order to keep them quiet, and drove them out.

The trip of the old Sacristan wasn't easy while transporting the two tots even though they were sitting peacefully in the perambulator while wetting with their saliva the sugar. Wiping sweat off his forehead with his sleeve, the old man continued pulling the perambulator over the cobble-stone road with the two ten month old boys jolting in it.

When he found himself in the yard of an orphanage located in Subacius Street, he totally forgot about his weariness even though, just a short while ago, he had to stop at least ten times in order to rest. At those moments, he kept consoling himself he would be able to get rid of this heavy burden in his life.

Sacristan wasn't in time to even approach the door of the orphanage, and some tall woman with a gaunt face appeared in the doorway. A few long, deep wrinkles on her forehead were telling about her difficult life. Her stern gaze was drilling right into his eyes, "Honorable Citizen, where do you think you are taking these children?!"

Without thinking much, Sacristan stated, "To your orphanage."

"We don't receive children. Do you understand?!"

"I don't care if you do or if you don't," Sacristan retorted, "I brought them here, and I'm going to leave them here! What do you want me to do with them?! Just as someone had left them to me, now, I'm going to give them to you."

"I don't know who had brought these children to you, but I know well you won't be able to leave them here," the ghost-like woman stated in a strict tone of voice. Now, Sacristan had no doubts it didn't appear to him she was acting rude.

"This is your responsibility to give refuge to the innocent foundlings," said the old man while taking out of the perambulator one little boy holding him by his armpits.

However, he didn't have time to lower the child on the ground, who was already able to stand on his own, when he heard the loud voice of the woman, "Sir, stop acting willfully or I will call the police! They won't stand on ceremony with you. In addition, you will have to pay a fine. And if that is not enough for you, they might put you in jail. We already had some cases like that. We know well our duties, and no one is going to tell us what to do! So now, are you going to take your child out of here in a friendly way, or you think you would rather have me take the measures related to the administrative interference?"

Stupefied old fellow didn't know what to do or say.

Then she commanded, "Why are you standing like a stone? Seat the child back into the perambulator. You need to come inside and see the situation for yourself. Otherwise, you are going to get some wrong ideas about us. Also, I have to register this incident officially."

The old man seated the child back in the perambulator, gave to the both little boys some more sugar cubes, and followed the woman along a wide, darkish corridor.

Soon they ended up in a rather small, modestly furnished room. There were only a writing-table with a couple of chairs and a wide, massive bench standing along one of the walls there.

The woman showed Sacristan the chair asking him to sit down. Now, she was talking to him in a much softer voice. Without any delay, she reached for a sheet of paper in the drawer and began asking him questions after what she recorded all his answers in writing.

When she inquired what the names of the twin boys were, the old man only shrugged his shoulders.

"Hmm… it seems very strange that the sacristan and the dean of the church have not baptized the children yet. Isn't it the customary thing in any church?" she expressed her surprise.

Then she began moralizing him, "Those children have been with you for a long time now. And they still don't have names?! I see how you take care of the poor children; they have not been baptized, they have no names, and the only thing that is on your mind - how to get rid of them! It looks like you don't care about their further destiny. In that case, you could just leave them somewhere next by the fence where they would die, thus, freeing you from taking care of them."

"I could not do that!" exclaimed Sacristan. "They are people and not some kind of kittens or little dogs."

"Well, if you possess such a sensitive heart, then, let's go and I will show you something."

The woman with the old man walked in silence to a big garden full of children. Surprisingly, it was so quiet there it seemed one could hear a bee buzz by.

"Let's take a close look at those kids here," she offered.

Sacristan for a while was staring at the few dozen of the thin children there, who had obviously been exhausted because of a long starvation.

"Well," broke the silence the woman, "do these live ghosts tell you about anything? There is not one or two of them here but about forty. In spite of that, it is so quiet here, isn't it? Now think – they all are live creatures, which means that if they were healthy or, at least, if they had enough to eat, they would play and scream like all normal kids do, thus, filling this garden with life. Instead, this place resembles more a cemetery with the dead little bodies that are still lukewarm and lounging about. We had four times more children before. Majority of them we succeeded evacuating through various organizations and adopting with families. Several weak children died. We have quite a few more of them on the way there, too. About ten of them total are lying in bed, I would not be mistaken by saying, doomed to die, just waiting for their sad fate to take them away from us forever. We are helpless to save those unfortunate. And the only things they need are food, vitamins, and medicine which we do not have. Let's go back inside – I will show you those dying children. These children in the garden are the lucky ones in comparison to the ones you are going to see now. I think we could find some guardians to a few of our children here. But who would agree to take a bedridden child!?"

They walked into the room where about ten beds were standing. There were children lying in them with gaunt, sallow faces and eyes sunk deep into their little skulls. Sacristan began feeling very uneasy in this death room.

The woman was obviously used to this kind of environment. She walked from one bed to the other and stroked heads of the dying children. She was shaking her head more than she was talking even when some of the children mumbled in their week voices asking for something to eat.

As they approached the last bed, they saw a child whose skin had been turning blue. His eyes were motionlessly fixed onto the ceiling, and his lips were opened as if he was still trying to utter some words. However, his last, unfinished request was already frozen in the air. Probably the little one had been calling for help and, without having received it, he just remained in the same posture forever.

The woman moved his little hand with the spread apart little fingers to make certain he was no longer alive. And indeed, he was not only cold but also hardened like a limb of a tree.

She only rocked her head with sadness and said, "This little boy has already finished suffering all his pains on Earth. Who knows, maybe he is better off than all the rest of the children still remaining in this room. Look at this worn out with hunger little ghost face! Ask those little lips what was his last wish. Don't be afraid – come here and close his still seemingly suffering eyes. Come on – someone has to do this. Just try - and you will understand how difficult it can be!"

The woman took Sacristan's hand and placed his stiff with old age fingers over the eyes of the little, dead boy. He reluctantly closed the lids over those eyes that not so long ago were blooming with life; they were ready for the eternal sleep and darkness.

"Sir, now that you have seen everything yourself, you should be able to make the right decision," the woman said.

Upon leaving the room, Sacristan pulled two cubes of sugar out of his pocket that he had been saving in order to give them to the twins to prevent them from crying when he was going to leave them in the orphanage. Then he placed the sugar right on a gaunt chest of one of the children when he was passing by. The poor boy's chest was barely heaving.

The woman grabbed the sugar and said, "We share food between all children equally. This time, I'm not going to make any exception, either."

When Sacristan found himself outside, he was feeling so overwhelmed with grief he forgot to even say goodbye to the woman. He just trundled away with his two boys without turning to look back at the worker of the orphanage, who was still standing in the doorway.

It was midday, and the sun was so mercilessly scorching the old man's shoulders it appeared that there was not just the thin fabric of his shirt, but something much heavier had been placed over his back. Nevertheless, Sacristan was too agitated to be able to react to the heat. Time from time he kept running his hand over the top of his head or wiping his sweaty face with his sleeve.

He didn't stop to rest even though he was quite tired. The sun in a meanwhile kept scorching as if it was trying to take vengeance on Sacristan for his evil intention in relation to those two poor boys.

Only when he drove onto the bridge over Vilnele River, the hollow rumbling of the wheels of the perambulator woke him up from his apathy.

He stopped and breathed into his lungs the stuffy, hot air, but that didn't help him to recover his strength. On the contrary, the sweat stood out on his forehead again. Suddenly, he felt very tired.

Sacristan had been walking such a long distance that even his shoulders bent down, and his legs were getting heavy as if filled with lead. His head began to swim, and his heart was beating somewhat with interruptions. His tired eyes could see only the heated cobble stones on the bridge that were shining with the intense heat.

Even the trees with their leaves withered were lined up on both sides of the road like some guards observing the strange triplet that was seemingly forgotten by God even though one of those three had served Him all his life at the church.

The other two of the three still had no time to do any good on this Earth, but they had no time to sin, either. In spite of that, God's watchful eye did not notice them, too. Who could know what kind of destiny was awaiting those little boys at this initial stage of their life? The twins were making just the first steps of their life stretching far ahead of them, and it was unknown at that point if it was going to be covered with fragrant petals of roses or their sharp thorns.

The twins began fighting while sitting in the perambulator which woke Sacristan up from his reverie. Obviously, his interference was necessary to appease the two tots.

After calming the children down, he began pulling the perambulator further up the hill while breathing with difficulty.

When he passed the hills of Uzupis and found himself in Olandu Street, first thing he saw in the distance was the dome of the Sts. Peter and Paul's Church that looked so festive against the serene sky.

However, the old man was so exhausted he was not paying attention to this beautiful view, and the twins were still so small they could not get a grasp of the beauty of the nature or understand that they could enjoy and admire it, too.

Finally, the perambulator being pulled by Sacristan rolled into the spacious yard of the parsonage. At that exact moment, Dean happened to be standing at the window. When he saw Sacristan returning together with the little boys, he without feeling what he was doing, exclaimed loudly, "Deun, send our suceour!" ("God, send us help!")

Of course, no one could hear his call for help in Latin.

Dean didn't leave the window until Sacristan disappeared in the doorway. And even then, he remained standing in the same spot. His eyes were anxiously wandering through the empty yard while, in his mind, he was weaving a plot what to do with those children next, who for over two months now gave him no rest.

Dean was waiting for Sacristan to walk into his room, so he could get his questions answered. But Sacristan wasn't showing up as if trying to tease him. Then Dean thought he might be feeding or trying to put the children to sleep after this long and difficult trip.

However, one and then two hours passed away, and Sacristan didn't come. During this time of waiting, Dean decided to walk over to Sacristan's room himself in order to inquire why he had not left the children at the orphanage.

Having lost his patience to wait any longer, he went to Sacristan's modest room. Without knocking on the door, he opened it himself and approached the matter right away, "Why didn't you leave the children in the orphanage?"

"What orphanage are you talking about?"

"Did you go to the orphanage?!" Dean asked gazing at Sacristan, his eyes wide open with surprise.

"Yes! I went to the orphanage, but I discovered there a cemetery instead! My old heart could not let bury those poor, little boys among the rest of the little, live corpses of the other children there. Moreover, I had suffered such a huge shame and vexation that even now I can't find peace. Only when being there I realized what villains we are. I have little time left to live on this Earth. Soon, I will have to stand before God, and what I am going to say to Him? God had sent these little children to us, so that we would take care of them. Instead, we had been looking for the way how to get rid of these innocent twins not taking into consideration at all what fate was awaiting them. We have even forgotten about our main responsibility which was to baptize those children."

The first thought that came into Dean's head after hearing Sacristan's reproachful words was to rail at him for such insolence. However, for some reason that he could not understand himself he was unable to do this.

Moreover, he was standing and listening to him talking. A thought crossed Dean's mind how this old man had dared to say things like this without fearing him, since he had been only his servant for so many years! Being stunned by his unexpected, brave words, Dean still couldn't get back to himself.

Sacristan finished his long talk and fell silent waiting for the punishment because of his straightforward utterance directed at his so called 'monarch', on whom his future depended.

However, to his big surprise, Dean was silent.

At first, Sacristan thought that Dean was probably getting ready for a huge storm, thus, building his fury up, so that he could totally knock him down.

The minutes were slowly passing by making Sacristan afraid of the upcoming fury, but no words escaped Dean's mouth.

Finally, the fear took over, and Sacristan realized he should be more obedient since he had nowhere to go at his age. It seemed to him all he could do anymore in life was eat. And if he wanted to do just that, he had to work for his food. However, being so old, he could no longer do any physical work. The only job he was still suitable for was serving the church, which didn't require of him having a good health.

The only other option for him was to go begging. He still could sit by the church door with his hand stretched out asking with humiliation the passersby for some charity.

Scary future was awaiting Sacristan, who had devoted his entire life serving the holy church. If Dean dismissed him from his duties, he would not have anything left to live for.

Those scary thoughts swimming in his head made him forget his previous feelings; he bowed to his destiny and mumbled in a quiet and meek voice, "Padre, please forgive me for the reproaching words that dared to escape my mouth. What had happened was that the orphanage had refused to receive the children. And I'm glad they didn't let the twins stay with them because what I've seen there will never fade away from my memory. You won't believe – the children that are in those premises now have been dying from starvation. They don't even look like normal children; they look more like barely warm corpses. My heart was overflowing with blood when I was looking at them. I also saw there a dead child with his mouth opened. He had probably been asking for food or for help, but no one rendered it to him. First of all, because of not having enough food at the orphanage, they obviously couldn't receive any more children. Second, after seeing all the misery there, I couldn't agree myself to leave our children to die there. It would be better to throw them down from the bridge into the river like some kittens, so that they wouldn't suffer. If you still wish to get rid of these children, then kick me out together with them. I would be walking in the city contacting its residents door to door with a bag over my shoulder. Hopefully, I would be able to save those unfortunate twins from starvation or from being placed into that disastrous orphanage where only the imminent death would be awaiting them. I just could not give them away to a place like that where they could die. I guess, such had been the will of God for me to take care of them until my legs are still moving and my eyes still can see the road I'm walking on."

"Stop talking nonsense!" Dean cast an angry look at the old man, who appeared even older after today's event. "Who is kicking you out from here?! I just wanted to help you because I had seen how you had been tormenting yourself over those children. If you want, you can continue taking care of them. God forbid that they die or anything bad happen to them. It's unfortunate the times are so difficult now. If not for the war, some nice family would definitely take these two little boys, who are as strong as bells, to live with them. But as far as baptizing goes, I have to notice it has been not only my fault but yours as well. You have always been closer to those kids. Therefore, you could have reminded me about that. But it's not a problem – we can baptize them any time. You could even come in with the children tomorrow before noon, and we will baptize them. Indeed, they have to have names. We will make sure they are going to have the most beautiful names possible!"

The next day, Dean in good spirits met Sacristan with the twins at the church.

"I'm glad you aren't late," he greeted Sacristan first while standing at the altar. "So what names are we going to give them?"

"I don't know, Padre. Whatever names you have chosen will work for me."

"I can't believe you haven't chosen the names for them! Not good," Dean answered quickly in a little unsatisfied tone of voice. It was obvious he was anxious to perform the ritual of the christening as soon as possible in order to free himself of this responsibility.

"Padre, you said yesterday that you were going to name them the most beautiful names imaginable. Therefore, I didn't even think of any names because I had thought you already had the names for them."

"Well, let's not waste time. Just name any names you deem to be fit," said Dean impatiently.

"I don't know. One of them could have the name Baltramiejus. It's a nice name, and there was a saint with such name as well," Sacristan offered.

Dean agreed with the suggestion of Sacristan right away. He didn't really care what the names of the twins were going to be. He just wanted to get rid of this obligation that was now giving him pangs of conscience.

However, neither one of them could come up with the second name as fast as they did with the first.

Dean asked Sacristan already for the third time, "How are we going to name the other little boy?"

It appeared Sacristan wasn't in a big rush to answer his question. He could not come up with any suitable name for the other twin boy.

In a meanwhile, Dean was yawning while trying to drive away boredom. Sacristan as if on purpose could not think of any name. Then Dean took the initiative into his own hands and uttered the name that first came into his mind, "Let's baptize him as Peter."

"Well, St. Peter's name sounds good to me! So it's Baltramiejus and Peter," repeated the names of the twins Sacristan.

"But maybe it's better to call them Peter and Paul?" Dean expressed the unexpected idea that suddenly came into his mind. "The twins could have the names of the saints of our church!"

"That's an excellent idea!" exclaimed Sacristan. "Peter and Paul. The twins have been found in the yard of the Sts. Peter and Paul's Church and, thus, they should carry their names. Probably the heaven itself is sending these names to them. The boys will be later thankful to us for giving to them those beautiful names of the saints especially because they have happened to be the twins."

Thus, after the pretty long debate, the twins got their names, and from then on, neither Sacristan nor Dean was calling them just 'boys'. The only bad thing now was that not only Dean was mixing their names, but Sacristan as well didn't know which name belonged to which boy. If they had to call one of them, they would use any one of the two names that came first into their mind.

When the children got a little bigger, they often both would come running even if only one of them was called. The boys themselves didn't know which one of them was Peter and which one was Paul! They didn't understand that their church guardians were the ones to blame for this confusion since Dean and Sacristan often called the same boy by the different name. After all, their foster children looked so similar - just like the two peas in a pod.

Sacristan dressed them in the same clothes, and he also kept buying them exactly the same toys as well. He did this in order to prevent them from fighting over their stuff.

At last, Sacristan realized it couldn't go on like this forever, and he needed to know what name belonged to whom.

Therefore, he bought dark colored pants to one of them and light colored pants to the other one, whom he called Peter now. This way, he figured that the other boy with the dark little pants was supposed to be Paul.

It seemed the problem was finally solved, and everyone was happy, including Dean, who had warned Sacristan quite a few times before that the twins must know their real names.

Nevertheless, the boys continued mixing up their names. The boy with the light pants was supposed to be Peter. However, when

Sacristan called Paul to come to him, Peter would run towards him instead. Then, Sacristan had to explain again to each of them they must remember their true names in order to avoid confusion and future problems.

In spite of all his efforts, the very next day, the story would repeat itself, and the twins would call each other the wrong names again.

However, all their cunnings soon came to the surface. It turned out that the twins had been switching their little pants. This way, Paul when wearing Peter's pants, would turn into Peter for a little while and vice versa.

All the time changing their pants, the children got again totally mixed up with their names themselves. Besides, Sacristan realized, too, it wasn't the good way to set the names for the children. Now, he started looking for the other methods to do this. It was especially difficult for him to distinguish the little boys because he was old and could barely see. Most likely, only their biological mother with the help of her instinct could recognize who was who. However, it was impossible to do this for a man almost in his seventies who could also barely hear anything anymore.

One boy soon injured his leg which swelled preventing him from walking for a while. In a few days, though, he could walk again but only with a limp.

Sacristan decided that now was the best time to impart to the boy his name. He began calling the boy Peter even though, now, neither one of them knew what his real name was to begin with.

Sacristan felt sorry for the limping boy. Therefore, he often sat him in his lap and stroked his head. In addition, he would give him a bigger piece of sugar than to the other twin.

The other boy - Paul - was becoming jealous since his brother was getting more attention and love from the grandpa than he did.

Therefore, little Paul also began to limp which caused the old man to get mixed up, and he would place Paul in his lap instead. Now, he would caress Paul and give him a big piece of sugar while calling him Peter.

However, the deception soon was discovered since the old man noticed that both little boys were limping. When the swelling of the boy's leg went down, he didn't know which one of them had really been injured.

Sacristan at last realized he had been tricked over by the clever twins.

His health in a meanwhile was declining rapidly while life was getting more and more difficult. He could hardly take care of the lively, little boys. And there was no one to help him cope with all the troubles, too, even though the war was almost over. After all the big confusion, life was very difficult and if not for the Dean, in no way he could have made it with those little kids.

Lately, some young woman dressed in black had been coming to the church every Sunday. She liked to play with the twins, and she would give to Sacristan some food. A few times, she even handed him pretty significant amounts of money stating that she was feeling sorry for those little boys and regretted she could not take them home with her. Sacristan was very happy she was so generous to them.

As the Bolsheviks replaced the Germans, Julija's situation worsened, and she became apathetic. She ceased visiting her children as if she had totally forgotten about them. Sometimes she felt sorry she didn't leave with Captain. At those moments, tremendous longing would overwhelm her, but then she would try to reassure herself she had made the right decision by not going with him to Germany. She was glad she stayed at home with her loved ones.

Sometimes Julija would get overwhelmed with an urge to tell about her children to her uncle and aunt. She wished she could confess to her beloved guardians, thus, stopping the endless haunting of pangs of conscience forever. However, as soon as she thought about this, the fear set in. Surprisingly, she was feeling weaker now than five years ago when she, being almost a teenager girl, had managed to overcome such huge difficulties in her life. Even though she was over twenty years old now, she was terrified of having to deal with any more problems.

Just not long ago, her dream had been to restore to life her business at her tailor's shop and build her own independent life. She had been planning to move away from Verkiai to Vilnius and take her children to live with her.

However, it was not meant for her dreams to come true. As the governments have changed, the Bolsheviks requisitioned a lot of their grain and farm animals. Later, when Lithuanians took power into their hands, their government laid tributes also, and Polish legionaries after that totally destroyed their farm in Verkiai. In fact, that was when the last, decisive blow was hit to Julija's family when they were attacked at night, and their last cow with almost all their supply of grains were taken away. The only grains that left to her family were those which had been hidden by her uncle. There was no doubt, Julija and her guardians would have to face death if they didn't have any food left.

This last incident caused irreparable damage to her uncle's health. He became very nervous; every little thing agitated him. Soon after, his heart began to limp, and he got a couple of heart attacks.

Of course under those circumstances, Julija with her aunt had to walk almost on their tip toes around the house to make sure Uncle was surrounded by the peaceful environment. Aunt was hiding from him everything that could cause even minimal discomfort to him.

During the last months, Julija almost didn't leave the house. As her uncle lay down, she was spending a lot of time at his bedside reading books to him in order to keep him entertained. When he would get asleep, she would muffle herself up in her big shawl and rock in a rocking chair until she fell asleep herself while still sitting in it.

The days were going by, boring and looking all the same, even thought life in the city was in full swing already. Some people were able to rise above their routine and live a little happier than they did during the war.

In a meanwhile, little Paul and Peter had been growing up as fast as dough would rise on yeast. The healthy boys could not understand that their guardians were rapidly getting old and could barely move around the church anymore. Sacristan often could not get up without someone helping him after he was kneeling for quite some time at the altar.

He realized the time was coming soon when he wouldn't be able to take care of the boys, who were becoming more mischievous every day. They were no longer content with playing only in the churchyard, but they often went to play on the other side of the stucco fence, which created the dangerous situation, since that fence was running along the busy street.

As the boys were getting bigger, they were also becoming more independent. The old Sacristan, on the contrary, was growing weaker and weaker, and he could not keep up with them anymore.

Some strangers often would bring the twin boys to the old man after finding them running in the street which was giving even more troubles to him.

However, Sacristan didn't dare to complain about that to Dean being afraid that he would make him take the children back to the orphanage.

Still, he was very worried about the twins since he could no longer take care of them. In spite of that, he kept driving a thought of tying to get rid of them away.

Most of the time, he had to give up his daytime nap. He began closing the small gate of the churchyard, so that the boys couldn't run out to the street. Then he would sit down himself in the yard by the big entrance gate that used to be locked during the regular days of the week. This way, he could watch the twins playing there. Only a little, metal gate next to the big gate was always opened all day long, thus, allowing people to come in and pray or just look at the magnificent interior of the church inside.

The church was considered to be the masterpiece of Lithuanian Baroque. The interior there had the masterful compositions of over 2,000 stucco figures and ornamentation created by famous Italian sculptors and architects. There was no comparable church in the entire capital of Vilnius, and it could have easily competed with the other famous churches of Europe! No wonder, many guests from abroad kept visiting the Sts. Peter and Paul's Church.

One day, Sacristan was watching the twins in the churchyard and began dozing on the bench in the shade of old lime-trees. Once in a while he would open his eyes a little and make sure his naughty twins were nearby and didn't leave to the street.

The boys in a meanwhile were jumping and screaming while playing care-free.

Sacristan didn't even notice when through the small gate a couple dressed in modest but elegant clothes walked in. They were in their forties. He could notice gray hair by the temples of the man which made him appear even more solid and intelligent. The woman walking next to him was about five years younger than him. Her high hairdo and tall heals made her equal in height with the man, who was already pretty tall.

After being woken up by the echo of their steps in the yard, Sacristan with curiosity watched the elegant couple walking towards the main door of the church. During the last months of the disorder in the city, it was uncommon to see people like that walking around. The man with the woman didn't even glance at the old man sitting on the bench.

They concentrated their all attention to the façade of the church. Before entering it, the couple even stopped to read the memorial plaques bricked into the wall by the entrance door. Then they quietly exchanged a few words and disappeared inside of the church.

The man and the woman spent over an hour inside of the church. The time was going so slow for Sacristan; it seemed that not one but at least three hours passed by until he saw the couple again in the doorway of the church.

They were not in rush to leave the sanctuary, though. Instead, both of them walked around the church inspecting every its corner outside. They stopped by the painting on the outside wall of the church depicting horrible plague of 1710 in Vilnius City.

Sacristan was observing every couple's move. He had nothing else to do but to see them with his eyes through the churchyard and into the street.

However, to his big surprise, the man and the woman were not in any kind of rush to leave even after checking their big yard.

Now, they walked to Sacristan, politely greeted him, and sat down next to him on the same bench. Then they made some comments about the lonely, faded away painting on the outside wall of the church. They also asked a lot of questions even though Sacristan could not answer the half of them.

It seemed to Sacristan the couple enjoyed talking to him while resting on the bench in the shade of the big trees of the churchyard. A gentle breeze felt so refreshing.

The woman was less eloquent. She was listening more than talking and would put in a word only once in a while just to follow the etiquette. The man was very politely representing the entire course of their conversation. However, at the same time, he appeared somewhat insisting. He talked a lot about architecture and art of this and some other churches he had seen in Vilnius.

While they were sitting and talking, the twin boys ran up to the bench. They were expecting to get some treats. Often, the other people used to give to them candies and cookies or treat them to some sweet rolls.

"Good boys!" the woman exclaimed with excitement in her voice. "I have something for you. Come here," she opened her purse and began rummaging in it.

"Yes," uttered Sacristan, "they are good, but they also are unlucky, honorable Madam."

"Why would they be unlucky? They are so handsome. In fact, they look identical like two drops of water. It's difficult to believe they could be unfortunate."

"Well, if you knew their fate, then you would agree with me," Sacristan added.

"Why are you talking this way about them? No one knows how their lives could turn out to be in the future," the woman answered while looking at the twins.

"Of course, no one can predict their future," agreed Sacristan, "but my heart has a presentiment their childhood is not going to be easy."

He shook his head and continued, "I'm getting too old to take care of them. Not much time is left for me to live in this world. Together with my eyes closing, the page of their book of childhood is going to close, too. I'm the closest person to them. When I'm gone, they will become total orphans."

"What happened to their parents?" the man, who was very attentively listening to Sacristan talking, asked.

"Of course, they had parents or they would have not come into this world," in a sad voice spoke Sacristan. "However, we don't know anything about them. I found those twins abandoned by the door of our church five years ago. Back then, they were so tiny, maybe five or six months old. They could not walk yet. Sometimes I want to call their parents villains, but only God knows the real reason behind their cruel action. Therefore, He is the only One who could judge them for their behavior. I think I found those children right on time. That was when thousands of refugees had been moving through Vilnius. No charity organization could harbor these poor children. Many of those organizations evacuated into the depth of Russia themselves. Soon after Germans had occupied Kaunas, all the squares became crowded with poor people and refugees. Even the families with small kids were sitting among them under the opened sky. That was when I found those twins by the door of our church. I have no idea who had brought them there. Maybe their mother herself had done such an evil thing since she had had no way of feeding them. But it could be that their parents had died, and some other people brought them to our church. Our Dean during sermons kept offering the parishioners out of the pulpit to take the little boys home in order to bring them up, but he never succeeded finding such generous people. I tried to give them to the orphanage myself. However, they too, didn't take the boys since they hadn't had enough food to feed their own orphan children. I saw those live, little corpses awaiting death to save them from the starvation. Therefore, I myself didn't want to give our healthy, lively twins into the clutches of death. Thus, I've been taking pains over raising them for five years now myself. We, too, had to go through some hardships and even experience hunger sometimes. However, God was merciful to us and sent some compassionate people who didn't let us perish. During the most difficult times when the entire country had been devastated by war and was steeped in the biggest poverty, they subsidized money and food. Now, things are getting better, and the skies above our city are beginning to clear up. We no longer have to be afraid of death or ask ourselves what we are going to eat tomorrow. It seems I could live now, but the past hardships have aged me prematurely. The old age keeps bending me to the ground and whispering into my ear, 'Where are you, the old man, going to leave your twin boys? Who is going to take over bringing them up after you pass to another world?'"

Tears appeared in the old man's eyes, and he continued, "Soon, I will have to leave this world, and these little boys are going to be at the will of the cruel fate. Who is going to wipe their tears away? Who will feed them and provide them with the shelter? Please, God, be merciful to them. Don't leave those poor twins to face their destiny alone."

Now, the woman was also deeply touched, and she could not keep herself from crying. Tears filled up her eyes, and she, like through some mist, could see only the silhouettes of the running around boys. She was thinking to herself that if there was only one of them, someone might take him home. But who would want to give a home to the twins?!

"Yes, indeed, it's the sad story," finally uttered a man in a hollow voice that sounded like it was coming from underground.

The woman wiped her eyes with a fragrant handkerchief and asked, "As far as I understand, you are very concerned about the further fate of those twins. Of course, you have got used to them over the years. Would you be able to part with them if needed?"

"It goes without saying that it would be very difficult for me, being at that age, to separate with them. But I have to think about their future, too. In any case, death is going to separate us. Therefore, they would definitely be better off if there was someone to take care of them. If I could just find people like that, I would be able to die in peace. Now, that I don't know what is awaiting them makes me fear death. So far, there were no benefactors who would want to make those boys happy. I have no other choice but to wait until my last breath for some good people to come by."

"What if we decided to take care of them?" the woman asked.

"Rozalija, what are you talking about?!" the man didn't let his wife drive herself into the subject, and he fixed his inquiring gaze at her. His voice sounded totally different than before; now, it was half strict and half fearful.

"Adomas, we've been looking for a child to raise before," implored her husband the woman.

"Dear Rozalija, think about the consequences! We were talking about taking one child, but there are two of them here! And they are five years old. That age won't work for us. Do you remember that we talked about finding an infant who would never be able to find out his origin, and we didn't want anyone knowing about that either."

Then he turned to Sacristan and said, "Sir, my wife and me can't have children. That is why we would like to adopt a child. Moreover, we own significant assets, and we would like someone to inherit these assets. Thus, the child growing in our family would have a huge responsibility to carry in the future."

Then he looked at his wife and continued, "Rozalija, I can't believe you are taking this so light-mindedly. Those boys would remember about their past life here. Besides, there are two of them! When they grow up, they would have to share the inheritance. They would not care about ideas and hard work that a few generations of our family line had put in order to build up our wealth. I'm afraid they would find out about their past when growing up together because they would be able to discuss their childhood memories. They could even bear malice towards us later in life because we had brought them to our home, or they could despise our family's dreams and goals by treading our relics under foot."

"Adomas, I don't agree with everything you've just said. Our parents, grandparents, and great grandparents lived honorably. There is no reason for you to worry about someone disrespecting their past. They are just the little boys, and we would raise them to be decent people. Their characters and personalities would depend mostly on the environment they would be living in. It's been a few years we have been looking for a little boy now, but it's been also virtually impossible to please you so far."

The wife was speaking in support of the boys, who were still playing in the churchyard not suspecting their destiny was being decided for them.

Sacristan didn't interfere with the conversation of the man and the woman. He just listened attentively to their every argument trying to soak up all the details.

When it became totally clear to him what the couple's agenda was, he calmly slipped into the conversation, "Of course, it would be nice if both of the little boys could grow up together. Not every couple would do such a thing for them. However, if your initial goal has been to find a child, then you could take just one boy instead of two. This way, it could be easier to find parents for the other boy as well. At least, I would be at peace that one boy's life has been put in order. I don't think your fears the boy would remember his childhood are well-grounded. You could tell him later on that he grew up at his grandpa's, and you took him into your home after his grandpa passed away. You could even promise him to show the place where he had spent his first years of life when he grows up. If he would have some memories from his early childhood years, longing could weigh down on him until the rest of his life. Therefore, you could find some similar church and show it to him later. Those boys have never seen anything else but this church and its yard. On Sundays, they see many people, and a few of them sometimes treat the boys to some sweets. One more advice to you – if the boy would ever remember his brother, you could make up hundreds of various stories. You could even make him believe he had never had a brother!"

"Still, it's not known how the new environment could affect the little boy. And what would we say to the other people about the sudden appearance of the child in our home!?" tried to stay adamant Rozalija's husband.

"Adomas, let's take one of the boys," Rozalija entreated her husband. "He is right – we could make up some story depending on the prevailing circumstances. If to think so, we have not been in Warsaw even once during all these years of the war. Instead we lived with my father in the village. I think now is the time to move back to Warsaw. For this reason, we can't sell the factory. But when my father dies, we could sell his farm. Since my father had bought it not very long ago, I don't feel any sentiments in relation to it. We shouldn't raise the boy at the farm because people there could tell him about his past. We could buy a small estate somewhere close to Warsaw and we could tell to our neighbors there I bore a son during the war. Please, dear, let's take one boy home with us. We are getting old. Therefore, it's probably even better he is not an infant any longer. There would be much less problems raising him, and it would appear he is growing faster. You yourself expressed a desire to have a helper. If I could, I would gladly take both of the twins. We could find enough stuff to do and food to feed all of us."

"Rozalija, it is out of the question taking the two boys! I have been looking for the successor not with the intention that he would divide my inheritance which I have been planning to leave to him alone. He is going to have some responsibilities, too, and that is to represent our assents and prevent our family's name from disappearing. Only under those conditions, I would adopt the boy, thus, giving him my surname to bear and to preserve from dying it out."

"Adomas, let's take one of those boys. I understand your concerns. Don't think I am some kind of thoughtless person. You won't make mistake if you listen to me now – I promise you."

Finally, he yielded to his wife, "Okay. Which one of them have you chosen?"

"They look so similar. I can't decide," Rozalija answered.

"Well, maybe we should ask for their guardian's help? He could advise us which one of those boys to pick."

Then, the man turned to Sacristan, "Would you be so kind as to help us decide which one of the twin boys you would like to keep at the church?"

"I can't tell which one is which. Sometimes I mix up their names myself. At one time, I kept dressing them up in different color clothes in order to discern them. However, those rascals would switch their clothes between themselves, and nothing good came out of my ruse.

Thus, neither I know which name belongs to which boy nor they know that themselves. The only thing I can tell you for sure is that one boy was baptized in Peter's and the other in Paul's name. They have got those names because they had been found by this church which is Sts. Peter and Paul's Church. So the dean of the church and me found it to be meaningful to give them namely those names. However, it's up to you which boy you want to take home and which name out of those two you would like to call him. This way, there would be put a stop to the confusion of their names as well."

"Okay," agreed the man and looked at his wife, "I like name Peter better than Paul. And what do you think, Rozalija?"

"Yes, I like this name too. We could call him Piotrus, just like they do this in Poland," she answered.

Then the man looked at Sacristan and said, "We are not going to choose one boy over the other. Can you please call Peter? Whoever comes here, will be fine with us."

"Peter," Sacristan called, and both boys ran up to him.

"Which one of you is Peter?" Rozalija asked.

"I am!" unanimously answered both little boys.

"This boy is going to go with us. His face is cleaner," Rozalija rushed to one of them, fell down on her knees, and began kissing his cheeks. Her eyes tearing up, she kept repeating, "This is Peter, my little son. This is Peter..."

Thus, the fate of the twins was determined. One boy's face was clean, and the other's was not. Probably his brother accidentally had soiled it while playing, thus, at the same time, ruining his entire future. He himself now became Paul that didn't bring him good luck, either.

Little Peter couldn't understand the reason behind the endearment or the stream of the loving words of this unfamiliar to him woman, who so unexpectedly showered him with the kisses.

Only when grandpa Sacristan reminded him about his unknown parents, the little boy woke up from his astonishment.

"Peter, say something! This is your mommy and your daddy. Say hello to them. They have come here to pick you up. I told you before they were coming! You will be happy with them. No one will dare to hurt you because your parents will protect you and take care of you. All you'll need to do is listen to them and respect them."

How long Peter had been waiting for this moment and how many episodes of meeting his parents he had created in his childish mind! And here his long awaited mamma was kneeling right in front of him with tears in her eyes. However, those eyes were radiating joy, and the tears were rolling down her cheeks because of happiness.

Little Peter was standing, not being able to move, also shackled by chains of happiness. Before, he had imagined his meeting with his mother somewhat differently, though. He'd thought he would be jumping and playing with her.

Now, he was looking at her falling into tears, and he began crying himself. However, those were tears evoked not by mortification but by love and happiness. He didn't even feel when his little arm opened up widely, and he hugged her neck.

"Mamma!" Peter cried out so loudly that even an echo in the churchyard reiterated his heart-rending voice. It appeared as if all the saints had heard the cry of joy coming up right from the bottom of his little heart, and they answered in approval, "Maa... amm... maa!"

Paul, who had been standing next to grandpa Sacristan and observing the scene sprang, too, with his arms apart towards the woman screaming, "Maaamma!"

However, grandpa was in time to grab him by his clothes. Holding him in his arms, he began explaining, "Paul, this is Peter's mamma. Your mother is going to come later. She is still looking for you, and she is going to find you very soon."

"Grandpa, I am Peter! This is my mamma! Let me go," he was trying to get out of Sacristan's embrace and run to the woman, who was still kneeling on the pavement in front of his brother.

"Listen to me!" Sacristan attempted to appease him. "You are not Peter. I called you this way many times because I used to mix you up with Peter. If you really were Peter, your mother would have recognized you. It means the other boy is Peter. But don't despair because your mother, when she finds you, is going to recognize you, too. Now you understand why I can't give you to this Madam? If I gave you to her, then what would I tell to your real mother when she comes here looking for you? She is coming soon. Peter's parents told me they met her and she told this to them herself, didn't she?" Sacristan asked and looked right in the woman's eyes.

"Yes, indeed. We met one woman who was looking for her son by the name Paul. She had so many beautiful presents in her hands! You mamma is probably better than I am because I have not brought anything to my son Peter. If we meet your mamma again on the way back, we will tell her where to find you."

This way, she managed to convince Paul that soon he would also be a happy, little boy, just like Peter.

When all of them settled down, Sacristan asked the couple, "When are you going to take the boy?"

"We would like to spend one more day in Vilnius. I think tomorrow in the late afternoon, we could come back here if that's okay with you. I think there is no reason to postpone this matter. What do you think about that, Adomas?"

"Yes, I think too there is no reason to delay. We should get him out of here as soon as possible. He is our son now, and we must start taking care of him immediately. In fact, why would we even have to wait until tomorrow? We could take him today, right now! We are not going to leave him here at all. I hope you have nothing against this, Sir?"

"To tell the truth, I don't want to part with him so suddenly. I would love to spend some time and caress him before leaving. However, if fate demands that he must leave today, then so be it."

"Well, Rozalija, I think it's time to go. We've already spent too much time here."

"Grandpa, do you have some toy to give to Peter that could remind him of you?" asked Rozalija.

"Unfortunately, I had never had enough money to buy toys for them. Therefore, they have been growing up without any toys. They just played together," Sacristan answered.

"It's too bad," regretfully noticed Rozalija, "but who knows - maybe it's even better this way."

"Once upon a time, I carved out of wood to each of them a little soldier. If they didn't lose them, then maybe one is lying somewhere around. Paul, go look for it," Sacristan asked the little boy.

Grandpa didn't have to urge him twice. He like a bullet speeded through the churchyard. Not even five minutes passed by, and he was back with the two wooden soldiers in his both hands. One of them he gave to Peter, and the other he was squeezing in his hand as if somebody was trying to take it away from him.

"Paul, say goodbye to Peter –to your best friend with whom you have enjoyed playing together."

However, Paul didn't stay long close to Peter, who was standing next to his mother and holding her hand. It appeared as if they were total strangers now.

It was difficult to say what was happening in the boys' little hearts at the moment.

Grandpa pushed Paul on his shoulders urging him to step forward the direction of Peter, and he walked carefully as if just now learning to take his first steps. Peter was also encouraged by his parents to move towards his brother.

As the little boys approached each other, they hugged one another over their shoulders as if wrestling. Then they looked into each other's eyes, kissed each other, and parted.

Peter's new parents took him by his hands, walking each on his both sides, and all three of them were headed through the little gate when Paul suddenly ran up to his brother and with tears in his eyes, without saying a word, gave him his own wooden soldier to take away, too.

Thus, the twins parted.

Stooping old Sacristan, holding the little boy by his little hand, was standing and looking at the going away man and woman with the little boy in between them. Tears were rolling down both Sacristan and Paul's cheeks watching Peter disappearing far ahead in between people and trees growing along the pavement of the street.

Little Peter was walking proudly holding hands with his new mother and father. He was filled with joy that he had never experienced before. It was the first time he got out of the tall, thick stucco wall surrounding the Sts. Peter and Paul's Church.

This was the totally new, unfamiliar world to him, and he loved it! In every step, Peter saw something new. However, he didn't dare asking questions to his new parents. If he was walking with his Grandpa Sacristan, he would definitely bug him all the way. But now, Peter was only once in a while furtively glancing at his daddy and then at his mammy. They appeared to him better looking, smarter, and stronger than any other passersby. However, he was reluctant to express his thoughts loudly. Instead, he was keeping them a secret deep in his heart.

Nevertheless, as soon as Peter saw a river flowing by for the first time in his life, he exclaimed, "Mammy, look the sky is below - on the ground!"

"Sonny, this is not the sky but the river," Rozalija said smiling.

"This is water, Peter," his father added.

"Can we drink it?" Peter asked.

"We can drink it, and we can bathe and even swim in it."

"Wow! How much water," Peter was devouring with his eyes the Neris River while admiring its swift current moving between the green banks.

Even people passing them by on both sides of the street appeared to Peter somewhat new, beautiful, and interesting.

When they reached the center of the city, his patents took Peter to the confectioner's shop. Even though the assortment of candies was not abundant there, his little eyes got glued to the boxes filled with different sweets. He was standing at the counter not being able to take his eyes off of the dainties.

When he was walking back in the street with the candy in his mouth, this time, the environment didn't seem to interest him that much. Most likely, it was because he had to 'digest' all the new things he had experienced in such a short amount of time. The impressions had stirred up a real chaos in his head. He was also feeling tired from walking such a long distance for the first time in his life which caused him to become a little phlegmatic.

His parents noticed the difference in his behavior. After exchanging a few words, they went to a hotel the name of which seemed so strange and difficult for Peter to pronounce that he didn't even try.

All three of them passed through the rather dark corridor and climbed wide stairs to the second floor that was brightly lit up by the daylight. Then they entered anther long, darkish corridor with many doors on both its sides. Almost at the end of it, they stopped at one of the doors on the right side.

Peter's father pulled a key out of his pocket, unlocked the door, and let him walk first into the room. There were two beds and a little table with two chairs inside. A big mirror the size he had never seen before was hanging on the wall. But what Peter liked the most about that room was the abundance of the sunlight in it.

The room at the church he used to live in had always been dark; no sun rays ever could penetrate inside there through the two low windows almost reaching the ground. On one side of the yard, there was a tall stucco wall enclosing the churchyard. And on the south side, there was standing a tall house blocking the sun, too. Only when looking up high, Peter could see a little patch of the sky which he used to look at mostly during cold winter days since he had no warm clothes to go outside to play. In addition to that, the yard of Sacristan's home was so tiny and heaped up with all kinds of junk that it had been possible to only cross it on the narrow path well-trodden right in the middle of that rubbish.

However, the twin brothers used to get bored of sitting in the dark room all winter long. Therefore, they half-naked would run outside where they stuff their mouths with snow or swallow icicles. Sometimes those kinds of pranks would give to one or both of them a bad cold or even a high fever. But no one used to treat them with any medications or call a doctor. In those cases, Sacristan used to say a prayer asking God to eliminate the sickness and, thus, their treatment would be over.

Soon, Peter with his new guardians went to the restaurant to eat supper at their hotel. His mother and father had trouble teaching him how to use a fork since he was used to eating with his hands. His parents had to teach him many other things from the start as well.

Peter obediently carried out his mother's and father's wishes even though they sometimes bored him. When upon returning to the room he was seated on the chair, Peter soon got tired of listening to his new mother and father talking. However, just as he would get tired soon, he would also come back to life quickly and start running, jumping, and playing like any child of his age.

Then suddenly, a deep sadness took over Peter, and he could barely keep himself from crying. He was feeling such an intense longing that if he could, he would gladly go back to Paul. But in his little heart, he knew it was already too late to change the course of events unfolding before him.

He continued obediently sitting on the chair until his eyelids began sticking together, and the sleep surmounted him.

Soon his father brought from somewhere a folding-bed that his mother covered with clean bedclothes, and he was lain to sleep. He didn't even feel when he drifted into the world of sweet dreams.

When he woke up, the first thing he saw was bright sun rays which were coming into the room through the big opened window. In the beginning, he couldn't make out where he was. However, as soon as he saw the familiar faces of his mother and father looking at him from above, he instantly remembered yesterday's events.

Suddenly, a mantle of sadness took over his consciousness again. Not being able to cope with the huge change that tumbled over his fate, Peter burst into tears.

His guardians could not appease him for a long time. He was not answering their questions; he only cried. And as soon as he began to calm down, he started asking them to take him back home – to the Sts. Peter and Paul's Church. He said he no longer wanted to go anywhere with them.

After long persuasions, his persistent guardians succeeded in reassuring Peter to continue his journey to his new home.

From then on, his new life began. It was so different from his life with Sacristan, and he had to get used to this new style of living.

His parents not only taught him courtesy rules every day but they also trained him to be orderly and clean.

Now too, as soon as Peter ceased crying, he was taken to the bathroom where his mother washed his face with cold water and soap.

Of course, Peter didn't like it. When his mother gave him a soaping, he tried to cry but the tears didn't help him; his mammy did to him what was necessary.

It wasn't easy for Peter to get accustomed to his new responsibilities since he didn't know what the water really was for. At his old home, it mainly had been used for drinking. His Grandpa Sacristan would give him and his brother a bath in a big trough only once a month. And only once in a while, when his face got very dirty, Grandpa would wash the dirt away with his wet hand and wipe his cheeks with his sleeve.

Therefore, no wonder, little Peter had never got used to cleanness. It seemed to him a normal thing to have a dirty face or hands, and he never realized that somewhere else the different order could prevail.

They had their breakfast brought to them straight to their room, and the unwonted rules were limiting him all over again. Peter had already learned how to use a spoon, but eating with the fork caused him the most trouble since he could not understand its true purpose. According to him, it was more convenient to eat straight with the fingers. The forks and knives were turning in his hands and even falling down on the ground. Besides, it was very difficult to get them into his mouth. However, eating without using those strange, uncomfortable tools was out of the question, just like washing his face without the soap.

After breakfast, Peter began sobbing again which forced his guardians to make a serious decision to leave immediately with the afternoon train even though they had planned to stay a couple more days in order to explore Vilnius.

Until two o'clock, they had not left the room. But the circumstances made them pack their suitcases quickly and hire a coachman.

Peter really liked traveling like this. It was the first trip in his entire life, and his eyes were shining with joy. A smile began playing on his lips. He was beaming while sitting in between his parents on a soft leather seat looking around with childish curiosity.

Soon, this most interesting journey ended. Nevertheless, an hour later, the other one, even more interesting took its place.

Now, he was sitting in another carriage of the train in his mother's lap and gazing through the window at the passing by houses and trees that kept changing each other as if always rushing somewhere. But the most interesting thing was for him to observe the houses running as if they were competing with each other. He couldn't understand this visual effect, and it seemed to him it had to be this way that the buildings had to be running just like the train itself was.

However, the suburbs of the city soon ended, and wide, large forests exchanged the buildings and houses. Then, the planes and meadows with meandering brooks overgrown with bushes and grasses stretched out before his eyes. He was looking with curiosity at herds of cows and flocks of sheep grazing in the lush fields. He also saw quite a few horses grazing right next to the railroad track; Peter was used to seeing the horses. Only they used to be harnessed to a cart and trotting along the street that was going along his church. Here, the horses were standing free, but for some reason, their front legs had been tied up together. He was wondering what had been the purpose behind this.

Peter's mother sitting next to him was showing and explaining a lot of things to him even though he wasn't asking her any questions.

Once in awhile, the train would pass some village or town with a tall tower of the church stretching high into the sky.

Thus, they continued moving fast ahead until it became totally dark. The train kept tapping with its wheels up the sleepers, and it appeared they were talking between themselves in their own language that Peter could not understand.

Soon, the sun set in the horizon, and the people in the carriage began dozing. Some of them were lying on the benches; the others were sitting their bodies rested against the walls, and many of them probably being already asleep.

A bed was made for Peter on the bench, too. Being rocked by the carriage springs and hypnotized by the constant, monotonous sounds of the wheels beneath him, he didn't even notice when he drifted into sweet sleep taking all the impressions of the day with him into the world of dreams.

He woke up only when the sun had already been risen pretty high above the horizon, and its rays were gently tickling his face.

For a while, he couldn't understand where he was and what had happened to him. It seemed to Peter he had still been tired which evoked in him a desire to cry. However, after looking around, he restrained himself from showing any kind of feelings to those numerous strangers around him.

About one hour later, all three of them were standing on a platform of some small train station. A few of the other passengers who alighted from the train quickly disappeared. Soon, only Peter and his mamma were standing alone in the station waiting for something because his daddy had gone somewhere. After a long time of waiting, he finally showed up together with a cart. Then, all three of them got in it and left.

It seemed to Peter their trip lasted a very long time. Sometimes, the horse was trotting but, most of the time, he was walking pretty slowly.

Thus, being jolted badly in the cart which caused even his sides to hurt, the sun mercilessly scorching above, they finally reached a white house sunk in old, tall trees. This was where their journey ended.

As the cart with the horse stopped by the white pillars, some unfamiliar, old man came out of the house. He wasn't as old as his Grandpa Sacristan, but his head also looked the same white and resembled a blooming apple tree in spring.

The old man kissed Peter's parents without noticing him sitting in the cart where only his head was sticking out of the hay, the thick layer of which was covering the bottom of it.

At last, he noticed Peter, too.

"Who is this man sitting in the hay over there?"

Peter's father walked up to the old man and whispered something into his ear. Then, he lifted Peter out of the cart, and all four of them walked into the house, where they found themselves in a big and very beautiful room. A table there had been covered with a white tablecloth, and the chairs also upholstered with white fabrics. On the walls, there were hanging huge, incredibly beautiful paintings that Peter got lost admiration in. The floors seemed to be slippery; they were shining so much it appeared he was standing on ice. Peter just could not have enough of those surroundings there.

He was seated on one of those soft chairs covered with the white sheet, and he had to listen to his parents talking to the old man for a long time even though he couldn't understand what the conversation was about.

Finally, supper was served, and he was taken to the bathroom where his face and hands were washed with soap. Peter couldn't understand why his mamma was doing this since it seemed to him his hands were still clean. True, his face had got dusty during the long drive there, but he still was asking in his mind the same question why he had to wash himself so often.

The food tasted very good. The only thing that burdened little Peter was that he had to eat it with the fork.

During all this time at the table, they talked a lot. His daddy was talking the most, and his mammy would put in a word only once in a while. Peter noticed there were a lot of dishes there. He himself ate out of the three plates and drank out of the two glasses.

No matter that it was still pretty light outside after they ate their supper, he was put into a soft bed. Being tired after the long trip, he without thinking about anything was fast asleep.

While he was sleeping, his guardians were talking long even after dark since Peter's destiny was being determined. Finally, his parents with the old man came to an agreement to sell the estate and buy another one somewhere close to Warsaw. Now, they wanted to take their little son away from here without any delay. They didn't wish him gaining any new memories about this place, but the main thing was that his mother and father wanted to isolate their child from the neighbors and other local people who had known them for a long time. Peter's parents were paranoid those familiar people could reveal their secret to their son, telling him they were not his real parents.

Thus, as soon as the sun had risen, the one horse cart rolled out of the estate again secretly taking Peter away on another unknown trip.

Again, he was on the road, ready for a long travel not even knowing the purpose behind all this. For the second time, he found himself at the same train station. However, Peter didn't even notice it since, in his head, the chaos of the last events was still reigning.

The same tiring traveling by train continued and already started to bore him. However this time, it lasted only five hours. Again, he saw through the window caravans of houses and various buildings running fast in front of his eyes making it look pretty much the same like before.

Finally, the train slowed down its speed and stopped all together. Next thing, Peter and his parents were making their way through the crowd on the platform there.

When they walked to the big square of the train station, his parents found a light horse-carriage, and soon, all the family was flying fast along the street. Peter thought he got back to Vilnius, and he was going to see Paul and Grandpa Sacristan. He began dreaming of telling them about all the impressions he had experienced.

Being absorbed in his thoughts, he didn't notice when the carriage stopped by a big building.

His daddy paid the coachman, and they found themselves in a splendid hotel where they lived for the entire week.

During that time, he wasn't allowed to go outside. He was spending all his time with his mammy, and it wasn't boring to be with her at all since she was reading to him many nice fairy-tales. She also talked to him about a lot of new, interesting things.

His daddy would leave every day while he was still asleep, and would not show up all day long. And even if he returned to their room during lunchtime, he stayed there for a very short time. Then he would leave again. Therefore, Peter almost didn't have opportunity to talk with him. When he finally returned home, it usually was so late that Peter was already asleep.

Sometimes, his father would leave even late in the evening. However, to Peter's big surprise, he saw him one morning upon waking up. As soon as Peter opened his eyes and sat down in his bed, his daddy walked up to him and started a conversation, "Get up, Peter. Enough to sleep! We are going home today."

"Are we going to be on the road again?" asked Peter in an unhappy voice.

"This time, sonny, we are going to be on the road for the last time. It won't take long, too. You don't like it to be in the hotel anyway; there is no yard to play here. Don't you want to find some friends to play with?"

Thus, Peter moved to their new home – the five room apartment. The smallest room was allotted to him personally.

In that apartment, they lived for two years. After that, his mother's father – the grandpa -- sold his beautiful, white home in the country that enabled his parents to buy a house fifteen kilometers away from Warsaw.

It was rather a small estate where his new grandpa moved to live together with them. Peter quickly made friends with the old man, who became his best friend now.

Peter was growing up in a good home, being taken care of by his rich guardians. He had no idea what poverty or crime was. He was attending museums, theaters, and listening to the music. During the breaks in the foyer, his guardians would explain to him the meaning of the play or teach him how to listen to the music.

Years were passing by, and Peter finished primary school. When he later entered gymnasium, his parents and he moved back to live to their previous five room apartment in Warsaw.

By now, he forgot all about his past life in Vilnius, and he never even mentioned anything about Sacristan or Paul.

He became very much attached to his grandpa, and he would always anxiously wait for upcoming Saturday because his parents would always bring him to the grandpa's estate where they would spend weekend themselves as well. Peter was always reluctant to leave back to the city for the period of an entire week after visiting out in the country. He loved spending time with grandpa in his beautiful place!

When Peter had still been a little boy, he liked running around the park there, but the most he had been fond of was his summer vacations. The country-side was fantastic! There was a beautiful, big park with the widely branched out trees of a hundred years' standing close to the grandpa's house. And behind the park, a narrow brook was murmuring with a little man made dam which had created a pretty good size pond. In that pond, grandpa had been spawning fish, and Peter loved spending time there, too.

Often together with the sunrise when light, white fog was sitting on the surface of the water, he would get into a little boat and row into the bed of rushes or fish and admire the nature. Once in awhile, a couple of ducks would settle on the water in the pond, and they cackling gaily would plunge in this small area of the water. Peter only had to sit quietly in his boat hiding in the thicket of the rushes so that he would not scare those beauties away since the slightest move could easily frighten them.

He also loved taking a walk through an alley of old lime trees where a lot of small squirrels had made their comfortable homes in the hollows. The little creatures liked to thrust out their little heads and follow with their little, round, black eyes the youth lost in thought passing by.

But most of all, Peter loved to swim in the transparent water of his grandpa's pond during the warm summer days. Luckily, his grandpa's estate was in a pretty remote area and away from the city and the other residents' settlement. Therefore, neither animals nor people would disturb the water there.

The local folks from the closest village were going to swim in their own small lake that was located in a close proximity to that village. During hot weather, even people from the city often came to spend some time by that lake as well.

For some reason Peter, who was being called by the name Piotrus when he moved to live in Warsaw, didn't find any friends there. He was mostly lonely and reserved when in the city. In a way, his parents liked him staying away from the doubtful influence of unfamiliar youth. It seemed to his parents that they had succeeded inoculating him with their own ideas and good values.

They didn't realize that while Peter was maturing, his outlook on life was changing too. His mother and father thought their son's childhood memories had faded away forever a long time ago.

However, on the contrary – those memories about his life at the church began haunting him particularly intensely at this time in his life. The waking up memories about Sacristan and Paul made him even a little oppressed. Sometimes it seemed to Peter he was often wading through some mist of his enigmatic past dreams.

He even began feeling as if his parents were hiding something from him, but he didn't dare asking them anything about it, being afraid to cause them any pain.

In a meanwhile, Paul in Vilnius was loitering around farmers' market being in the watch for gullible citizens in order to unlade their pockets. No wonder, he would choose most crowded places there.

He didn't always sleep at Sacristan's place by the church. Now, he constantly roamed in the streets. Sometimes, he would steal some small things at the stores. In order to survive, he also had to resort to various fraudulent activities and cheating.

In the very beginning, when Peter with his new guardians had just left, little Paul was missing him tremendously. Sometimes he used to hide somewhere and cry bitterly all day long. He became sad, and even Sacristan was often enable to cheer him up.

For a long time, he was anxious to meet his mother, too, whom he had imagined to be very similar to Madame Rozalija.

Paul kept asking Sacristan when his mother was going to come to get him also, just like Peter's mother had got him. However, time was passing by, and his mother wasn't showing up.

Eventually, he ceased asking about his mother, and her image in his mind slowly began dying out, leaving only a hard scar in his heart due to his unfulfilled expectations. His grandpa Sacristan also stopped talking about his mother coming to pick him up.

As if it was not enough, the weight of years kept oppressing the old man. Sometimes, he would stay in bed sick for days at a time.

During those times, Paul had to replace his grandpa even though he didn't like doing chores at home and at the church. In spite of that, he always attentively listened to Sacristan's instructions, and if he was unable to accomplish something, he would come back to his grandpa and tell him about it.

But in a way, Paul already took over all the Sacristan's responsibilities. He was performing his duties at the church but he also would go to buy food at the store or the farmers' market that was located very close to the church. He became so smart that he often managed to make arrangements with the shopkeeper to borrow some groceries from him.

Constant lack of money made Paul think of the ways making it on his own. On Sundays or during various holidays when large crowds of pilgrims gathered at the church, a lot of beggars would come to the churchyard, too. They would sit down on the ground by all the entrances to the churchyard and the church itself and they would cover the entire outside steps begging for the charity.

A lot of the times Paul, too, would sit down among them with his thin arm stretched out and look at the passersby as if he was their obedient servant.

"Honorable Madame, please help the poor," he would say to passing by parishioner.

Often, the people would throw some coins down into Paul's ragged cap displayed on the pavement in front of him.

However, most of the time, the other beggars would drive the competitor away. Once in a while, Paul would get a thrashing, and he, howling loudly, would move to another place.

In spite of all the difficulties and inconveniences in relation to the begging, Paul didn't refuse from his new occupation since it had been bringing him pretty good revenues. Mainly because of this he and Sacristan no longer had to starve. Moreover, his earnings derived from begging in the churchyard enabled him to pay his debts for the groceries.

One year later, Paul turned into a real pro in begging! He mastered a great number of various cunnings by watching the other beggars twisting their extremities, thus, making themselves look crippled. However, when the Mass was over, they would miraculously become normal again.

Paul began imitating them, and he became very successful in doing that. Soon, he became like an artist since he could in a masterly fashion change not only his expression of the face but also the appearance of his entire body! Even people who had known Paul could not recognize him when he was sitting at the entrance of the church begging for money.

He made people think he was mutilated or that he had been deformed at birth. He would wrench his arm or legs the way that not every artist of the circus could do the same! And he would do this with his face as well, making himself look rather like mentally ill.

Sometimes he would stuff his mouth with something in order to change expression of his face which in turn would make even his eyes look different. One moment, they would be smiling meekly while begging, and the other moment - they would shed tears. He could also screw up just one his eye where it would become barely visible, or he would distort his face by turning it to the side and stretching his chin out. The other trick that he used a lot was his favorite grimace where he tried to make an impression he was unsuccessfully hiding his teeth behind his lips because they had been protruded.

Paul grew his hair long which he would rumple when need arose along with putting some makeup on his face. For example, he would paint a dark circle below his eye making it appear he had a black eye or glue moles and birth-marks that made him look very sorrowfully.

He no longer was being chased away by the other beggars. On the contrary - now, he became the boss in his churchyard. The other beggars were striving in order to take their places next to him since, then, the coins kept jingling not only into Paul's raggedy cap, but they also were falling into theirs' caps as well. Pretty soon, Paul was considered to be one of the best beggars there.

However, the beggars did not stick all the time only at the Sts. Peter and Paul's Church. They in crews used to go to the various villages making up their own caravans of travelers, especially during the times of the religious holidays. They would sit down at the local church in some village in a few rows and beg, beg, beg.

Those beggars not once asked Paul to go together with them. However, he was true to his principles. He had an obligation that didn't let him leave his church, and that had to do with his grandpa Sacristan, who had not been getting out of his bed for a few months now. He was basically dying in their room resembling a basement which sun rays could never reach.

Paul took a good care of his grandpa; he not only was supplying him with the food, but he also was bringing the money home that he had to spend in order to buy that food. Paul was becoming more mature, and he was proud of being able to take care of his grandpa Sacristan.

One day, Paul returned home with good earnings after a church festival. He was in high spirits and was planning to make his grandpa glad. However, as soon as he walked inside, he noticed that Sacristan was very sad.

Paul tried to talk to him, but it didn't make him feel any better.

"Grandpa, is anything hurting to you?"

"Yes, sonny, my heart is hurting. Probably it smells a rat."

"What do you mean? You and me should rejoice in this warm, beautiful day," Paul said.

"You say it is the beautiful and warm day. Is the sun shining outside, too?" Sacristan asked him.

"Yes, grandpa, it is shining. Not a cloud in the sky."

"I wished I could see the sun at least once before I die. But it's impossible since it never looks inside to this dismal room."

After a short silence, Paul offered, "Grandpa, would you give it a try and get up? I will help you with that. We will go outside, so you could enjoy the sun for a little while."

"My eyes will never be able to rejoice at the sun. I feel I won't be visiting this Earth for very long. Soon, I'm going to see God Himself."

Suddenly, Paul remembered when, as a child, he used to play with little mirrors. An idea came to his head that he could probably direct sunrays through the window into the grandpa's room using a mirror. Being afraid his plan would not work, he didn't reveal his idea to Sacristan.

Paul opened the window, and the warm current of the air intruded inside of the half basement smelling like mould.

Then he secretly took a mirror off the wall, went outside, and got onto a roof of a lumber-room that was pretty high up. There was plenty of sunshine everywhere around; Paul tried a few times to move the mirror in his hands, and then, he aimed it at the open window of their room below.

He fixed the mirror propping it up on its both sides with little rocks and left it on the roof of the shed. Then he radiating with joy ran back to his grandpa.

He was expecting to see Sacristan overwhelmed with joy as well. Instead, to his big dismay, Grandpa appeared frightened.

As soon as Paul entered the room, he began to groan, "Sonny, I'm probably already dying. I can see sun through the window. I know it can't be happening since the house in front of us that had been blocking the sun all the time is still standing. It's one of the two – either I'm dying or it is a miracle! I always wanted to see the sun before I die, and here God has fulfilled my last wish. Most likely, though, I'm seeing it just in my imagination. Paul, my Dearest Son, please don't leave. Stay with me a little. Come closer – I want to look at you for the last time in my life."

"Grandpa, this is really the sun. You wanted to see it, so I placed the mirror onto the roof of the shed and pointed the sunbeam straight at your window. Now, I will be diverting the sunshine to you every day!"

"Boy, you are so smart, sonny! I've learned a lot of things during my long life, but I've never heard about anything like that."

Sacristan turned his head and gazed at the sun ray his eyes radiating with joy.

In a meanwhile, Paul walked on his tip toes to his grandpa and sat down on his bed.

Now, both of them were watching the sun ray slowly moving towards Sacristan's bed. They also could hear organ music; it was at the intervals being filled with the singing of the chorus as well, thus, merging into one miraculous, harmonious totality. Sometimes the sounds of the music were quiet, and sometimes the entire room was filled with them making the two hearts in it melt.

Those sounds were coming from the Sts. Peter and Paul's Church where the Mass vespers were coming to an end.

Finally, the beautiful melodies ceased, and the lonely, golden ray abandoned the darkish room with the two quiet souls hanging in it.

Paul knew he had to leave and sit down with the rest of the beggars asking for the money since the parishioners were just about to pour out of the church.

However, he refused from his easy money and remained sitting next to Sacristan, who for the first time in his life had asked him to stay by his side.

The last seven years drew Paul and Grandpa Sacristan together more than ever before. Sacristan had never punished or scolded Paul no matter how naughty he would be at times. He had only patiently explained to him that this kind of his behavior had been difficult to tolerate and asked him to behave.

Because of Sacristan's gentle disposition and, also, since Paul didn't have anyone else as close to him as his grandpa, he became very attached to him.

Now he was setting the mirror on the roof of the shed every day in order to bring some sunshine into the dark half basement room where his grandpa was living his last days.

Sacristan was talking about leaving this Earth more and more often. Probably he wanted to accustom Paul to what was coming up. He also gave a lot of advice to him on how to live further after his death. Sacristan came to an agreement with Dean of the Sts. Peter and Paul's Church about Paul taking over his responsibilities to serve during the public prayer at the church.

Nevertheless, Paul had different plans for his future, but he didn't want to make grandpa upset by voicing his objection to him.

The sad day had finally come when Sacristan's voice was getting weaker and weaker. Soon his body strained itself both directions as if he was using all his strength to make himself comfortable in bed. His eyes got fixed onto a one point above, after what his entire body suddenly became limp, and his hand slid off of his chest down onto the bed by his side. Grandpa Sacristan remained staring at the ceiling.

Paul was waiting when Grandpa's compressed lips would start moving again that, just a short while ago, were still communicating to him. Not hearing a word coming out of his mouth, Paul took his Grandpa by his cold, unfeeling fingers and shook him a little. However, his hand was as heavy as lead.

Now, Paul had no doubts his Grandpa bade farewell to this world, leaving him totally alone to will of the cruel fate.

Paul jumped off the bed clutching his hands together as if they were frost-bitten and began moving backwards toward the door. Being driven by some inner fear, he didn't even notice when he found himself outside. Only when in the churchyard, he came back to his senses and completely realized what had just happened.

Paul wiped cold sweat off his head with his sleeve, collected all his strength, and while all trembling with grief, he stole back into the room.

This time, though, he didn't get frightened seeing Grandpa lying motionless in bed. On the contrary, he seemed to be very close and dear to him.

Paul didn't feel when his legs brought him to his Grandpa's bed where he fell down on his knees. Weeping loudly, he tried to wake him up repeating the same words over and over, "My Dear Grandpa, my Beloved. Please, talk to me! Don't scare me, don't leave me alone here!"

Tears squeezed his throat, thus, silencing his moaning. For a while, he couldn't utter a word. Paul buried his face in Sacristan's chest and continued crying bitterly.

After having a good cry, he felt a little bit better. However, after a short while, he began talking to his Grandpa again, who remained indifferent to his grief.

In the afternoon on the third day after Sacristan's death, a cart harnessed with two black horses stopped at the side gate of the churchyard that Dean had rented earlier. Four men carried out the black coffin with the remains of Sacristan and placed it onto the catafalque under the baldachin. Dean himself seated Paul next to the casket there.

The church bells ringing that were seeing off the zealous servant of many years standing to his last journey, the catafalque gave a start. Soon, it was moving faster and faster its bound with iron wheels loudly rumbling over the coble-stone road, going away from the Sts. Peter and Paul's Church and drawing nearer to the Antakalnis' Cemetery where grave-diggers had already been waiting armed with their shovels.

No one was following the casket; there were no relatives and no loved ones. Nobody knew where Sacristan had descended from or who his parents had been. In a way, his fate was similar to that of Paul, who was the only one to see him off. He was sitting next to the coffin and holding onto it in order not to fall off the catafalque.

Thus, there was no one to mourn over the old Sacristan. Only mighty sounds of the church bells were still unceasingly ringing while announcing his last journey to his rest place at the cemetery.

Just the way the catafalque hastily came rolling to the Antakalnis' cemetery, the same hurriedly, without even opening a lid, the casket was lowered into the grave.

Paul was standing alone on the edge of it listening to the sounds of the two shovels throwing the soil down while making hallow noises when hitting the top boards of the casket.

Half an hour later, a small fill was poured together, and a new, wooden cross was erected on one end of it.

Paul, his head hanging low, was standing quietly. He neither was moaning nor shedding any tears as if he was totally indifferent to everything that was happening around him.

The catafalque had been clattered away quite a while ago. Probably it was already taking remains of another deceased person for his eternal rest to some another cemetery. The grave-diggers had also deserted the cemetery leaving the fill tidied up.

Now only the lonely orphan boy was standing next to it. There had been no one left in the entire world to take care of him. From this day on, Paul had become his own master, and he had to manage his life using his own discretion.

As if it was not difficult enough already for him at that moment, a crow flied passing by right over his head and disappeared between two trunks of pine trees that merged into one thick body of a trunk right down close to the ground. Its loud, ominous voice disturbed the dead silence at the cemetery.

This sound woke Paul up from his thoughtfulness. He looked around and mumbled quietly while kneeling on the ground by the freshly made grave, stretching his arms forward, "Grandpa, get up. Let's go home. Don't leave me alone in this hostile world. I don't know how to live further without you. I'm too young to be on my own. Why don't you say something to me? You used to be nicer to me before. Tell me what I have to do now, where I have to go..."

No one answered his incoherent words.

Paul stayed a little longer weeping and complaining to his grandpa. He also reproved his dead grandpa for leaving this world, while still lying over the ground fill himself. The wet sand got stuck to his cheek, but it dried out quickly and fell off.

However, no matter how long someone had to grieve, there was always an end to it. The same way, Paul had to cease crying and blaming his fate.

He summoned up all his strength, shook off the sand of his clothes, and wiped the tears that had already started growing dry. Then he slowly walked out of the cemetery.

Half an hour later, together with the sun going down, Paul returned home. It was so empty there, and he was feeling so lonely that he didn't even eat supper. Instead, he lay down on the grandpa's bed with all his clothes still on.

Having folded his hands under his head, Paul fixed his eyes on the ceiling that was beginning to get dark and lay for a long time until he got asleep.

After this biggest shock in his life, Paul didn't leave the room for three days in a row. No one came to visit him, and no one comforted him in his big grief. Only hunger managed to drive him out of that wet basement room on the fourth day's morning.

He had wished to die himself in his grandpa's bed of starvation, but it turned out that his imagination was not enough to accomplish his determination.

As Paul found himself in the street, he discovered nothing had changed there during his time of grieving. Life was in full swing just like before, and carefree laughter could be heard around.

Just by being in this kind of environment, his heart slowly began coming to life. Some kind of instinct shook Paul out of his apathy. No person could ever vanquish time that was capable of healing all the wounds – bodily or those of the soul.

No wonder, the same happened to Paul. He also got under the influence of the vigorous life that was moving him forward together with the rest of the people around.

He went to the store and bought himself some food. After eating, Paul felt much stronger and didn't want to stay in the darkish room for a minute longer.

A beautiful August morning greeted him filling his soul with the new energy for living.

It happened to be Sunday as well, the very time when people were beginning to gather at the church. Of course, the beggars had also been taken up their usual places next to the central door of the church.

They like always were stretching their hands in front of every passerby. Having put resigned expressions on their faces, they were begging for money. Of course, the same one passerby not always could afford to dole out a few beggars there. However, about half of all the parishioners were throwing coins into the caps of those begging outside the church.

Without waiting any longer, Paul also sat down among the beggars himself. Like the rest of them he, too, changed his expression of face which made him look like a totally different person.

Beggars took advantage of the generous people, and Paul had quickly assimilated this method of begging himself. As soon as he

Violeta Treciokaite "The Secret of One Grave"

would notice some nicer dressed person, he too would use all his talent and eloquence in order to move that person to tears.

It wasn't easy for Paul after his grandpa's death get back to his usual occupation right away since he was still feeling some unexplainable heaviness on his chest. However, life was forcing him to leave all this behind and get hold of its future threads with his both hands as soon as possible.

Since Paul was late to get a good spot in the churchyard that morning, he was sitting a little further behind the other beggars who had been lined up making up the front row. Therefore, his cap was a little further away from those passing by along them people which meant that the fewer coins were reaching his cap, also.

That alone made him wake up from his torpidity which was only driving him to perdition.

Soon though, his talent of begging came back to him, especially when he noticed a very well-dressed woman walking in through the main gate of the churchyard.

Paul instantly set a suitable for the beggar expression of the face and moved into the front row pushing the other beggars on both of his sides away from him.

As the beautiful madam approached the front door of the church where the beggars had been concentrated the most densely, she with a sign of compassion on her face passed every single one of them and placed a coin in every cap on the ground. Those who had no caps in front of them were holding their wizened, bony hands stretched out towards her.

As the madam approached Paul sitting on the pavement, she placed the biggest coin into his palm he had ever received. His heart began beating fast with joy, and he squeezed the coin tightly in his hand. Then he with a lightning speed stretched out the other hand, and the unfamiliar benefactress inserted another coin which was even of bigger value than the first one. In addition to that, she even smiled at him. This smile filled up his entire heart with some remarkable warmth that woke up some human feelings in his heart.

Suddenly, he brightened up and, for a split second, he forgot what he was doing in this churchyard. It wasn't common for the beggars to smile, but he couldn't overcome his feeling of happiness that was now easy to notice in his eyes and in the expression of his face.

The service at the church began, but it wasn't as full of people as it used to be during most other church festivals when pilgrims could not fit inside, and many of them would stand in the churchyard, which usually would also be almost full.

A few late persons once in a while kept still walking into the church.

The beggars never used to go inside the church even during the Mass. Instead, they would pray in their work places while begging on the ground in the churchyard. It turned out they had been praying more than the people in the church since they never missed a Sunday. Sometimes a few of them would come even during the middle of the week to beg by the main entrance of the church where they would whisper under their noses all kinds of prayers asking the Lord to alleviate their suffering. In spite of that, the Almighty for some reason remained unmoved by their supplication and didn't grant mercy to anyone of them. They remained to be the same poor beggars just as they had always been.

Because of the Madam, who had given him so much money, Paul made an exception to the tradition in relation to the begging.

He so wanted to see her again that he impatiently waited for the service to start. As soon as the Mass began, he quietly stole through the tall, widely opened front door inside of the church.

It was pretty crowded with the people inside, especially right beside the door. Paul with difficulty squeezed his way through those praying into the middle of the church where there wasn't as many of them.

Even though they were standing about a meter away from each other there, his curious eyes could not find the benefactress that some unknown power was drawing him to.

Paul kept working his way deeper and deeper into the front of the church. To his big dismay, he still couldn't find her.

Having lost his hope to see this sweet, elegant Madam, Paul cast his look to the left, and here she was standing next to the column!

Suddenly, pleasant shudders surged through his entire body, and he felt the color flowing into his cheeks. He couldn't look at her longer than for a few seconds. However, those few seconds poured so much warmth into his soul that his heart began beating so fast he even got frightened.

In order to avoid her noticing him, Paul moved a few steps backwards. Then he changed his place of observation all together, moving to the other side of the column; he walked to the confessional that was standing next to the wall. It was much darker there. Thus, hiding in the shadow of the confessional, he was devouring with his eyes her every move.

He could not understand why she caused such a revolution in his heart, and now, he didn't know himself what was that what he wanted from her!

He admired her to his heart content while she was observing the priest performing the religious ceremonies at the main altar.

Then she pulled a small prayer-book out of her purse, quickly turned some pages over with her beautiful, dexterous fingers, crossed herself, got down on her knees, and began praying.

Paul knew she could not see him. Therefore, he was looking at her openly and without feeling shy. The longer he was observing Madam, the more he admired her. In his mind, he was comparing her with Rozalija, whose image like through some mist was standing in front of his eyes. He remembered how she had taken away Peter, and he wished his mother was like Rozalija. He still had once in awhile been dreaming of her searching for him.

Paul continued looking at the elegant, unknown woman wishing she would take him away from here which would make him the happiest boy on the entire planet! He would love her with all his heart; he would listen to her and do all the chores at home for her such as buying groceries, peeling potatoes, and washing floors. He would never let her do any of those dirty jobs! And he would treat her even better than he had treated his Grandpa Sacristan.

Paul was thinking he would give to her all the money he had collected while begging to the last coin.

An idea about some other kind of life never crossed Paul's mind. He didn't realize this woman had never peeled potatoes or washed floors, or did the like by herself. Moreover, her bed had always been made for her and meals prepared as well. In addition to all this, if someone had told him now she was his mother by blood, he would think that person was totally insane!

Paul didn't know that the only thing needed at this magical moment was to run up to her and utter a cry 'mamma', and it would be sufficient to make his all dreams come true!

He could not know she had come to the church not only in order to pray or to dole out the beggars that had always been plentiful by all the churches. This Madam came here to get her children.

All these years, Julija had prayed to God asking Him to line up for her all the events and the circumstances of her life that would enable her to take her boys home with her. She always dreamed of the times when her aching heart would be able to rejoice at the most precious feelings of the motherhood again. She didn't have a presentiment, too, that the love of her life was now secretly looking at her out of the dark corner!

It was fated that neither Paul knew this Madam was his mother nor his brother Peter learned that his real father had been teaching him Latin and German lessons in Warsaw. In the beginning, Peter didn't even like his teacher because of him insisting on high standards.

However, when Peter graduated with the golden medal, he realized he had to be thankful to his teacher for his achievements. The only thing both the teacher and his student didn't know was that they were the father and the son, too!

This family had been so broken-up and so scattered through the two countries that no one could find out anything about anyone of them.

After Robertas had left Vilnius, he himself had no idea if Julija had given a birth or not, let alone to the twins!

Paul also could not realize his mother he had been dreaming about every day and even during the nights was standing only a few meters away from him!

The Mass was coming to an end since the chorus was singing the last canto to honor St. Mary, being accompanied by organ music. He deeply regretted the secret, intangible visit with Madam was coming to an end. With his head hanging down, Paul carefully slinked out of his lurking-place, where he had been feeling like in heaven while trying not to attract anyone's attention. Before, he always used to control his actions when inside the church during the service which made him feel uncomfortable. But this woman made him feel totally different. He just wanted to be himself when in her presence.

He quickly walked to the churchyard and sat down among the other beggars on the ground. Now, he was anxiously waiting for the fancy Madam to come out of the church.

As soon as the people began struggling to come out through the front door, Paul set such a sorrowful expression of his face that it would have definitely frightened him himself if he just looked at that moment in the mirror. His intention was to direct attention of as many people to himself as he could in order to evoke their pity.

This time, he didn't care about the charity. His whole attention was geared not to miss the woman, whom he wished was his mother.

And he saw her coming out the door. However, she soon stepped into the crowd and was carried away by it.

Julija walked around the church. She was expecting to see her boys running around somewhere in the churchyard. She was determined, this time, to take her twins home.

She was nervous and excited at the same time thinking her sons had grown up significantly during this long time she had not seen them. In her mind, she could picture them playing in the churchyard - being healthy, bright, and jolly, just as they had been before when she used to come to visit them often during the years of the war.

Not being able to see them outside, she decide to walk to the Sacristan's place. The closer she was getting to it, the faster and harder her heart was beating in her chest, and her legs began to bend down while trembling hard.

Julija was feeling totally lost when she approached the arch shaped doorway leading to the half basement of the old stucco building with the low windows. She could feel the sultry smell of damp mould that was beginning to get into her nose and even tickle her throat.

She was standing in front of the door hammered together out of the thick boards that were in some places covered with whitish mold.

Julija didn't dare to open it. She took a deep breath, lowered her head, and flattened her hot cheek against the cold stucco wall. Soon, she felt her entire body beginning to grow numb with cold.

Having received her balance back, she tried to knock on the boards of the door, but her hands were trembling so hard she had to wait until she would come down a little bit. In order to appease the agitation, Julija bit her thumb until she began feeling pain.

She already had questions and words prepared to say beforehand; she knocked quietly on the door. For a while, she listened attentively, but she could not hear the slightest rustling coming from behind the heavy closed door.

She thought that maybe those sitting inside could not hear the knocking, and she gave another try, only this time, it was so loud she felt sharp pain in the joints of her fingers.

However, no one answered again.

She didn't know what to do now – to give it another try or to return to the churchyard and keep searching for her boys there again.

While Julija was standing and trying to decide what to do next, her hand instinctively tugged at the big, ornamental, metal door handle to make sure the door had been locked.

Nevertheless, to her biggest astonishment, the heavy door very easily opened up slightly. She didn't close the door but was gradually and carefully opening it wider.

However, she didn't dare to walk inside through that door right away. Instead, she stopped on the threshold as if being stunned.

The time was counting the seconds peacefully as if waiting to see what this woman was going to do next.

At last, Julija decided to come into this small, beggarly room that had been filled with stuffy air. In addition to that, she could also feel some unpleasant smell of fermentation that seemed to be getting not only into her throat but also into her eyes.

After habituating herself a little to this horrible smell, she began looking around. The surroundings there were also nightmarish! The walls were blackened due to dampness and mould. The two narrow windows were reaching the ground, enabling those staying in this room to see mainly only the legs of the people who no doubt used to rarely pass by in this secluded corner.

Through those windows that most likely had not been washed for years daylight could hardly penetrate inside. The floors were rotten in a few places, and the boards would swing every time she made a step. Obviously, they were rotten underneath as well.

In one corner, there was a pretty wide bed with half blackened mattress on it. A pile of some rags was laid over it.

In the opposite corner, there was standing a caved in stove. Its fallen down bricks were lashing around the same room. Next to the stove, there was a table hammered together out of plane boards with a smoky pot sitting on the top of it. A few dirty spoons with pieces of bread that had been covered with mold could be seen there, too.

Julija walked closer to the table and leaned over it to look inside of the pot where she saw some liquid, over the top of which together with the inner walls of the pot itself, white mold had been growing thickly. It seemed the mold was everywhere - starting with the outside of the front door of this room and ending up in this pot!

She bent down and smelled the broth which made her gagging. Then she walked to the bed and sat down onto the edge of the gray mattress. After gently passing over the top of the mattress, she with sadness in her eyes looked at its dirty, coarse surface. Her eyes worked down onto the pile of rags sitting in the middle of the caved in bed, and she noticed familiar little, ripped pants.

She quickly grabbed them into her hands and pressed against her breasts like some precious gift. Julija recognized it was the one pair of the little pants she had sewn secretly from her aunt with her uncle and brought to the church herself.

Not feeling what she was doing, Julija quickly dug up the entire pile of clothes. However, she could not find another pair of the little pants that she had brought then in, also.

Without waiting any longer, she in a hurry thrust the little pants into her purse and began to sob.

Having covered her face with her palms, she sat for a while trying to tame her grief because she didn't want her children to see her looking like this.

Soon, she was already feeling more relaxed while she was waiting for her twin boys or their guardian Sacristan to walk in.

In a meanwhile, Paul was searching with his eyes for his fairy among the people in the churchyard. He even went outside to the street behind the stucco fence looking for her. The crowd was breaking up right outside the main gate and moving away in different directions.

It never occurred to him to look for her in his own room! However, fate was merciless to Paul, not allowing him to meet his mother when he needed her the most.

Not being able to find her, he went back to the churchyard and sat down close to the main entrance of the church.

He was sitting with his head down feeling wild pain in his soul. This time, though, he wasn't asking passersby for the money. Nevertheless, the coins kept unceasingly falling into his cap until all the people left the church.

Finally, the beggars also poured all their booty into their pockets and, with an entire crew, headed across the churchyard towards the gate. Some of them were helping themselves walk with a cane or just a simple stick of a tree.

They didn't leave Paul behind as well since they knew the old Sacristan had been dead, and there was no one and nothing that could bind the orphan boy with this church any longer.

To those beggars he was a real asset. Therefore, they literally dragged him along clustering him around.

As if feeling something bad coming up, Paul didn't want to go with them. But the beggars did their best enticing him away while treating him with tidbits.

Soon, they found themselves next to two carts harnessed with horses, waiting behind the stucco fence of the churchyard.

All the beggars clambered up into the carts. Paul wasn't in rush to leave since he didn't know what to do after that.

The beggars invited Paul going together with them. When he refused definitely, the biggest one of them jumped out of the cart, seized him by a scruff of his neck, and cast him into the cart.

Paul gave a frenzied scream, but his mouth was quickly closed with someone's hand and some rags thrown over his head, too. Thus, no matter how loud he would had called for help, no one could have heard him screaming with the wheels of both carts rattling over the cobble-stone road being trotted by the two horses, thus, making an impression the entire city clattered.

When the church was left far behind, someone took the rags off Paul's face and threatened him that if he didn't cease sniveling, he would be taken back to live in his previous conditions.

Overwhelmed with fear, he stopped crying. He turned back and was looking at the Sts. Peter and Paul's Church that was getting smaller all the time. However, the dome of it was still visible vaguely through the branches of the trees for a long time. Every time it hid itself, it would come back again for a short while as if waving goodbye to Paul.

Soon, the cupola disappeared out of the sight all together. Now, Paul was seeing only unfamiliar places until the city streets ended. He had never gone further than a few blocks away from the Sts. Peter and Paul's Church. Therefore, he had no chance to see any forests and fields in the open.

The further they went, the more the environs were changing. Finally, they entered a dirt road in the pine tree forest where Paul no longer had to listen to the loud, rumbling clatter of the wheels.

Even though for some time his ears were still stuffed, but soon, he could distinct the sound of the forest, murmuring its melodies that he was hearing for the first time in his life; he could not get enough of this peaceful feeling taking over his tired soul. In addition to that, the pine trees were spreading a particular and a very pleasant smell that Paul was enjoying, also.

One beggar was very nice to him and even gave him some cookies. No one was threatening or intimidating Paul anymore in spite of him being so far away from the city where nobody could protect him from any kind of abuse.

He was no longer being taken away by force, either. Now he was considered to be a member of this big family of the beggars, whose lifestyle had been to travel from one little town to the other, where they would come to the church of that town on Sunday after spending the weekend there as well.

On the weekdays, they would attend a farmers' market. The scheduled days for the market differed from town to town, thus, making the beggars hop from place to place. That is how they had come to Vilnius the past weekend, where they had visited quite a few of churches since they were plentiful in the capital city. Of course, the beggars didn't miss the farmers' market there, too.

Spending their time in the farmers' markets enabled them to gather significant amounts of money. Neither one of the beggars became rich, but they didn't struggle either. No matter of that, they always tried to make others think they were starving.

Moreover, once in a while, they would have such big feasts that even well-off farmers could envy them.

This time, too, they arrived to a nice meadow with a few tents already showing white on the green dark grass. A few horses had been grazing while tied up to the trees growing close to the tents.

As their two carts were approaching the camping place, loud cries greeted them, and the humped, bow-legged, and blind began coming out of the tents and bushes. A couple of blind creatures hurried to meet the two carts filled with the beggars. They kept jabbing with their sticks the ground while moving the direction that the voices of those arriving were coming from.

The meadow was quickly filled with the various noises being generated by those crippled creatures that had been situated in this wonderful refuge of the nature.

The two horses of the new arrivals were also unharnessed, and two lame men tied them up to the long chain. Then they helped Paul to climb out of the cart.

As soon as he got onto the ground, he began feeling little needles poking his legs that had been grown numb after the long sitting during the entire journey; he almost fell down.

Soon, he was able to walk around, though, feeling pretty good since no one was paying attention to him.

While he was slowly circling the camping place, a thought crossed his mind to run away from there. However, as soon as Paul walked further from the meadow and into the forest, fear took over making him return.

When the sun was hidden behind the trees, Paul began feeling rather hungry. He had neither loved ones nor any acquaintances among those many crippled people.

Being tormented by the hunger, he came close to the beggar whom he hated the most not because he had a very deformed face but because he was the one who had grabbed Paul earlier and threw him into the cart. He also had pushed his palm rudely against his mouth then, too.

Nevertheless, the starvation made Paul to reconcile with him, and from then on, he was not retreating from him a step.

After noticing this, the robust fellow stroked Paul's shaved head gently and asked, "Are you hungry, brother?"

Without waiting for the answer, he continued, "I'm not surprised. Such is destiny of all the beggars – to beg and to suffer cold, hunger, and disdain. However, tonight you won't have to suffer the hunger or disdain. Today we are having the celebration! Look – they are already lighting the fires. Soon they are going to make supper, and we are going to eat! Just wait a little bit; you must be patient, my little brother. Go to the camp-fire and make yourself warm. It's going to be cold at night. Besides, you could get some snacks from those cooking over there. Let's go to the place where the smoke is coming out."

He didn't need to keep persuading Paul any longer, who had learned to adapt himself to the circumstances when still living with his grandpa Sacristan.

Paul quickly found himself by the bonfire that was crackling merrily while, with its red tongues, licking the branches piled up high above his head.

For a while he was sitting on the ground, but when the fire flamed up good, he had to move back because the heat was becoming unbearable.

When the camp-fire produced a lot of live coals, a few big coppers were placed on stones with pieces of meat floating in the clean water. Soon they were bubbling vigorously; even the lids kept dancing on the top of them. The water was dripping over the sides and right down onto the coals that, sputtering and squeaking in all kinds of voices, were dying out, after what they would soon burn merrily and brightly again.

There were three such bonfires kindled with all the beggars gathered around. Many of them were sitting on the grass, and the others were hanging half-way on their crutches.

Suddenly, a squeaking sound of a violin was heard next to the one camp-fire. Some inexperienced hand was trying to play, which irritated a few beggars.

Someone cried out, "Shut up!"

However, another voice replied, "Let him practice! I don't mind him playing."

Thus, the little violin died away only when the coppers were taken off the camp-fire. The pleasant smell of the boiled meat dispersed through the entire meadow.

Then the meat was taken out, cut into pieces, and placed into big bowls. Now, it was arousing the appetite of those gathered around even more. Having had nothing to eat all day long, Paul's mouth was watering. He could not take his eyes off of the meat making everything around appear dark in color due to the starvation.

The cook who was working by the coppers noticed Paul observing avidly her every move. She quickly trimmed the meat off the bone leaving some sticking to it. Then she threw it down onto the grass in front of Paul.

After turning over a few times in the air and then sliding over the ground, the bone got covered with the withered grass and pine needles.

However, there was no time to hesitate, and Paul grabbed the hot bone that had just been taken out of the copper, which even made his eyes tear up.

Without releasing the bone out of his hands and not even blowing cool air on it through his mouth, Paul kept pulling with his teeth pieces of meat away from the bone. In the beginning, he had to release the bone out of his hands a few times. Holding the bone only with his teeth, he was beating his burned fingers down up his knees. The next thing, he would have to release the bone from his teeth and then rub with his hand his scalded lips.

Finally, the bone cooled down on its own. However, now the meat didn't want to come off since it had not still been completely done. In spite of that, hungry Paul with the biggest appetite continued pulling it off the bone.

After eating the most of the meat, he continued sucking on the bone which made his entire face greasy.

After everybody fortified themselves, the real feast began. In between all the three camp-fires, there were bowls placed with the remaining meat right on the grass covered with two bed-sheets.

Soon, bread and a few big one liter bottles of vodka were brought in as well. A glass was being filled half way and sent from hands to hands. During the first round, everyone was drinking the same amount in spite of their age or gender.

For the second round, the women were not drinking anymore, and the old men got only a half of the previous dose.

Pretty soon, all the bottles were lying empty on the grass. The camp-fires were not burning as brightly, too.

Probably it wasn't necessary anyway because the bodies of those around were spreading much more warmth and energy now than they had been before.

All the beggars began bustling and, soon, they were in such agitation that they were trying to shout one another down. Everyone wanted to be in the center of attention. Gesticulating with their hands, they were arguing about something.

Then, a few more big bottles were brought in. As the beggars kept emptying them one after the other, the camp-fires also continued going out. Luckily, someone once in a while would throw a little of dry brushwood over the top of them in order to keep at least the light on.

As the feast had reached the culmination point, the violin got into hands of another person who made it weep bitterly. The blind beggar was playing it now, and the violin was sometimes crying like a baby and sometimes bleating like a sheep.

Since this time the music was making everyone happy, all the noises ceased, giving space to the violin express itself. And it kept sobbing like some disappointed girl or laughing in all kinds of voices, at times, resembling those in the nature.

Then a humped girl about sixteen years old sprung up next to the violinist and began singing the St. Mary's song.

Soon after, two more singers with an accordionist and two clarinetists joined them. One singer had no leg and the other was a young boy blind on his one eye. The man, who had no leg, was standing on the wooden stick that had been fixed to his amputated extremity, and he was leaning slightly forward while holding onto another stick. And the boy was all the time digging in his nose before he started to sing. It turned out that all the three musicians were blind and only one of them could see a little bit with one eye which would happen only during daylight.

In the dark, it resembled a country-side band, especially because they performed their repertoire so successfully for which they had neither prepared themselves nor rehearsed beforehand.

At last, some dancers showed up, too. Someone threw more wood into all the camp-fires, and in their light, the entire camp was having a good time in their own way.

Hump-backed, lame, single-eyed, and those with wrenched out extremities were dancing. The other words, all who could stand on their legs were moving and stamping ground under their feet. Everyone was dancing the way they knew or, better yet to say, danced even those who didn't know how to dance.

Everyone was in high spirits including paralytics who always used to be sour. Nevertheless, this evening their faces were also radiating with joy. Everyone got not only to eat enough of meat but, also, to drink vodka to their hearts' content, enabling them for a while to forget about the wrongs the Mother Nature had endowed them with.

As soon as some woman sat down, a drunken man was trying to kiss her. Those women who had a lot to drink were generous, allowing the men touch them above their knee. There were some of them, also, who left the campsite and went deeper into the dark forest in order to give themselves up to the call of the nature completely. Some couples moved away from the site thinking of only fooling about a little, but then, one of the women got raped. Everyone at the camp-fires could hear her calling for help while screaming out of the darkness.

However, no one was in rush to rescue her. Instead, some rebukes were heard at the fire blaming her for going there in the first place.

"She doesn't need to pretend she is a saint. Just wait – soon, she'll come down..." some old man added rudely.

And indeed, pretty soon, both the man with the scratched skin on his face and the woman with tousled hair returned. In spite of this, they appeared to be happy; even though the nature had mutilated them physically, it had still left those feelings to them that all the human beings were bound to experience the same way.

Finally, the moon came out from under the clouds, and it was not necessary to throw the wood into the camp-fires so often.

The feast was in the middle of its full swing, and no one wanted to go to sleep yet. After having his stomach stuffed full with the meat, Paul didn't think of leaving the campsite, either. He liked watching the other people having fun.

He was the only healthy person there. Paul didn't realize that the beggars took him together with them not because he could enjoy being different; they wanted him to become just like them, who after cursing their fate, always tried to take vengeance on those not crippled.

The night was coming to the middle, and Paul's eyelids began sticking together. Not being able to stay awake any longer, he walked to the cart, climbed inside, lay down on the hay, and covered himself with rags. Then he instantly went to sleep.

While sleeping soundly, he didn't have any dreams, and he woke up only early in the morning after something heavy tumbled over him. It almost crushed him to death.

Turned out it was the beggar. After having crawled out with much difficulty from underneath of him, Paul got asleep again since it was still the sweetest early morning sleep hours.

He woke up only when the sun was already high in the sky. At once, he could not perceive where he was.

After stretching his body and rubbing his sleepy eyes with his fists, as he always used to do at home, Paul climbed out of the cart leaving the beggar snoring there loudly. He was stinking so badly that Paul couldn't stay there any longer anyway.

The entire camp was still asleep, and loud snoring could be heard here and there once in a while being interrupted by the whistle coming from someone's nose.

However, those noises didn't wake up the residents of this campsite.

Paul was the only one who wasn't sleeping. Lending his ear to the sounds around him, he could also hear horses once in a while snorting on the edge of the forest and barely audible, faraway bark of a dog. Then, those sounds would die out, and the entire surroundings would sink into somber silence.

However, Paul wasn't paying much attention to the environment. He walked to the camp-fires with the smoke still coming out of all the three of them. The grass was so badly trampled down in between of them that, in some places, it had been pulled out with its entire roots. The sheets were still on the ground all dirty and with the pieces of bread and meat lying on it. The picked bones and the empty bottles also could be seen further on the grass.

Paul got down on his knees and began cramming everything that he came across into his mouth. Soon, he was feeling full again. Since he already had experienced hunger being in this company, he decided to hide some food for himself. Therefore, he wrapped a big piece of meat and bread in some paper that he tucked under the hay in the cart where the one-eyed beggar was still snoring with his legs and arms wide apart.

Not having what to do, Paul was lounging about the area. Soon he found himself in the wide field. There was so much sunshine around.

He took a couple of deep breaths of the fresh, cool morning air and passed his palm over the bent grass that breeze was playing with. Suddenly he felt free of his past. Overwhelmed with joy, he broke into run through the field looking upwards at the wide, vast blue of the sky.

Thus running, he ended up by a small murmuring brook that, in some places, was winding through thick brushes. Only when the creek blocked Paul's way, he stopped running and began walking along it until he reached the place where there were no bushes stretching by the water.

He waded in the brook up to his knees for the first time in his life, rejoicing at the beauty of the nature and observing the water rushing into unknown distance, while it was gently caressing the skin of his legs.

When he returned to the camp, everyone was already up and running. No one had seen him leaving, and no one paid any attention to him when he came back, either. No beggar asked him if he was hungry since everybody cared only for themselves.

Therefore, Paul realized he should never forget about his well being which prompted him to hurry to the place where food, remaining from yesterday, had been gorged down by the beggars wasted after the last night's drinking. A few of them were throwing up while holding onto the trunks of the pine trees.

Even though he wasn't hungry, he still kept stuffing his mouth with food, too.

Later in the day, the camp-fires flared up again, and the new batch of meat in the coppers got placed over the flames. It was already spreading a pleasant smell throughout the entire area.

When the evening came, they began having fun as they had the last night.

Thus, they were drinking, eating, and dancing for three days total, and only in the afternoon of the fourth day, the camp was disassembled.

Soon after, the entire caravan of the carts was making their way through the forest, moving towards the highway.

Thus, a long and difficult journey began that lasted for a few years. The string of carriages was getting smaller all the time, scattering the beggars through different towns along the way.

Helping themselves walk with canes and sticks, they moved from village to village teasing dogs and begging for food and money.

After traveling like this for some time, Paul also had to separate with the remaining beggars. His guardians now were a one-eyed man and a stout, humped woman who treated him with cruelty. The woman actually was a little more tolerable, but the man turned out to be the real beast. He would whip Paul for every trifle – for collecting too little money and for coming back too early even though he had never returned before the sunset. Paul was afraid, however, to wander alone in the unknown vicinity after dark.

During the summer, life wasn't as bad since he didn't have to suffer cold. But there were problems with food because his guardians would not give him anything to eat when he came home, and they didn't feed him in the morning upon him leaving, too.

Therefore, he learned to save some food for himself such as a slice of bread and a piece of flitch or an egg. Then, after passing a first big bush or a hill, he would sit down behind it on some rock and eat before starting to take on his usual duty as a beggar.

Things would get really bad during the winter time, though. The wind could blow through his rags easily, and his legs would ache badly after freezing all day long while begging outside. They often become swelled, too. As if it was not bad enough already, his head would get covered with scabs that dribbled all winter long. Only during summertime, they would heal for a period of a few months.

Not once, the single-eyed beggar tried to mutilate Paul. One time he broke his arm, the second time his rib, and the third – dislocated his leg. However, all these injuries healed up without leaving any traces of disablement.

For a while, the one-eyed man had big losses since Paul could not go begging. He was limping which in a way made his guardians happy because they thought he would remain crippled, just like them, forever.

One year later, though, he ceased to limp. In spite of that, his guardian did not hurting him anymore. Most likely, the one-eyed man changed his mind because he himself began feeling unwell. Sometimes, he would spend from a few days to a week lying sick in bed which saved Paul from being maimed.

Now, the old beggar had to be nicer to Paul, so that he would continue feeding him and his humped companion woman. She didn't go begging through the villages as Paul did every single day; she would go to sit only for a few hours at the church on Sundays.

However, her earnings were always scanty and never enough to buy food for all three of them. In addition to that, they had to get forage for the horse, fix the wheels of the cart, and obtain some clothing for themselves.

Paul, to the contrary, used to bring a significant amount of money. When he begged in the churchyard, the copper coins would fall into his cap all the time. And during the farmers' market days, he would prepare the real show; he would walk on his hands, wriggle like a snake, and play various pranks trying to keep gawks around happy. Sometimes, he would change expression on his face or make himself look like a hunch-back. Then, the money was falling down unceasingly, and he was bringing home his cap full of coins that his guardians would always take away from him.

Of course, they couldn't afford to get rid of Paul because he was the only one who had been supporting all three of them.

However, deep down in their hearts, they knew that one day he was going to leave them even if they mutilated him. In that case, he would probably even take vengeance and run away earlier.

Therefore, his guardians decided to keep taking advantage of Paul for as long as the circumstances allowed them to do that.

Being afraid to lose Paul, his guardians refused to go with the other beggars to Vilnius no matter that it was the middle of the summer - the time when villagers had been swamped with numerous field chores. They didn't even have time to attend the church on Sundays or the farmers' market. Instead, they were toiling in the fields from the early morning until late in the evening. Then, on Sundays, they were resting after the heavy work of the previous week while trying to collect their strength for the next week.

In a meanwhile, the city residents worked less, and they rested more. A lot of them would go on vacation out in the country, and the rich were going to the seaside or the Carpathian Mountains, or even to famous resorts abroad. That was precisely why the beggars kept coming to the towns and big cities where churches and farmers' markets never lacked people.

During his years of begging, Paul visited a lot of villages and towns and he stayed a few times in many of them.

He had also been twice in Lida City where he had spent two months the first time and a month the second time.

Paul preferred staying in the city rather than in some village. Towns appeared more exciting to the young boy, and traveling from village to village began to bore him.

However, Paul didn't mind sitting at the doors of the churches where, every time some woman passed by, he would make a sorrowful expression on his face and stretch out his hand towards her.

If a woman was walking with a boy of approximately his age, Paul always showed him his teeth or tongue when she didn't see it. If the boy didn't react to this, Paul would sometimes spit in his face or throw a little rock at his back upon him walking away.

Paul liked farmers' market days the most, though, where he used to feel himself to be the real master of the situation. Often he managed to perform his part so brilliantly that people would surround him in a thick circle making it difficult for those behind them to watch the show. At those times, the money was falling non stop into his ragged cap on the ground.

Unfortunately, Paul didn't have any use out of his efforts since very seldom he was able to hide a few coins from his guardians while they in turns watched him performing his tricks. Either the hump-backed woman or the one-eyed man was guarding the money and emptying his cap once in awhile.

However, Paul was used to giving away all his money already since the times he had lived with his grandpa Sacristan. But then, Sacristan would give him some money, too.

The new guardians, though, never gave him a farthing.

Soon, Paul learned to be more clever; he began hiding as much money as he could whenever he had opportunity to stash away some of his coins.

As he was maturing, this kind of exploitation by his guardians and flogging after that, too, no longer could agree with him. That was when he started thinking of escape. He no longer paid any attention to his guardians' threatening to hurt him in case he tried to leave. They never failed to remind him, also, that all the beggars had known him, thus, making it impossible for Paul to hide from them as well.

For a while, it worked, and Paul thought there was no way for him to ever break away from this slavery.

Twice a year, all the beggars used to gather together and have their meetings. Sometimes, they would argue, but at the end, they always used to come to an agreement. Those kinds of meetings, as a rule, would be crowned with a feast.

The springtime feast always used to be scanty and last only one night, but after the autumn gathering, they would have a good time for a few days in a row and sometimes even for an entire week.

The spring coming to an end, most of the beggars used to be in poor health. Their bodies covered with ulcers, raggedy, and mangy, could only arouse disgust. Their horses, too, would be so overdriven they could hardly pull the carts. A few of them had even died.

That was when the money Paul gathered came in especially handy for the beggars since they could buy another mangy horse. If there was any money left, it would often be divided between those brothers and sisters in their crew who needed it the most. Some of them had an illness or were coping with some other hardships.

However, during fall meetings, the beggars would feel and look much better. Majority of them used to even dress up, and only their feebleness or crippleness served as the proof they had been wronged by God.

Nevertheless, those beggars probably would never agree to exchange their lifestyle for that of the small farmers' since they didn't have to perform any physical work. All they had to do was walk leaning on their canes and sticks from one village to the other. They also had the carts with the horses which were their only significant assets that they never separated with.

This way, Paul spent three years of his life while living together with those wronged by God. He had completely forgotten about his life in Vilnius, and only once in a while, he would see the splendid interior of the Sts. Peter and Paul's Church as if through the fog in his dream at night. The beauty of the interior of the church he had been growing up in was so exceptional, he had never seen anything like it while traveling through the numerous other churches during the past few years.

He didn't really remember the exterior of the Sts. Peter and Paul's Church since he truly had paid attention to it only once from the distance when the beggars had kidnapped him three years ago.

Lately, Paul began intensely dreaming of running away to Lida. When lying in bed, before getting asleep, he often was making plans for escape in his head.

However, the opportunity never presented itself, and he had to postpone the fulfillment of his plan.

In spite of growing up in Vilnius, he didn't know the city because Sacristan had never taken him out behind the walls of their churchyard. The only time Paul had the opportunity to go a little bit further had been when the grandpa passed away and he, after burying him, had to walk alone from the Antakalnis' Cemetery back to the church.

Thus, Paul never had a chance to get to know this great city. It almost seemed to him that it comprised only of the Sts. Peter and Paul's Church and a few surrounding streets. Therefore, he was paranoid the beggars could find him there quickly since they used to occupy almost the entire churchyard during various church festivals.

Therefore, his all hopes were directed now towards Lida City.

During the last meeting in spring, the beggars were trying to talk Paul's guardians into going to Vilnius together with them. In the beginning, they didn't agree, but later, they said they would think about it.

Listening to them talking about going to Vilnius, Paul got scared. After choosing a moment, he implored them not to go there which made it a turning point for his guardians in making their final decision. Now, they no longer worried about Paul escaping from them while in Vilnius.

A few days later, Paul and his guardians were already driving through the streets of the suburb of Vilnius.

Paul was sitting in the back of the cart lost in thought and in a bad mood. Imagining Vilnius to be twice as small as Lida, he wasn't even looking around. He had not expected any kind of a good outcome here.

The long drive, however, made him finally pay attention to his surroundings. As Paul looked to the right, he saw a great number of railroad tracks with numerous carriages hooked together sitting on them. He was surprised to admit to himself that he liked what he was seeing.

And as they entered the city, it appeared as if there was no end to it. Paul had thought that after driving through a several streets they would hit the fields again, but instead, all he was seeing were hundreds and thousands of houses and buildings of different sizes.

Now, he wasn't looking down; he with curiosity observed what was happening around him.

They passed under a cement bridge running over their heads, and he heard a train rumbling loudly above. Then he saw a web of streets with tall houses on both sides of them.

Paul looked around but could not see anything else except the stone and brick buildings everywhere around, and he realized he drove into Vilnius from its other side. That was the reason why this time he couldn't spot the Sts. Peter and Paul's Church the view of which had accompanied him when he was leaving Vilnius three years ago.

As soon as they passed shacks of the outskirts of the city, the sidewalks full of people greeted them. The coachmen were scurrying both directions; the light horse-carriages were flying by on their rubber wheels. There were also other carts in the streets loaded with goods being pulled with difficulty by the large sweaty horses. The drayman most of the time walked next to the horse once in a while pulling the reins and cracking with a whip over the weary animal's back.

To his big surprise, Paul didn't see even one church. Even when passing the Gate of Dawn (Ausros Vartai), he didn't notice that it was actually the church.

Only when they were approaching Hale market (Hales turgus), he sensed they were coming close to some distinct place of the city. Before even entering the market, Paul could see the trade boiling everywhere, since the people were selling goods right on the sidewalks.

Paul and his guardians walked to the main gate of the Hale market with men and women streaming in and out.

They saw a good spot a little further away from the entrance with a few beggars already sitting there, their hands stretched out to the passersby.

As they noticed Paul with his two guardians, a few of the beggars fixed their wrathful gazes on all three of them entering the farmers' market, and one man even shook his fist in the air trying to drive Paul, the one-eyed beggar, and the humped woman accompanying him, away. However, Paul didn't leave him unanswered. He grinned and stuck his tongue out teasing that shameless creature.

He almost paid a price for his impertinence since one of the beggars on the ground tried to hit him with his cane. Luckily, the distance between them was pretty big, and the cane was too short to reach him.

When the three of them finally situated themselves in some remote place, not many people were dropping coins into their caps.

Paul kept looking around while in his new place and not putting out enough efforts in order to make more charity even though his guardian woman was nagging him to put to work his tricks.

In spite of that, Paul didn't show his abilities until the late afternoon when they moved to beg at the Gate of Dawn Church where many other beggars were already sitting on both sides of the entire street running along the long building of the church.

This time, Paul with his guardians occupied a better place, which enabled them to collect much more money.

When it became dark and people began scattering, Paul with his guardians headed to their designated place to spend the night. Having passed under the already familiar railroad bridge and an old cemetery, they found themselves in a rubbish-heap of the suburb with the mountains of garbage showing everywhere around. There were also a few more carts of some other beggars there, and a few horses were grazing next to them.

This was the place where beggars used to stay; no one was driving them away from there. Therefore, many of them often came and camped there.

This time, though, the area was half empty. They could see only one small camp-fire smoking where, most likely, supper was being prepared.

Beggars could not kindle big bonfires since there were not many places to find wood around here. The other option they had was to buy the firewood.

Paul also had to obtain some wood first in order to cook their supper. Since it was already dark, and he didn't know how far the forest was, Paul headed back towards the city. Soon, he found himself next to the stone wall of the cemetery.

After climbing over it, he was standing under big trees hardly being able to see anything because of the darkness. He began feeling very uncomfortable in this kingdom of the dead where it was so quiet. Only far away, he could hear city murmuring that was even more stressing the dead silence in the cemetery.

Paul his heart shaking with fear kept carefully stepping over the fills of the graves and passing along the little iron fences. In the moonlight, he was looking around while moving deeper into the cemetery in search for some butt of a board or an old, halfway rotten wooden cross. He was thinking of taking some fallen down wooden fence if he was lucky to come across it.

However, as ill luck would have it, he could find neither the crosses nor the pickets of the fences that would be suitable for the firewood.

Paul continued climbing the hill with the massive crosses made out of granite. All the fences that he came across happened to be made of iron as well.

His efforts were not in vain, though. As soon as he reached almost the top of the hill, a tall, thick wooden cross blocked his way. Paul didn't even think of trying to break it. Nevertheless, when passing by, he leaned on it in order to catch his breath. To his big surprise, the cross began swaying.

Not thinking much, Paul gathered all his strength, set his both hands against the cross, and gave it a push.

The cross, making a loud, squeaking sound, fell down taking Paul together with it on the ground.

It turned out the bottom of the cross was almost completely rotten. There was no time to reason. Paul had this huge cross on his back, under the weight of which his legs began bending. He tried not to think about it much while he was dragging it down the hill. While stumbling over the cement barriers and small fences made of stone, Paul continued his Golgotha journey, stooping due to the weight of the heavy, old cross that had finished serving its time with its mission for someone's soul.

At last, Paul all covered in sweat, dragged the cross with utmost difficulty to the brick fence surrounding the cemetery. Then he somehow managed to put the cross onto the top of the fence and throw it to the other side of it. It was pretty easy for him to jump over the fence without the cross weighing his shoulders.

When on the other side of the cemetery, Paul gave a deep sigh of relief and quickly looked around.

It was quiet. Again, he thrust the heavy cross on his back and concentrated his all attention to carrying it along the empty, narrow street.

On his way, he passed a couple of young girls and a few teenage boys. No one of them dared to comment on him carrying the cross. Paul was thinking that for some unknown reason he would not give his strange burden to anyone even if they tried to take it away from him.

Having stopped only a few times to rest, he finally delivered the cross to their campsite where he hacked it up into pieces with an axe. Soon the cross was already burning with two small pots boiling over it. A pleasant smell was coming out of them which made Paul's mouth salivate. He just kept adding more of the cross wood into the fire in order to speed up the cooking.

After the tasty and substantial meal, he made his bed this evening under the cart where he lay down with all his clothes on. He covered himself with old rags that were stinking like sweat and mould. However, smell that was coming from the numerous piles of the garbage superseded the smell of his coverlet.

This time, though, he didn't get asleep at once as he used to when feeling rather dead-beat after a long and difficult day. Now, he was thinking about Vilnius. All kinds of plans were interlacing in his head about getting away from his odious guardians.

After learning that Vilnius was a very big city as well, Paul was no longer linking his destiny to Lida. He decided to stay here, only he still didn't realize how he was going to put his plan to fruition.

He didn't sleep a wink until the early morning with all those thoughts swimming in his head. Only at the dawn, the sleep surmounted Paul sending him to the kingdom of pleasant dreams.

When he woke up, he didn't even feel any lack of sleep. On the contrary, his heart was singing!

After breakfast, Paul in high spirits went to the Hale market where he didn't sit idly as he had done in the early afternoon yesterday. Instead, he right away put his talent to work by playing pranks and performing various tricks.

All day long, Paul had a big crowd gathered around him allowing pickpockets to make quite a fortune as well.

Many people laughed to their hearts' content while watching Paul's performance, but there were some of those who had to cry upon coming home and discovering their money was gone. Often, when someone was not paying attention, some thief would easily clean that person's pockets. Therefore, it was a good idea to be especially vigilant at the farmers' markets.

While begging in Vilnius, Paul continued earning a lot of money that his guardians, constantly staying beside him, kept collecting every few hours. However, they never offered to buy him a candy or a sweet roll for all his efforts.

Days and weeks were passing by. Paul's guardians were immensely happy with him making so much money, but neither they nor Paul suspected some eyes had been avidly observing them, and someone had even secretly followed them to their place of stay. They didn't know that the plot regarding Paul's abduction was being intensely prepared.

Thus, one day after seizing an opportunity when there were little people around Paul, some man with a huge bag filled with all kinds of junk was walking by. As he approached Paul with his guardians, he dropped the bag on the ground and brushed his dry forehead with a sleeve of his shirt. As he was trying to lift the bag, he pretended he was unable to do so. He looked around and then he fixed his eyes on Paul, "Young man, would you help me to take this bag to my cart? It's very close from here on the street."

Since Paul didn't give a stir, the man pulled a zloty out of his pocket and showed it to him.

"Take it. I will pay you; just help me, please, to get this bag to my cart."

Paul didn't rush at the money; he only glanced indifferently at it as if the man was applying not to him. However, the eyes of the hump-backed woman were shining with greediness. She grabbed the expensive coin out of the man's hand and nagged at Paul, "Dear, go help this nice man to take his bag to his cart!"

Paul got up lazily, with reluctance and picked up the bag by its corner. Then he carried it away through the market-place. Soon, the unknown man and Paul found themselves by the cart with a coachman standing next to it.

The man asked Paul, "Would you get inside the carriage, so I could hand you the bag?"

Not suspecting anything wrong to happen, Paul jumped inside of the light horse-carriage with its top on. Instantly, two men appeared seemingly from nowhere. One of them brought Paul down to the back seat covering his mouth with his palm, and the other one heaped up him with the bag which was so big it almost covered both of them. Then the coachman quickly whipped the horse on his back legs. The animal adroitly waved his tale and broke into a run rushing through the street full of people. Luckily, no one got under the wheels of the carriage.

After flying like this for a few hundred meters, the men took the bag off Paul's body and uncovered his mouth. However, as soon as he straightened himself upright, he heard a clicking sound of an unbending automatic knife, and its blade flashed by his side.

Then, the strict voice warned Paul, "Don't try to escape, or this knife is going to make a hole in your side. Do you understand?!"

Paul remembered that at the moment he had been abducted he had not felt any fear; his abduction wasn't a new thing to him since it was happening for the second time in his life. However, after seeing that big knife pointed at him, his forehead got covered with cold sweat, and he mumbled quietly while shaking with fear, "I'm not trying to escape."

"Great. I'm glad you understand," uttered the man while folding the knife and putting it back into his pocket. "If you'll be smart, you could have a much better life with us than you've had with those pitiful beggars. But you'll have to listen to us."

The carriage finally stopped. One of the men got out of it first, and then he asked Paul to climb out of it, too. The three of them walked through a big gate with a smaller gate fixed in it, and now, they were standing in a small, square yard that was surrounded with a tall, stucco wall. The man who walked in the last locked the door of the little gate behind him.

Paul looked around and saw the only door in the yard in front of him. Soon, they were already walking along the narrow, long corridor where Paul was hardly able to see anything after entering it from the daylight. At last, they stopped at a big door covered with iron ornaments.

The room on the other side of the door resembled a warehouse with stuff sitting on shelves and boxes in every corner stacked up to the ceiling. They could hardly walk through all that stuff on the floor with a little path left among the boxes and bags, leading to another similar door.

As they opened that door, Paul saw a narrow, steep staircase going up to the second floor where they entered a two room flat with a kitchen all crammed with furniture.

In the middle of the first room, there was a big table covered with an expensive burgundy color tablecloth. Four chairs with soft seats upholstered in fuzzy fabric of the same color had been standing around the table.

An ancient wardrobe that most likely had belonged to some dignitaries, with their family's coat of arms carved out on the top of it, was parading in the middle of the front wall. On the other walls, two big oil paintings in golden frames were showing off nicely as well.

However, the most beautiful thing to Paul seemed to be a huge chandelier hanging low over the dining table. A great number of glass ornaments, fixed to its golden plated frame, were sparkling in the sun.

Finally, a tall and wide book-stand full of old books was taking up space along the entire opposite wall. One could say this room looked, felt, and even smelled like a dwelling of the nineteenth century.

Another room was smaller and furnished with up to date furniture. A cumbersome writing table was standing by the window there with a very unique inkstand on it – the mermaid holding in her hands a dish that could also be used as a small vase. Also, an electric lamp was sitting there, too.

A door to the balcony facing the street was next to the table. Along another wall, a rocking chair and two more simple chairs were standing. The last piece of the furniture in the room was a soft sofa that obviously belonged to the set of the furniture in another room. In the middle of the third wall, a stove was mounted with capacity to warm up both of the rooms.

After Paul was seated on the chair, one of the two men sat down leaning comfortably back on the sofa, and the other one in the rocking chair.

He was the one who began the conversation applying to Paul, "If you comply with our requirements, your life could turn out to be much better than that which you lived up until now. Otherwise, we would have to take drastic measures. But if you listen to us, we'll create such great conditions for you that you have never dreamed of! You no longer will have to wear your rags, too. We'll dress you nicely, and you will have good meals every day. Of course, nothing is free in this world. But don't despair – we are willing to train you. We saw how you lived, and we felt sorry for you. You shouldn't continue staying with the beggars for the rest of your life. You could learn our ways of making money, and you won't have to make people laugh in the streets. I think you are going to forget your previous life very soon. It was obvious no one really cared about you before. People you were with yesterday had wanted only the money that you used to earn for them by being the clown and making others laugh at you. I can reassure you that you would never be bored with us, and we wouldn't lay our hands on all of your money, also. True, you would have to give us a certain amount of it every day, but the rest of it would be yours. Moreover, we would help you to earn that money. So what do you think about our offer?"

"I don't care – I agree. To tell the truth, I don't have a choice but to accept your offer. Those beggars abducted me three years ago. Since then on, my life had turned into real hell," complained to them Paul. "I tried to escape a few times, but they kept threatening me they were going to find me anywhere. There are so many of those beggars that it's almost impossible to hide away from them. I probably lucked out by getting here with you. I hope you can protect me. I no longer want to beg myself. My guardians used to take all the money away from me and beat me up, too. But if you are going to treat me this way also, I will definitely run away from you."

"Oh no, we would not hurt you! I hope you don't mind us saving you from your cruel guardians," the man said.

"But where am I going to live?" Paul asked.

"Don't worry about that. We are going to take care of you. For a while, you could stay here. Do you like this room?"

"I do. To tell the truth, I've never lived in such a nice place yet."

"I'm glad we have come to an agreement," the man noticed. "Well, let me introduce myself to you. Others call me Bik." Then, he pointed his finger at another man sitting on the sofa, who had not uttered a word during all this time. He only smiled once in a while.

"And this is Mik. I hope you won't mix up our names. What is your name?" he continued.

"Paul. This is the first time I'm hearing names Bik and Mik. It's easy to remember such short names."

"Paul is a nice name, too," noticed the man sitting on the sofa.

All three of them talked for awhile longer. The men were inquiring about his life in detail. While Paul was describing to them what injustices he had experienced, both of them were only shaking their heads in compassion.

During the time they spent together, Paul had not been insulted once. On the contrary, both men were taking his opinion into consideration as if he was equal to them.

Paul liked it since it was the first time in his life he was feeling to be a full-fledged person.

After lunch that all three of them ate hastily, they went out to the city. The two men really kept their promises. They bought him a modest, inexpensive suite and new leather shoes. Just yesterday, Paul could have only dreamed about the outfit like this.

On the way home, the men bought him a portion of ice-cream that he was licking slowly enjoying every bit of it.

He also got a haircut; the barber with clippers shaved his head leaving only a black tuft on his very forehead.

As they reached their flat, Mikas waved goodbye leaving Paul with Bikas.

Next day, Paul woke up late after seemingly the first time in his life having slept so comfortably and peacefully.

After breakfast, he dressed up with his new clothes and put on his nice shoes that he was still lost in admiration with.

As soon as they went out, Bikas bought ice cream to both of them. They walked around the city looking at the nice buildings, but this time, they didn't drop at any store. They just strolled about the streets without any particular purpose in their minds.

They did the same for a few more days, and then, the two men began teaching Paul different subjects. First of all, Bikas opened an ABC book and showed the letters to Paul. He also was showing him how to write.

In the beginning, Paul had difficulty mastering the new things. He thought he would rather be doing some heavy, physical work instead of tormenting himself with the reading and writing.

However, Bikas was very persistent. Because of his efforts, Paul began making progress in English grammar.

In addition to that, Mikas started coming in and teaching Paul his new occupation. He was spending a few hours every day showing him some tricks of an illusionist. This science was much easier for Paul to master. Only the first two weeks were more difficult, but after a couple of months, he achieved a lot.

Mikas spent especially much time showing various tricks with cards. Often, he would stay with Paul up until midnight teaching him swiftness.

In time, Paul got really bored with learning to write and read. However, he realized Bikas and Mikas wouldn't feed him here for free. Paul really wanted to go out and be among people. However, Bikas always worked with him until noon teaching him intensively grammar that was so difficult for him to learn.

Moreover, Paul couldn't understand why he needed all this education. In spite of this, Bikas tried to convince him he had to know how to read and write which would be needed in the future.

Mikas teachings, to the contrary, turned out to be so interesting that Paul would almost automatically do all the exercises ten times in a row, and he was never bored.

Pretty soon, he mastered them so well that Mikas announced it was time to apply his knowledge in practice. Paul received the news with gladness. He was happy he would not have to study so much anymore.

Nevertheless, Bikas opposed to Mikas' wishes demanding to have Paul completely ready.

Thus, the third man who was teaching Paul acrobatics appeared. The arena was made for him in the warehouse on the first floor where a steel rope was stretched out from one wall to the other for Paul to walk through.

In the beginning, he had to learn walking on the rope until he could keep his balance. Of course, it also took him some time to master it. He would fall down hundreds of times until he finally managed to walk from one end of the rope to the other without falling of it once.

Then, the program in the field of acrobatics expanded, and Paul was also being taught walking through the walls. He had to quickly run up and down through the boxes stacked high, jump from on stack onto the other, and make a leap off the box and grasp with his both hands big hooks fixed into the walls there.

Paul wasn't succeeding in the beginning; he had to suffer numerous bruises and even a few serious wounds until he mastered the art of the acrobatics.

In spite of that, he patiently followed his new teacher's instructions. Only well after midnight, he would get to bed and then sleep like dead.

Then, the next day, he would do exactly the same. Thus, half a year passed turning Paul into a totally different person. Now, he could read and write pretty well, play cards splendidly, and even do all kinds of magic!

Another six months later, he would never fall off the steel rope or the boxes when jumping onto the wall. Also, he would never miss to seize with his hands the hooks in the wall.

Nevertheless, his learning didn't stop. He was being taught new things all the time. Bikas even showed him how to eliminate ink on a paper and how to transfer a seal from one document to another.

Despite many more things for Paul to learn, he also knew some tricks of his own, which were impossible to master even for his teachers. For example, he could change the expression of his face beyond recognition, cry like an infant, and then talk like a grown up man. He could perfectly imitate woman's talk, laugh, and wail. Moreover, he could miaow like a cat and bark like a dog.

Sometimes he used to make it appear as if a dog attacked a cat. The other times, he would cackle like a chicken or crow like a rooster. He also could bleat like a cow or a donkey and neigh like a horse. One time he made sounds resembling those of a mare after her foal moving too far away from her. Paul was able to mimic the entire herd of animals, and he could do that so perfectly that no one could tell it wasn't real!

Another thing that he was good at, he could place both of his legs on his head at once. He also could scoop up with a spoon some soup and pour it into his mouth just by using his toes! None of his teachers could do anything like it.

Finally, the day had come when Paul went making money with Mikas for the first time. He could not wait for this day to arrive.

Thus, they came to Kalvariju Market. Paul had never been in such a big market in his entire life.

The whole main street there was flooded with people, and live trade was happening there. He didn't see any big animals being sold, only a lot of country folks on sidewalks with their baskets full of eggs, butter, chickens, ducks, a few of geese, and a turkey. Some sellers were holding in their hands the small goods such as pocket knives and various shining pins or cheap beads made of glass.

On ragged looking man was selling new shoes that probably had been stolen. It was easy to sell such items fast since the trade was going intensely.

A few beggars were sitting by the wide gate of the entrance to the market, and they were looking impudently to every shopper's eyes.

It was even busier in the center of the market where people could by anything their hearts desired.

However, in the outskirts, impoverished merchants were sitting right on the ground next to the fence. They had their legs under their body looking like some Moslems that had lined up all their junk in front of them right on the grass. There were so many various merchandise there it was impossible to even enumerate all of those articles. One could even buy there such small things like used and, later on, straightened out metal nails and some other knick-knacks.

The fences served as show-cases with all kinds of stuff for sale hanging on the top and sides of them: chains, used carpets, quickly daubed oil paintings, lamps, their shades, and all kinds of ornaments made of paper.

In the central aisle of the market, there were hundreds of tables covered with tarpaulin and all kinds of merchandise displayed on them.

One could buy there not only needles with buttons; multitudes of silk and woolen materials were changing colors in the hands of the buyers. Also, suits made of expensive fabrics were alluring the eyes of many people. In other words, the market was bursting with goods.

As far as one could take in, there were carts everywhere. The unharnessed horses were eating hay out of those carts while snorting loudly. A few other horses had bags with their fodder hanging down their necks.

The carts were also heaped up with all kinds of goods and earthly blessings. The untied bags were spreading heavenly smell of freshly baked bread. In some carts, rams exhausted after the long trip to the market were lying on the straws together with pigs that were covered in lather. Every time passersby touched the animals, they would grunt as if complaining about being tired of their bothersome caresses.

On the other side, cows were lined up in entire rows with calves tied up to the edges of the carts. They had already been used to the constant touching and didn't pay much attention to the people.

In the other rows on their carts, people were weighing apples, pears, and ripe tomatoes that were making everyone's mouths water just by looking at them.

A lot of simple women were jostling one another with their goods - the eggs, butter, chickens, geese, and turkeys - that were teeming here in comparison to the place by the street or at the entrance to the market.

Unceasing cackling of the hens could be heard here and there and, once in a while, even a rooster would break into song probably foreboding his upcoming death. Being induced by his voice, geese would start cackle around, too. The cows, also, were unceasingly mooing and bleating in frightened voices as if blowing a trumpet. Horses would answer them by neighing in one or the other place. Sometimes they would even begin to kick each other, thus, setting up a clamor, but people always interfered and quickly suppressed their aggressive behavior.

Some buyers, clustered around a fatty animal, were trying to convince their owner to knock down the price. Then they would leave but always come back and shake the owner's hand firmly, taking away their purchase with them.

Usually the trade between the men was friendlier than that which was happening between the women. The woman purchaser would not want to let a fat hen or goose go but she also would not want to pay the price the seller woman had been asking for. Thus, both of them kept torturing the poor bird while pulling it both directions. Sometimes, the women would even get in a fight rattling against each other.

Thus, the market was spouting and bubbling while giving opportunities to steal some stuff for tramps and mixed-matched vagabonds, too. And there were plenty of them around. One could even hear once in a while moaning of those who had become the victims of the thieves. Sometimes, the scoundrels would just grab a wicker basket filled with already bought goods and rush through the crowd of people. Then, some woman would be running after the thief shouting and entreating people to hold him back.

However, the tramp would never get flustered even in the worst case scenario. Moreover, he would himself start screaming, 'Hold the thief!' and point at his own companion running empty handed in front of him.

This way, they would manage to escape with their booty. However, if they sensed they were going to be caught, they would drop the stolen stuff and run as fast as their legs could carry them. They knew that big problems were awaiting them otherwise.

Paul was walking with his teacher through this autumnal farmers' market that was bursting with the earthly blessings. Having passed his theory examination, he came here to put his ability in practice. Before starting his occupation, though, he was following Mikas in the market with his mouth open in amazement. He had never been in such a huge farmers' market.

Soon, while wondering around, both of them came by chance to a merry-go-round that was surrounded by a lot of children. They were clinging all around the low fence and gaping at the other children flying by in the circle. Some of the children on the merry-go-round were sitting on the plastic horses, the others in little carriages behind those horses, and still others were sitting on mystical, big, colorful birds.

Paul had opportunity to see many merry-go-rounds, but he had never seen such a magnificent one. Many times before, he had watched children enjoying care free time on those kinds of roundabouts.

Even though he could not take his eyes off them, he didn't dare to ask Mikas to let him swing together with them.

However, Mikas himself guessed Paul's wish since he asked, "Would you like to go for a ride?"

Paul didn't answer anything; he only shrugged his shoulders a couple of times in response.

"This is the first time I'm seeing the boy who doesn't want to go on the merry-go-round!" Mike noticed in a surprised voice.

"I'm not refusing to go; I just simply don't have any money," said Paul with sadness.

"It's not a big deal. I could borrow you some money and you could pay me back after you earn your own money."

After receiving some money from Mikas, Paul was already sitting on a white horse while holding onto its mane and flying in the air, feeling like in some enchanted fairy-tale. It was the first time in his life when he was enjoying the pleasure of being carefree like most of the other children. He was very grateful to Mikas for this moment of happiness.

Mikas also bought Paul a lollipop candy. It was the clear, red rooster on a small stick that he was licking while following him.

Then, they came to a place where men were playing cards on small tables surrounded by crowds of curious people.

The game was in its tightest point when Paul and Mikas somehow scraped their way through the crowd to the table where Mikas quickly occupied a place. He had been a frequent card player here. Therefore, he had no problem getting the seat at this table.

He almost always used to win, and sometimes he faked his loss because it made him feel bad being ahead of others all the time.

However, there were times when he went down to cunning where he would switch cards so quickly that no one could ever catch him.

Paul was standing behind Mikas and watching him playing over his shoulder. He was admiring the agility of Mikas' hands and the dexterity of his fingers. It almost appeared as if he wasn't even touching the cards.

After observing the men play for about two hours, he got a little bored and went to another table to watch the others playing cards.

A lean, short man with small moustache was sitting there who with his thin fingers promptly threw down four cards on the table. One of them happened to be the ace of spades. The rules of the game had been very simple – whoever guessed the card correctly, that person got paid ten groszy. If no one guessed right, then the juggler would get the money that was already displayed on the table.

Paul knew very well how to play this game because he had been trained by Mikas for a long time.

After having studied for a good half an hour that man's way of playing cards, Paul began feeling sorry he had no money to play with. With aching heart, he returned to Mikas, who kept winning money while sitting at his own table.

Mikas lifted his eyes, smiled at Paul, and said, "You are back? Here is ten groszy for you. Go buy some roll or candy for yourself."

After receiving the money, Paul didn't rush to the counters where the sweets were being sold. Instead, he went to the table where the men had been throwing out cards out of a deck.

There were still a lot of gawks standing around who kept feverishly flipping cards while staking their money. However, hardly any of them succeeded in guessing the card right.

Now Paul got in line to play cards. Soon, it was his turn to place his ten groszy next to the money of the juggler with the mustache. Four cards were placed on the table that he needed to find the ace of spades among. His heart began to tremble when he had to open that card. However, there was no time to delay since the other men were ready to place their money on the table, too.

With the trembling hand Paul opened the card. It was the ace of spades! His eyes brightened up, his heart began beating fast out of happiness, and he didn't notice when he grabbed two ten groszy coins from the table.

According to the rules of the game, a person who guessed correctly had the right to guess for the second time in a row without waiting in line for his turn to play again.

For the second time, the cards were thrown on the table, and again, Paul put another ten groszy into his pocket.

The third time, the juggler performed his throwing of the cards very carefully. Nevertheless, the third time, too, the riddle was solved which left the juggler scratching his head.

Therefore, the fourth time he was shuffling the cards so fast that it was impossible to catch his movements. In spite of this, the right card was flipped over again, thus, enabling Paul to guess the fifth time out of his turn!

This time, the juggler took all the measures trying to lead Paul into error; he was throwing the cards for a long time from one place to another.

Finally, four cards were again lying in front of Paul's eyes. This time, though, he didn't know which card was the ace of spades. However, he didn't fret himself about it since his pocket no longer was empty. Without guessing, he opened the king of diamonds.

This time, Paul fell out, and the juggler renewed stuffing his pockets. However, not for long since Paul stood in a line again.

Of course, he guessed right again and had already sixty groszys in his pocket that he was now raking with his fingers while the smile was playing on his face.

As Paul placed the money on the table, the juggler pushed it back towards him, leaned with his chest over the table, and hissed at him angrily, "Get out of here, you snot!"

Nevertheless, those standing around the table protested expressing such huge dissatisfaction that the juggler had to give in.

Thus, the cards were thrown seven times. Seven times Paul guessed the ace of spades. And seven times Paul put a ten groszy coin into his pocket!

This way, Paul spent about an hour playing card game, but that time didn't go in vain since he had earned pretty solid amount of money.

After the conflict with the juggler, he didn't stand in line any longer; he returned to Mikas, who was still playing.

The day was going to an end, and the farmers' market was getting deserted. At last, Mikas had to stop playing, too. He just like Paul was satisfied with the results of the day since he had made more money than him.

"Well, Paul, we can go to some restaurant and have a meal. My stomach is growling like an angry dog. You must be hungry too," he said.

Thus, they walked through the rather empty farmers' market. As they were passing the juggler, Mikas uttered a cry, "Henikas! How things are going?"

"It would be good if not for this snot walking next to you," he pointed with his finger at Paul.

"He is not the snot; he is my student. I understand your frustration, though, and we could talk regarding him not playing with you anymore. You are welcome to join us for dinner to discuss this matter. We'll have a drink, a nice meal, and at the same time, we'll be able to celebrate the expansion of our circle of the acquaintances."

Thus, all three of them went to a fine restaurant where a decanter with brownish alcoholic beverage and a couple of bottles of dark beer quickly appeared on their table. A bottle of lemonade was ordered specially for Paul because he had loved it so much. Then three schnitzels were brought in, which stimulated an enormous appetite in all three of them.

First of all, Mikas and Henikas had a drop after what they both wrinkled up their noses. The drink in the decanter happened to be very bitter. In a meanwhile, Paul had half of a glass of the lemonade the gas of which went to his nose right away. After licking off his sugary lips, he followed the example of the other two his companions and with relish began guzzling his food without paying any attention to what was happening around him.

During the supper that lasted for long time because Mikas with Henikas ordered more drinks, they were discussing the latest events and only sun going down they left the restaurant both red in their faces.

For a while, they were waking in the street together. Then, Paul separated from the two of them in the Ozeskienes Square.

For the first time in his life, he returned home alone with no one checking on him. He didn't drop at any other place even though he had plenty of free time. Some instinct was driving him to his flat in spite of no one waiting for him there since Bikas was gone somewhere for two days, also.

Therefore, Paul knew he could get home at midnight and nobody was going to reproach him for that. Despite this, he was in a hurry to get to their empty flat waiting for him under a few locks and keys, behind the big door with metal ornaments.

While playing with the coins in his pockets, he was feeling joy in his heart, knowing he was the sole owner of this money. He had never experienced such a feeling before. True, he had made much more money many times before, but back then, he had known that the money didn't belong to him. Therefore, it had not made him happy in spite of it being earned only because of his resourcefulness and cleverness.

In good spirits, Paul walked up to the gate of his yard; it had been decorated with black metal grating. Before opening it, he stopped and attentively scanned the gate thinking it would not be easy for someone to break in.

He took his key out of his pocket, unlocked the gate, and carefully slipped into the dark yard locking the gate behind him again.

Next thing, he already was in the tall warehouse on the first floor of the house. The warehouse was now half empty since the rope had been stretched out from one its wall to another. Paul was practicing to walk on it every day, sometimes a few hours in a row. After being exhausted from doing it, he often didn't even want to look at that rope.

By sense of touch he climbed the dark staircase, walked into his room, and got comfortable on the sofa. Without turning on the light, he looked through the window at the darkening sky and plunged in thought.

As if through the dream he suddenly saw his faraway life at the Sts. Peter and Paul's Church. The feeling of wild longing squeezed his heart when he remembered the moment of parting with Peter. He recalled how after that separation with him he had waited and waited for his own mother to come and get him, too. How many times he had dreamed of some miraculous fairy descending from the skies, folding him in her arms, and never letting him go!

He could even hear clearly in his mind her saying through tears, "This is my beloved son!"

However, the time was passing by, but that fairy with her arms stretch towards him wasn't showing up. Only for a short while during his begging times, the picture of some woman that he had dreamed of being his mother used to appear before his eyes.

In his mind, he also recalled his abduction by the beggars and years of very difficult life with them. Those had definitely been the worst times of his life. Back then, he had been too small and, thus, not able to protect himself from his offenders. Just those memories about his life begging among the indigent, dirty, and uneducated people made him shiver. But the worst part of it had been that he had to walk dressed in thin, raggedy clothes with no decent shoes on.

Luckily, all this remained only the painful memory now. He no longer was waiting for winter with fear, and he didn't have to walk barefoot during summertime as well. Also, people no longer were paying attention to his scanty clothes which in turn didn't make him blush because of that. On the contrary, now he was feeling equal to the majority of those people. He no longer had to be a laughing-stock allowing others taunt him. Instead, he also could look others in their eyes proudly. Having his own money, allowed him to feel his value and not to be an obedient servant of the beggars while trying to get into favor with them.

He firmly decided not to allow anyone to exploit his labor anymore and always think about himself first! Paul finally realized that no fairy is going to come to him in order to rescue him.

Sitting comfortably on the sofa in the dark room, he was playing with his coins while pouring them from one palm into another. The clanking sound of the money in the silence of the room sounded almost like music to his ears.

He no longer was dreaming of his mother who could take him with her into some nicer, warmer, and brighter world.

Now, his thinking shifted to that of the huge power of the cold coins that were talking to him in a very friendly and reassuring manner. While ringing in his palms, they were beckoning him to stay with them and obtain much more of them, promising him in return to never forget him or disappoint his hopes! It didn't matter how he had earned the money. The most important thing was that the more of it he had the more respectfully he was treated by others. Even when they were feeling hatred towards him, no one of them dared to express it. Paul realized money was the most powerful thing the will of which obeyed all.

He remembered Mikas' teachings about the value and the power of the money. This kind of psychology had taken a root in Paul's consciousness so quickly he could not have even imagined there had been different laws of life that made people better and happier if they had just followed them.

Paul's life had left big wounds in his soul, and he was unable to heal them using his still immature intellect.

For years, he had no opportunity to live among decent people that could show him some examples of sacred ideals. All he could get from the people surrounding him were hatred, violence, greediness, and inoculation of the power of the money.

The teachings of the beggars had worked. Having his own money for the first time in his life, was just like having the crumbs of that big power. However, they made him feel a full-fledged person.

He noticed that when he found himself at any counter where goods were being sold, a sales person would be going out of his way in order to please him. Even if that sales person happened to be three times older than him, he would turn into an obedient servant to the power of Paul's money.

The situation changed drastically, though, if some old centenary man, wearing raggedy clothes, showed up at the same counter. As he stretched out his bony hand towards the sales person asking for the charity, the ireful, disdainful stare of the sales person would meet him in response.

After throwing into his cap a copper coin, the sales person would look at the poor, old man in such a way it was obvious he was letting him know the indigent people were not desirable fellows in his store.

Paul had experienced this on his own skin. He himself had to beg for money so many times in his life that the memories of those moments were stuck forever in his head. Neither time nor different lifestyle could ever obliterate them.

However, the experience of collecting the charity used to be much different when he performed in front of people. At those times, they would throw the money into his cap with joyful smiles, their eyes shining with happiness.

Thus, he spent about two hours in the dark making his own conclusions about life.

Besides Bikas, Mikas, and Paul, no one else used to come to this flat. Before leaving, Bikas had warned Paul very strictly not to go anywhere alone. Therefore, he diligently carried out Bikas' wishes and went somewhere only together with Mikas, who had been his only friend at this time.

Paul was getting tired of sitting at home alone since Bikas used to leave for a day or even for a few days in a row every month. Paul didn't know where he was going because Bikas never told him anything about his frequent trips. It appeared that he didn't share much about this with Mikas, either.

However, Paul noticed that after those trips, things stored in the warehouse would disappear, and sometimes new boxes would fill it up as well.

Those operations used to happen always at nighttime, and Paul was helping Bikas to carry the lighter boxes into the yard himself. When there was more work involved, Mikas also would come to give them a helping hand.

Paul wasn't really sure what Bikas was doing since neither Bikas nor Mikas ever let the cat out of the bag. Bikas himself used to refer to his business as being engaged in trade. However, carrying the boxes secretly at night, while trying not to make any noises, seemed very strange to Paul. Mikas also never talked about his friend's occupation. He only told to Paul that Bikas was a very smart man, and that in the future, Paul was going to become just like him – a very clever person, who would never be at a loss.

As far as Mikas' occupation went, he told Paul that he had been engaged in some random jobs.

Since Paul used to spend a lot of time with him, he had an idea what kinds of jobs he was talking about. When opportunity offered, Mikas would clean up pockets of some gullible citizens. Especially he liked to do this in crowded places such as framers' markets.

In spite of that, Paul liked Mikas very much. He loved going out to the city with him where he would spend an entire day together.

Even though Paul was still doing his exercises walking on the rope and jumping from boxes onto the walls in the warehouse, he liked to practice ruses of cards as well.

He was doing pretty good already and could put to practice all his tricks. However, he wasn't fond of sciences being taught at the traditional school. Everything there seemed to him just a waste of time.

In spite of that, as soon as he learned to read and write, he realized he had been wrong thinking this was not necessary to know.

During the past six months, Paul had got very attached to Mikas and Bikas. He had never heard a harsh word from either one of them. They had always been polite to him and never insulted or hurt him.

There were some differences between his two friends, though. Bikas appeared to be more serious which called for Paul's respect towards him. As about Mikas, Paul had treated him friendlier that Mikas as if they had been equal in many aspects. In addition to that, Mikas was always in good spirits. He often used to jab his elbow into Paul's side or smile at him tenderly and wink his eye trying to keep him in good mood, too. He also would buy him some sweets once in a while.

With those thoughts Paul slowly got up off the couch and turned on the light that illuminated the room so brightly he had to blink his eyes for a few seconds.

Then, he rubbed his eyes with his fists making himself to get used to the light. He pulled a stack of cards out of the drawer and began adroitly throwing them onto the table. It was working so well for him that he no longer had to repeat it over again.

Therefore, he shoved the cards into his pocket, lazily walked to the mirror hanging on the wall, looked at himself, and distorted his face into a grimace that made him laugh at himself.

Next thing, he found himself in the warehouse that was halfway empty at this time. Like some leopard he made a few big leaps and adroitly jumped onto the rope swinging from one side to the other, thus, forcing him to spread his arms both ways in order to keep his balance.

He swiftly ran across the entire length of the rope, jumped onto the wall right off the rope, and grasped the iron beam with his hands after what he got back onto the rope. Then, he hopped a few times up and down and performed a backwards somersault which landed him on the rope again.

However, he didn't wish to be engaged in the rope-walking for long either. Having done the most complicated jumps so perfectly that many equilibrists would envy him, Paul returned to his room and sat down at the writing table where he began rummaging in the drawer.

There he found his ABC book he had still been studying, but after turning over a few of the pages, he again threw it back into the drawer.

Reading seemed to be the most difficult of all his exercises. He wished he could read all the books in his room that had been sitting on the book shelves there. Some of them were thick and written in a very small letters. Paul didn't even try to read the titles of those books.

He pulled out a few thinner books and looked at their front covers. However, no one of them attracted his attention. Paul already wanted to leave when the front page of one book with a beautiful colored picture on it caught his interest.

Every page inside of the book was illustrated as well, and the pictures themselves were so beautiful that Paul was unable to get enough of them.

Curiosity surmounted him. Not being able to resist the temptation to find out what the book was about, he opened up its first page and read loudly the title written in big letters. It said 'Fairy-tales'.

No one had ever told him stories, and it was not surprising he didn't know anything about the fairy-tales. Therefore, he got no impression of any kind after reading the title of the book, either.

However, just by looking at those beautiful pictures, his inner voice was telling him something very interesting was being revealed in this book.

And Paul wasn't mistaken since this was Grimms' Fairy Tales which had contained a lot of wonderful stories that had long been famous among the little and the juveniles.

Paul took the book and began reading its first story while lying on the sofa which he read through slowly and with utmost difficulty from beginning to end. It made such a big impression on him that he instantly started reading the second one which he finished well after the midnight. His eyes were sticking together, and he didn't even notice when he got asleep.

Only the next day after waking up late, he lazily got off the sofa. He went to the kitchen and washed his face with cold water. He still couldn't get quite used to that because, since the times when he had lived with the beggars, his body wouldn't see the water or soap for weeks in a row.

Then he went downstairs and began his usual morning gymnastics on the rope. Mikas had asked him to do this every day for at least an hour.

Only after coming back to the kitchen, he hastily made himself breakfast which he had learned to cook while living here. He not only had to make the breakfast meal but dinner and supper as well.

After eating, he had a lot of time left for himself. Since it had been strictly forbidden for him to go alone out to the city, he again took the yesterday's book into his hands and quickly got absorbed in it.

Paul sat with the book until Mikas came to check on him well into the afternoon.

Entering the room, he greeted him cheerfully, "Hello, my friend! This is the first time I'm seeing you reading a book without being forced to do so which, I think, shows a big progress! Are you planning to become a scientist? What are you reading by the way?" He walked up to Paul and took the book out of his hands.

"Oh, that's what it is!" he exclaimed. "The Grimms' Fairy Tales. I've heard about this book before. It's very appropriate for your age. Just don't start believing the fairy-tales."

"I understand myself they are just the fairy-tales," Paul agreed. "If to think so, there are no charmed princesses in the world that can be turned into white swans or giants who are bigger than centenary trees. In spite of that, I enjoy being with those characters and watching them conquer all the obstacles they encounter on their way, at least, in my imagination."

"It's good you've found the pleasant occupation, but you mustn't forget about your primary duties, too!"

"I'm not forgetting about my responsibilities," argued Paul, "and I have to listen not only to you but to Bikas as well. He said that if I don't learn to read and write, I will never be able to deal with uncertainties in my life since I won't be smart enough for that."

"I like the way you think and that you follow Bikas' advice, too. He is experienced in life, so you can learn a lot from him. Here is some money for you. This is your today's pay," Mikas said throwing a half zloty coin next to Paul.

"What do you mean 'my today's pay'? I haven't even left the flat today. How could I have possibly made any money?"

"Do you remember when yesterday at the restaurant the juggler Henikas promised to pay a zloty to you every day when you didn't show up at the farmers' market?" Mikas asked.

"Then why did you give me only half of the zloty?"

"You see, my Dear, there is a law in commerce stating that someone who act as a go-between gets a part of the pay. Since I played the part in this matter that has benefited all three of us, I'm in title to the pay."

Paul objected, "It's such a small pay already, and you are taking a half of it! If I had known about this deal, I would have never agreed to do it for that amount of money since I could make much more money myself by participating at the card games in the farmers' market."

"My friend, you don't know all the circumstances that we should take in consideration. And as far as the half of the zloty that I had appropriated from you goes, I think I haven't wronged you too much. I have always treated you to some sweets or paid for some other things for you," Mikas answered.

Paul continued sticking up for himself, "You see, if I was allowed to go out any time, I would also find the way to stuff my pockets with the money. In that case, I also wouldn't grudge spending money on you."

"Okay, you won," yielded to him Mikas. "You should be firm and not give way to those who try to take advantage of you. Here are twenty more groszy for you," he pulled the money out of his pocket and placed it on the sofa. "Now, I hope you won't feel any harm being done to you since we shared it like the real businessmen."

"It feels better now," Paul agreed.

"Tell me, Paul, what are you going to do with this money. If to think so, you don't really need anything. You have clothes, and you are not starving, either."

Paul scratched his head and said, "Bikas says money is the biggest power on the planet. Therefore, I shouldn't go wrong by having more of it. After all, I could buy you and him some presents, thus, returning the favors to you. Also, I could buy stuff for myself."

"I see you are turning into a man on a large scale. I have to go now," Mikas said and left Paul alone again in the flat where he got absorbed in his fairy-tale book.

Thus, years were passing by with Paul continuing to perfect his education. In addition to this, he learned to box. He no longer was the servant to Bikas at home even though he still liked preparing breakfast for them both. Lunch and dinner he used to eat in the city since he rarely was at home during the day and especially during the evening time.

Paul didn't have to listen blindly to Bikas and Mikas any longer. Most often, he worked on his own. However sometimes, he helped them robbing shops and cleaning people's pockets in busy places. He was able to climb to any floor of any house through its wall that none of his partners could do. After taking glass of the window, he could enter any flat or premise. Also, he could easily unlock any lock. All he needed to do was to see the key that was needed to unlock that particular lock, and he could make it himself.

And if there was some alarming situation, he was able to get out without being hurt.

In a meanwhile, Bikas and Mikas had happened to get behind bars a few times, but Paul never abandoned them, and once, he managed to even abduct Bikas from the prison.

Soon, Paul became so famous in the criminal world he gave no rest to the police even for a minute. They always followed on his heels not being able to catch him.

He did a lot of crimes but neither one of them was tied to a murder. He robbed many shops, restaurants, cash registers and cleaned out a lot of pockets of various coachmen. How many documents he forged; it would be difficult to even count them all!

It was unknown how long this kind of fury would have lasted if not for one large incident with the police when a policeman was murdered during a robbery of a big bank even though Paul hadn't even participated in it.

Bikas and Mikas had been meddled with that robbery after what they got a few years in convict prison.

Therefore, Pas was being watched even more vigilantly by the police, too. As soon as they got a hold of him, metal chains were placed on his wrists.

Nevertheless, even now, he managed to slip away out of their hands when they were passing a fence that was stretching along the street when on their way to the Police Department. At that moment, Paul kicked a policeman into his stomach. Then, he himself adroitly jumped over the fence, and by the time the policeman collected himself, Paul was already clambered upon the balcony into a third floor after what he disappeared into the flat there himself, thus, succeeding to run away from the police officer.

Now, Paul didn't have any doubts he could not get back to his own flat where they had arrested him just a few hours ago. His hiding place was no longer a secret to the police.

He didn't know where to take shelter, especially because now he had been kept an eye on from all the corners. In addition to this, he had no means for living. All his money that he could live on for a long time remained in Bikas' flat.

Paul had to find the way out of this unexpected situation without delay. Instantly, various ideas began swimming in his head. However, in order to put them to work, he needed money.

Up until now, he always used to figure out something quickly and easily. However this time, after finding himself in such strange circumstances and with the metal chains still on his wrists, Paul was feeling puzzled.

He realized he could not show up looking like this in public, and it was not easy to get rid of those heavy things since he had no tools to cut them off.

Luckily, he had been able to escape and hide away. He waited in his hiding-place with utmost anxiety and only well after dark, he went outside to the alley.

For a while, Paul was knocking about in the city until he succeeded in finding himself at one familiar pickpocket's place, and he helped him promptly get rid of his annoying chains.

Having those heavy, uncomfortable things on, Paul had been beginning to feel lost. However, as soon as they were taken away from his hands, he felt as free as a bird.

Now, he couldn't delay even for one minute since his stomach had been growling for long time already, and he had no one grosz in his pocket.

In spite of that, after spending only two hours without the chains on his wrists, he already had so much money he could live on it for an entire week. However, in order to bring about his plan, he needed much more money.

Without putting it off, Paul began implementing his plan. He had already foreseen long before a robbery of cash registers in two shops and a burglary in one flat. The details to accomplish this were not completely thought out by him yet because of the lack of time to do it, but he also knew he had to act fast.

Of course, the uncultivated soil could not bring the desired harvest. Therefore, it was not surprising when he found the cash registers at the stores to be almost empty. Only the burglary of the flat gave him the significant profit that allowed him to carry out his plan.

Soon, he was already sitting in a first class carriage of a train looking through the window at the changing views. He was staring avidly at the flying by villages and homesteads along the wayside. Paul remembered when as a little boy he used to walk from one thatched roof hut to the other with his little bag on a rope over his shoulder while making dogs bark. How much misery and disdain he had experienced while growing up without intercession and without an appropriate care!

Paul was amazed at himself what a big difference was between him, the little beggar then, and him now – the experienced eighteen-year-old tramp knowing how to put to work all kinds of ruses, who was now sitting in the comfortable first class carriage, dressed nicely and with the money in his pocket.

Thus, Paul arrived to Grodno but he didn't stay there for very long and kept traveling from town to town. However, he never stayed longer than for a month even in big cities such as Warsaw, Krakow, and Lvov.

Most of all, he liked to earn his living in Warsaw, though, since this megacity could offer the most opportunities that even his native Vilnius could not. The only problem with Warsaw was that he had to obtain the same accent the locals living there had, which would have enabled him to become a full-fledged representative of the dregs of a society there. This had been his only occupation since his early childhood that was in his blood and in his flesh.

Life made him learn to quickly adjust to the new circumstances since time was ahead of him. However, Paul dreamed of living in luxury which required a lot of his resourcefulness.

He loved to dine in good restaurants and sleep in first-class hotels. Moreover, his traveling required a lot of money. Lately he frequented going to Zakopane where a lot of tourists liked spending their vacation.

Paul would join them roaming about the mountains until he would learn if they had money, after what he would steal it and disappear himself with his booty.

He never got engaged in the small stuff. Even when after hanging onto some group of tourists he succeeded stealing someone's wallet there with just a little money in it, he always pretended that he had found it on the ground or had seen left somewhere by someone, and then, he would return it to its owner without taking any money out of it. This way, he knew he would not arouse any suspicion, thus, making people be extra cautious with their money which made it very difficult to get in any kind of relationship with them.

During summertime, he often went to the sea-coast where even more people used to gather. Paul thought he had especially good opportunities there.

Thus, he spent two years knocking about all over Poland. Especially he liked the big cities, but he never refused going to crowded farmers' markets in the small towns that never lacked gawks, too. They were the ones he was always after.

Often, he would steal money even from people praying in the churches, or he would just get into a dense stream of them coming in or out of the church.

However, he could take advantage of religious feasts only on Sundays. In addition to that, the big cities, also, could offer him the opportunities to make some money not only in the farmers' markets but in the streets there, too.

When he arrived to the seaside, it was the very climax of the season. There were so many people on the beach it appeared that not only half of the Poland but also half of the Germany was there as well. He could hear German being spoken everywhere around.

As soon as Paul found himself there, he began assessing and monitoring the environment.

He was walking half naked, his shirt over his shoulder, and looking around. As ill luck would have it, the sun was scorching mercilessly.

However, he remained persistent and kept looking for the suitable opportunity to steal something.

Once in a while, he would wipe his sweaty forehead with his shirt thinking it was virtually impossible to find anything worthy in this kind of environment since it was highly unlikely people would carry big amounts of money with them to the beach.

Walking in this world of the naked, Paul realized there was nothing for him to do here. He even began to regret thinking he had made a mistake by coming on the beach. What could he steal there - a bath-robe, and umbrella, or a swimming suite? He could make hardly any money on those items, let alone live sumptuously.

He was getting angry at himself he could not make any money today even though most well-to-do men used to come to this resort in order to rest, to suntan, and to breathe the sea air.

Paul didn't need such things for himself; he came here being driven by different intentions.

Nevertheless, he loved evenings when the restaurants filled with people. There he could have a good meal and drink to his heart's content. There were also different clubs in the city that offered various games, but Paul wasn't too fond of those kinds of activities.

But when some card lovers gathered, it always improved his situation. However, the game never lasted long since he would manage to win most of the money there, after what he would run out of the things to do very soon.

This time, Paul decided to take a swim before leaving and, thus, to say goodbye to the Baltic Sea.

He quickly threw off his clothes, ran in big leaps over the white beach sand towards the sea, and jumped into the water.

Soon, the big waves were already rocking Paul while, once in a while, lifting him up high into the sky and then plunging him into the depth where he could reach with his feet the fine sand of the bottom.

Nevertheless, Paul wasn't enjoying the swimming as much as the others who had come here on vacation were. He was bathing in the sea not because of the pure enjoyment of the carefree pleasures the summer had to offer but because the sun was scorching mercilessly in the sands on the beach.

For a long time, Paul was diving in the salty water not being able to completely cool down his body, since the water had also warmed up during the day.

When he was finally back on the shore and putting his clothes on, a few girls passed him running noisily, and one of them - with a beautiful mess red hair - suddenly shouted at him, "Peter!"

Paul glanced at the girl standing about ten steps away from him and didn't answer anything. At first, he thought she took him for somebody else.

Nevertheless, she again uttered in a surprised voice, "Oh my God! How did you end up here?"

"Just like anyone else," Paul answered.

"You had told me you were not going to go to the sea. Have you changed your mind?" she asked stretching her hand while greeting him.

A hundred of thoughts instantly flooded Paul's mind at once and materialized into one single idea that this girl could very well be some adventurer, just like him.

For a split second, he wanted to retort to her sharply in order to end their strange conversation.

However, as soon as he saw her tender, pleasant, and very intent look, he didn't dare to be rude. In addition to that, she enthralled him not only with her sweetness, but with her beauty as well.

For a while, he was standing dazzled, not being able to comprehend what was happening.

As always being very resourceful, he instantly refrained from making an urgent decision to say something inappropriate. Instead, his face brightened up like the sky after a big, dark cloud passed over it.

Paul said in a timid voice of a bashful youth, "My dear, time can be your enemy just as it can be your friend. Therefore, we all sometimes change our plans."

"I don't understand you, Peter. When I invited you to go with me for a week to the sea, you didn't want to go. Remember - you said you had more important things to do that were related to your education. I thought you were going to study the science of law. To tell the truth, it hurt my feelings then when you refused to go with me. Any other girl wouldn't even talk to you after this!"

"Janka!" the voice of one of her girlfriends reached them coming from the sea. "Come here!"

She waived at them splashing in the water.

Seizing the opportunity, Paul set his talent to work. He quickly opened up his 'speaker', "Dear Janka, I agree I was wrong by misleading you but, believe me, I didn't do this just to cause you the pain. When you left, I began feeling so lonely. The longing weighed down on me, and I decided no studies at the law faculty could fill the empty space in my heart. I wanted to see you right away! Even though I expected you would meet me with the words of rebuke, I am ready to fix my mistake now."

"I'm not angry at you, Peter," she said. "Actually, I am very happy you are here. I hope you are not in rush to go anywhere. Let's sit down and talk."

She was the first to sit down on the loose sand heated by the sun. Then she asked, "When did you arrive here?"

"Today, and the first thing I've done was I came here and even had a swim! It was so nice to rock on the waves. Go have a swim with your girlfriends, too. I will wait for you here."

"I like being with you more than with them. I have found them here, in this resort town, so I would have somebody to go swimming with. In the evenings, we play tennis. We go dancing once in a while, too. It's so much fun! The dances take place under the open sky in the pine forest. Not only youth but the older people come there, too, and every one of us dances the way we can. They have more fun activities this year than they had last year. Where are you staying this time? Or maybe you are in the same villa as you had stayed last year with your parents?"

"No," he said while lying down on his back. "The villa is too expensive for me to rent all by myself. I am staying in a hotel this time."

Janka lay down next to him on her side.

"You've got such a nice suntan, like some mulatto girl. I've never seen you looking so good," he said.

"You really like it, Peter?" she asked while stroking her flat stomach.

"I could kiss your bronze body all over right now," he said turning his head to look at her.

"You've had plenty of time to kiss me before, but you have never done that," she said gazing deep into his eyes.

"I had not dared to do this. And now, I'm afraid you are still mad at me."

"Peter, a kiss has its magic power to dissipate all anger and madness."

"Okay, I will prove you I can act like a real man."

"Go ahead," she said, "or I can run away from such Don Juan, which would probably make my girlfriends laugh."

"I don't think they are going to laugh seeing a real knight next to you! On the contrary, they might get jealous."

"Promises, promises…"

"You don't believe me?" he asked.

"You act somewhat different today. For some reason, you even look different. Moreover, you are so cold towards me after such a long separation. I don't know how to react to your indifference; it feels as if you are not happy to see me at all," Janka said in a concerned tone of voice.

Paul also turned on his side facing her, and their eyes united in a long gaze. Then his eyes slid down her face, neck and stopped on her round, bronzed shoulder. He could see her nice breasts heaving rhythmically under her bra.

Paul raised his head with his wet hair full of white sand, leaned forward, and gently touched with his lips her heated by sun shoulder.

At that moment, her fingers with the beautiful, long nails got in between his hair and stuck into his skin; the long, reddish color hair waves hung down covering his face. They were tickling Paul's cheek in this warm, gentle sea breeze.

Since there were people swarming around, Janka was feeling shy to become too intimate with him even though her heart was hungry for his endearment.

She overcame her desires and quickly sat down after what Paul lazily and reluctantly did the same. He regretted this pleasant time had lasted so shortly.

Their conversation ceased for a while, and now the one and the other were sitting while thinking their own thoughts.

That was the first time Paul lost his mental equilibrium. Finding himself in this puzzling situation, he didn't know what to do next – keep silent or talk. And if he had to renew the conversation, then what was that which he had to say to her? He wasn't very good with the women even thought it hadn't been a novelty to him having the most intimate affairs with a few of them already. However, it had happened in totally different circumstances where he didn't have to feel shy.

In general, he wasn't too attracted to the women. The big role in this had played his unwillingness to spend money while pursuing the relationship with them. Those expenses had seemed to be totally unnecessary to him.

In his mind, Paul was still debating if he should give himself up to the passion of love. After all, she could have really considered him to be her fiancé, playing the role of whom for a while, he would have most likely benefited greatly!

The only thing that made him wonder was the possibility of looking so alike with some another person that didn't allow even his loved one notice the difference!

Paul could not believe that which was happening right in front of his eyes! He still was having his doubts, though, thinking that there was the possibility he had met someone as deceiving as him. However, he decided to continue pretending he was that person she considered him to be thinking to himself that if he had been able to save himself out of the most puzzling situations before, he could succeed in getting out of a scrape here, too.

Janka was the first to utter, "Well, what are you thinking about, Mr. Future Judge?"

"I would like you to soften your terminology. For example, you could start calling me Mr. Lawyer," said Paul trying to show her he was more inclined towards intercessors than those condemning other people.

"You were the one who always dreamed about justice for all. I remember you becoming indignant at the lawyers that had defended some degenerated individuals. Generally speaking, I think if one is right, he or she doesn't need a lawyer, and if he is wrong, then no lawyer could help him anyway. However, cleaning the society from those kinds of dregs would benefit us all."

"I agree with you," he said nodding his head.

"I personally feel sorry for those poor unfortunates that are constantly being tangled up in the web of crimes," she resumed talking again. "I think that our society would benefit more from helping them than from trying to destroy them. Someone should stretch their firm helping hand enabling them, at least, for once in their life to feel some tender, loving feelings coming from others. Instead, looks like they are just being run down like some homeless dogs."

"My views on this subject have changed quite a bit, too," Paul assented to her. "When I look back, I think I had been mistaken about some of my attitudes towards the life of those misfits of the society. Probably my perception of the same subject is going to change even more as I study the law. You see, Janka, I have never had an opportunity to have anything to do with the criminals. All I know about them I have derived from various books. I realize that as I proceed with my education in the field of justice, the broader horizons are going to open up before my eyes making me come to the new conclusions. Right now, I consider myself to be the person with not completely formed outlook on life yet. Therefore, I would rather not draw any conclusions for that matter at this time."

"I wished my daddy could hear your reasoning now. He would definitely be proud of you! He always considered you to be the perfect member of the new generation. He also told me you are self-confident which was making him worry a little bit that it could cause you some problems in the future. But it sounded like a compliment to you at the same time."

"Of course, I have deep respect for your father, Janka. However, I don't understand why he is so concerned about my views. It is for me to decide what course in life I must take, and no one else can do this for me."

"Peter, please don't say things like this about my daddy! He had meant well. He has known you from your very childhood when your parents had bought the Kerciai estate and moved in to live there, thus, making you and your family our neighbors. Peter, do you remember the first time you and me met? I personally will never forget that! If you love and respect me at least a little bit, you mustn't talk this way. I realize you are the only heir to your parents, but I'm not poor, either. I'm getting my parents' estate they have in the country, and my brother is going to inherit their textile factory. No matter you are richer than I am, I won't allow you to say anything bad about my beloved parents, who wish you well."

"Forgive me, please, Janka. I didn't have any intentions to disrespect your parents. I have no slightest grounds for doing anything like that. Believe me - by saying those words, I didn't want to hurt your father. What I had in mind was that I am a live person, and I must think for myself. Imagine how you would feel if we got married and you would have to carry out all my wishes undermining your own wants and desires? In my opinion, every person is equal and, therefore, he or she should understand each other's needs and wants. Any kind of dictatorship is foreign to me. And as far as my family goes, I don't have any superiority complex in this area, either. My intentions towards you are the most noble. They are related to love and respect, and I'm going to keep acting in those parameters."

"Peter," Janka quickly changed the subject, "you shouldn't stay in the sun for so long. Put your shirt on. I will bring some cream and rub your shoulders with it."

Janka adroitly leaped up and ran towards her stuff that had been left lying in the very heat of the sun, next to the dunes. Soon, she returned to Paul carrying the jar of cream in one hand and her clothes hanging on her other hand. Then she rubbed the cream on his shoulders.

"Thank you, dear. I feel bad your girlfriends are having fun in the sea, and you are sitting in the scorching sun because of me!"

"To tell the truth, I've been swimming every day. I could miss my bathing in the sea once, especially when you are here!"

"Well, you won't have this kind of opportunity during wintertime. Look – you girlfriends are waving at you," he noticed and pushed her by her shoulders towards the sea.

Janka broke into run through the white sand and then over the water splashing it to all directions. As the water got up to the middle of her thighs, she lost her equilibrium, uttered a scream, and fell into the wave.

While she was bathing in the sea, Paul dressed up. He was sitting, his gaze fixed on the horizon where the Baltic Sea was meeting the sky, and thinking about Janka. He couldn't understand what kind of a girl she was. Was she just pretending or her fiancé and he really were as alike as the two peas in a pod? Doubt set in again, and he decided that, most likely, she was just an adventurer, some very experienced 'tern' of the summer seaside, who had just made up this entire fantastic story about her and him! During his lifetime he also had various opportunities to get in some unexpected situations. Nevertheless, this one exceeded all the previous ones! He had never even dreamed of running into such an unbelievably strange and interesting adventure!

Paul decided to play this game until the very end. He figured that soon every his question would be answered one way or the other. If everything was true what she had already revealed to him, he could warm his hands against her. And in that case if she happened to be just some resort town bitch trying to entangle the chosen by her victim into her cobweb, then soon, this adventurous tern would be unpleasantly surprised upon discovering she was cooing not to an innocent pigeon but to the falcon experienced in the same field. Then, this beautiful brown-haired lady would be spiting because of her foolishness.

He was wondering how she could fall into someone's arms without analyzing that person first. This appeared to be a very brave and dangerous move to Paul. At the same time, he knew that if she turned out to be just a useless star of the resort, then both of them would end up disappointed.

The flow of his anxious thoughts was interrupted by Janka running straight at him and splashing some drops of water on his face.

Smiling joyfully, he asked in a loud voice, "Have I made you wait here for too long?!"

"No, the time went by so fast, most likely, because I was watching the beautiful 'tern' diving among the waves in the sea right in front of my eyes. I wished I was an artist so I could perpetuate your image on an immortal canvas. However, since I don't have that kind of talent, I was only selfishly enjoying this view."

"It amazes me how drastically you have changed in such a short amount of time!" she said looking deep into his eyes. "This is the first time I am hearing such pleasant compliments coming from you that make my heart melt. Where have you learned those romantic things?"

"Loneliness is not always a bad thing; it can turn you not only into a romantic person but also into a poet! Where else one could pour out his thoughts if not onto paper?" Paul said.

"It looks like you are full of creative energy. And in general, Peter, you seem to have changed. You've become more interesting than you were before! You used to always talk about the social morals, philosophical problems, the law, and now, it seems that just all of a sudden, you've acquired a broader outlook on the world," Janka could not stop wondering at him.

It was not easy for Paul to compete with this highly educated and well-bred girl. In spite of that, he tried to stay on top and not let her knocked him down. Still, he would often run out of words and lapse into silence. After being driven into a corner, he thought this brave girl was cunning.

Thus, while they were talking in a friendly manner, the sun tilted over to the west side and was approaching the horizon. Its rays were hardly spreading any heat now. The wind also had died down, and most of the people had been already gone.

Finally, Janka offered, "Well, we should go home, too."

She got up, put on a simple but very elegant bath-robe, shook her hair while looking upwards, and stretched her hand down to Paul in order to help him get on his feet.

As soon as Janka looked at him standing, she snorted laughter through her nose, "Peter! You look so weird. This is the first time I see you dressed like that! You resemble some summer resort adventurer; they are frequent birds on every beach during this time of the year."

"Why don't you compare me to some hobo?" cut her off Paul.

"Peter, please don't get upset with me," she seized his head with the palms of her hands and turned his face towards her. "Please, smile at your Janka. This is not my fault you look like a hobo today. No matter how you look, though, I like you anyway. I just wouldn't want any of our acquaintances to see you looking like this."

"I'm sorry, Janka. I didn't think of dressing up when I was going to the beach."

"That's okay, Peter. This is not some kind of a fancy reception where people compete with each other while showing off their clothes. Today, I look not any better than you myself; my hair is dispersed like that of some witch. I know you are going back to your hotel now. Would you come to eat supper with us in two hours? I can only imagine how surprised my daddy will be upon seeing you!"

"Let me see you to your place, Janka. I don't know where you are staying," he said.

"We are at the same villa as the last year," she answered.

"I thought, I'll just ask," he said thinking their meeting was over forever.

Soon, they walked into a nice pine forest.

"Well, you don't have to walk me any further. I can already see our villa," she said pointing at the white wooden building showing through the trees.

"See you soon, Janka," he turned away to walk the opposite direction when he heard her voice coming from behind.

"Are you going to leave without giving me a kiss?"

"I was afraid someone can see us here," he answered.

"Who could possibly see us in this forest? We don't need to feel shy in front of these pine trees; they are not going to betray our secret."

The watchful Paul's eyes quickly scanned the environment around in order to make certain there had been no trap set for him. Lending an attentive ear to the sounds, he slowly walked towards her, took her by the waist, and pulled her towards him.

Paul could feel her breathing as his face was slowly getting closer to hers. Janka's tight breasts were resting against his wide chest. The next thing, their hot lips united, and Janka's eyes closed up.

Paul's eyes, on the contrary, opened up widely, and he pricked his ears, too.

He was kissing her for quite a long time while turning her to one side, then to the other, as if being afraid someone could stab him from behind.

Janka was melting in the arms of her beloved, but Paul carried out this act without experiencing any pleasure.

Finally, she tore herself away from him and mumbled incoherently, "I'm so happy you are here. I'll better hurry to give my parents the pleasant news about your arrival. Please, come soon. I will be counting minutes."

Janka sent him with her hand a kiss in the air and ran along the curvy narrow path towards the villa.

Paul waited until he could no longer see her disappearing between the trunks of the trees and showing up on the curve of the path again. Then he quickly walked the direction of the villa, also.

As he found himself behind the last thick bush, he decided not to proceed any further.

In front of him, there was a big square in the middle of which a small, elegant villa was standing with a pointed tower facing upwards. It looked very beautiful against the background of golden and pink clouds, helping to create almost a surreal picture of the spectacular sunset. The villa itself had one floor with a terrace above it right next to the tower, which had been decorated with the fanciful architectural ornaments.

Paul was looking at Janka jumping up and down and swinging a branch of a bush, looking like some little girl, before she disappear behind a big glass door shining in the sunset.

Then he rushed back to the pine forest, and a half an hour later, he already was in his modest, little room on the second floor that he had been lucky to rent out for a very little money.

He didn't even need a big room just for himself alone. A rather worn, dark color suit was hanging right on a peg-board mounted there on the wall.

Under a narrow bed, there was a half empty suitcase with a few clean shirts in it. Paul had been getting ready to leave and he'd made sure he had some clean clothes. Now, that caring of his came in very handy.

Paul picked the best shirt that he had worn only a couple of times before; therefore, it still looked almost like bra new. However, there was totally a different story with his suit. As soon as Paul took it off the hanger, he realized he could not come wearing it to that white, elegant villa.

Next thing, Paul was already carrying to his room a black suit that he had just rented from an owner of the hotel. The suit was made of a very nice material and looked almost new.

Paul washed himself up good with soap, dressed up quickly, and polished his shoes that appeared looking still pretty decently. After that, he admired himself in the mirror for some time.

He had never had an opportunity to wear such a nice suit. Therefore, he could not move away from the mirror.

Even though he was already dressed, but he still had a lot of time left before meeting with Janka. Therefore, he continued stamping in his room while trying to kill some time.

At last, he pulled out of a pocket of his old pants a pretty big knife with an automatic spring. Before slipping it into the pocket of his new pants, he pressed with his thumb on the safety lock located on the side of the handle. Instantly, he heard the clicking sound, and the blade shone in his hand.

A thought crossed his mind that if Janka saw him now, she would be scared of him to death. In spite of that, he cold-heartedly placed the knife into the right pocket of his jacket.

Then he went into another pocket of his old pants and pulled out a metal ferrule tool designed to be worn on the knuckles of a hand; he had had to resort to using it when being attacked before, and he had never separated with it since then. It had proved to serve Paul as the efficient weapon in helping him knock out a bigger and stronger rival than him.

Paul slipped it on the knuckles of his fingers and gently punched the palm of his other hand. Then he placed his metal thing into the pocket of his pants. He thought of it as of the safest and most convenient way to arm himself.

He used his knife only in the most critical instances since it was very easy to kill a person with it, and Paul had never done this type of offence in his life yet. He was well aware those kinds of crimes could rarely get buried in archives. Instead, they would constantly be right on the very top of all the stacks of the cases the lawyers would be working on.

Paul had always been very cautious, therefore, this time he also got ready for the worst, just in case.

Before leaving, he for the last time cast a glance at himself in the mirror, gave a wink to himself, and walked out of the room.

On his way to the villa, he also dropped at the barber's and had a clean shave. He asked to be sprayed with the best Eau-de-Cologne after what he left totally content with the way he looked.

Whistling light-heartedly a joyful melody, he was walking along a barely trampled down and already the familiar narrow forest path with the tall, slender pine trees growing on both its sides. Their coniferous branches were letting the sun filter through while shedding the long streaks of golden light. The pathway ahead of him appeared so beautiful and peaceful.

As Paul approached the villa, he first walked around it through the forest in order to familiarize himself with the building.

When he was already standing at the front glass door, he saw inside of the hall a young man who was playing table tennis with Janka.

The unfamiliar youth glanced at Paul, grabbed with lightning speed the little ball flying at him, and yelled joyfully, "Peter! I can't believe my eyes!"

He placed the bat onto the tennis table together with the little ball and began moving towards Paul his hand stretched out to greet him.

"See?" Janka's voice was heard, "I told you he is here!"

"Okay, sister. You won! I'm gonna buy you a box of the best chocolates in town tomorrow. In this case, it was worth going even for the bigger bid!"

"I can't believe you are here! You were so settled on studying that, in no way, I was expecting to see you this summer at the sea," he pattered with excitement while firmly pressing Paul's hand.

Now, Paul was almost sure he was being mixed up with some another person who had been very much alike as him. Nevertheless, a slight doubt Janka might had prepared this young man for their meeting was still tormenting him.

In spite of that, Paul continued pretending he was the same person by the name Peter they were considering him to be.

He was slow and very careful when talking to them trying to assess the situation and gather as much information as he could. Mainly, he was touching only the subjects he had already been familiar with.

"There is a law in the nature stating that everything changes constantly. Therefore, I had decided to change my mind, too, and have a vacation instead of sitting cooped up in the room. There will be enough time for my studies in the fall. I would rather be together with you enjoying every day that flies by so fast!" Paul said.

"I think you did the right thing by coming here. Your mind needs some rest just as you body does," said Edvardas patting Paul on his shoulder. Then he turned to his sister, "Janka, it's your turn to entertain our guest, and I'll better go tell your parents he is already here."

As soon as Edvardas disappeared in the long corridor, Janka jumped up to Paul, fixed her shining eyes on him, and began talking, "You are looking fantastic! Nothing like when I saw you at the beach. For a split second, I even began doubting it had been you. Edvardas would have a good laugh if he saw you then. Peter, I would love to kiss you, but I don't even dare touch you when you look so elegant."

"Don't exaggerate, Janka. It hurts when you say that I looked funny at the beach. I was exactly the same person then, just as I am now! I for example, don't perceive you to be any different inside no matter if you had a wet hair or a hair-do, which means that you are always the same precious to me, no matter what. In my soul, I think of you very highly."

"Peter, stop picking on me, please! You know that I love you just the way you are. No man is capable to love as passionately as a woman can! Think - if I didn't love you, would I notice any differences in you? And even if I noticed those differences, I wouldn't bother to tell you about them because of that simple reason that I wouldn't care! But now, since you are my fiancé, I must tell you many things, and I do this not to make fun of you. Simply, the way I see it is that, even though we have two separate bodies, we have to have the same feelings for each other."

"Your thinking is correct. However, I was feeling very comfortable wearing my old clothes when on the beach since I could roll on the sand with them. Imagine if I did this while dressed in this suit. Everyone around would probably think that I was either crazy or drunk."

However, Paul was unable to finish talking when steps in the corridor were heard.

Paul turned to look back and saw a tall woman about forty years old dressed in an elegant dark color wool dress. Her face was already beginning to wither. She was smiling, and he could see a few small wrinkles showing in the corners of her eyes. However, her figure was still so beautiful that many young ladies could envy her!

A man a little taller than her was following this noble lady; he appeared to be about fifty years old. His hair was wavy, thick and, by his ears, it was completely white. The man wasn't wearing a jacket, only a shirt, and was carrying a folded magazine in his hand.

As soon as the noble lady walked gracefully into the hall, she exclaimed in a very pleasant voice, "What an unexpected and very dear guest! Hello, hello, Peter. I'm glad to see you healthy and in good spirits!"

After the official part of the greeting, the hostess asked, "Peter, why didn't you come straight here upon your arrival?"

"I'm sorry, Madam."

Janka jabbed her elbow into his side and whispered into his ear, "You should call her mother."

"I am sorry, mother," Paul mumbled in a barely audible voice and pricked up his ears after hearing himself utter the word 'mother'. He had never in his entire life called anyone 'mother'.

However, since he had been used reacting quickly to any situation, he didn't get lost this time, either.

"It had been so hot in the train and then in the crowded bus that I became all sweaty. Therefore, I didn't want to show up here looking like that and feel miserable all evening long. Even Janka when she saw me at the beach said I looked pitiful. I just had to take a swim in the sea first in order to come to life. Again, I beg your pardon, mother. I didn't mean to insult you."

"Supper will be served in about half an hour. Janka, you are still in your bath-robe. Please, go change your clothes!"

Janka excused herself and left. The hostess turned to everyone and asked, "I think it can be too stuffy in the dining room. Should we have our supper in the terrace instead?"

"When the weather is like this, there can't be any better place to eat than that in the terrace," her husband agreed. Then he turned to his son and said, "Edvardas, take Peter upstairs, and I will ask to serve the supper for us there."

Paul followed Edvardas along the corridor. At the end of it, there was a narrow staircase leading upstairs.

Soon, both of them were on the terrace. There were two tables standing on both sides of it. On the right side, there was also a very beautiful bronze statue sitting on a half meter high pedestal with three girls depicted on it. One of them was holding a flower, and the other two were stretching their arms towards it. On the other side, there was growing a widely branched out palm tree which was taking up almost the entire corner of the terrace.

Edvardas joined together the two tables in the middle of the terrace and placed the chairs around them.

The next thing, a maidservant came in wearing a white, impeccably clean apron and covered up both tables with one white tablecloth that made everything look even more elegant and bright since the very last rays of the ready to go down sun were falling onto the white tablecloth making it look slightly pink in color.

On the east side of the horizon, the bottom of it was all deep red and looked as if being splashed with raspberry juice. The pine forest was spreading a pleasant smell of resin. In addition to that, once in a while a gentle, warm, refreshing breeze coming from the sea would bring refreshing humidity. The sounds around also cooperated with this fine evening so perfectly fit for the family gathering - even the forest was rustling its evening song that would die out and come back on with every gust of the gentle wind .Thus, everything around was breathing of romance.

However, Paul was not able to rejoice in this wonderful environment. He wasn't paying much attention to the sounds or the view, and he didn't draw the fragrant air into his lungs like some of the others there did after having walked up to the railing of the terrace and leaning forward with their hands on it.

Instead, he was measuring the height of the terrace with his eyes thinking to himself how fast he would be able to get down on the ground if the need arose.

He no longer had any doubts, though, that he got into the fireside of the noble and decent family.

Soon plates with food were being lined up on the table. The host with hostess reappeared; he was carrying a bottle of cognac, and his wife - a crystal vase filled with chocolates that she placed in the middle of the table.

Janka's father asked everybody to sit down wherever they wanted.

At that moment, Janka showed up in the doorway. As soon as Paul saw her, he opened his mouth wonder-struck. He had never seen such a beautiful girl in his entire life!

She was wearing a sky-blue color wool dress. On her chest, two rows of pearl beads were shining. One row was girding her neck, and the other was lying on the edge of her décolleté. Half of her hair on the top was nicely gathered together and pinned in the back with a big, golden pin incrusted with rubies. The rest of her hair was let down reaching the middle of her back which helped stress the beauty of her face. When she turned her head, the rubies appeared in her hair looking like the big drops of hardened blood.

On the left side of her dress, she had another golden pin showing with a light green color diamond in the middle of it. Her bare up to her elbows arms were decorated with golden bracelets and a diamond ring was shining on her hand.

She walked up to Paul smiling and felt the pleasant aroma of the expensive Eau-de-Cologne spreading from him.

With the sunset in the background, her hair turned even more pretty color. However, Paul was mainly preoccupied trying to estimate how much her jewelry was worth.

As she sat down next to him, the host filled up little crystal glasses and urged everyone to have a drink.

The sun was already way below the horizon line, but the white tower next to the terrace was still bathing in its red rays that resembled blood.

The festive supper began during which they talked more than they ate. Of course, it was not easy for Paul to pretend all the time he was the other person. He was trying hard to learn as much as he could about that other person by the name Peter this family had been erroneously considering him to be.

During this long meal that lasted until midnight, he learned a great deal.

Upon leaving, Janka's parents offered him to sleep over in their house. When he politely refused, the hosts asked him to come for breakfast in the morning.

Of course, Janka walked him outside where he had to perform all the duties of the fiancé again.

This way, an entire week passed by, during which they practically didn't get separated. Janka was very happy with his attachment towards her. It never occurred to her he had his own secret agenda.

She was feeling sorry that, after a few days, she had to leave back home with her parents. Paul was feeling upset, too, since they had spent so much time together, and besides the huge expenses, he didn't get any use out of it. He was almost out of all his money now.

The next day, he came to see Janka in the afternoon and found her alone in her room lying on the sofa and reading a book.

As soon as he appeared in the doorway, she leaped up, ran towards him, and grabbed his hand, "Sit down, Peter. I'm so happy you are here! I was feeling so lonely without you."

"The villa is always full of people. You shouldn't feel lonely," he said.

"My daddy with my mom went to the beach, and our maidservant went to the farmers' market to buy some food. I've been all by myself here waiting anxiously for you to come. We could go walk on the seaside and have a swim, too. I will leave the key for the maidservant in our secret place. Therefore, we don't have to wait until she returns home."

Paul took Janka by the waist, pulled her closer to him, and began kissing her passionately on her lips.

After a while, he was becoming more and more persistent which for the first time evoked her resistance, "Peter, stop it! You are getting too far."

"Janka, I love you, and I can't imagine my life without you. Why are you avoiding my closeness?"

"Peter, what are you talking about?! Don't you trust my feelings for you?"

Paul again twined himself around her and tried to kiss her on her neck. However, frightened Janka again freed herself from his embrace.

"Peter, please stop it! You have never been like this before. What has got into you!?"

"What do you want me to stop doing?" He asked. "Are you still thinking to marry me or not?"

"Peter, what are we talking about here? Have you for some reason lost trust in me?"

"I still trust you, but before we get married, I would like to know more about you. It makes me wonder why you are trying to get away from me. You've been going dancing with your girlfriends until midnight. What happen after that I can only imagine..." he expressed his frustration.

"Yes indeed, I went dancing a few times. Edvardas always went with me there, too. Therefore, we returned home together with him. There is nothing bad in having a little fun on vacation. In spite of that, I always remained faithful to you. You can ask my brother; he'll tell you the same."

"Of course, Edvardas will be on your side. It can't be the other way – he is your brother. However, your coldness seems suspicious to me. Before you would not retreat from me, and now, you've just of a suddenly become so distant."

"Peter, don't say things that aren't true."

"My dear, I would like to believe your words, but all I see now is that you are pulling back from me."

"Peter, you are wrong. On the contrary – you are getting more precious to me every day! Your rebukes are not well-grounded."

"Okay, I will do whatever you say – I won't touch you anymore," he said.

"You can still kiss me as you did before, Peter."

Janka moved closer to him, looked tenderly deep into his eyes, and kissed him gently on his lips herself.

Paul didn't leave her unanswered; he kissed her back passionately again making Janka's heart flutter. And for a few seconds, their loving feelings towards each other returned. But then, Paul started becoming more aggressive again.

Janka would gently free herself of his embrace being afraid to hurt his feelings. However, Paul was determined to accomplish his plans at any cost.

Thus, he brought her down on the sofa, but Janka managed to get out from underneath of him. She quickly jumped to her feet, and Paul got up after her.

She was all red on her face and breathing heavily. Paul understood that he could win more by ruse.

Therefore, he abruptly turned around and, looking down, he walked towards the door.

Frightened voice of Janka caught up with him, "Peter, where are you going?!"

"I'm leaving. I understand I was wrong trying to force you make love. I don't think it's the right thing to do since you don't really love me. You have just killed our love. I don't see any reason for us to continue our relationship."

After uttering those words, Paul grabbed the handle of the door. However, he was in no time to open it since Janka ran up to him, obstructed the door with her entire body, and began entreating him, "No! I will not let you leave being in this kind of mood. Peter, you are wrong. God is the Witness I am faithful to you."

"I don't care about any witnesses. I know what I feel and why I'm feeling this way. There is a reason why you are like a stranger to me at this moment. And don't feed me with your empty promises! No one needs your hypocrisy. I'm stronger than you – you better move away..." he said all frustrated.

"My God, Peter... you are frightening me. You have never been like this before. Despite that, I love you anyway. I can't imagine how I could live without you. Please, don't despise me. I think that probably some evil, jealous tongues led you into error."

Paul resumed talking, "I don't think you are taking it seriously. This is the last time I'm talking to you because I'm leaving Poland. In a couple of days, I will be abroad."

He seized Janka's hand in order to move it off the door handle when her other hand twined around his neck. She burst into tears and mumbled in a barely audible voice, "Please, don't leave me. Do whatever you want with me. If you walked out now, what would I be able to tell to my parents? What would they think about us? Oh my God, I'm so unfortunate!"

On one hand, Paul was triumphing in his heart of hearts he was able to conquer this girl from such a noble family, who had an opportunity to enjoy an easy life. On the other hand, in his mind, he was laughing at her thinking how devastated she was going to be later on upon learning the bitter truth of him. He was rejoicing the fate was going to mock her just as it had done to him during the course of his entire life. Instantly, Paul recalled the times when he had lived his migratory life of the tramp, like some ragged dog being hounded by everyone.

At last, he took Janka by the hand, walked her to the sofa, and seated her, after what he began kissing her wet from tears cheeks while whispering gentle words at the same time. He didn't let her totally come to herself. As soon as she began calming down, he hurried to take hold of her feelings completely.

After yielding to his passion, she took her downfall deeply into her heart. Only because Paul was almost all the time with her, she didn't get completely depressed.

A few days later, Janka made peace with her situation. The only bad thing was that when the time came for her to go home, Paul unexpectedly told her he had received a letter from his friend in

Gdansk where he was writing about a misfortune that had befell him. He was asking Paul to come and stay with him for a couple of days.

Paul tried to find Janka's jewelry in her room, but all his efforts were in vain. And he badly needed money. Two weeks without doing his usual activities that had enabled him to get some money not only exhausted all his savings, but also put him in debt to the owner of the hotel, who kept persistently demanding him every day to pay rent and even threatened to kick him out.

Finally, Paul succeeded to convince the owner to let him stay there one more day expressing his surprise to the owner that the money his friend had sent him hadn't reached him yet.

Of course, he wasn't really expecting any money because there was no person in the entire world who could send it to him.

Paul was hoping to get some money from Janka's family instead. He decided to give it a try and expressed his concern to her parents he had to go to his friend almost with no money when his friend, most likely, needed it badly.

As soon as Paul mentioned about the money, Janka's father asked, "How much money do you think you are going to need, Peter?"

"I'm not sure. It depends on what had happened to him. I don't think he would ask me to come for no reason. He is just not that kind of person. It would be nice if you could borrow as much as you can, and I will return it to you as soon as I get back home," Paul said.

"I don't have much money right now with me, but I could spare you five hundred zloty. I hope it will be enough, and if it's not, than you could send me a telegram to my home," Janka's father answered.

"I think it should be plenty," smiled Paul.

In the afternoon, he saw off the entire Janka's family home.

Having left alone and with the money in his pocket, Paul roared with laughter. He was thinking of leaving right away on one of his numerous 'tours' without even paying to the owner of the hotel. However, it was such an unbearably hot day he could hardly breathe. Being all sweaty, he decided to take his last swim in the Baltic Sea, wait until the evening, and then come back for his things in order to whirl away from this resort where he had such a great time for over two weeks he could not ask for anything more!

Whistling a lively melody, kicking little rocks lying in his path, and sometimes even giving a jump, he was walking towards the seaside where the other even more interesting adventure was awaiting him.

The beach was full of people. In some places, he had to make a big curve in order to pass the groups of men, women, and children lying or sitting on the sand.

This way, he finally walked to the edge of the water. Then he sat down. As he looked around, he saw a woman with a beautiful tan sitting about two meters away who was staring right at him.

However, when he looked at her, her eyes turned to the sea.

Paul didn't dare right away to ask her to watch his clothes while he was going to bathe in the sea. Instead, he lay down on the sand that was so heated by the sun he had to move often.

When he cast his glance again at this lonely woman sitting on the white sand, she smiled at him and said, "The sand is hot, isn't it?"

"I feel like in a frying pan," he agreed staring at this beautiful woman, who appeared to be about thirty five years old.

Word after word, they began talking and Paul asked her to guard his clothes. Then he got into the water and was splashing there for a long time like some girl. The water was as warm as tea. Therefore, it was not surprising he forgot about everything around including the money in the pocket of his pants.

Paul got out onto the shore only when he got tired, but he wasn't feeling cold as it used to be most of the times when he took a swim before.

As he was walking towards his stuff, the woman asked him from the distance, "Have you got cold?"

"Oh no, the water is very warm. I simply got tired swimming all the time. If I would just lie peacefully and let the waves rock me, I could spend the entire day in this kind of water! But since I am a hyper person, I can't stay still for a long time. I love diving in the waves!" He said while running his hand through his wet hair.

"I'm glad you had fun swimming," she said.

"Would you, Madam, like to do the same? Now is your turn, and I could watch your clothes."

"I already had a swim. But I would gladly have some lemonade to quench thirst. Someone told me it's being sold behind that dune over there."

She was ready to get up in order to go search for the lemonade, but Paul jumped to his feet first and said, "I will find some lemonade for you!"

He quickly grabbed his pants and started putting them on while already moving the direction of the dunes, and he heard her voice after him, "Wait; take the money!"

"Don't worry, Madam. I have some!" he shouted back and disappeared running behind the dunes overgrown with bushes and shrubs.

Paul was gone for a pretty long time. Then he showed up with the two bottles of red lemonade; he was coming from the completely opposite side which startled her when she unexpectedly heard him saying behind her back, "Here is your refreshing living water. You should drink it now while it's still cold."

"I'm so thirsty, but I don't have anything to open the bottle with. Maybe you have a knife?" she asked.

"I don't," he said, "but I will find the way to open it. I'll go ask people around."

Even though Paul had a knife in this pocket, he didn't want her to see it which could make her think something bad about him.

He tried to please her, secretly wishing he could enter into a more close relationship with this lady, just as he had done with Janka. After all, there was no real necessity for him to go anywhere yet.

Paul borrowed a pocket knife and opened the bottle for her. She gracefully took it from his hand and offered another bottle of lemonade to him.

"Thank you, Madam, I'm fine. The seawater permeated my every pore. You will get thirsty later; there is plenty of time until the evening. The lemonade is going to be warm by then, but it's better than nothing. At least, you will be able to wet your palate."

She drank almost all bottle of the lemonade, took a deep breath into her lungs, and said, "Wow! It's so cold and refreshing. I'm going to pay you for the lemonade now."

The woman pulled a little wallet out of her purse. When she opened it, he fixed his avid look on the contents, but he couldn't see any big bills, and his curiosity instantly abated.

"Here is half of a zloty," she stretched her hand to him with the money in her palm.

"Madam, I'm not rich, but I can afford to buy you a bottle of lemonade."

"Thank you," she said putting the money back into her wallet, "I didn't wish to insult you."

The conversation that had started between the two of them didn't come to an end. On the contrary, it was going on further.

Paul didn't have any idea the fate brought him together not with just some casual woman but with his biological mother!

The easy money was on his mind, but Julija was struck by his similarity with that of Robertas. As soon as her eyes had met with the eyes of Paul for the first time, shudders of excitement passed through her entire body. It seemed as if Robertas himself was gazing at her.

She wanted to spend as much time with this youth as she could.

"We've been talking for a while now. My name is Julija," she said stretching her beautifully tanned arm to him. It looked a little wet from sweat that was shining in the sun. "I've come here from Vilnius for a few weeks' vacation."

As soon as Paul heard her mentioning Vilnius, his heart fluttered. However, he as usually didn't lose his self-control and showed no emotions.

"I am from Gdansk myself," he said, "and my name is Paul. I would love to travel, too, but except Gdansk, I have not been anywhere else. This is my first trip that I had been preparing myself for two years. I hadn't had any money to go anywhere. So I worked during summertime as a stevedore at the harbor, thus, saving money for coming here on vacation. There had not been any other way to make the money since two more years are left for me going to school."

"Paul, what are you studying?"

"I'm studying the law."

Julija became even more curious now; thousands of various thoughts began rushing into her head. She was wondering about the similarity between him and Robertas; she wanted to know if there was any possibility he was her son. But then - how he could end up so far away from Vilnius?! Now, Julija urgently wanted to find out about Paul as much as she could.

She could not throw off a possibility, too, of him being Robertas' son, whom he might have had with some another woman.

Then she remembered Robertas telling her about his family, who had owned a saw mill before the war. However, according to this mysterious youth's talk, he appeared to be poor.

She decided that the World War I could have impoverished his entire family, just as it had caused many problems to her family, also.

Not being able to find the peace of mind, she brought herself to ask, "Paul, you said you had dreamed of traveling and you had to work at a seaport loading goods in order to earn money to come here. Don't you have any family or other close people who could help you? I hope I'm not too intrusive with my questions. You don't have to answer them if you don't want to."

"No, I don't have any secrets. I'm just afraid you would get bored listening to my meager biography. But if you really wish to know, I can tell you a little bit about myself. I was raised in Gdansk where I still live with my father and my mother," Paul was lying. "My father works as a joiner at the port, and he makes pretty good money there, but the problem is that my mother is ill. Lately, she has been spending more time in bed than on her feet. Besides that, my education required a lot of money, too. It's very difficult for our family to survive on only one income. I don't even talk about the clothes; I'm the only one out of our family who is dressed halfway decent. Our food is not enviable, too. I couldn't say we are starving, but we also never get enough to eat. That's the environment I currently live in."

"Hopefully when you are done with your studies, your life is going to take off," she said.

"Of course, everybody cherish their hopes for better life, but I have to think logically, too. I don't believe I will be able to find a good place to work at after finishing my education since I don't have any acquaintances that could help me find a good job. Maybe I will succeed getting the worst position possible in some small office, and that's the best I can do. But for now, I could probably get a job only at the customs in the sea port. At least, such is my dream while I am studying to get my degree in the field of law."

"Paul, don't despair – everything is for the best," she tried to encourage him.

"I'm not sure about that."

"Why are you painting your future in such dark colors? Think positive."

"I love talking to you," he said. "Time has passed by so fast. What should I call you - Miss Julija or Madam Julija? As about me, I would like you to call me simply Paul. I'm used to being called this way at the university, by my parents, and all my friends. When I worked at the sea port during the summertime, my co-workers used to call me Paul, too."

"You can call me either way; I wouldn't get insulted. The time I've spent with you wasn't boring at all. On the contrary – it went by seemingly unnoticed," she said.

During the last minutes of their conversation, she tried not to touch the deeper social problems since it was important for her just to find out about Paul's past life, namely, if there had been any relation to Robertas. However, at the same time, she didn't feel comfortable inquiring him about it in the straightforward manner.

The sun was no longer spreading warmth, only the light, and very little people were left on the beach. The time had come to abandon this place for the two of them as well.

At last, Julija with Paul got up, too, which meant she had to part with him without being able to find out any more details about his personal life. She didn't want to separate with him yet, but she didn't know how to find a reason to hold him back, either.

Julija refused to believe their paths were going to go different ways forever.

Therefore, she took a risk and asked, "Paul, I'm sorry for my curiosity, but where are you staying?"

"Behind this fancy White Foam hotel," he pointed with his finger, "there is a small village of fishermen about a kilometer away from here. There is the one and only shabby hotel in it where I am staying."

"Great! It turns out we go the same way," she said.

"Then, I could see you to your place, Miss Julija," he offered.

"That is where I am staying – in the White Foam."

"Wow! It must be a very nice hotel," Paul noticed.

"I like it! My room is on the second floor. I spend some time on the balcony every evening before I go to sleep listening to the sounds of the crashing waves and breathing in salty air of the Baltic Sea. It's so calming!"

Thus talking, they approached the White Foam hotel which was triumphing with its beautiful exterior and surroundings. It was obvious not everyone but only the selected ones were allowed to enjoy the stay here.

"Well, we are here," she said.

"It's too bad we have to part," Paul noticed with sadness in his voice. "Just like many others who bump into each other and then separate for good."

"To tell the truth, I don't want to part with you. I think I owe you a favor for buying me that lemonade," she noticed. "For some reason, I have a feeling our conversation isn't over. I would like to hear more about your life, and I want to tell you some things about myself too, of course, if you are interested in learning something about me."

"Miss Julija, you can't imagine how much I'm interested in learning more about you. I could probably listen to you talking all night long and never get bored! Besides, I have no doubt your life is more interesting than mine."

"Would you like to come to the White Foam restaurant this evening? We could continue our conversation there," she offered.

"I would love to, but I'm afraid my clothes aren't suitable for this kind of luxury. My suit that I have in my hotel room is rather shabby. They probably won't even let me in when they see me dressed like that."

"I will help you with this," she said, "just let me know if you are available tonight."

"I can come any time. Those four faded color walls in my room can't keep me inside."

"Then I consider it as a 'yes'," she said smiling, "and I'll be waiting for you in the lobby of the second floor at eight o'clock in the evening. Just in case if the porter asks you, tell him please you are going to the room fifteen. See you soon, Paul."

The first thing he did as he returned to his hotel, he went to its owner, who met him very passively. Obviously, he didn't want to hear Paul entreating him to stay another day free of charge.

Nevertheless, as soon as the owner saw Paul's beaming face, he fixed his inquiring gaze on him, but he still didn't get up off his chair in order to meet him which he always had done every time a guest walked in.

"Sir, I've come here to pay the rent; I've finally received the money order."

After hearing those his guest's words, from whom the owner of the hotel had never expected to get the money for the past four days, he instantly and drastically changed and became so sweet like some healing balm to be smeared over a wound.

This time, though, Paul wasn't talking much. He paid for additional two days ahead, said good-bye, and left.

There was plenty of time, and he didn't need to rush. Therefore, he went to the buffet and bough two portions of sausages and a cup of black coffee. Then he quickly gulped everything down which made him feel better since hunger had been starting to make him feel feeble.

When Paul returned to his gloomy room, he felt good for the first time during his entire stay here. Now, he no longer needed to be afraid of being kicked out on the street by the owner of the hotel. Moreover, for some reason, he began feeling as if he came home and not to the temporary room that he had to rent in the midst of his never ending traveling from town to town.

He fell down onto his narrow bed and heard the usual twittering sound of the metal wires and coils inside the mattress which had annoyed him every time he would move. Nevertheless, now, this squeak appeared somewhat pleasant to him.

Paul was lying on his back with his hands under his head and staring at the ceiling.

Hundreds of thoughts were swimming in his head. First, he remembered the events of this morning: parting with Janka, kisses and caresses, the tears as if her heart had been feeling they were separating forever. Paul could already picture in his mind Janka meeting her real fiance Peter, who no doubt would be listening to all her rebukes with his eyes wide open out of astonishment, upon their next date.

Then he gave an angrily laugh thinking both of those molly-coddles deserved just that. He was glad that now he was not the only one who had been wronged by fate like some homeless dog. He wished he could see the drama happening between those two representatives of the upper class of the society, who had never had opportunities to experience the true meanness being inflicted on them by others.

He wished he could get between them again and do some more damage to their relationship. Suddenly, a new thought crossed his mind that was probably exactly why he had been born into this world – to cause problems to the others!

Then he asked himself a question - who he was. The answer came – nobody. And then, another answer followed telling him that, at the same time, he was all in one: the beggar, the thief, the clown, the swindler, the hypocrite, the gambler, the blackmailer, and only devil knew who else!

An idea crossed his mind he would probably be able to play a role of a decent person as well. Now he was almost proud of his achievements thinking that not many people on this earth could accomplish so much in their lives in such a short amount of time! He wondered how so many different characters could possibly find a place in this one body of his!?

Paul also had a scary thought coming into his head to go find that spoilt person by the name Peter and, with one prick of his knife, eliminate him from this world. After that, he himself could become the dandy, marry this little red-haired monkey Janka, and begin living the modest, innocent, and boring life in high society!

He pulled his big knife out of his pocket and pushed a small shining button on the side of its handle. The crackling sound of the metal was heard, and the blade of the horrible knife shone in his hand. After turning it a few times in his palm, Paul bent it back.

He decided the path of the murder was too drastic even for the person of his occupation. But what if he could just change the appearance of Peter's face, for example, by scalding his face and eyes, so that nobody could recognize him? However, he understood such a criminal act would make him even unhappier person than he had ever been! Paul remembered his times of begging when he had to walk his blind friends holding them by their hand. He could not imagine anyone being unhappier than someone who could not see.

Therefore, this way of dealing with the situation appeared unacceptable to him. But the thought of living his life as a decent person still seemed very captivating. However, he didn't know how to go about implementing it – was he better off leaving Julija and going to Warsaw to look for the opportunities there or cooking up something with his new victim?

One thing Paul was absolutely clear about, though, was that he needed a lot of money in order to put his plan to work, and Julija appeared to be the one who had lots of it. It couldn't be the other way if she was able to afford staying in the most expensive hotel in the town!

Paul wondered if she was some rich widow or maybe just a spinster which seemed very surprising to him that no one had noticed the beauty queen like her! Then the next thing, he made a decision not to let her go off his radar.

With those promising thoughts he got up off the bed and began dressing up in a hurry. The white shirt had already been worn by him a couple of times and, therefore, it wasn't completely clean. Not having the other choice, he had to content himself with wearing it that night.

Looking pretty beggarly, he was already standing at the front entrance of the White Foam hotel, and the door-keeper stopped him as he was trying to get in. However, as soon as Paul told the man the number of the room Julija was staying in, the door-keeper politely bowed, moved out of the way, and showed with his hand a wide staircase leading into a second floor.

When Paul walked to the second floor, he saw through the glass door an unbelievably beautiful lady sitting under a huge palm tree branched out clear up to the ceiling in the spacious lobby.

He didn't recognize her at first. But as soon as he stepped onto the polished with wax parquet, down on which he could even see his reflection, the lady got up gracefully off the soft armchair and slowly began moving towards him.

With a smile on her face, she uttered," Wow, you are so punctual! It's eight o'clock sharp now."

Paul could not believe his eyes this was the same Julija he had met at the seaside. He never in his entire life had seen a woman dressed so splendidly! In her hair gathered together high on the top of her head, she had expensive pins with colorful gems that were changing colors on their tips every time she moved her head. Ruby earrings like two drops of blood were handing down to the middle of her neck, looking as if they were just about ready to fall onto her halfway naked shoulders. In the middle of her chest, there was shining a big pin studded with various gems, which was holding together an elegant velvet shawl.

Julija was wearing long dress reaching clear down to the floor. Only the tips of her black shoes where showing from underneath of it. Her waist was wrapped with shiny black material making her look even slimmer.

Paul had almost to screw up his eyes as if looking at the bright sun.

"We are going to go to the restaurant," she offered after he didn't answer her.

"I don't know if you would like to show up with me looking like this at the restaurant."

"Don't say things like that. Besides, I've already reserved a table. We can have a good time listening to the music, watching people dancing, and we could even dance, too!"

Paul followed her along the corridor that was leading to the restaurant at the very end of it, located on the same second floor. As soon as they walked inside, the eyes or everyone there turned to Julija and followed her to their very table.

Right away, a waiter presented himself, leaned low forward complaisantly, and asked, "What would you like to order?"

"Well, Paul, what are we going to order? What do you wish to drink?"

"To tell the truth, I'm not hungry," Paul answered.

"We'll order something to eat later. For now, please bring us a little glass of liqueur and cognac and also some good chocolates and roasted almonds."

The order was delivered at a lightning speed. As soon as the waiter left, Julija raised her glass filled with the liqueur and said, "Paul, let's have a drink to our acquaintance."

Jazz began playing, and couples one after the other were coming out to dance in the middle of the restaurant where there was a round circle floor area, polished, slippery, and shiny, with many people already dancing on it. It appeared as if suddenly the entire restaurant had come to life with people laughing and talking loudly.

"How do you like it here?" she asked.

"It feels like heaven," he answered.

"Indeed, it's nice here. My restaurant in Vilnius is less modern, but also not any worse than this one."

"Do you own a restaurant?" Paul's eyes became wide open.

"I own a restaurant twice as big as this one and also a hotel that is three or four times as big with a parking lot for ten cars for the convenience of the guests. Have you ever been to Vilnius?"

"No, Miss Julija, I've never had an opportunity to be anywhere else but in Gdansk," he had no other choice but to lie in order to keep his past life of the beggar and thief a secret.

"That's right! I've already asked you this before. I suppose there is a reason why they say 'long hair but short wit'," she said jokingly. "Paul, have your parents ever lived in Vilnius?"

"No, Miss Julija. My father was born in Gdansk, and I doubt he had been any further in his life than that. My father doesn't know anything else in Gdansk but the harbor where he works. My mother is German by her descent, but I'm sure she has never been to Germany. As far as my father goes, he wouldn't even know the name of the city of Vilnius or where it is located. However, I've heard a lot about Vilnius myself from the history classes at my gymnasium. When I had studied the history there, it had seemed to me I had traveled to Vilnius for a short while in my mind. Polish history is closely related to that of Lithuania. I remember them teaching us about Polish-Lithuanian union. The grand Duke of Lithuania Wladyslaw II Jogiello had been the King of Poland as well and paved the way to the Poland's Golden Age. During my history lessons, I had always wondered about Vilnius, the famous ancient city. I remember devouring with my eyes the pictures of the Cathedral, the Gates of Dawn, St. Ann's Church, and the narrow lanes with arches there in our textbooks," Paul was passionately talking while gazing at the corner of the ceiling as if he was turning pages of his history textbook at that very moment.

"I also remember the St. John's Church with the tallest bell-tower in Vilnius and the Sts. Peter and Paul's Church that my own life is somewhat related to," he added.

As he pronounced those words, Julija gave a start, and a powerful current of excitement surged through her entire body. It seemed to her she heard an inner voice telling to her, 'that's where he had been abandoned'.

Suddenly, she hid her reddened face in her palms.

A huge diamond ring flashed in front of Paul's face that instantly attracted his attention.

"Are you okay?" he asked.

Julija quickly restrained herself and said, "A piece of almond got stuck in my throat making me choke. Let's have a drink."

She lifted her glass without waiting until he picks his and emptied her liqueur. Then she asked, "Please, continue talking."

"I was telling to you about Vilnius that I had in my imagination," he said.

"But you just mentioned that your life has been in some way tied up with Sts. Peter and Paul's Church. Can you elaborate on that a little more?" she sounded anxious since some inner voice whispered into her ear this was her lost beloved son.

"It's simply a coincidence my name is Paul, just like the name of that church in Vilnius that I have never seen in my life and only in the picture of the history book."

Now, Julija realized he wasn't her son and he had nothing to do with Robertas, either. She believed him when looking into his pure eyes so much resembling those of Robertas; Paul appeared to be too naïve to contrive.

Dancing couples returned to their tables as the music ceased playing.

"Paul, I hope you don't mind I am asking so many questions about your past when I have not told you anything about myself yet. You haven't even asked me anything. Aren't you interested in who you are sitting with at this table?"

"Miss Julija, I simply don't dare to pry about your life hoping you'll tell me about it yourself. This is a perfect moment to do this, and if you are ready, I am anxious to hear it."

"My life, Paul, is much longer than yours, and I have accumulated more stressful episodes, too. You are handsome, young, and your entire life is still ahead of you. It seems to me that the most beautiful days of my life have already gone. Now I can only recall the best moments of my life from the past and rejoice at them."

"Miss Julija, you shouldn't complain about your life. You are going against all good nature has gifted you with. You are beautiful, rich, respected by others. Is all that too little for you?! Everyone is looking at you and envying you right at this minute. You are shining like a star blinding with your jewelry all these people around!"

"You are right, Paul. I am shining, but this light isn't spreading warmth to anyone. It's just as cold as that of the moon. Yes I'm rich, but I am also unhappy. I would prefer happiness over all my riches. My life has been pretty turbulent; I've had short moments of happiness that I had to pay over the full measure for. I had loved, and I had been loved too, but still, I had been left alone. When I had been young, I had been a rich bride, but this didn't bring me happiness. Then, I lost almost all my wealth. Later on, the times changed, and I became rich again, even richer than I had been before the war. Besides the hotel I was telling you about, I own four best tailor shops in Vilnius together with fashion salons attached to them. I live in a beautiful home near Vilnius with a beautiful park outside of it where white and black swans swim in its ponds. I don't walk on foot but drive in limousines that I have ten all together! I go on vacation to Switzerland, Italy, Carpathian Mountains and meet whims and caprices of all the rich people. However, I don't feel happy. I don't have any relatives or other close people, and no one asks me to help them. True, I am being often invited to various parties and social entertainment events where I feel highly respected. But that is not enough for me to be a completely happy person. Many rich, old men had proposed to me, but I didn't want to sell myself to them. There were some young men who had wanted to marry me, too. However, it didn't take me long to figure out they had been more interested in my assets than in me personally. I could not be happy with someone like that after I had been madly in love with one youth, to whom I gave myself completely away, but he left me anyway, " Julija fell silent.

"What a villain!" Paul squeezed his hand into a fist. "Show him to me, and he will never have peace in his life!"

"You are young, Paul, and you don't know life yet. Let God judge him," Julija said placing her little, soft hand on his fist which Paul could feel quickly melted down like steel from the heat.

"I know," she continued, "you wouldn't be able to do anything like that. You are a good person. Hopefully, fate won't spoil you."

After hearing her talking like that, sweat stood out on Paul's forehead. Thoughts flooded his head whispering into his ear that he was much worse after what he had done to Janka. He realized he had no right to judge others.

Paul was surprised this woman made such a huge impact on him. She appeared to be practical, life-seasoned, but at the same time, she was innocent like a young girl. He was wondering how she could fall for his pretence to be a decent youth!

"Paul, I hope you don't mind me being so open with you. You honestly told me about yourself, and I wanted to pay you back the same way."

"Miss Julija, all your secrets are safe with me. After sharing them with me, you will feel much better."

"You are right," she said. "Therefore, I will share with you one more thing. But first, tell me what you are thinking of me. Do you find me to be attractive?" she asked and slipped down her shawl uncovering her bronze shoulders.

"You are gorgeous!"

"Paul, look at me – I'm just a doll that people like to look at. But wash all my cosmetics off, take all my jewelry off, and no one is going to look at me anymore. Sometimes when I come back from the parties, restaurants, and theaters, I stand before the mirror and ask myself who I am and what my purpose in this world is. Probably, I was born into this world just to be fed and smartened up in order to shine. Sometimes I feel so empty, not able to create anything worthy, and torn away from society like a dry branch of a tree. What accomplishments could I gift to humanity that I would be able to remember when I get old? Only empty desert is going to be around me with hungry wolves howling from ambush, waiting for me to die. Such is going to be my finale. However, I can't do anything about it."

"Miss Julija, you are too strict to yourself when you should enjoy every day of your life, since we live just once!"

"In a way you are right," she agreed. "Besides, that wasn't my goal to cry on your shoulder when I had invited you to come here. Let's better dance!"

"Do you mind people seeing you together with me dressed like this?"

"On the contrary – having in mind my age, I should triumph dancing with the young partner like you!" he retorted.

As soon as the music began playing, Julija got up and called the waiter with a movement of her head, who instantly presented himself at their table.

"When we finish dancing, bring us two beef-steaks, a glass of cognac, and a bottle of cold lemonade, please."

Then she headed to the dancing floor where a few couples were already spinning, and Paul followed her.

Julija's beautifully tanned arm touched Paul's shoulder, and next thing, they were already flying on the parquet. There were still just a few people on the floor, and the majority of the people at the tables were watching Julija and Paul dance.

Some of the guests in the restaurant could recognize Julija since they were used to seeing her every day of the past week when she was coming there alone dressed in fancy, different clothes every single time. This evening, though, she was here with this youth dressed in very modest clothing that didn't seem to be suitable for such a luxurious restaurant.

Julija and Paul danced about fifteen minutes and returned to their tables where their food was delivered for them without delay.

After they finished eating, Julija wiped her lips with a napkin and excused herself to go to the bathroom after what she returned with the lipstick back on her lips.

"Let's have a drink, Paul. We need to warm up our brain," she smiled at him, emptied a half of the glass, and placed an almond into her mouth.

At that time, the lights began to gradually go out, and finally, it became completely dark. All both of them could hear were only the sounds of the music and the steps of those dancing.

Julija was sitting all tensed up in the dark with her hands on the table anticipating Paul's hand to touch her hand.

Paul badly wanted to kiss her, but he had to fight his instincts with his teeth clenched. He could hardly withstand the pressure of his feelings.

The lights came back on revealing Julija still sitting all numb with her eyes fixed on the table.

"Well, it's time to go home; it's getting late," she said.

"I'm going to pay for the food and drinks," Paul offered.

"Oh no, the staff here is going to charge my account. You are my guest. I invited you, and I'm going to pay for everything myself."

Julija got up first, and Paul followed her to the glass door where she stretched her hand out to him and said, "I had such a great time with you. I won't forget you."

Julija gently squeezed his hand, smiled tenderly, and walked away along the same corridor they had come here, leaving Paul standing all dazzled.

When he returned to his little room, he fell with all his clothes into his bed where he lay until it began dawning. A lot of various thoughts not making much sense were swimming in his head, and if someone asked what he was thinking about, he would not be able to answer.

He got up late with a headache, washed his face with cold water, and ate in a simple dining-room of his hotel.

As Paul got outside, a hot, sunny day greeted him. In spite of that, he didn't go to the beach but crossed the fisherman village and went to the pine forest. There, he lay down in the shade of the thick pine tree and stayed there until lunch.

Paul couldn't understand what was happening to him; it didn't even occur to him he was in love with this mysterious woman. The only appreciable thing he could feel was some unexplainable longing that was tormenting him. The memories about yesterday's evening were all the time interlacing in his head sometimes gently caressing his stormy feelings and sometimes making him feel unusually lonely.

Thus, exhausted with his thoughts, he walked back to his hotel where a pleasant smell of cooking food was coming from the dining-room.

When he walked inside, he saw the dining-room crowded with people; mainly the fishermen and not holiday-makers had occupied all the tables there. They had not even changed their clothes after coming straight from the sea, and the stench of the fish could be felt around.

Some of them were avidly gulping borsch soup, and the others, their entire bodies over the tables, were loudly smacking their lips and washing the food down with foaming beer, sounding like pigs devouring swill.

After eating, some men were giving loud belches; they were stroking their stomachs with their greasy hands while leaning back. It was so smoky inside of the dining-room with the low ceiling it appeared as if there was no air to breathe there at all.

In one corner of the premise the men sitting around the table were already pretty drunk and laughing loudly. A couple of them were arguing while trying to prove something; they gesticulated with their hands energetically.

Paul wasn't paying much attention to this boring, 'gray' public in the dining-room. After finding a place to sit down at the table next to some other people, he hurriedly ate a meal he had ordered and walked away from this noisy 'beehive', rattling with dishes.

Then he returned to his room, lay down, and got quickly asleep. However, bad dreams tormented him not letting to rest properly.

When he woke up and went outside, terrible heat greeted him. He didn't seek refuge in the forest this time. Instead, he walked by the White Foam hotel and went straight to the beach that was teeming with people, just like yesterday. They were everywhere – in the sea, in the dunes, and on the beach itself.

Walking among the people, Paul was looking around trying to find Julija.

He passed the place where both of them were sitting before; he recognized it by a knoll of the sand that he himself had poured together and stuck some sea shells around. Their place was empty.

Paul stopped for a short while feeling immense heartbreak. In his mind, he was debating what he should do next – keep looking for her or run away from here, and if to do the latter, then where to go next?

Then he kneeled on the sand by his little hillock, dropped his shirt on the ground, and began making another circle of the shells around it; he was wondering if he should go to Warsaw in order to reunite with Janka. At the same time, he regretted he would never be able to see Julija again.

Suddenly, he heard a voice from above, "Hello, Paul. What are you doing here?"

"Oh hello, Miss Julija," he uttered and jumped to his feet.

"Looks like fate ordained to thrown us back together. There is a saying that no one can hide from his or her destiny," she spoke in good spirits.

"To tell the truth, I've come here looking for you," he said.

"I came here in the morning myself, but you were not here. I don't know why but time was dragging for me so slowly after yesterday when we had had such a great time. I think, I had been too open with you at the restaurant. I have to admit I have never told my secrets to anyone else but you. No one in the last twenty years has learned from me even half of what I told you yesterday in one hour! You probably thought – what a silly woman!"

"Your guess is not correct. I think after a woman shares her pain with a person she can trust, she feels liberated as if a huge stone went off her heart. In your case, you are not risking anything since soon each of us is going to go our own ways. Even if after our separation I wanted to reveal your secrets to the others, I wouldn't be able to find anyone who knows you. Therefore, no one would get interested in your life story. The impact, of course, could be completely different if the same information would be passed among acquaintances because it could multiply like some virus or bacteria. Some people can make mountains out of molehills!"

"I think I would be the same sincere with you even if you lived in Vilnius. For some reason, meeting with you made me lose my balance. Would you like to have a swim with me?" she asked. "It's so hot that there is not enough air to breath. I've already swum three times and still want to immerse myself into the water."

"Where did you leave your stuff? Aren't you afraid someone can steal it?"

"It's a trifle. It's just my bath-robe and a purse with a little bit of money and cosmetics in it."

The next thing, Paul was already walking after Julija further and further into the sea until she immersed herself under the water and began making splashes with her feet.

Thus, Paul and Julija kept meeting every day on the beach, and in the evenings, they would go to the restaurant where she was shining like a star again blinding not only him but also all other guests around them.

This way, two weeks passed with them not separating from each other even for one day. During that time, they never became angry with each other. Contrarily, they became so attached to one another that every time Julija and Paul separated, they would anxiously wait for tomorrow to come so that they could be together again.

However, time was ruthless to both of them, and the day had come when Julija said she had to go back to Vilnius in a couple of days.

When the evening came, Paul offered her not to go to the restaurant but to see the sun on the beach which made Julija very happy.

And even after the sun went down, they remained sitting on the loose sand. At that moment, a refreshing, cool breeze blew out from the South. It was becoming stronger and stronger very fast. Next thing, it gathered some dark clouds above their heads that lightning crossed with its illuminating flash, and the rumbling of the thunder was heard.

The wind kept getting stronger; the sky was now flashing unceasingly.

"Are you cold? You can put my jacket on," he offered.

"But then, you are going to be cold."

"I'll be fine," he covered her with his jacket but didn't take his arm away off her shoulders.

Since she didn't show any signs of resistance, he pulled her closer to him and put his arms around her waist. Again, she didn't object to this kind of closeness.

Now, their conversation came suddenly to an end.

Both of them were sitting plunged in thoughts looking at the distance where the sky was merging with the sea.

The storm was getting closer. Paul brought himself to become even more intimate with Julija; he squeezed her thigh in his arms.

Julija answered him by placing her head on his shoulder after what he couldn't handle it any longer. He found her lips and glued his hot lips to hers.

After the first passionate kiss quieted down, the strong wind blew wailing from the side of the black cloud that brought in the first big drops of rain. The sea really began to rage as if threatening this couple in love that unknowingly was breaking the law of decency.

"Paul, we should leave now," she said when another bright lightning crossing the dark clouds that had gathered right above their heads. The thunder was imminently aiming at them.

Julija was the first to get up. Paul followed her example. Then he was walking next to her while holding her arm.

As they reached the White Foam hotel, it was already raining cats and dogs.

Julija took his jacket off her shoulders and offered, "Come in to my room, and you can wait there until the rain stops. You can't go back to the fisherman village in this kind of weather."

Paul didn't refuse. He obediently followed her. As both of them approached the front desk, she asked for a key.

She was the first to walk into her suite where she turned on the light. Instantly, a big chandelier lit up the unbelievably huge room looking more like a hall with two rows of soft chairs lined up along the two walls.

In the opposite corner by the glass door leading to a balcony there was a small, round, polished table standing on one leg. Its surface was shining in the artificial light of the chandelier as if it had been made of glass. Next to it, along the wall, a narrow sofa with a tall back was standing, and two soft chairs were on the other side of it. Another corner was filled with a big, widely branched out ficus plant with two armchairs facing each other underneath it. In the middle of the room, a big Persian carpet was spread out that was literally blooming and bursting out with all kinds of colors.

Just now Paul noticed a white marble statue standing close to the door in the third corner between the rows of the chairs. It was about one and a half meter tall with three beautiful girls on the pedestal trying to catch a pigeon that had been fixed to the wall right above their heads. The wire holding the bird was a little bent down from its weight.

"Would you like to see the entire suite?" Julija asked.

"I would love to!"

She took his arm and walked him to another door, "This is my bathroom with the shower, and this door leads to my cosmetics room."

The cosmetics room was pretty big in size with mirrors standing next to each wall. There was an oblong table covered with glass in the corner there, too, loaded with an army of little bottles, scissors, tweezers, sprayers, and all kinds of other trifles and various small things the purpose of which Paul didn't know let alone to know their names. In this room, it was possible to see yourself in all the sides.

Then she took him to the bedroom where two low but wide beds were standing put together in the middle of the room. There were also two huge four door wardrobes there. On both sides of the beds, there were standing low rise dressers covered with glass. The bed was already made and a light kimono robe was lying on the low soft stool right next to the bed.

As they returned to the luxurious living room, Julija asked, "How do you like my suite?"

She offered Paul to sit down and pushed an electric button on the wall.

"Heavenly! It's difficult to believe some people live like this."

A quiet bell was heard, and when Julija opened the door, the servant asked, "How may I help you, Miss Julija?"

"Please, bring us something to eat: smoked ham, hot hunters' sausages, a bottle of good cognac, chocolate, bourbon wine, lemonade, and two portions of salad."

After receiving the order, the youth servant bowed down and quickly but quietly left. In about five minutes, before a real conversation between Julija and Paul even began, a small cart loaded with dishes rolled into the hotel suite.

The servant promptly placed some plates and bottles on the table leaving the rest of the stuff on the cart that he pushed closer to the table. He poured some spirit on the sausages and lit them up;

they instantly got engulfed in blue flames. Then he opened the bottles, bowed down, and swiftly left.

"Paul, let's refresh ourselves. I personally am very hungry."

While the last little tongue of the bluish flame was dancing on the meat, Julija filled their little glasses with cognac and urged him, "Let's have a drink. It will warm us up from inside."

During their late supper, the storm outside was raging while threatening with thunder and lightning, and the rain was pouring right onto the glass of the windows. However, the roaring of the Baltic Sea far exceeded all the other noises. It appeared as if the entire White Foam hotel was shaking.

Soon, the hunters sausages disappeared from the plate and the bottle of cognac was standing halfway empty.

Both Julija and Paul's brain got hot. They were feeling satiated and content.

"Miss Julija, I would like to tell you something very important. May I also ask you to turn off some of the lights in the room; they make my eyes hurt."

She turned off the chandelier leaving only a small lamp, fixed to the opposite wall, on that had been covered with a frosted glass. The entire huge room submerged into twilight.

Julija sat down next to him on the sofa and asked, "Is it too dark now?"

"No, it's just right," he answered.

The lightning was time from time illuminating the room and leaving it dark again in between the flashes.

"Didn't you say you wanted to tell me something important?" she asked.

"Yes I did, but I'm afraid you won't approve my feelings for you."

"Take a risk," she enticed him to talk. "I want to hear about your feelings for me."

Paul took Julija's hand into his, squeezed it tightly, and looked attentively deep into her eyes.

Then he lowered his eyes onto the floor and asked in a timid, barely audible voice, "Miss Julija, I love you."

For a while neither one of them uttered a word. Only noise of the crashing waves was disturbing the deaf silence once in a while being drowned with the faraway rumbling of the thunder.

Surprisingly, the darkness in the room was now beginning to complicate the situation making both of them feel awkward.

At last, Paul broke this uncomfortable silence, "You have given me no answer yet."

However, she didn't say anything again. She only shrugged her shoulders a couple of times and continued looking in front of her, somewhere in the middle of the room.

"Why aren't you talking to me?" he asked getting impatient.

"I knew you were not indifferent to me, but I never expected you to admit it," she answered at last.

"How could you possibly know about my feelings for you?"

"I'm no longer a sixteen-year-old girl who is not able to see things like that. I just felt it."

"Miss Julija, I can't believe this has happened to me. I have never loved anyone in my entire life. Every time we parted for the night, I felt some unexplainable longing. Then, every time I saw you again, my eyes lighted up. I can't imagine how I will be able to separate from you. In addition to that, I don't have any friends who I could share my dreams and concerns with. You have been the only person who took my loneliness away for a while. Moreover, you are capable of haring me out, and I loved our sincere conversations! I will never forget those wonderful days spent with you. I'm not sure if you like listening to me since I have never been good at expressing my feelings. I hope I'm not burdening you too much."

"Paul, you can't imagine how happy I am hearing you talk like this. Now that I know I'm being loved by you, I must answer you the same way in return for your sincerity. I love you dearly, too. It's only sad our love lasted for such a short time. Tomorrow is the last day we can spend together because the day after tomorrow we must part and only God knows if we will ever meet again. And if it's not meant to be, then I want you to know that I wish you a lot of happiness in your life. I understand that we would not be able to enjoy our relationship for long in either case. You are young, Paul, and your love would go out just like a match which burns brightly for a few seconds and then goes out. In spite of that, I love you with all my heart and all my soul! I will always be glad I had an opportunity to spend two unforgettable weeks with you that will never fade away from my memory. I hope we will separate like good friends. The storm is over now, and you may go back to your hotel. I would like you to have a good rest and, then, come and see me early in the morning."

Julija was the first to get up off the sofa, and Paul followed her. When they walked to the door, he bowed down, took her small, soft like a down hand, and kissed it.

At that moment, she also kissed him on the top of his head. When Paul straightened himself up, he saw her eyes filled with tears. He couldn't leave when seeing her crying; he hugged her waist with both his arms, pulled her close to himself, and gently kissed her on the lips. He didn't dare to express his passion.

When Paul left, heartbroken Julija, her hands shaking, filled up her little glass with cognac, drank it to the bottom, fell on the bed, and began weeping bitterly. Pretty soon, she was crying convulsively with her face buried in the pillow, trying to suppress her loud sobbing.

When Julija finally calmed down a little, she got up with difficulty, walked to the window, and looked outside through the curtain. Not being able to see a soul alive, she opened the balcony door, stepped on it, and even leaned over the railing to see if she could spot Paul standing somewhere outside on the pavement. After being assured he wasn't there, she walked back inside and then to the front door of her suite.

Then she returned to the sofa and sat down. However, tears began strangling Julija again and she, feeling restless, walked to the bedroom where she took off her clothes leaving them right on the floor. She put her nightgown on and fell onto her bed but didn't have strength to cover herself with the blanket. Now, she gave way to the tears, her face buried in the pillow again, grieving her unhappy love that had so unexpectedly stirred up her feelings.

In a meanwhile, Paul was sitting in a hallway holding his palms over his head and thinking what he should do next.

Then he walked back to the door of her suite and knocked on it quietly a few times. When Julija didn't answer, he pushed the door, and it opened up itself. To his big surprise, it wasn't locked.

Paul walked inside the dark room on his tiptoes. Through the opened door of the bedroom, the hollow sobbing could be heard.

Carefully like a thief he slipped into the bedroom where Julija dressed only in her gown was lying on her bed with her face hidden in the pillow.

He quietly walked up to her and gently placed his hand on her shoulder. Paul wasn't in time to say a word when she jumped up and, looking at him with her eyes wide open in astonishment, asked, "How did you end up here!? What happened to you?"

"Yes, something has really happened to me, and I've come back to tell you what it is. The door happened to be unlocked. If you don't want me here, you are free to turn me out of your suite."

"I would never turn you out!" she exclaimed. "What happened?"

"I'll tell you but, first, please tell me why you are crying so grievously as if you have buried someone."

"Yes, you are right. I've buried you in my bleeding heart."

"My Dear, I don't want to die."

"I have placed you in the best place in my heart, though," she said.

"I've come here to talk not about death but about life. While sitting outside in the lobby, I came to a conclusion that I don't want to live without you being present in my life. And that is why I've come back to you."

"Paul, what are you talking about?! Are you sure about that?"

"I am sure! I have been thinking only about you for the last two weeks. I love you, and you love me. What else do we need? I want us to get married and be happy."

"Paul, how could I be your wife? I am much older than you! Maybe I could make you happy for ten years, but just knowing we are not meant to be together, would make me unhappy. I could not handle that. Please, let's not talk about it," she entreated.

"I'm not asking for anything else from you – just be mine," he got on his knees and placed his head in Julija's lap.

"My Dear, I can't become your wife," she said while tousling his thick hair, "but you can ask for anything else your heart desires. If you wish, I could give you money to go to Switzerland, Italy, or Paris."

"Do you find anything wrong with me? Why don't you want me?"

"There is nothing wrong with you," she said. "But it would definitely be something wrong with me if I allowed it to happen. Why don't you want to take the money? I have enough of it. I could make you the luckiest youth."

Paul began kissing her knees with his hands wandering through her thighs.

Julija was trying to suppress her passion and implored him to stop being so daring but Paul didn't hear her supplication.

He continued passionately caressing her trembling body while showering her with the kisses.

Julija for the last time gathered all her strength; she put her arms against his wide, muscular chest ready to offer resistance to his passion.

As she opened her eyes, she saw burning desire in his eyes, too. For a split second, it seemed Robertas was again with her! The memory when they had been making love on the Sapezinka hill many years ago vividly flashed in her mind.

Gradually, her arms began to bend until they totally collapsed under his weight, and Paul got total possession of Julija's feelings.

The Baltic Sea was raging while menacing them with this act of sacriledge.

The next morning as soon as the sun came up, Paul was the first to open his eyes. He saw Julija sleeping by him and remembered how they had reveled in the passion of love all night long.

Again, they spent the time together completely devoting themselves to each other, and that day turned for them into their honey day. They enjoyed every minute laughing, making love, and swimming in the sea.

However, the time to part had come, and again, Paul begged Julija to marry him. However, she was adamant in her belief that their age difference could bring no happiness to either one of them.

"Paul, I already gave you myself all. Please, believe me – this is for your own good."

"I believe you, Julija, but I refuse to disavow my feelings. You will be mine no matter what! Yes, I will go home and find the way to get some money even if I had to commit an offence. Please, don't say we are parting forever! You are like the sun to me – how could I want to lose you?! You are my happiness; I must be with you. I love you so much that no one else could love you like this! I could carry you in my arms. I would spare my life for you!"

"Paul, I appreciate you but, please, don't go to Vilnius. Better wait for me to come here next summer, and we will be together again. In a meanwhile, I don't want you working at the seaport. Therefore, go to my bedroom and get from my purse as much money as you need. In a meanwhile, I will walk to the owner of the hotel and order the car."

When he opened the wardrobe door, he saw a lot of jewelry on the shelf there that blinded him for a second with their bright sparkling.

Instantly, he forgot about everything in the entire world. He had never seen so many precious gems in one place!

Compelled by instinct, he grabbed the jewels with his both hands. Then he suddenly stopped wondering what happened to him just of a suddenly.

However, he soon forgot about all the scruples, and the jewelry was already in his pockets.

Now he felt like running away which meant he would part with Julija forever because of some spangles that for a while made him forget about everything, including her. Those gems had belonged to her, and he stole them from her, from the woman who was supposed to be the most precious to him in the entire world!"

Some imperceptible power forced him to put all the jewelry back on the shelf. Instead, he picked her purse that was lying there too, took out of it one hundred zloty, put the money in his pocket, and left the remaining three hundred zloty in her purse.

He was still standing by the opened door of the wardrobe not sure why he was doing this. After all, he could take the three hundred leaving her only a hundred zloty.

A thought crossed his mind that if he had happened to be here the first day they had met, all her jewelry and money would had been gone. Then, he would have disappeared together with all his plunder.

However now, he peacefully put her purse back, closed the door of the wardrobe, and went back to the living room.

Soon, Julija returned and informed him, "The limousine will be here in half an hour and we will have to leave. Would you, please, help me gather my stuff? The maidservant is coming to take my luggage, and I don't want her to see any of my things."

When they went to the bedroom, Julija opened her purse and asked, "Did you get some money?"

"One hundred zloty," he replied.

"You should take more; you are not going to get very far with just one hundred."

"It will be enough; I'm not used to squandering money. Moreover, I don't even have where to spend it. And it should be enough for my trip back home."

"Well, you know better," she was pleasantly surprised learning he was so economical.

Julija took the jewelry into her cupped hands and placed it into her purse. Before closing it, she walked to Paul, who was standing by the window and looking outside and said, "Paul, take this jewelry, it will come in handy to you."

"What could I do with it? If someone saw me wearing your jewelry, they would start laughing at me."

"But you, Paul, could sell it and make a significant amount of money."

"I have money," had said pretending to be naïve.

A thought he was too innocent crossed her mind. Then she wondered if he would stay that way if they actually got married. How long would he have the strength to fight the power of the money? Probably not even a year later, he would turn into a greedy dragon.

She quickly snapped her purse and care-free threw it on the bed. Then, she wound her bare arms around his neck and began kissing him passionately.

However, their pleasant moment was interrupted by the maid, who knocked on the suite door. She came to pack Julija's things into the suit-cases. Soon, the limousine arrived as well where the twelve big suit-cases were crammed not only in its luggage carrier but inside of the car itself, too.

After long and tearful good-bye Julija got on the very back seat of the limousine and was looking at Paul standing in the middle of the street all the way until the car turned around the corner leaving only his image in her mind.

After arriving in Vilnius, Julija was often reliving her vacation memories thinking of the time ahead when she would be able to see Paul again.

Even though Julija was spending most of her time at home, her good acquaintance Gertruda quickly learned about her arrival from vacation. Both of them had met at a party ten years ago and had been associating closely since.

As soon as she entered the waiting-room in Julija's home, she began lively chattering, "Miss Julija, I'm so glad you are back. How was your vacation? Please, tell me all about it."

Gertruda kissed her girlfriend on her cheek and resumed her clattering, "You have such beautiful suntan. And in general, looks like you don't get old, Julija; you just keep blooming. I have to admit I envy you. Your beauty, like the Aurora Borealis, probably charmed quite a few young men during your vacation. But I've come here not in order to be carried away by your beauty. Every woman is a competitor to each other. One way or the other, I'm here to infuse some warmth into your heart."

"Thank you, Gertruda, for your pleasant compliments you've showered me with so generously."

"Julija, you can't imagine how much I have been waiting for you to return from your vacation! I'm not sure if I have told you about my teacher who had taught me Latin twenty years ago and whom I had fallen in love with. Back then, I had been very young and stupid. I had thought that being rich gave me right to disrespect my teacher. Thus, with my impudent behavior I had managed to antagonize my love from the very beginning! I've made some more mistakes later, too, which changed the entire course of my life. I wished I would had been more gentle with my words when talking to my teacher back then, and I would probably be happily married to him now! Can you believe, Julija, three days ago, I met him totally unexpectedly in the street after so many years! I asked him some questions about his personal life. When I learned that he was not married, I was silly enough to tell him I would divorce my husband in order to be with him. He refused me motivating that he would never participate in breaking up another family. It turned out to be he is now highly educated person with the doctor's degree in Philosophy from the University of Warsaw. Moreover, he manages the entire department of Philosophy in the University of Warsaw and teaches there Latin and German languages as well as philosophy. He is very interesting to talk to. I'm throwing a party in his honor this Sunday. That is why I've come to you - to invite you to participate there, too. You never know what's going to happen – he is not married, and you are a free bird, also. He is no longer young, but he is not old, either. Therefore, you both would make a perfect couple!"

"Gertruda, thank you for the invitation and your concern for my happiness, but I have never complained to you about being unhappy or wanting to get married. I'm very content with my life now! And as far as the marriage goes, I don't intend to shackle myself with the marital chains. I prefer to stay free!"

"Julija Dear, it's too bad since you both seem to be meant for each other. Despite this, I'm not going to bother you about that anymore. Do whatever is best for you, but you still must come to my house this Sunday."

When the day of the reception at Gertrudas' house came, Julija put on a very simple but elegant dress in order not to attract anyone's attention. This was the first time when she gave so little attention to herself since her only adornment was just her long ball gown. Besides it, she wasn't wearing any jewelry as she always used to do before.

She got into a limousine that took her to Gertruda's splendid home. Julija didn't have any desire to go to this reception. Therefore, at one point, she almost wanted to ask the driver to take her back home. However, at the same time, she was feeling obligated to her girlfriend Gertruda, whom she had known, as it seemed to her, for ages.

A man-servant who was standing at the widely opened main entrance bowed down as soon as he saw Julija, whom he had known for a long time. Right away, he invited her to come into the luxurious lobby with statues made of bronze and marble standing in every corner.

Julija was well familiar with this house.

As soon as Gertruda saw her girlfriend, she graciously took her by the arm and introduced her to some of the guests Julija had never met before.

"Now let's go I will introduce you to one more person. I told you about him yesterday."

Gertruda took Julija by her arm again and walked with her to some grayish haired man. He seemed somewhat familiar to Julija. However, as soon as Gertruda uttered his name, Julija instantly became dazzled.

"Miss Julija, this is Mister Robertas." Then she looked at him and said, "Julija is my best girlfriend. Remember - I told you that I had wanted to introduce her to you."

Julija didn't hear Gertrudas' words; only some rumbling was sounding in her ears, and it began getting dark in her eyes, too. She wasn't even able to stretch her hand to him, and she only moaned in a quiet, painful voice, "Oh my God..."

"Julija, what has happened to you?" Holding her by the arm, Gertruda asked in a frightened voice. "Are you okay?"

"I am feeling giddy. It will go away... Probably I've spent too much time in the sun. It had happened to me before, too."

"Mister Robertas, please, help me walk Julija to that little table over there. It should be more comfortable for her to sit down now. I am going to get her something cold and refreshing to drink."

With their help, Julija was brought to the remote corner where two soft chairs were standing on one of which she was seated.

"How are you feeling, Julija?" Gertruda asked.

"Thank you. It has already gone away."

"Thanks are to God! You scared me so much; my hands are still shaking. I will give an order to bring some cold kvass. It usually refreshes as soon as it wets the palate."

A clay pitcher was brought in with a clay cup together, and Gertruda poured a half of it of kvass and gave it to Julija.

After Julija had a few sips of this tasty drink that was a little sour and sweet at the same time, her eyes really brightened up.

At that moment, more guests walked in through the front door, and Gertruda had to leave the two of them.

Julija was holding the cup in her hand afraid to lift her eyes and look at him.

Robertas was still standing beside the chair and holding the back of it firmly with his both hands; he didn't dare to say a word. He was feeling so stunned, so broken he could hardly stand on his both legs.

"How are you feeling, Julija?" the voice of Gertruda approaching them fast was heard.

"Great," she answered as if nothing had happened.

"I'm glad you are feeling better. I have not finished introducing you to each other," she chattered out lively.

"We have already got acquainted with Mister Robertas. I can't complain – he is a very pleasant person. However, I still can't get back to myself. I hope Mister Robertas is going to forgive me for my unwariness; I've made him stand for so long. Please, sit down Mister Robertas. Gertruda, I think you should take care of the other guests. They need you more than we do, don't they, Mister Robertas?" asked Julija looking at him with strained smile on her face. Now, he appeared to be even more confused.

The new party of guests burst into the lobby. Gertruda again retreated, and their conversation came to an end but not for long this time.

"Mister Robertas, please sit down. I feel very uncomfortable when you are standing. It seems as if you want to run away from me, and I am holding you from doing that. Believe me – I won't be bothersome. We can touch only pleasant subjects. Tell me please how you are doing. I've heard a lot of nice things about you and your achievements in science. I have to admit I'm proud of you! Very little people refuse from easy commercial profits and do difficult scientific work. Your policy is very praiseworthy. "

"Yes indeed, I've succeeded in achieving pretty high level in science. You would think anyone should be happy with that. Not me, though! You mentioned commerce thinking that I had been involved in it before. This is not so; I have never had anything to do with the commerce. It had been only the myth that I had created myself. I could tell you more about it but, I guess, there is no sense in doing that now. I would rather take advantage of our unexpected meeting and learn how you spent the past twenty years. Of course, I realize you had to go through a lot of heartbreak because of my actions that you would never be able to forgive me."

"Obviously, during those more than twenty years a lot of water flowed under the bridges. The terrible war swept through, which shook the entire Europe. Then, a few years had to pass by in order for life to get back on track. As about me, I never was mad at you. I had probably been the biggest culprit myself of everything that happened between us. I had been only sixteen years old then; no wonder I had not realized the consequences I would have to deal with later on in my life paying a huge price for my irresponsible behavior. I had been madly in love with you and had felt like an innocent child or any girl or youth feel when they experience their first love. How could I under those circumstances be angry with you? On the contrary - I had adored you; at times, I had been afraid of merely looking in your eyes. When I realized I had been left alone and without any help in such a difficult situation, I saw salvation for a while only in death. Nevertheless, even at that critical time in my life, I didn't blame you. You remained my shining ideal to me. As you can see, I am still alive and well. It means nothing bad happened."

They talked for a long time, and Julija told him in detail about her life. However, she never mentioned anything about one thing that interested Robertas the most.

"Julija, you have told me so much about yourself, but there is one more very important subject to me that I still would like to know about."

"I don't know, Robertas, what is important to you. Let me know – I don't have any secrets from you. And even if I had something I had wanted to keep to myself, it has died out by now. Therefore, there is no reason hiding what we both already know. Of course, I could have forgotten to tell you something. In that case, forgive me please – I had to suffer through so much."

"Julija, I don't know if you would like to discuss this, but I really want to know about it. What I mean is that before we had separated... had you been expecting a child then? What happened after that?"

"Yes... I had given a birth," Julija said and cast an inquiring look at Robertas, whose forehead was covered with drops of sweat.

At that moment, she felt sorry for him when looking at his tired, full of grief face. After all, maybe he hadn't been as guilty as she had thought.

Then, Gertruda's husband showed up in the middle of the lobby and loudly asked all the guests to go to the second floor for the feast.

Without being able to find out anything in the concrete, Robertas rose up from his seat after Julija, wiped his forehead with his handkerchief, and followed her. She looked like some beauty queen walking with her head up high triumphing, and he resembled a shadow following her from behind with his head down.

As they approach the wide staircase, Julija stopped and cast a glance at the totally confused Robertas, and she pitied him.

In order to distract him a little bit, she asked, "Robertas, please help me climb up these steep stairs." Then she nudged him on his side with her slightly bent arm letting him know he can take her arm.

As soon as he placed his hand around her arm above the elbow, Julija pressed it closer to her side, and she could instantly feel his hand shaking. Then she pressed it even harder to herself showing him she was not indifferent to him. If not for the last encounter at the seaside, she probably would had renewed her relationship with Robertas right away since it turned out that the feeling of her first love had still been lying deep in her heart for all these years! Now, it was getting out into daylight from underneath of all the layers of events and relationships with other people; her love for Robertas was beginning to smolder, warming her heart more and more.

Unfortunately, there was no other convenient opportunity for them to continue their important conversation. At the end of the reception when the guests began leaving, Julija also bid farewell to Gertruda and left. Robertas saw her off and helped her to get into the limousine.

"Julija, I think we should meet. I hope I could mitigate the situation for you. May I ask you for your address? I could come and visit you tomorrow, or we could meet somewhere."

"Where are you staying in Vilnius? I could give you a lift, and we will make arrangements in the car about our next meeting."

"I'm staying at "Viktorija" hotel. It would be nice if you could take me there, of course, if it's not too far away from your route home."

"According to the policy of my business, it is my responsibility to serve my guests. I own the Viktorija hotel. Therefore, I would be glad to deliver you to the very front entrance. I could come and see you tomorrow, but I don't know the number of the room you are staying in since I still don't know your last name."

Upon parting with him, her heart began trembling when he bent down to kiss her hand.

Julija returned to her house in Verkiai. The next day after breakfast she arrived at the Viktorija Hotel where Robertas was already anxiously waiting for her.

As soon as he heard knocking on the door, he threw a magazine to the side. He was amazed seeing Julija dressed in a white dress and looking so beautiful!

"I have started waiting for you a long time ago even thought I had known well you were not going to come before this time."

As soon as Julija sat down, Robertas resumed their yesterday's interrupted conversation, "Did you give a birth to a girl or a boy?"

"Men usually like sons better; they make them proud. And I gave birth not to one but to two sons! However, back then, there was no one to rejoice with over their coming into this world. We were forgotten by others. Therefore, I could not experience much happiness in relation to their birth. It was rather an unwanted birth – like some burden to every one of us. Therefore, I had to hide my pregnancy from the entire world. Then, the war came; hardships began piling up one after another. It's still difficult for me to recall those days of misery that terrify me every time I remember them."

Suddenly, Julija hid her face in her palms and burst into tears.

Robertas, seeing her like this, was at such a loss that he didn't know how to comfort grieving Julija.

When she calmed down a little, he asked, "Did the children die?"

"No, they lived. Probably they are still alive."

"Where are they?"

"I don't know. I had been in such a regrettable state back then. If not for the war, I would have been able to support them. Not getting any help from anyone, I took the boys to the Sts. Peter and Paul's Church and left them by the door of the sacristy there. It would be difficult for you, Robertas, to understand what huge pain I had suffered, how much I had had to endure! I had been so lonely, forgotten, and abandoned by everyone. I had been just too young and inexperienced in life then. I had been afraid of everything, but the most I had been worried about was that my guardians could find out about my children. If you were there, you could have at least advised me what course to take in regards to that, but I had been left totally alone with the two children! Even under those circumstances, I had been able to take care of them for about six months without anyone finding out about them."

She fell silent, gave a deep sigh, and then continued, "When I submitted my children to their fate, a dean from a pulpit at the church accused refugees for abandoning the twins. Vilnius then had been full of people leaving because of the raging war. Later on when Germans occupied the city, I was so disappointed in life that I could not even think about the children. In spite of this, maternal instinct soon woke up inside of my heart, and I began giving a sacristan financial aid because he had provided a shelter for my little boys. However, when Germans retreated from Vilnius and the governments changed, my family situation got significantly worse. We lost almost all our assets. Only our homestead in Verkiai that had also been totally robbed was still barely surviving which didn't let my aunt and uncle be totally destroyed. However, when apathy took a hold of me the second time, I couldn't find strength to recover as fast as I had done before. Only because of a lucky coincidence and with the help of some good people I was able to take care of my tailor shop which put us back on our feet very soon. Around that time, I also got back my hotel with the restaurant. That is when my life began flourishing. I no longer was a teenage girl but a grown up woman capable of reasoning and making my own decisions without anyone interfering with my business affairs. That is when I decided it was the best time to bring my boys home, but as ill luck would have it, it was already too late. I had not known then that if I had only come to the Sts. Peter and Paul's Church on one particular day just a few hours earlier, I would have found one of my sons there because the dean of the church had still seen him early in the morning on that day. The dean told me that my other son had been adopted by some nice couple prior to that. They had had no children of their own. The sacristan who had raised our boys had been already very old and sick. For a while, he had not been able to get out of his bed. Therefore, our little one had to beg for money sitting at the front door of the church which had helped them both to survive. When the sacristan passed away, our boy probably lived all by himself in that damp half basement. I've been there – the poverty there had been so horrible it's impossible to describe it. Our son had been a good boy, better that you and me put together. Because of our fault he had to suffer so grievously. To this very day, I can't forgive myself for the crime I had committed. I've lost not only my children but the peace of mind, too."

Julija began crying bitterly again covering her face with her hands. However, this time, her sobbing didn't last long since all her tears had been already cried out.

Then Robertas also told her his side of the story in detail admitting that he, too, had highly regretted for the meanness he had done with his cruel behavior. Only now, he revealed to Julija he had never been the son of the factory owner and, instead, he had lived in a very poor family. Therefore, he couldn't even dream about the marriage. As about the abortion, he had not had enough money to pay for it, also, in order to help Julija, even if he had sold all their family assets. He was explaining to Julija that, later on, when he had been lucky to get a job, it had already been too late for him to help her. Being chased by fear, he forgot about everything, including his sacred duty to Julija, and ran away from Vilnius all together. Then the war descended upon Europe. Nevertheless, thanks to good luck, he succeeded in putting his life in order.

After having finished his story, he fell on his knees and asked her for forgiveness as well as for her permission to find their sons. He was very afraid she would never pardon him for the suffering she had to go through because of him.

"It's too bad our life worked out this hapless way, but I think destiny already had punished us for our wrong doings. If not for the war and our inexperience in life, we could hug our sons now when they are already grownups," she said.

"Would you let me find them? And you wouldn't drive me away, too?" he asked looking in her eyes pleadingly.

"They are not only my children but yours as well. What right would I have to separate them from their own father or forbid them to experience your love?!"

"Julija, you have an unbelievably noble heart! I've done so much damage to your life, and you don't even bear any malice toward me. I'm proud of you. We are gonna find our children, and we all are going to be very happy! If you have nothing against it, we could even get married."

"It could be a little late already," she answered. "I fell in love with one youth. The only bad thing is that he is very young, and I'm afraid he could be just temporarily blinded by his love towards me. The reason why I've fallen in love with him, too, was because he looks just like you when you had been young. Even now, when I am looking into your eyes, I see the look of his eyes. The only difference is that your eyes appear tired and his are lively, bright - just like yours had been when we were young."

"You say he is young and looks like me? Is it possible that..."

"No, Robertas, I've already found that out," she cut him off.

"Don't rush into the relationship," he asked. "You had already experienced the heartburn of love. He might be a good person. However, he also has right to know the truth about you and me. If he finds that out later from someone else, it could be a huge blow to him. He probably wouldn't be able to forgive you. Think before making such a drastic move in your life and know that you always have me as your devoted friend."

Julija spent the entire morning with Robertas. Then she invited him to have lunch at the restaurant where they set another date for the next day in the afternoon.

After taking care of some business in the city, Julija only in the late afternoon returned home where an unexpected surprise was awaiting her.

As soon as her limousine stopped by the veranda of her house in Verkiai, not having a presentiment of anything just about ready to happen, Julija walked into the waiting-room where she saw Paul standing by the window and smiling at her.

This was the least she was expecting! It was just too much for her to handle at once – she had no time to habituate herself to one man, and the other one was already making his way into her life! She was getting too overwhelmed with all the latest events that so unexpectedly caught up with her.

However, Julija didn't give herself away. Instead, she pretended to be pleasantly surprised. Smiling, she stretched her hand to him which Paul kissed a few times.

"I have never expected you would come to my home, especially because it has happened so soon. How long have you been waiting here? And how did you even found out where I live?!"

"I've been standing here for about an hour and a half now. Maybe it doesn't seem like a very long time, but it felt like an eternity to me! I guess if I was in someone else's house, I would feel totally different. Every little thing here excites me since I know it's related to you. Having had enough time to think while waiting for you, I was dreaming about the moment I would see you again, but you arrived so quietly and unexpectedly that I even forgot to grab flowers I had bought for your earlier," he said and walked fast to the window.

He took the bouquet of already a little bit withered flowers off the sill and ceremonially presented it to Julija.

Smelling the beginning to droop blossoms, she said in a little excited voice, "Thank you, Paul, for showing your attention to me. I have to admit I don't get flowers often. Therefore, this has moved me."

Julija took him to the second floor to the guest room. There, she opened a wide glass door facing the terrace through which cool evening air began flowing into the room. The air coming from outside brought in pleasant smell of pine trees and water from a pond that was overflowing widely all directions and even right under the terrace.

"You, Paul, are probably not only tired after you long trip but also are hungry. I will ask for the supper to be served to us. In a meanwhile, you can stay on the terrace and enjoy the nature."

Left alone, Paul walked out to the big terrace hanging right over the pond; he leaned over the rail of it and scanned with his eyes big, widely branched out flowers growing on both sides of the pond. It looked like some greenhouse with its roof on down below. Then he lifted his eyes to look at the tranquil forest dozing on the west side, and on the east side, he could see a small village far away sinking in lush trees. It appeared as if the little houses there covered with thatched roofs were nestling up to the ground and looking like some mushrooms in the forest. About half a kilometer away, Vilija River was flowing freely with its banks in some places overgrown thickly that sometimes made the blue ribbon of it disappear under its green clothing.

He noticed two snow white swans swimming towards him from that part of the pond the view of which was covered with the corner of the house and the terrace. They were headed to the other side of the pond where a beautiful apple tree orchard was growing with the little apples already beginning to make their knots and pasting thick all over the trees. There were also some cherry trees among them; their red branches were drooping down from the weight of the berries. In some places in the orchard and along the pond, there were going a few paths covered with gravel and black currant bushes growing along them.

As soon as the beautiful swans noticed him standing on the terrace, they swam up to him. Most likely, they were used to getting treats from people feeding them down from the terrace.

"How do you like it here? Isn't it a romantic place?" Julija asked coming out onto the terrace.

"I'm feeling like in some fairy-tale. Before, I could not even imagine this kind of beauty! It seems to me I'm dreaming with my eyes open. You live like some princess," he replied.

"I myself love this home. I spend most of my time here even though I always have a lot of business matters to take care of. Therefore, I have to go to the city almost every day, but it's not such a big deal to me anymore since I don't have to waste a half of day getting there as I used to do before, when jolting in the one horse carriage. Now, I spend about an hour rocking in my limousine until it takes me to the very center of the city," Julija explained. "Well, let's go and eat. The food has already been brought in. Tomorrow, if you won't be lazy to get up early, you could see a magnificent sunrise which turns this place into the real miracle!"

She was the first to enter the splendid salon where the supper had already been served together with a bottle of cognac.

As soon as the two of them sat down, she herself filled up their little glasses and urged, "Paul, let's have a drink to your arrival."

"To my happy arrival," he corrected her.

"Of course, the happy one," she agreed and smiled looking deep into his eyes.

Then she drank half of her cognac and chased it down with kvass.

For some reason, the conversation wasn't happening between them, and both Julija and Paul were sitting in low spirits. Julija knew the reason of the coldness in their relationship, but Paul didn't, and he was seeking an opportunity to enter into more intimate relation.

He wanted to hug and kiss her, but at that moment, it appeared to be not very convenient time to do this. He was racking his brain over how to mitigate the prevailing tense atmosphere.

Finally, the supper ended. Julija got up and said, "Paul, you need to have some rest after the trip. Let's go I will show you your room."

"Julija, why are you so indifferent to me?" Paul asked in an agitated voice while getting up and taking her hand. "You are acting as if I have committed some offence against you. My dear, I've come here not to be welcomed by you in such a cold manner. I've come to you in order to ask you to marry me. We had almost agreed to do this while we were at the White Foam hotel. Have you forgotten what had happened between you and me there? I love you beyond your wildest imagination and can't imagine my life without you!"

Paul tried to hug Julija around her waist but she took his hand off.

"Paul, wait! I have to tell you something. You are right – we indeed discussed the question of marriage, and I have never told you I would marry you. I must tell you that the circumstances have changed, thus, saving me from making the wrong decision. Think yourself what kind of couple we would be. I'm already thirty seven, and you probably aren't even twenty years old. I can tell this merely by looking at your moustache and a beard that you probably just recently began shaving. Paul, I would like to be totally honest with you. I indeed had fallen in love with you, but that had been more like loving someone else in your body. You look just like him; only, that another person had been dating me about twenty years ago. That was the man I told you about when you and me were at the resort town. Remember – I told you about the man, with whom I had been madly in love with, and who had left me. Believe it or not, I met him unexpectedly just a while ago!"

After hearing these Julija's words, Paul released her hand that he was holding tight in his hand, and he collapsed on the chair. Then he suddenly jumped back to his feet as if being bitten by a venomous snake. His eyes fixed onto Julija's face were glaring with wrath.

Suddenly, a knife clicked in his hand. Seeing its sharp blade shining, Julija almost fainted. She grabbed the back of the chair with her both hands. For a while she was standing all shaking, and then, she began slowly moving backwards.

Paul made a few steps towards her holding his horrible knife which was glowing in the twilight and threatening with death.

"Paul, my dear, I can't believe you could kill me! Please, put the knife away!"

"No, Julija, I'm not going to kill you. I love you, and I could not live without you. You are going to be mine no matter what! But I'm going to settle accounts with that villain, who had hurt you before. He mustn't stand on the way to our happiness!"

"Paul, I haven't told you everything yet. Let me explain you something, and you will realize yourself that you and I could not be happy together. This way, the fate itself is going to solve everything for all of us. I have no right to hide anything from you, thus, jeopardizing your future, too. For God's sake, hide that knife, please!"

"Okay, but let me make a confession to you first. I hope you won't push me aside after finding everything out about me. Otherwise, I'm going to keep my word and put this knife to work in order to eliminate my rival," after saying this, Paul folded down his knife and slipped it back into his pocket.

He took Julija by her trembling hand, walked her to the table, filled the glasses with cognac, and began telling her his life story, "Julija, everything I told you about my life before is a lie from the beginning to the end. To tell the truth, I don't even know how old I am. I don't have any parents living in Gdansk. I don't know my real biological parents, but I am sure they are real scoundrels, much worse than I am. If you would only knew how much I had waited for them to come and take me home when I had been just a small boy! In my imagination, I had idolized them, but they had never come to pick me up. I used to see them in my dreams at night. Sometimes my mother in my dream would descend from the sky, hug me, and take me back with her to the kingdom of God. Nevertheless, every time I woke up, I got disappointed seeing only my grandpa who would reassure me anew by saying, 'Soon, your parents are going to find you'. However, always the same stinky half basement would welcome me again."

There was a long pause, and then he continued, "I'm not sure who I am. The only thing I am sure about myself is that I am a foundling. My childhood was very beggarly since I lived only with my grandpa. When he passed away, beggars abducted me. They broke my bones twice trying to make me crippled just like them, but God saved me both times. Thus, I spent a few years while traveling together with them across the villages and towns begging. Luckily, I was very clever. Therefore, they kept dragging me along with them half-naked and half-starved. Then, swindlers of the city abducted me away from the beggars. I could say that, in comparison to the beggars, I got into the good hands. I was taught to be just like them, too – the swindler. And I did really well! There were all kinds of moments in my life. Sometimes I was even feeling happy and, therefore, grateful to my parents for leaving me, which in turn let me lead the life I was living then. My new guardians once in a while would fall into the police hands and I had to use all my talents and new skills when rescuing them out. I was growing more shifty and resourceful. Therefore, I could easily take care of things like that. In spite of me excelling in my occupation, the police began persecuting me, too. Finally, my guardians were taking part in a big bank robbery and were caught again. That time, I was unable to rescue them from the police. Then, it was my turn – my hands were chained as well. Nevertheless, I was lucky to escape after what I began traveling from town to town. My knife had served me quite a few times, but I am not a murderer. I haven't killed anyone and would not want to do this or be back living like the tramp. I could become a good person when living with you, Julija. Otherwise, my only source of living remains to be my profession of the juggler; that was what I have been diligently taught to do for years, and this is the only thing that I know well. Also, I must confess to you that I am not from Gdansk but actually from here, the Vilnius. I had been abandoned in the churchyard of the Sts. Peter and Paul's Church."

As soon as Julija heard these words, she felt as if someone hit her on her head. Suddenly, it began humming in her ears. Feeling giddy, she fainted and almost fell of the chair.

Paul rushed to her, grabbed a glass with kvass off the table, and poured a little of the liquid into her mouth. After that, she regained the consciousness and opened her eyes.

"Now you see, Julija, what kind of person I am. If you will repudiate me, I will sink right back into the abyss and resume doing the same I have been doing all these years. Now that I've found you I don't want to let you go as long as my heart keeps beating in my chest!"

"Paul, were you there alone or with another little boy?" Julija asked quietly in a trembling voice.

"I lived with my grandpa sacristan."

"Try to remember if there was another boy living with you," she said anxiously looking at him.

"I'm not sure. I remember a woman dressed in black clothes who used to bring grandpa a bundle. Then she would give me candies. That's right..." he ceased talking and fell to thinking, "once she gave me less candy than to another boy. I tried to take the candy away from him, and she promised to give me more candies the next time which calmed me down at that moment. I can't remember now if she came after that again or not, though."

"So, there was another boy with you there?" Julija insisted.

Paul again plunged into a reverie. He sat for a while with his hands over the top of his head, and then he uttered in a dispirited voice, "Yes, there was... but I remember everything like through the fog. Some woman with a man came and took that boy with them. They were his parents. I remember now very clearly how they were walking away with him in the middle, holding him by his little hands. I was looking at them going away and cried out of jealousy because he had found his parents. My grandpa kept reassuring me that my parents would come and get me, too. However, after my grandpa passed away, there was no one left to support or encourage me. Gradually, I lost any kind of hope. Only once in a while, I saw in my dream my father wearing a black suit. He had a short moustache.

One time when begging I saw a woman dressed in black at the Sts. Peter and Paul's Church. She placed a big coin into my palm and gave me a beautiful smile. I liked her so much I instantly wished she was my mother! As soon as the Mass started, I stole into the church and watched her from afar. I still remember the sad look in her eyes which sometimes reminds me your eyes. After that, I never saw her again because, that very day, I was abducted by the beggars and, against my will, had to part with Vilnius for a few years."

Julija couldn't bear the heartbreak any longer. Wringing her hands, she quietly moaned and broke into tears.

Paul standing beside her began comforting her as best as he could. However, Julija seized his hand, squeezed it in her palms firmly, and pressed it to her chest. Then she with difficulty uttered, "Thank you, it will go away soon."

A few minutes passed. She took a deep breath and resumed talking, "Paul, I know you rail at your mother. Of course, you have the right to do this; your mother has earned this. But do you think you could forgive her if she turned up in your life? Or you would never be able to forget the wrong that she has done to you?"

"Yes, Julija, I called down curses upon her during difficult times in my life. However, I don't feel hatred towards her. My grandpa had always talked very highly about all mothers and, at those moments in my imagination, I used to see my mother surrounded by the bright light of her halo. In my childhood memories, I had portrayed her to be somewhat sublime. Later when I grew up, I didn't think much about her anymore. Only once in a while then I would threaten her with all the thunders, thus, cursing her. In spite of all this, if I saw her now, I would forgive her right away every bit of what she has done to me by leaving me. Maybe at least now, after so many years have passed, my childhood expectations and dreams that had created so many magnificent pictures of my mother in my imagination would finally come true. "

"Paul, my dear child!"

Julija embraced Paul and showered with thousands of kisses his cheeks, forehead, and eyes forgetting everything in the world out of happiness.

Paul also answered her with kisses, only they were passionate, but she was too overwhelmed with joy to notice that.

At last, Julija came to her senses and realized what was on his mind since he didn't know the real reason for her excitement.

Therefore, she decided not to delay a minute longer and revel to him her secret.

Julija freed herself of his embrace and turned the light on.

Then she walked back to him, unbuttoned his shirt, uncovered his right arm, and began carefully examining it. After she couldn't find what she was looking for, Julija slowly collapsed on the chair and mumbled under her nose in a dispirited voice, "I don't understand…"

"What are you, Julija, looking for? I have only a cross tattooed on my left arm. To this day, I have no clue who did this to me and why!"

He pulled his arm out of his shirt and showed her the mark of the already almost faded blue cross on his beautifully tanned skin. After seeing it, she almost fainted again.

Now, Julija had no doubts Paul was her son!

"You see it?" he asked her.

"Yes, only I don't understand why the tattoo is on your left arm and not on the right."

She began to remember when her little son was shrieking at the top of his lungs until he turned blue when the tattoo youth she had brought in to tattoo the crosses on her twins' arms was pricking him with the needle. After finishing one cross, Julija and the youth changed places trying to calm the infant down. This way each one of them ended up on the different sides of the crib. In any case, it was obvious to Julija now that Paul was her son!

"I don't know why the cross mark is on my left arm. I don't remember ever receiving it."

"Paul, this is difficult for you to understand, but I know why you have your cross on your left arm. The woman whom you have told me about and who used to give you candy, as well as the one you were looking at during the Mass in the church was me! The woman whom you called down curses on is also me. I am your mother you had been waiting for so anxiously in your childhood!"

Having heard these words, Paul sprang aside from Julija and fixed his surprised look on her.

Julija continued, "I am the cursed mother, who abandoned you together with your twin brother."

Powerless and helpless, she was sitting feeling totally crushed, when Paul began laughing uncontrollably.

When his hysterical fit went away, he said, "It's impossible! Where are the proofs?! Please, tell me that you have just created this story in order to leave me for the second time."

"No, Paul, from now on, I will never abandon or leave you. Moreover, I believe we could find your twin brother. Tomorrow you are going to meet with your biological father. O my God, it's such a happiness I have finally found my son! You were so similar with your brother like two drops of water. Even I had difficulty telling which one of you was Paul. I know how we could find your brother! We are going to place your photograph in the newspaper, and we will mention the mark on his right arm."

"Oh, no!" Paul exclaimed. "We don't need to resort to that. I know where my brother is."

After saying this, Paul began retreating backwards until he hit the door of the terrace. Suddenly, he remembered Janka and got scared of the consequences that could complicate the whole their situation even more drastically.

"No, I won't go to see my father tomorrow. Instead, I will go to Warsaw and find my brother."

"Paul, you really know where your brother is?!"

"I'm not totally sure, but I think I could find him. His name is probably Peter. I've heard a lot about him."

"Yes, Paul. His name was Peter since in your childhood your grandpa sacristan used to call you both Peter and Paul!"

They sat talking sincerely for a long time, however, Paul didn't reveal to Julija under what circumstances he had learned about Peter.

At midnight, with an aching heart, Paul found himself in a small but very cozy room. Nevertheless, to his big surprise, he wasn't feeling happy after finally finding his mother, about whom he had been dreaming for so long. On the contrary, now, he was getting angry his mother took his first love for a woman away from him. There had been no day or even an hour since the time Julija and him had met he would not think of her. She had always been on his mind. And just of a suddenly, his entire dream collapsed and went to pieces!

He was lying on the sofa with his clothes still on until dawn, but even when the sun shone inside his room, he was still wide awake.

Suddenly, the door quietly opened up and Julija appeared in the doorway. She didn't dare to go inside. Only when Paul turned his head towards her, she walked up to him and said, "Good morning, Paul. Why are you dressed? You can't rest well with the clothes on. You probably didn't sleep well?"

With difficulty getting up, Paul mumbled under his nose in an unhappy voice, "I haven't slept at all."

"Are you sick? Maybe something hurts to you?"

"Yes, my heart hurts. I have never in my entire life been so unhappy! I don't even know if I am glad that I have found you. At least, I am sure of the reason why my heart is crying – it's because I have lost my beloved."

"Paul, my Dear, you've found hundred times more than you have lost. Your mother is the only one for you in the entire world!" she sat down next to him, hugged him around his waist, and kissed him on his cheek. "My dear son, you have found the motherly love the power of which you couldn't even comprehend! I also hardly had any sleep. A few times during the night, I walked on my tiptoes to the door of your room, so that I could only listen to you breathing. Not being able to hear anything and reluctant to disturb your sleep with my rustling, I returned to my room feeling glad you were so close to me. Paul, you can't imagine what enormous love you have discovered; it will never stop burning for you! It's not the same love that appears only for a moment and then goes away. The mother's love for her child is the strongest love of all! The mother's love is the queen of all the loves that crowns her child with halo, and it never grows cold or dies out. This is not the same love your beloved woman can provide you with which fades away or even goes out all together as time passes by. This kind of passionate love a person can experience many times in his life. But mother's love ignites only once and blazes with the same intensity until her eyes close for eternity. Therefore, Paul, you shouldn't feel sorry for finding your motherly love!"

"In a way I can understand what you mean. However, you have your truth and I have mine! I have never been surrounded by the halo of the motherly love before. So far, I have experienced only love that had flashed for a short moment and drowned my heart in its flames. I have loved you as my sweetheart without whom I was feeling sad and lonely to the point I wanted to cry. However, as soon as I lost my beloved you and found in you my mother instead, I felt even lonelier than before even though I knew you love me dearly. I don't know why you are so distant to me, and I don't feel any warmth coming from you, either. Now, I feel as if being abandoned in some faraway desert with my heart weeping. Before, I was like in a beautiful oasis where my heart wanted to sing and bathe in the fantastic dream. I don't even feel love towards you anymore. I can't imagine how I am going to live from now on; I am even afraid to think of my future."

Julija pressed her cheek to his face as bitter tears began quietly running down her face that dampened his cheeks as well. For a while, both of them were sitting glued to each other looking like some immovable creation of the Mother Nature.

When Julija calmed down a little bit, she asked in a trembling out of grief voice, "Why can't you forgive me?"

"I have already forgiven you a long time ago. You shouldn't even burden yourself with the thoughts like that."

"Thank you, Paul, for your sincerity and kindness. I will do everything I can in order to make you love me as a son should love his mother. Now, undress and lie down; have some sleep. I won't let you go anywhere today. For some reason, my heart feels that my other son's life has been much easier than yours. Therefore, I must give you more of my love and attention than to him."

"Thank you, mother; it's very kind of you to say this. However, I won't go back to bed. I would rather enjoy the sunny morning on the terrace."

"Sure, I will go with you. Just put your jacket on. It's usually cold outside in the mornings."

Paul took his jacked with him and walked to the terrace hanging above the pond. There, he covered Julija's shoulders with his jacket, stretched his arms to the sides, breathed damp air deep into his lungs, and exclaimed in a fascinated voice, "Momma, how beautiful it is in your place!"

The morning was incredibly nice. In the serene sky, like swans in the pond, little, white, fluffy clouds were floating just above the horizon. The surface of the pond below was wrapped in mist that appeared like steam rising up from the boiling copper.

Only faraway mooing of cows was disturbing this peaceful scene. Somewhere close, also crowing of a rooster was heard with hens accompanying him with their clucking. And the forest far ahead appeared even greener than yesterday. Somewhere on the edge of it they could hear rattling of wheels, and a crow cawed a few times right behind the pond in the orchard after what an entire flock of sparrows flied over their heads making noise with their wings. Then, they landed on the roof loudly chirping, thus, also taking part in creating the harmony of the morning.

Julija wasn't paying much attention to those sounds, but Paul was listening to every one of them.

After breakfast, Julija put one hundred zloty into Paul's pocket and gave him a ride in her limousine to the train station.

Next day, Paul was already in Warsaw. As soon as he found himself in Marszalkowska Street, he rented a big room in a luxurious hotel. Then he found a phone number of the Kerciai estate and ordered a call from there.

He was lying on a sofa when, less than an hour later, the phone rang. Paul answered, "Is this Kerciai?"

"Yes, it is. This is Peter talking. How can I help you?"

"Yes, you are the one who I would like to talk to," Paul said. "I have an urgent matter to discuss with you. I am in Warsaw now in 'Niagara' hotel, room number thirty six. We could meet here or anywhere you prefer."

"Sir, I'm sorry, but I don't understand what it is in regards to. You could tell me that now on the phone. Or if you have something important to discuss with me, you could just come to Kerciai. The bus runs here four times a day. Besides that, I'm sure there are other ways to reach us. Kerciai are not that far away from Warsaw."

"I understand, Mister Peter. I'm afraid our meeting could be not very pleasant. Therefore, you have right to decline it. I guess, if you can't come today to meet with me, then I will have to go to your place in Kerciai. But I have to warn you that my visit could give your parents a huge blow, and that would be entirely your fault. We are adults, and we can solve problems ourselves. I've come here all the way from Vilnius just to see you and have a half an hour conversation with you. If you told your parents a person has come from Vilnius who wants to talk to you, they probably would get a heart attack. But if I were you, I would definitely talk with me first!"

"Is this some kind of an ultimatum?"

"You can think anything you wish," Paul answered, "I could tell you who I am right now, but we still would have to discuss this in detail. Believe me – you would like to know this!"

"Okay, I will be there," Peter agreed.

Without telling anything to his parents, Peter got into his car, and soon, he was already at the best hotel in Warsaw.

He wiped cold sweat off his forehead with his fragrant handkerchief, gave a zloty to a porter who was politely holding the door widely open for him, and walked into the spacious lobby. Then he climbed the wide staircase onto a second floor and found the room thirty six.

There, he stopped at the door hesitating to knock on it. However, there was no reason to delay, either. Therefore, he quickly and pretty loudly knocked with his trembling hand.

First, he could not hear any rustling behind the door. Only after a while that seemed to last very long, Peter he heard a voice, "Come in."

Peter timidly opened the door, walked inside, and saw an elegantly dressed youth standing by the table in the middle of the room.

Immediately, Peter got rooted in the spot with his mouth opened not being able to even greet him.

"Peter, you don't need to introduce yourself to me, and as about me, you are going to find out who I am during our conversation. First of all, I would like to thank you for coming to talk to me."

As soon as Peter approached the table and sat down on the chair that Paul had offered to him, Paul sat down, too, and fixed his attentive look on Peter, who looked exactly like him!

"Peter, I will go right down to the point. You are my brother."

As soon as Peter heard these words, he jumped up off the chair as if being poured boiling water over his entire body.

"Don't be surprised – you are going to learn more of those kinds of stunning things. I don't want you thinking that I called you in order to require from you some of your assets. Even though we are twin brothers, I have no right to your foster-parents' inheritance. You don't have to worry about that. You and I both are the foundling twins, and your current guardians had adopted you."

"There is no proof of that!" exclaimed infuriated Peter.

"I have plenty of proofs! One of them is that I have found our real parents that you also must meet. Such is every child's obligation, and later on, you could do about that whatever you find appropriate. If this is not good enough proof for you, then your guardians could confirm some other things, too. I would like to ask you, Peter, if you remember anything about our separation when your guardians had taken you away together with them. I personally remember something very vaguely as if through the fog. However, even if you don't remember anything about that, it's not a big deal. I found out from our biological mother there is a cross tattooed on your right arm. Do you have it? If you don't have it, then you can consider all this to be a mistake, and our conversation is over. I have the cross like that tattooed on my arm which our mother had ordered to be done to us."

"Yes, I do have the mark like that," gasping for air answered Peter.

"You could probably argue that I found out about this mark on your arm from somebody else," Paul said.

"Didn't you tell that you have come here to talk to me from Vilnius? But how did you find out about me?"

"From Janka. I had met her at the seaside, and she had thought then that I was you."

"And you have taken advantage of that?.."

"Yes."

"You damn scoundrel! " Peter jumped off his chair and grabbed Paul by his throat.

Then Paul hit him with his fist on his stomach, and Peter fell down on the floor.

Finally, Peter ceased writhing, got up, and sat down back on the chair.

Paul pulled out his knife, pushed the button on its side, and it made a clicking sound when unbending automatically.

"Do you see this toy? I've made a hole with it to quite a few of dare-devils! But I'm not going to do the same to you. However, I have to warn you that you must stop jumping at my face!"

For a while, silence reigned between them, and then, Paul continued, "I know myself I am a scoundrel. However, it would have been all the other way around now if your guardians had chosen me over you! In that case scenario, I would call you a scoundrel. But it is the way it is. However, this is not why I've come here. Now, that you have found out a little more about me and about your own past, I would like to tell you also more about your real parents, our parents by blood. Our father manages a faculty of philosophy at the University of Warsaw. He is an honorable person, don't you agree?"

Instead of answering him, Peter slowly began moving backwards toward the door.

"So you are leaving? You don't want to find out everything to the end; you don't want to hear anything about your mother? She is a noble person, just like you. Only I alone am a scoundrel," saying these words, Paul hit the table with his fist so hard that even an ash-tray jumped up into the air. "Your guardians were spoiling you; they dressed you in nice clothes. Various teachers taught you different subjects at school and at the university. You have never experienced hunger. You didn't know what hardship was. You always have been taken care of until you have grown into this dandy boy. During all this time, only hardships and misery were surrounding me and poisoning my blood with hatred. Since my early childhood, I had loafed with a bag over my shoulder hungry, ragged, being run down by everyone like some little mangy dog. What good could have my guardians taught me? They had been jugglers. Therefore, no wonder, they taught me the same stuff they had been doing for years themselves - to steal from shops, banks, and people. They also taught me to play cards. In fact, I superseded my teachers and became a better juggler then they had ever been! It's difficult to enumerate all the mean things I have done to others! If you have just known one tenth of what I've done, you would be shocked! However, you have to realize that if your guardians had not taken you with them back then, you most likely would have been just like me now – the juggler. When you had happened to do something wrong at the time you were growing up, your guardians had helped you every step of the way by teaching you what was right and wrong and telling you how you had to fix your mistakes. As about me, if I had played some dirty trick, my guardians praised me and even gave me an incentive to continue doing the same."

Paul and Peter talked for a very long time until they agreed to go to Vilnius together to meet their biological parents.

Next day, both of them went to the store and bought for their mother a present - the expensive golden pin with three gems. After that, they left for Vilnius.

During the trip, the conversation wasn't happening between the two of them, most likely because both of them had such different outlooks on life.

Thus, they arrived to Vilnius in silence where Paul took Peter to a hotel, and he himself went out in order to buy one more present for their mother for his remaining money.

He checked out a lot of stores and didn't find anything he was interested in buying. However, he was not ready to give up yet. He walked into a jewelry store where on the counter under the glass various adornments were sparkling.

There were a very few people in the store – a couple of women and three men looking at the jewelry.

Then, one more man walked in and asked, "Have you got the bracelet?"

"Yes, Sir, I did," the salesperson took out of the safe a golden bracelet with greenish gems that were changing colors.

The buyer without even trying to bargain, paid a big amount of money, placed the bracelet into his pocket, and left the store.

Paul followed him from behind, and in his mind, a plan had already been created to get this piece of jewelry from that man.

Paul followed him all the way to the Viktorija Hotel. Without knocking on the door, Paul slipped inside of his unlocked room. The man wasn't even in time to say anything when Paul hit him on his head with a brass knuckle. Since the man turned his head slightly towards Paul, it directed the blow to his temple even though Paul was trying to hit him on his jaw.

The man didn't let out a sound and fell down on the ground. Then, Paul pulled the bracelet out of the man's pocket, quickly wiped away his fingerprints with his handkerchief, and slipped out the door the same imperceptible way he had got in.

As Paul found himself back in the street, he felt as if nothing had happened; he had been used to the incidents like that. Especially now, when his brother was staying with him, he didn't even give a second thought of what had just taken place.

Paul and Peter ordered a taxi and, in a half an hour, both of them were welcomed by their mother's open arms.

Soon, she was already entertaining them at dinner not being able to find words to express her happiness.

Julija told them everything in detail about how she had met Robertas and how she wanted to commit suicide after he left her, and how fate rescued her from such a horrible death. She went on telling Paul and Peter about the time when she gave a birth to the twins and the numerous hardships she went through. In spite of that, she was determined to elbow her way through life. However, the war blazing, she felt totally destroyed and had no other choice but to leave her twins at the church, thus, hoping that some decent people would take

Page
340

them. Julija continued her life story telling to her sons how long she was looking for them while placing advertisements and even hiring a detective whom she had promised a big amount of money for finding at least one of her sons. Unfortunately, all her searches went in vain, and she had to reconcile herself to her destiny.

Then Peter told them how stunned he had been when he had found out from Paul about their father, and it turned out that he had been his teacher at the gymnasium where he had been teaching Peter Latin. Moreover, during last few months while he was studying law at the University of Warsaw, Peter often used to go to the lectures of his father, who had advanced in his career and became a doctor of philosophy. Peter expressed his deep admiration in his father and told his mother he was immensely proud of him!

The only thing that bothered Peter now was he could not believe his father had done such a horrible thing to their mother. All the time, Peter saw in his teacher integrity, and he might have even inherited some traits of character from him such as diligence, attention to details, and persistence. It appeared to Peter the manager of the faculty of the philosophy had superseded all the rest of the professors and teachers at the university since he had been living alone, without a family, and had been totally devoted to the science.

Nevertheless, now, he could not comprehend that what he was hearing about this person whom he had been almost worshiping.

"I can't believe he could do something like that," Peter uttered. "However, it is possible there had been some secret in relation to all of this, and I hope, our father is going to reveal it to us himself. I've known him for ten years, and I don't think he is a bad person!"

"My dear son, I can tell you how everything had happened. You are right – he is a good person," Julija said, and then she told them in detail everything she knew about Robertas from his own recent tale.

She told her sons how their father after finishing gymnasium could not find a job. While he had been studying there, he had impoverished his parents so badly there were days they lived half-starved.

No wonder, he could not help Julija. There had been no way he could marry her when living in such poverty, either.

Julija wasn't able to finish the story since a maidservant walked into the guest room and told her she got a phone call.

When she came back, she said to her sons, "You can have a walk in the orchard. I have to go to Vilnius urgently. At the same time, I will drop at your father's and let him know you both are here. I'll ask him to come for a visit tomorrow."

Having concealed a fact the police called her because of a murder case at the Viktorija Hotel, she got into the limousine and left.

In a meanwhile, Peter and Paul walked onto the terrace to enjoy the view and wait for their mother to come back.

However, Julija wasn't showing up. And then, the maid came and let them know their mother was going to be home late and that she was wishing them good night and sweet dreams over the phone.

Only when it got very dark, both of them walked into a big, spacious room full of flowers, prepared especially for them.

Their bed was made for both of them to sleep together on a wide sofa. Both Peter and Paul could not get asleep for a long time, but the conversation wasn't happening between them, too. In spite of them being twins, they didn't have mutual things of interest to talk about. Even though Paul's life seemed to be more adventurous than Peter's, neither one of them said a word lying in the dark each of them with their own thoughts swimming in their heads.

Finally, Peter got asleep. Paul wished he could turn on the other side, but with Peter lying next to him, he couldn't let himself the luxury of doing this.

Lying on his back, he was listening to various sounds coming inside through the open window. Faraway barking of dogs, a song, and clamor of young people reached his ears.

Midnight approaching, all these sounds gradually were dying away until they ceased all together, and dead silence of the night took over.

Suddenly, he heard the noise of the coming car that was getting more and more pronounced until it could be heard already in the yard. Then it stopped, and Paul could discern the bang sound of the car door. For a short while, he was listening to the sound of the steps that quickly died away, too, and the night enveloped everything in the somber silence again.

Finally, Paul's mind surrendered to the sweet sleep.

Next day, both Paul and Peter were sleeping long since no one woke them up.

Peter was the first to wake up. He turned on his side and, thus, woke his brother up, too.

Both of them greeted each other out of politeness and got up. They washed themselves up and ate breakfast during which they were not talking much again. Julija appeared to be not talkative as well even thought Peter inquired about her yesterday's late, urgent leave.

As soon as they finished eating, Julija finally broke the silence; she took a deep breath and uttered in a dispirited voice, "My dear sons, I must impart terrible news to you. You are grownups. Therefore, you should be able to handle that. Yesterday, the police called me up on the phone because of a murder that had taken place in my hotel. I didn't tell you earlier because I didn't want disturbing you. However now, I feel is the right time to tell you the sad news. The murdered person is your father!"

As soon as Julija said it, Peter jumped off the chair and began retrieving backwards.

"This is a huge blow to our family," Julija continued. "This is the true irony of fate – just as your father was getting ready to enter his family, it was meant for him to die right on its threshold. At least, Peter was lucky to get to know him as his teacher, but you, Paul, have never had an opportunity to meet him in person. Therefore, Paul, I worry about you more since you have been wronged by fate. In addition to that, you have been growing up not knowing parental love. Now, you have to experience the other blow. I have not slept all night long thinking what to do now. I have to admit, I was going to keep this murder a secret from you. I'm calling down curses upon that villain who commited this crime!"

Julija burst into tears.

"I curse this damn murderer of our father, too!" uttered Peter. "With me being a jurist, I must find that scoundrel, so that he could be punished by the goddess of justice even if my entire life would be spent chasing him!"

Paul, all shrunk back, was listening to the curses of his closest family members suspecting he was to blame for the murder of his own father. He remembered how he, with all his might, had hit the man on his temple and, then, he robbed him afterwards.

His head began buzzing, ringing, and humming. Everything was spinning around. It seemed the ground opened up before him. He instinctively wanted to hold on to something but couldn't find anything he could grab in order to get some sense of security. There was no one he could expect to provide him with some comfort for his aching soul, either.

The entire world was going against him! No matter which direction he was headed or what he did, every time, a new offence was following his actions.

Suddenly, he jumped off his chair and gave a scream of terror that pierced Julija and Peter's hearts. Having turned all pale and wheezing, Paul began rushing about in the room, not allowing them to come near him.

Maids gathered in, and some men were called in, too; with the help of the three of the men, Paul was seated on the chair. Being held by six strong arms, he was yelling out of immense pain, "Kill me! I'm the biggest scoundrel on this Earth! No matter where I go, the meanness follows me. I'm just an unfortunate beast that only brings pain and grief to those around him!"

After a lot of efforts Paul was finally calmed down.

The rest of the day was spent in the biggest heart-break but without any big psychical escapades as well. Paul remained sitting sunk all numb on the sofa until the evening.

Next day, the medical examination stated the death had been caused by cerebral hemorrhage. Robertas' body was released to Julija, who rented an apartment in the city in order to lay out his corpse.

Two days Robertas's body was lying in that apartment, but no one came to visit the deceased. Only three people didn't leave his side, and at the end, all three of them saw his body off to Rasos Cemetery.

They returned home to Verkiai when sun was already going down, and after the funeral supper, Paul asked his mother to let him sleep in the little room where he had slept before.

As soon as he got there, he locked himself in, took some sheets of paper out of a drawer, and began writing since he had made his final decision on how to proceed with his life.

Well after midnight, he heard quiet knocking on the door.

He quickly hid the filled up pages under the pillow. Then he walked to the door and unlocked it, "Mother, why aren't you sleeping?"

"Paul, I can't sleep when you are not sleeping. This is not the first time I've come to your door on my tiptoes, listening. However, as soon as I saw the empty bed through the keyhole, I got frightened and decided to check why you aren't sleeping. Maybe you feel bad, and nightmares are tormenting you? Paul, please lie down. I could sit in the chair next to you if that helps."

"Momma, I am asking you to let me be alone, just as you had let me before when I had arrived here. I promise that after that, I will be obedient; I will be as quiet as a grave."

"Paul, I don't know why but I have a predicament of something bad happening."

"Momma, nothing bad can happen to me. You will see – I will be the first to greet you in the morning tomorrow," he took her by her arm, walked her to the door, kissed her on her cheek smiling, and wished her good night.

Then he returned to his desk and finished writing his letter. After folding it, he placed the letter into his pocket and opened the window widely. The stream of cool, fresh air gushed inside the room.

On the east side, the sky was dawning when Paul finally turned the light off and lay down. As never before, he was feeling relieved and at peace, and he got sweet asleep.

He was sleeping so soundly that he didn't ever hear knocking on the door.

Being afraid Paul could had done something bad to himself, Julija called one of her maintenance workers and asked him to unlock his room and if it was necessary, to even break open the door.

Luckily, there had been no key in the door on its other side, thus, making it easier to unlock it.

Upon opening the door, they saw Paul still sleeping peacefully.

Having heard the rustling, Paul finally woke up and opened his eyes. At first, he could not understand what was happening. Only after Julija explained it to him, Paul smiled artificially and got up off the sofa.

He washed his upper half of his body with cold water which dispelled all his sleep right away.

During breakfast everybody's mood was a little better. Paul also was trying to take part in their conversation but, this time, Peter talked the most while remembering various episodes about their deceased father.

However, secretly Paul was anxious for the breakfast to be over, thus, hearing only bits and parts of Peter's tales.

Then, Paul was the first to get up from under the table. He told his family he had to go to the city. Julija offered to give him a ride, but Paul refused from her help asking her to stay at home and wait for his friend to call. He wanted his mother to tell his friend he was going to meet him in the Rotuse Square.

Paul looked deeply into his mother's eyes, thus, parting with her for good. Being afraid some unnecessary word could escape his mouth, he turned around abruptly and walked to the door with Julija following him.

Before leaving, Paul stopped in the doorway, once more looked into her eyes, grabbed her by her waist, and kissed her passionately on her lips.

After him kissing her, Julija was standing lost, not knowing how to react -- to scold him or to pretend nothing happened.

With immense sadness in his eyes looking at her, he kissed her gently on her cheek and, before closing the door, he muttered in a barely audible voice, "Farewell, my dear mommy."

Paul went to Vilnius by bus.

As soon as he found himself in the city, he hired a coachman, and soon, he already was in the Antakalnis Cemetery where he rambled for a long time until he found Sacristan's grave with a rotten cross standing on it. The twofold pine tree was still growing next to it, its two trunks shooting high into the sky out of the same stump that both of them had been sharing for so many years. Only now, it appeared much thicker than it had been twelve years ago, when his grandpa was buried there.

Paul had difficulty recognizing this place. Luckily, when he had still been living with Bikas and Mikas, he had found the grave and cut out a cross on one of the trunks of those pine trees. The cross had been almost overgrown with new bark and moss now, but Paul could still recognize the scar of the cross on the bark of the pine tree.

Now, he carved another cross on the adjacent pine, too, and pulled out some weeds on Sacristan's grave.

Then he walked to the watchman of the graveyard, gave him five zloty, and took him back to the grave.

"In a few days, a woman will come to you who will ask you to show her this grave. Please, remember where it is and show it to her together with these two pine trees."

After leaving the cemetery, Paul went to the post office and ordered himself a call to Verkiai.

He didn't have to wait for long. Not even ten minutes later, he already heard his mother's voice.

"Momma, this is me," he said.

"Paul, your friend hasn't called yet. But I'm glad you have called. It's already lunch time. You should go to the restaurant and have something to eat. Don't walk in the city hungry."

"Momma, I would like to ask you something very important. I went to the Antakalnis Cemetery where I have found grandpa's grave. He had brought me up. He is buried on the northern side of the cemetery next to a twofold pine tree where, twelve years ago, I had cut out a cross on one of the trunks of it. However, it is barely noticeable now since the new bark has grown over it. Today, I have carved another cross on another trunk of the same twofold tree. If you won't be able to find this grave, go to the watchman of the graveyard, and he will show it to you. Okay, mother?"

"Okay, Paul. But I don't understand why you are saying this to me over the phone. Why can't you and I go there together? I would be happy to put up there a nice monument."

"Momma, I wrote a letter to you yesterday, and I would like you to read it. Better yet, ask Peter to read it to you. I have to go. I'm sending you a thousand kisses. I will love you until my last breath."

After saying those words, he hung up the phone.

Julija right away went to Paul's room and found the sealed envelope in the pocket of his jacket. There was nothing written on the envelope.

Then she went to the terrace where Peter was sitting on a backed chair.

She gave the envelope to him and said, "I've just talked with Paul. He asked me to give this letter to you, so you could read it to me aloud. He sounded very strange as if he was leaving us forever. I am worried – my heart forebodes disaster. Read it! This letter should reveal a lot."

Julija sat down on a rocking chair, and Peter opened the envelope. He removed a few folded pages out of it and began reading in an excited voice, "The most terrible thing in life is when a person begins to fear himself after discovering who he is. I am one of those people. There are many evil-doers and villains in this world, but I supersede them all! I must take my mask off and reveal to you who I really am. I'm not going to list my numerous transgressions in this letter; I have done thousands of them. If all my victims came together and began complaining, shedding their tears, and calling down their curses on me, the ground would probably open up and swallow me in order to prevent me from fouling my own family nest. So far, God has been very patient with me, and he has been silent. And without his decision, ground could not swallow me. Since people who surround me at this time are too noble, I must pass judgment on myself, and no one would be able to change it. But before I do this, I must confess my biggest sins to you, or they will remain unknown, thus, the others could be unjustly accused for them. I would rather have those curses fall on me because I am the committer of those crimes. Unfortunately, even when I had wanted to do something good, it always turned out to be just the opposite way. I would love to be able to get rid of all those horrors, but they just don't leave me alone. On the contrary, they keep following me and trying to push me to do some new villainous acts! Just during the last two months, I have committed the horrible sins against you, momma, and against Peter, too, let alone my father. As about my brother Peter, I must confess that when I had met his fiancé at the seaside, I had dishonored her, too, by treading under foot her beautiful feelings that she had unknowingly given to her beloved Peter through me. I had taken advantage of her by deceiving her. I'm guilty of intruding into my brother's and her paradise of love. What could be worse than that?! However, I had done this not knowing then that Peter had been my brother. Still, it is not a good reason to justify myself. The fault remains to be the same, and no one could mitigate it. I'm not asking Peter to forgive me, and I must get the righteous repayment in another world for all my bad deeds I've done in this world. The only thing I would like to ask Peter – please, remember our innocent childhood. In the name of it, I implore you not to leave Janka. She will always love you the same way she has loved you until now since she had never known about you having the twin brother. You are a sensible person, and I am sure you will make the humane decision in relation to this. After this sin, another one followed, only this time, it was related to my dearest, beloved mother. What happened was that as soon as I had separated with Janka, I was going to take to my heels getting away from the seaside. However, another disaster had been already lurking and waiting to get a hold of me."

He ceased reading.

"Keep reading, Peter."

"This is about you, mother. Maybe I don't need to know this."

"Please, go on reading. I have learned about your misfortune, and I think I am to blame for everything," trying to suppress her tears, Julija urged her son to continue reading the letter.

Peter went on, "And one beautiful day, I took a hold of my mother's feelings, just as I had done to Janka. As soon as I became acquainted with my mother, mean thoughts crossed my mind. Luckily, I fell in love with her, which prevented her from experiencing the same Janka had experienced after she had met me. Thus, I neither robbed nor left my mother. Love turned out to be stronger than knavery. True love had taken over me and made me obey its laws. Since my early childhood, I had had to think not only about myself but about a responsibility of taking care of my feeble grandpa, too. From then on, every day, I had to puzzle my brains over how to earn some money in order to make living. Time passing by, though, I fell under the power of the money that turned me into its slave. Only when I had the money, I felt like a full and equal member of the society. I didn't know a different kind of life, and I was completely satisfied with it. It seemed to me that in order to survive in this world, one had no other way but to deceive the other person, and the more I hurt others, the better living I would make for myself. Examples in the nature confirmed to me the same since I saw hawks feeding on other birds, and wolves eating the other animals. I realized that if they refused from their prey, they would die. The same way, I realized that if I had left my occupation, I would also have perished. Nevertheless, I think, the man is the biggest predator of all! In order to satiate himself, he destroys the lives of others. To the contrary to the animals, though, he kills not only those who are weaker than him but also those stronger creatures than him as well. In order to eat, the man butchers animals, too. I understand that it is vile to disappoint a girl, but it is much worse to have your own mother as a lover! It gets beyond all the laws of common decency. Nevertheless, even this wasn't the biggest of my crimes against the principles of humanity which calls for the biggest punishment for me – the punishment by death. Some crimes could be mitigated if the criminal sincerely repents and becomes a better person. However, my last crime could not be mitigated or forgiven by any means! It is so because I was the one who had killed my father! Therefore, you did the right thing by calling down curses on me. Moreover, I curse myself now, too. I have to tell you that I must let you know how it had happened. When I had succeeded convincing Peter to go with me to Vilnius in order to visit our mother, we both went to a jewelry store where he bought an expensive present to our mother. Of course, I could only dream about buying something so luxurious to her since I had only ten zloty left in my pocket. But I also felt that I had to buy her something from me personally because I knew I had been guilty of being a bad son to her. At the same time, I continued loving her the same passionate way, just like before, when I had not been aware she had been my biological mother. Therefore, I went to one jewelry store in Vilnius with intention to steal something for my mother. However, as ill luck would have it, at that very moment, my father walked into the store, whom I had not known then yet. A bracelet that sales person handed to him caught my attention. Therefore, I followed my father to a hotel where I hit him on his head, took the bracelet out of his pocket, and left. I had not realized then that he had died on the spot from the impact. Thus, momma, I brought you that bloody bracelet that, most likely, Father had bought for you. It righteously belonged to you; only you got it from the wrong hands. I'm guilty even though I didn't realize I had killed my father, just as I had not known I had fallen in love with my own mother! In addition to that, I had not known Janka had been the fiancé of my real brother! What are the odds of experiencing the chain of such unbelievable coincidences happening one after the other in someone's life?! Probably it's not meant to be for me to become a decent person, ever, since only the transgressions and crimes have been accompanying me all of my life. Even my good intentions kept turning into bad deeds. I must voluntarily leave this world in order to prevent the new crimes from happening. My beloved momma and my dear brother Peter, I will no longer be able to commit new crimes because there is a very little time left for me to suffer on this Earth where the path of my life had been so difficult and thorny. I can already see a fiery disk of the sun of my life quickly moving towards the horizon, and I know it is the last sunset my eyes are looking at. The death resolution is horrible. However, it is fair and final. My dearest momma and my beloved woman at the same time, I am begging for your forgiveness while down on my knees kissing my mother's hands and the body of my beloved woman. I cannot imagine how much pain and suffering I have brought into your life upon you meeting me after so many years. Since I am still crazy in love with you, my only salvation is to leave this world in order to stop this series of disasters that keep piling on our family because of my fault. I don't want to deal with any more crimes myself, I no longer desire the love that makes me unhappy, and I'm not looking forward to living the life that brings me only grief, tears, and curses. Momma, I know you are the only one in the entire world who could forgive her gone astray son. Please, bury me together with my grandpa Sacristan by the twofold pine-tree in the Antakalnis Cemetery. A watchman of the graveyard will show you the place. After you are done reading the letter, come to the Sts. Peter and Paul's Church to get my body. You will find it where I had been deserted in my childhood. It's time for me to say farewell to my beloved mommy, my deceased father, whom I have killed, my honorable brother Peter, Janka, and my dear deceased grandpa Sacristan, too. Good-bye also to those who might find some nice words to say about me and not send down curses on me. Farewell to the bright sun who had been shining for me for twenty years. Good-bye the wide world, as well, where upon leaving you, momma, I kiss you a thousand times repeating tirelessly 'You are my Beloved Mother, My Momma'!!"

Julija couldn't hear the last words. Her mind went clouded, there was a ringing in her ears, and her head began swimming. Tears were squeezing her throat. Not being able to bear it any longer, she painfully moaned and started weeping while wringing her hands.

Then, she jumped off her chair as if going off her head; with crazy look in her eyes, Julija was running back and forth in the room helplessly snatching at everything on her way. Things kept falling out of her hands.

However, there was no time to grieve; Julija suddenly stopped in the middle of the room and painfully asked, "Peter, what are we going to do now?!"

"I think we should rush to the church. Maybe we can still save him!"

"Peter, let's hurry!" Julija grabbed her son by his hand and pulled him out the door. Both of them got into the limousine and rushed out to Vilnius, raising a pillar of dust.

Half an hour later, the limousine stopped at the iron gate of the churchyard.

As Julija and Peter quickly got out of the car, they could not notice anything suspicious by the main entrance of the church that had been wide open.

After taking a breath of relief, Julija walked through the gate into the churchyard.

Nevertheless, as soon as they found themselves in the yard, they heard a long-drawn, heart rendering cry, "Maamaaaaa!.."

Both of them were not in time to raise their eyes, and the body of a person flopped down onto the coblestone pavement after flying down from the roof of the church.

This was Paul. He was now lying on the ground not being able to get up; he only slightly lifted his head and quietly whispered through his pale lips," Momma, Peter..."

His head drooped, and blood gushed out onto the stones.

Julija ran up to her son lying on the ground with his bones broken, seized his bleeding head, and babbled moaning, "Paul, sonny! Why are you so cruel to me?"

"Dear momma, it was necessary. Take my hand; I can't feel it. I'm dying, and there is still so much that I would like to tell you. Peter, please promise me you are going to marry Janka," Paul fixed his painful, entreating gaze on Peter, waiting for an answer while feeling his life in big leaps was retreating away from him.

Peter was kneeling on his one knee with his head hanging down, but he wasn't in rush to give his brother an answer.

In spite of that, Paul concentrated all his strength in order to keep his eyes on his brother even though the light was already going out after a black veil had begun to cover his sight.

At last, Peter quietly mumbled, "Okay, let it be as you wish. I will marry her."

After that, a sad smile distorted with pain for a moment appeared on Paul's lips, and the black mantle of death covered the churchyard no matter that it was still brightly lit up by the rays of the sun.

Paul's lips, though, were in time to whisper some incoherent, incomprehensible words, but the only one of them that Julija and Peter could discern was the last one, "Momma..."

Then, his lips got limp, and his body became stiff.

Paul's body was lain out in Verkiai among a lot of flowers. In a couple of days, Julija buried him next to the grandpa Sacristan.

A few days later, the body of Robertas was also transferred from the Rasos Cemetery to the Antakalnis Cemetery and was lain to rest next to his son.

Peter stayed a week longer with his mother helping her finish funeral arrangements. However, the day came when he told Julija he had to go back home to Warsaw.

"Peter, my home is your home, too. Don't you like it here? Please, don't leave me in this difficult situation."

"I do like it here, mother, but I still have to go to Warsaw. My guardians are also very noble people. In addition to that, I have to finish university. Moreover, I have to keep my word that I've given to my brother and marry Janka. However, I will never leave you, and I will always be with you in my thoughts. I can't condemn your actions; you have suffered so much that you have already redeemed all your faults twofold. I realize how difficult it is for you now, but please, don't despair. Always remember there is a person in this world who thinks a great deal of you. Now that I've found you, I will never forget about you; I will be writing letters to you. Next summer, I will definitely come for a visit to Verkiai. Of course, then, we will also visit the grave where the three souls of our precious people are resting."

Peter tried to calm down his mother as best as he could. She looked aged at least ten years during just the last few days. Now, her hair was the same white like a blooming apple tree in springtime.

When Peter left, Julija shut herself in her room and didn't let anyone in for ten days. She refused to see even Gertruda, who came to visit Julija a few times. Julija refused to talk to her business staff people also when they came to discuss some urgent, important matters related to her hotel business.

Only when she received a letter from Peter, she finally left her room and went to the orchard where she spent a couple of hours by the pond.

Then she again retread into her shell and locked herself back in her room for another few days.

A month passed, and she finally began coming out to the orchard every day in the afternoon. Having covered her head with a black veil, she would quietly lounge for an hour through the orchard her eyes roving somewhere in the far distance. If she met someone on her way, she would not even notice the person passing by.

In the evenings when the sun was going down, she would go to the terrace and sit there stagnant in the rocking chair until it became totally dark, her eyes always fixed ahead in the distance.

Only when the fall came, Julija recovered a little bit from her helpless apathy. Again, she began receiving the staff members of her business who were coming to present various documents for her to sign.

After reading them attentively, she would sign some papers and reject the others asking her employees to make a decision on their own.

Soon, she got a letter from Peter where he was writing that he married Janka, and that she was getting ready to give a birth to Paul's baby. In his letter, he also indicated that Janka was still unaware of the fact the baby was not his. He said he was going to keep it a secret forever since he didn't want to disturb his wife's happiness. Everyone in their house, including Peter's guardians, had been anxiously waiting for their heir to come into this world.

While reading her son's letter, Julija rejoiced deep in her heart hoping that a boy was going to be born, thus, making it appear her beloved son Paul didn't die after all, as if he was just gone for the time being. Filled with joy, she didn't feel pain of Peter that was coming forth through his writing.

As the spring came, Julija received the happy news. It was Peter's letter notifying her that Janka gave a birth to a boy and that the entire estate of Kerciai was now blooming with the twofold spring!

Holding the letter in her hand, she was sitting on the sofa smiling, and her heart was singing joy!

In his letter, he also went on telling her that even though everyone was celebrating the birth of his son, his soul was suffering immensely as if it was not the springtime for him but the late fall.

For a split second, Julijas' heart trembled anxiously. However, as soon as she remembered about her newly born grandson, her soul was filled with warmth again, and she laughed loudly forgetting about all the wrongs life had brought to her before.

In her head, she was already making plans about having Peter with her grandson visit her next summer. She wished she could at least for a short while look at her grandson, who seemed to give her the new strength for living now.

She began anxiously counting days when Peter was supposed to come for a visit to Vilnius.

Instead, a new blow came into her life! It was the telegram that stated: 'Peter shot himself. According to his last wish, he has to be buried next to his father. Meet his body at the train station.'

Not only Peter's guardians but also Janka with her three month old son arrived to the funeral.

No one could understand why Peter had committed suicide. Julija was the only one who knew the horrible secret. However, in no way, she was going to revel it!

After Peter's funeral, her health deteriorated completely. She was terribly depressed again.

A few weeks later, she got a heart attack that made her bedridden for two months.

Being afraid she could unexpectedly die, Julija called in a notary in order to write up a will leaving all her assets to her grandson who, according to Peter's wish, had been baptized as Paul.

When a month later she received another heart attack, after which she could not leave her bed, Julija didn't hesitate to order an advertisement being placed in the main Vilnius newspaper to enter the competition for the best tombstone.

Very soon, hundreds of designs of the gravestones were laid on a little table next to her bed.

Julija carefully looked through the drafts a few times and chose a big, plain, and flat gravestone.

Soon, the quadrangular black granite tombstone weighing ten tons was ordered, on the top of which only a bronze oak tree leaves' wreath was placed. Under the wreath, it was written:

REST IN PEACE FIVE INNOCENT SOULS

As the ill fate would have it, one beautiful, crisp autumn morning, just after Julija finished making all the arrangements related to the placement of the gravestone, her own heart stopped beating in her chest.

She was also buried in the same grave and covered with the same heavy granite gravestone.

Violeta Treciokaite "The Secret of One Grave"

Violeta Treciokaite "The Secret of One Grave"

Violeta Treciokaite "The Secret of One Grave"

Violeta Treciokaite "The Secret of One Grave"

Violeta Treciokaite "The Secret of One Grave"

Violeta Treciokaite "The Secret of One Grave"

Violeta Treciokaite "The Secret of One Grave"

Violeta Treciokaite "The Secret of One Grave"